To my mother, Janice Kuhn—my best and greatest fan. Thank you for calling me the minute you finish reading my books and giving me your encouraging feedback...even if it's midnight!

And special thanks to my son Richard—thank you for allowing me to use your name.

For if our heart condemn us, God is greater than our heart…if our heart condemn us not, then have we confidence toward God.

—1 John 3:20–21

In *Uncertain Heart*, Andrea Kuhn Boeshaar has crafted a beautiful, heartrending tale that instantly draws readers in and doesn't release them until they've reached the final page. As always, this talented author blends sadness and grief with uplifting joy and gentle spirituality. If I were doling out stars, I'd give Andrea *four* for this one!

—Loree Lough
Award-winning author of
*Love Finds You in Folly Beach, South Carolina*
and *Beautiful Bandit*

A delightful story that touches on deep issues, all wrapped up in a satisfying romance. It captured me, a real page-turner.

—Lena Nelson Dooley
Award-winning author of
*Love Finds You in Golden, New Mexico*
and *Cranberry Hearts*

Rich in historical details, Andrea Boeshaar's stories always entertain! A great way to spend a weekend.

—Susan May Warren
Best-selling author of *Nightingale*

Captivating, charming, and deeply entertaining, Andrea's *Uncertain Heart* held me spellbound from the beginning. With warm, likeable characters, surprises sprinkled along the way, and romance that delights, this book is pure pleasure from start to finish.

—Miralee Ferrell
Author of *Finding Jeena* and
*Love Finds You in Bridal Veil, Oregon*

Author Andrea Boeshaar has penned yet another masterpiece. *Uncertain Heart* is a don't-miss read!

—Kathleen Y'Barbo
Author of *The Confidential Life of Eugenia Cooper*
and *Beloved Counterfeit*

Be ready for a pleasant journey back to 1866 Milwaukee, where Sarah, a young governess, is hoping to rise above small town life by immersing herself in big city culture and luxury. Andrea Boeshaar seamlessly weaves period detail with beautiful imagery, romance, and intrigue into this engaging story. It's exciting to see what happens when Sarah's dreams clash with God's plans. Didn't want it to end!

—Susan Miura
Reviewer, Faithfulreader.com

# ANDREA KUHN BOESHAAR

REALMS
A STRANG COMPANY

Most Strang Communications Book Group products are available at special quantity discounts for bulk purchase for sales promotions, premiums, fund-raising, and educational needs. For details, write Strang Communications Book Group, 600 Rinehart Road, Lake Mary, Florida 32746, or telephone (407) 333-0600.

Uncertain Heart by Andrea Kuhn Boeshaar
Published by Realms
A Strang Company
600 Rinehart Road
Lake Mary, Florida 32746
www.strangbookgroup.com



All Scripture quotations are from the King James Version of the Bible.

This is a work of fiction. The characters in this book are fictitious unless they are historical figures explicitly named. Otherwise, any resemblance to actual people, whether living or dead, is coincidental.

Cover design by Bill Johnson



Library of Congress Cataloging-in-Publication Data

Boeshaar, Andrea.
Uncertain heart / Andrea Kuhn Boeshaar. -- 1st ed.
p. cm.
ISBN 978-1-61638-023-6
I. Title.
PS3552.O4257U53 2010
813'.54--dc22

2010022554

First Edition

10 11 12 13 14 — 9 8 7 6 5 4 3 2 1

Printed in the United States of America

# One

*Milwaukee, Wisconsin, June 1866*

STEPPING OFF THE TRAIN, HER VALISE IN HAND, SARAH McCabe eyed her surroundings. Porters hauled luggage and shouted orders to each other. Reunited families and friends hugged while well-dressed businessmen, wearing serious expressions, walked briskly along.

*Mr. Brian Sinclair...*

Sarah glanced around for the man she thought might be him. When nobody approached her, she ambled to the front of the train station where the city was bustling as well. What with all the carriages and horse-pulled streetcars coming and going on Reed Street, it was all Sarah could do just to stay out of the way. And yet she rejoiced in the discovery that Milwaukee was not the small community she'd assumed. There was not a farm in sight, and it looked nothing like her hometown of Jericho Junction, Missouri.

*Good.* She breathed a sigh and let her gaze continue to wander. Milwaukee wasn't all that different from Chicago, where she'd visited and hoped to teach music in the fall. The only difference she could see between the two cities was that Milwaukee's main streets were cobbled, whereas most of Chicago's were paved with wooden blocks.

Sarah squinted into the morning sunshine. She wondered which of the carriages lining the curb belonged to Mr. Sinclair. In his letter he'd stated that he would meet her train. Sarah glanced at her small watch locket: 9:30 a.m. Sarah's train was on time this morning. Had she missed him somehow?

*My carriage will be parked along Reed Street,* Mr. Sinclair had written in the letter in which he'd offered Sarah the governess position. *I shall arrive the same time as your train: 9:00 a.m.* The letter had then been signed: *Brian Sinclair.*

Sarah let out a sigh and tried to imagine just what she would say to her new employer once he finally came for her. Then she tried to imagine what the man looked like. *Older. Distinguished. Balding and round through the middle.* Yes, that's what he probably looked like.

She eyed the crowd, searching for someone who matched the description. Several did, although none of them proved to be Mr. Sinclair. Expelling another sigh, Sarah resigned herself to the waiting.

Her mind drifted back to her hometown of Jericho Junction, Missouri. There wasn't much excitement to be had there. Sarah longed for life in the big city, to be independent and enjoy some of the refinements not available at home. It was just a shame the opportunity in Chicago didn't work out for her. Well, at least she didn't have to go back. She'd found this governess position instead.

As the youngest McCabe, Sarah had grown tired of being pampered and protected by her parents as well as her three older brothers—Benjamin, Jacob, and Luke—and her older sisters, Leah and Valerie. They all had nearly suffocated her—except for Valerie. Her sister-in-law was the only one who really understood her. Her other family members loved her too, but Sarah felt restless and longed to be out on her own. So she'd obtained a position at a fine music academy in Chicago—or so she'd thought. When she arrived in Chicago, she was told the position had been filled. But instead of turning around and going home, Sarah spent every last cent on a hotel room and began scanning local newspapers for another job. That's when she saw the advertisement. A widower by the name of Brian Sinclair was looking for a governess to care for his four children. Sarah answered the ad immediately, she and Mr. Sinclair corresponded numerous times over the last few weeks, she'd obtained permission from her parents—which had taken a heavy amount of persuasion—and then she had accepted the governess position. She didn't have to go home after all. She would work in Milwaukee for the summer. Then for the fall, Mr. Withers, the dean of the music academy in Chicago, promised there'd be an opening.

Now, if only Mr. Sinclair would arrive.

In his letter of introduction he explained that he owned and operated a business called Sinclair and Company: Ship Chandlers and Sailmakers. He had written that it was located on the corner of Water and Erie Streets. Sarah wondered if perhaps Mr. Sinclair had been detained by his business. Next she wondered if she ought to make her way to his company and announce herself if indeed that was the case.

An hour later Sarah felt certain that was indeed the case!

Reentering the depot, she told the baggage man behind the counter that she'd return shortly for her trunk of belongings and, after asking directions, ventured off for Mr. Sinclair's place of business.

As instructed, she walked down Reed Street and crossed a bridge over the Milwaukee River. Then two blocks east and she found herself on Water Street. From there she continued to walk the distance to Sinclair and Company.

She squinted into the sunshine and scrutinized the building from where she stood across the street. It was three stories high, square in shape, and constructed of red brick. Nothing like the wooden structures back home.

Crossing the busy thoroughfare, which was not cobbled at all but full of mud holes, Sarah lifted her hems and climbed up the few stairs leading to the front door. She let herself in, a tiny bell above the door signaling her entrance.

"Over here. What can I do for you?"

Sarah spotted the owner of the voice that sounded quite automatic in its welcome. She stared at the young man, but his gaze didn't leave his ledgers. She noted his neatly parted straight blond hair—as blond as her own—and his round wire spectacles.

Sarah cleared her throat. "Yes, I'm looking for Mr. Sinclair."

The young man looked up and, seeing Sarah standing before his desk, immediately removed his glasses and stood. She gauged his height to be about six feet. Attired nicely, he wore a crisp white dress shirt and black tie, although his dress jacket was nowhere in sight and his shirtsleeves had been rolled to the elbow.

"Forgive me." He sounded apologetic, but his expression was one of surprise. "I thought you were one of the regulars. They come in, holler their orders at me, and help themselves."

Sarah gave him a courteous smile.

"I'm Richard Navis," he said, extending his hand. "And you are…?"

"Sarah McCabe." She placed her hand in his and felt his firm grip.

"A pleasure to meet you, Mrs. McCabe."

"Miss," she corrected.

"Ahhh…" His deep blue eyes twinkled. "Then more's the pleasure, *Miss* McCabe." He bowed over her hand in a regal manner, and Sarah yanked it free as he chuckled.

"That was very amusing." She realized he'd tricked her in order to check her marital status. *The cad.* But worse, she'd fallen for it! The oldest trick in the book, according to her three brothers.

Richard chuckled, but then put on a very businesslike demeanor. "And how can I help you, Miss McCabe?"

"I'm looking for Mr. Sinclair, if you please." Sarah noticed the young man's dimples had disappeared with his smile.

"You mean the captain? Captain Sinclair?"

"Captain?" Sarah frowned. "Well, I don't know…"

"I do, since I work for him." Richard grinned, and once more his dimples winked at her. "He manned a gunboat on the Mississippi during the war and earned his captain's bars. When he returned from service, we all continued to call him Captain out of respect."

"I see." Sarah felt rather bemused. "All right…then I'm looking for Captain Sinclair, if you please."

"Captain Sinclair is unavailable," Richard stated with an amused spark in his eyes, and Sarah realized he'd been leading her by the nose since she'd walked through the door. "I'm afraid you'll have to do with the likes of me."

She rolled her eyes in exasperation. "Mr. Navis, you will not do at all. I need to see the captain. It's quite important, I assure you. I wouldn't bother him otherwise."

"My apologies, Miss McCabe, but the captain's not here. Now, how can I help you?"

"You can't!"

The young man raised his brows and looked taken aback by her sudden tone of impatience. This couldn't be happening. Another job and another closed door. She had no money to get home, and wiring her parents to ask for funds would ruin her independence forever in their eyes.

She crossed her arms and took several deep breaths, wondering what on Earth she should do now. She gave it several moments of thought. "Will the captain be back soon, do you think?" She tried to lighten her tone a bit.

Richard shook his head. "I don't expect him until this evening. He has the day off and took a friend on a lake excursion to Green Bay. However, he usually stops in to check on things, day off or not... Miss McCabe? Are you all right? You look a bit pale."

A dizzying, sinking feeling fell over her.

Richard came around the counter and touched her elbow. "Miss McCabe?"

She managed to reach into the inside pocket of her jacket and pull out the captain's last letter—the one in which he stated he would meet her train. She looked at the date... today's. So it wasn't she that was off but he!

"It seems that Captain Sinclair has forgotten me." She felt a heavy frown crease her brow as she handed the letter to Richard.

He read it and looked up with an expression of deep regret. "It seems you're right."

Folding the letter carefully, he gave it back to Sarah. She accepted it, fretting over her lower lip, wondering what she should do next.

"I'm the captain's steward," Richard offered. "Allow me to fetch you a cool glass of water while I think of an appropriate solution."

"Thank you." Oh, this was just great. But at least she sensed Mr. Navis truly meant to help her now instead of baiting her as he had before.

Sitting down at a long table by the enormous plate window, Sarah smoothed the wrinkles from the pink-and-black skirt of her two-piece traveling suit. Next she pulled off her gloves as she awaited Mr. Navis's return. He's something of a jokester, she decided, and she couldn't help but compare him to her brother Jake. However, just now, before he'd gone to fetch the water, he had seemed very sweet and thoughtful...like Ben, her favorite big brother. But Richard's clean-cut, boyish good looks and sun-bronzed complexion...now they were definitely like Luke, her other older brother.

Sarah let her gaze wander about the shop. She was curious about all the shipping paraphernalia. But before she could really get a good look at the place, Richard returned with two glasses of water. He set one before Sarah, took the other for himself, and then sat down across the table from her.

He took a long drink. "I believe the thing to do," he began, "is to take you to the captain's residence. I know his housekeeper, Mrs. Schlyterhaus."

Sarah nodded. It seemed the perfect solution. "I do appreciate it, Mr. Navis, although I hate to pull you away from your work." She gave a concerned glance toward the books piled on the desk.

Richard just chuckled. "Believe it or not, Miss McCabe, you are a godsend. I had just sent a quick dart of a prayer to the Lord, telling Him that I would much rather work outside on a fine day like this than be trapped in here with my ledgers. Then you walked in." He grinned. "Your predicament, Miss McCabe, will have me working out-of-doors yet!"

Sarah smiled, heartened that he seemed to be a believer. "But what will the captain have to say about your abandonment of his books?" She arched a brow.

Richard responded with a sheepish look. "Well, seeing this whole mess is *his* fault, I suspect the captain won't say too much at all."

Sarah laughed in spite of herself, as did Richard. However, when their eyes met—sky blue and sea blue—an uncomfortable silence settled down around them.

Sarah was the first to turn away. She forced herself to look around the shop and then remembered her curiosity. "What exactly do you sell here?" She felt eager to break the sudden awkwardness.

"Well, *exactly*," Richard said, appearing amused, "we are ship chandlers and sail-makers and manufacturers of flags, banners, canvas belting, brewers' sacks, paulins of all kinds, waterproof horse and wagon covers, sails, awnings, and tents." He paused for a breath, acting quite dramatic about it, and Sarah laughed again. "We are dealers in vanilla, hemp, and cotton cordage, lath yarns, duck of all widths, oakum, tar, pitch, paints, oars, tackle, and purchase blocks... *exactly*!"

Sarah swallowed the last of her giggles and arched a brow. "That's it?"

Richard grinned. "Yes, well," he conceded, "I might have forgotten the glass of water."

Still smiling, she took a sip of hers. And in that moment she decided that she knew how to handle the likes of Richard Navis—tease him right back, that's how. After all, she'd had enough practice with Ben, Jake, and Luke.

They finished up their cool spring water, and then Richard went to hitch up the captain's horse and buggy. When he returned, he unrolled his shirtsleeves, and finding his dress jacket, he put it on. Next he let one of the other employees know he was leaving by shouting up a steep flight of stairs, "Hey, there, Joe, I'm leaving for a while! Mind the shop, would you?"

She heard a man's deep reply. "Will do."

At last Richard announced he was ready to go. Their first stop was fetching her luggage from the train station. Her trunk and bags filled the entire backseat of the buggy.

"I noticed the little cross on the necklace you're wearing. Forgive me for asking what might be the obvious, but are you a Christian, Miss McCabe?" He climbed up into the driver's perch and took the horse's reins.

"Why, yes, I am. Why do you ask?"

"I always ask."

"Hmm…" She wondered if he insulted a good many folks with his plain speech. But in his present state, Richard reminded her of her brother Luke. "My father is a pastor back home in Missouri," Sarah offered, "and two of my three brothers have plans to be missionaries out West."

"And the third brother?"

"Ben. He's a photographer. He and his wife, Valerie, are expecting their third baby in just a couple of months."

"How nice for them."

Nodding, Sarah felt a blush creep into her cheeks. She really hadn't meant to share such intimacies about her family with a man she'd just met. But Richard seemed so easy to talk to, like a friend already. But all too soon she recalled her sister Leah's words of advice: "Outgrow your garrulousness, lest you give the impression of a silly schoolgirl! You're a young lady now. A music teacher."

Sarah promptly remembered herself and held her tongue—until they reached the captain's residence, anyway.

"What a beautiful home." She felt awestruck as Richard helped her down from the buggy.

"A bit ostentatious for my tastes."

Not for Sarah's. She'd always dreamed of living in house this grand. Walking toward the enormous brick mansion, she gazed up in wonder.

The manse had three stories of windows that were each trimmed in white, and a "widow's walk" at the very top of it gave the structure a somewhat square design. The house was situated on a quiet street across from a small park that overlooked Lake Michigan. But it wasn't the view that impressed Sarah. It was the house itself.

Richard seemed to sense her fascination. "Notice the brick walls that are lavishly ornamented with terra cotta. The porch," he said, reaching for her hand as they climbed its stairs, "is cased entirely with terra cotta. And these massive front doors are composed of complex oak millwork, hand-carved details, and wrought iron. The lead glass panels," he informed her as he knocked several times, "hinge inward to allow conversation through the grillwork."

"Goodness!" Sarah felt awestruck. She sent Richard an impish grin. "You are something of a walking textbook, aren't you?"

Before he could reply, a panel suddenly opened, and Sarah found herself looking into the stern countenance of a woman who was perhaps in her late fifties.

"Hello, Mrs. Schlyterhaus." Richard's tone sounded neighborly.

"Mr. Navis." She gave him a curt nod. "Vhat can I do for you?"

Sarah immediately noticed the housekeeper's thick German accent.

"I've brought the captain's new governess. This is Miss Sarah McCabe." He turned. "Sarah, this is Mrs. Gretchen Schlyterhaus."

"A pleasure to meet you, ma'am." Sarah tried to sound as pleasing as possible, for the housekeeper looked quite annoyed at the interruption.

"The captain said nussing about a new governess," she told Richard, fairly ignoring Sarah altogether. "I know nussing about it."

Richard grimaced. "I was afraid of that."

Wide-eyed, Sarah gave him a look of disbelief.

"Let's show Mrs. Schlyterhaus that letter...the one from the captain."

Sarah pulled it from her inside pocket and handed it over. Richard opened it and read its contents.

The older woman appeared unimpressed. "I know nussing about it." With that, she closed the door on them.

Sarah's heart crimped as she and Richard walked back to the carriage.

"Here, now, don't look so glum, Sarah...May I call you Sarah?"

"Yes, I suppose so." No governess position. No money. So much for showing herself an independent young woman. Her family would never let her forget this. Not ever!

Suddenly she noticed Richard's wide grin. "What are you smiling at?"

"It appears, Sarah, that you've been given the day off too."

# Two

"So now what?"

Sarah accepted Richard's hand as he helped her climb aboard the buggy. "You'll have to stay with me this afternoon. We'll have some lunch, I'll show you around town, and—"

"And you won't have to look at your ledgers for the rest of the day." In spite of the circumstances, Sarah found herself smiling.

"My, my, Miss McCabe, you're quite astute." With that quip he climbed into the carriage.

"And you're quite full of buffoonery, not that I mean that with any disrespect."

"Well, all right, then." The amusement on his face faded to confusion. "You mentioned your family in Missouri, but I thought you hailed from Chicago. Which is it?"

"Missouri, although I'd been offered a teacher's position at the academy in Chicago. I'd hoped to build my own life there. However, through some misunderstanding, my position was given away to another teacher. I'm here in Milwaukee because I saw Mr.—I mean, Captain—Sinclair's advertisement for a governess and I needed summer employment. So here I am."

Richard frowned. "The captain hired you on a temporary basis?"

"Yes. Why do you ask?"

"Well, because in the past year, governesses have come and gone at the Sinclair household, and I got the impression the captain wanted to hire someone more permanent. Then again, the captain is growing more desperate with each passing day."

"Desperate?" Sarah swallowed hard. What had she gotten herself into now? Wait until Jake heard about this. He and Luke had been conspiring all along, wanting her to teach school in some dusty

Western town. If employment here with Captain Sinclair didn't work out, her parents might sympathize with her brothers. Worse, she might have to go home and live in Jericho Junction if she couldn't support herself.

"Please don't be alarmed. The Sinclair children aren't a bad brood at all. The boys are just...well, boys. But the two little girls are sweet as can be. You'll see. As for the desperation part, you can understand the captain's dilemma, with a business to run, four children, a household staff—"

"Yes, I see what you mean." She thought more about it as the carriage bumped along the rutty street. "*Desperate* seems a fitting word."

Richard steered the buggy through the city streets and found himself enjoying Sarah's chatter.

"Perhaps the reason Captain Sinclair agreed to take me on *temporarily* is because I promised to give his children piano lessons at no extra charge. However, I also made it clear that I must be back in Chicago by the first of September."

He couldn't resist teasing her. "Are you saying that I have only until the first of September to steal your heart?"

Sarah held her gloved hand to her pink lips and giggled in the most amusing way. "Mr. Navis, the man who intends to 'steal my heart' will have to contend with my father and three brothers first. I highly doubt you're in a position for such an undertaking. I'm twenty years old, and none have succeeded so far."

"Understandable. A father and three brothers are enough to deter any man."

"Yes. A sad chapter in my life's story."

"I'm sure." Richard chuckled.

She peered at him through a narrowed gaze. "You know, you do remind me of Jake. He teases me incessantly. The day he left to go west on a fact-finding mission was a day to rejoice for me."

Richard smiled. "Yes, well, I wonder how many young ladies wished that I'd go west on account of my wit. In fact, I know of several who would gladly buy my ticket." He looked at Sarah and saw her grin. "So Jake is the missionary, not the photographer?"

"Yes, he and my other brother Luke are planning to permanently move into the Arizona Territory and spread the good news. Ben is the photographer."

"I'll try to keep them all straight from now on." With a sidelong glance in her direction, Richard gave her a smile, glad that he'd been able to lift her spirits.

"I must confess to missing both Jake and Luke after they left. They started a church in Arizona, in a little nothing town there, and they desperately need a schoolteacher. My father believes in my brothers' vision and encouraged me to take the position. I thought about it."

"You're not serious?" Richard felt a frown weigh on his brow. He had never known a young lady willing to venture into the untamed West. He'd heard the journey was laborious, even dangerous, and once they arrived, settlers found deplorable conditions—especially in the "little nothing towns" of the Arizona Territory. It certainly wasn't a place for sweet Sarah the music teacher. "I hope you're not considering it."

She gave him a curious look. "Why would you care if I am or not?"

For once Richard didn't have a quick comeback.

He drove the buggy to Grand Avenue, and they ate at a small establishment by the Milwaukee River. Tall-masted schooners, tugboats, and barges sailed up the sun-sparkled water, making for an appealing view, and with his present company, Richard couldn't remember ever enjoying a meal more.

Sarah sipped from her water goblet. "I have been talking up a lather, haven't I?"

Richard dabbed the corners of his mouth with the white linen napkin. "I don't mind."

"You're very gracious. But I've been quite rude. Imagine, monopolizing our entire conversation! Please forgive me, Mr. Navis."

Richard smiled. "Consider it done…and it's Richard. I insist. I equate 'Mr. Navis' with my father."

"All right, then, Richard. Tell me about yourself. I certainly have talked enough about me."

"I'm not so interesting." He sat back in his chair. "I live with my parents on a farm about five miles northwest of here. No siblings. I completed my education in May of last year, which earned me a certificate in accounting. But I hate accounting more than words can tell."

"Then why continue to work in that capacity?"

"Because I still owe the captain several more months of service." Richard took note of Sarah's bemused expression and further explained, "Captain Sinclair paid for my education." He leaned forward. "A friend of my father initially got me a job doing dock work. But as soon as the captain discovered I had a 'talent for figuring,' as he put it, he sent me to school."

"What a wonderful opportunity." Sarah's smile slipped from her lips. "But you hate it? The bookwork?"

"Yes, unfortunately I found out too late that accounting doesn't suit me, although I'm grateful for the education. Knowledge is never lost."

"I agree. But does the captain know you hate your work?"

"He does, except he wants me to stay on as his steward. The pay is good, so I'm trying to determine if I can tolerate bookwork long enough to make a living. I've been putting off making a decision as I'm indentured until the end of December." Regret filled him. It seemed like a long time to work so laboriously and feel so dissatisfied. "For now, I leave my fate in the Lord's hands."

"A good place for it." A giggle escaped her. "I think that's the most intelligent thing you've said since we met."

With the meal finished, they walked out of the little eating establishment and went back to Sinclair and Company.

Richard glanced at his pocket watch. "I, unfortunately, must get back to my books. I do apologize. But Captain Sinclair ought to be here soon."

"Thank you. You've done over and above in seeing to my welfare." She glanced around. "Can I browse a bit?"

Richard inclined his blond head. "Most certainly."

While he returned to the front desk, Sarah walked up and down the wide aisles of the store. In the back she discovered the manufacturing part of the business. Upstairs she found the chandlery office and met Mr. Smith. He explained the purpose of the chandlery was contracting for the shipping and receiving of various goods.

"How very interesting." There didn't appear to be any lack of opportunity here at the captain's place of business. A pity Richard didn't seem more ambitious.

Finally growing bored with her wanderings, Sarah took a seat near his desk. She watched him interact with the other employees and customers, noting the way he enjoyed making them laugh, or at least smile.

A tall, sun-tanned, and darkly handsome gentleman entered the store. He wore a white shirt with billowing sleeves and tan trousers tucked into knee-high black boots.

"Captain Sinclair..." Richard waved him over, and Sarah straightened. "May I introduce your new governess?"

Bewilderment filled her. But how could this be the captain? The man coming toward them looked nothing like the distinguished, heavy-set, older gent she'd imagined. This one had thick ebony hair that curled at his collar, and—she blinked—he had black eyes.

His dark gaze rested on her. "Governess?"

She pushed out a timid smile. "How do you do, sir?"

"Miss Sarah McCabe, meet Captain Brian Sinclair." Richard turned to his employer. "I'm afraid she's been waiting for you since early this morning."

His expression fell. "Oh, no...it's Wednesday." He sent Richard an accusing look. "Why didn't you tell me it was Wednesday?"

"Thought you knew that, sir. After Tuesday comes Wednesday...happens every week."

"Hmm, yes..."

Sarah wondered if Richard was attempting to get himself fired by such back talk. But Captain Sinclair didn't appear offended.

Instead he turned to Sarah. "Miss McCabe, I am terribly sorry about this...er...mix-up."

"Mix-ups happen." She felt suddenly intimidated in the captain's rather larger-than-life presence. "Richard has been a wonderful host."

"Good." Captain Sinclair eyed Richard. "My steward can be quite useful when he puts his mind to it."

He saluted. "Aye, aye, sir."

Sarah swallowed the urge to giggle.

The captain shook his head at him then refocused on Sarah. His eyes roamed over her face, and she suspected he liked what he saw. She looked downward, thinking her brothers wouldn't appreciate the man's open assessment. Nevertheless she felt oddly flattered.

Richard cleared his throat. "Sir, I took Sarah to your residence, and I'm sorry to report there was a problem with Mrs. Schlyterhaus."

The captain pursed his lips. "Is she acting ferociously again?" Looking back at Sarah, he sent her a good-natured wink.

She felt her cheeks grow warm.

Richard folded his arms. "Mrs. Schlyterhaus behaved more than ferociously. She was rude. Apparently she had no idea that Sarah was arriving today."

"Oh, I'm certain I told her." With one hand he kneaded his shadowed jaw as his gaze returned to Sarah. "I gave Gretchen your name and read your letter of qualifications to her." He frowned. "Or was that the last governess?"

Richard sighed audibly.

"Well, no matter. I'll take care of Gretchen when I get home." He smiled and stepped toward Sarah. "But to make up for my neglect, I'll take you to dinner tonight."

Richard spoke up before she could reply. "I'm afraid you have a previous engagement, Captain."

He grumbled and glanced at Richard. "The Harborths' dinner party?"

"The very one."

"That's right. Then why don't *you* take Miss McCabe to dinner tonight? Eat slowly, perhaps take a ride, and I'll make sure Gretchen has her room prepared by the time you return her to my house later."

Richard appeared to think it over.

"Captain Sinclair," Sarah put in, feeling like a burden that neither man wished to bear, "I really can't impose on Richard...again."

"Well, of course you can." A grin pulled at his mouth. "Richard doesn't mind, do you?"

He shook his head. "Not at all, sir."

"I don't mind occupying myself," Sarah persisted. "I sense Richard has other things planned." A sweetheart waiting for him to call on her?

She dashed the notion. Unlikely, given their conversation earlier.

"No, no, it's fine, really," Richard said. "Sarah, I'd consider it a privilege to take you to dinner."

"Of course you would." Captain Sinclair smiled broadly now. "The opportunity to take a lovely young lady to dinner doesn't knock at your door often."

Another desire to giggle emerged, and this time Sarah didn't squelch it. Obviously Richard and the captain had an uncanny rapport.

Richard gave her a smile.

"Good." The captain gave a clap of his hands. "Then it's settled. And don't worry about transportation home tonight, Richard," the captain added. "You may use my horse and carriage."

"I had planned to, sir." Amusement washed over his face.

"And put dinner and everything else on my tab."

"As you wish." A mischievous grin curved his lips.

The captain noticed. "But don't overdo it!"

"Not to worry, sir."

Captain Sinclair looked worried nevertheless.

Finally, he turned to Sarah. "I'm terribly sorry about all this." He reached for her hand. "But tomorrow morning will be soon enough for us to get further acquainted."

"Yes, Captain."

Releasing her hand, he bowed quite regally. Then he gave Richard a few more instructions, asked about the day's business, and whistled his way out the door.

After he'd gone, Richard turned to Sarah. He seemed to gauge her thoughts.

She didn't know what to think. Her new employer seemed cavalier, almost to the point of irresponsible. Still, there was something rather thrilling about Brian Sinclair. Walking past Richard, she gazed out the shop's window and saw the captain speaking to someone on the street. She heard his deep chuckle before he boarded a buggy. She wondered about his four children. Would she get along with them? Were they as capricious as their father and as ill behaved as his housekeeper?

She turned from the window to find Richard standing a few feet away.

"You look tired."

Worried more accurately described how she felt. "I guess it's been a long day, what with the travel this morning."

"Understandably so." He turned and pointed at the crude staircase. "There's a small room upstairs where we keep a cot. You might like to rest a bit and then freshen up or even change your clothes. The room is very private, so you needn't worry, and, seeing as your trunk of belongings is still in back of the buggy..."

"You're very thoughtful." How like her favorite big brother Ben he seemed at the moment.

She tamped down her uneasiness and followed Richard. *Everything's going to be all right... isn't it, Lord?*

# Three

Sarah sat back, having enjoyed a tasty meal of grilled trout and rice pilaf. "This is a lovely place. What's the name of it? You said it's the Kirby House?" She allowed her gaze to roam her elegant surroundings, admiring the plaster-coffered ceiling. The entire dining room was wainscoted and trimmed with shiny, dark walnut.

"Right. It's one of Milwaukee's finest hotels and eateries."

"I don't think I've ever eaten in such a fine place." A tremulous smile played upon her lips. Wait until the captain got the bill. They'd enjoyed hors d'oeuvres and sampled expensive rarities from the menu. Would he be angry? Richard certainly didn't seem concerned.

"Abner Kirby was the mayor of Milwaukee in 1864." He dabbed the corners of his mouth with his white linen napkin. "Now he owns this fine hotel, and he's known for his peculiar sense of humor. One suite he's named Heaven—it's the bridal suite, in case you didn't guess."

"Ah..." Sarah sipped her iced tea.

"Another is called Hell." Richard leaned toward her. "That room's often assigned to inebriates."

Sarah brought her chin back. Did he think to shock her? Well, it didn't work. She was, unfortunately, familiar with the term because of the saloon at the other end of Jericho Junction. The place drew drinking and gambling men and some women who felt hopeless with nowhere to go. Sarah and her family reached out to any and all of them. "I hope Milwaukee isn't home to many inebriates."

"Too many, I'm afraid. This is a city of beer-makers and rich beer barons."

"They manufacture strong drink here?" Sarah knew her father wouldn't approve of the practice.

"Yes, but don't worry. I'll protect you."

She arched a brow at his ribbing. "And who's going to protect *you*?"

"Me? From whom?" Richard took a drink from his water goblet.

"From my three brothers when they find out you've been speaking to me of drunkenness and beer."

"Now, Sarah!" For a moment Richard looked taken aback—even worried. But then when Sarah sent him a grin, he chuckled.

"You're teasing me. How refreshing."

"Why?"

"Not many young ladies seem to have a sense of humor."

"Well, I have to admit your quips do wear on me. But I'm probably more tolerant than most because of my brother Jake."

"Another quipster?"

Sarah nodded. "And he's unmarried. Need I tell you why?"

Richard dipped his head. "A highly intelligent fellow?"

She rolled her eyes.

They finished dinner and left the restaurant. Richard offered his arm and Sarah took it. She thought his arm felt muscular beneath her hand, hardly what she expected from a bookkeeper who sat at his desk all day.

He assisted her into the buggy.

"Allow me to take you for a ride through town. It'll give Mrs. Schlyterhaus more time to prepare your quarters."

"A ride sounds lovely." She gazed up into the darkening sky. The colors of mauve and slate were painted across the horizon.

"You won't be chilled, will you? The wind has shifted and is now coming off the lake."

"No. I'm fine." She marveled at how he always sought after her comfort. Her brothers might even be impressed.

"Good. I hoped you'd say that." Richard gave a slap of the reins and the horse started. The buggy jerked forward. They rode down a busy street with brick and stone buildings, some quite ornate, situated on either side of it.

"As you'll see, there are many bridges in this town, and quite a lot of them are under construction. A flood back in April washed five of them away into the Milwaukee River."

"How dreadful."

"Yes, and what's more, the flood caused a stir among what's known as the wards, which are ethnic sections of the city. Irish, German, Italian, and so forth. At one time there was a terrible clash between them, particularly between the Irish and Germans."

"So essentially Milwaukee's residents were at odds with each other?"

"More than that. Several years ago there were terrible fights concerning the location of certain bridges and which roadways would be connected. Those fights were known as the bridge wars."

Sarah found herself becoming interested in the history of this city since it would be her home for the next few months, but she was also amazed at the extent of Richard's knowledge. "You must read a lot of books."

"Some."

She smiled. "You're so entertaining. You ought to be a schoolteacher."

"Thank you—at least for the part about me being entertaining."

She replied with a roll of the shoulder.

"I find it gratifying to win smiles or laughter. My father taught me life's too short for frowning and fretting."

Sarah couldn't find an argument there.

Richard pointed out a few more attractions. The Spencerian Business College, where he'd obtained his accounting certificate.

"How long have you worked for Captain Sinclair?"

"Almost five years. He hired me in December of sixty-two, just as the war gained momentum. I signed on for a five-year indentureship with the understanding that the captain would pay for my two-year education—which he did. Now I must keep my end of the bargain."

"And you will." Sarah had no doubt. Smiling, she leaned forward and glimpsed several polished grand pianos in the large window and decided she'd have to stop in soon and have a closer look.

"So..." The conversation lagged. "So you're twenty years old and not married yet? I can't believe it."

Sarah sent him a stern glance. "If I hear one old-maid comment out of you, Richard Navis, I'll—"

"No, no, that's not what I find funny." He regarded her. "What's funny," he said in softer tones, "is that no man has succeeded in claiming you for his bride."

"I have my big brothers to thank for that."

Richard laughed, but moments later turned thoughtful. "Am I to understand you have no love interests back home?"

"Not back home."

"I hope you didn't lose your true love during the war."

"I didn't." Sarah knew he was fishing—but in the wrong creek. "Were you an enlisted man?"

"No. My father was, though. He's a decorated veteran. I stayed home to finish school and look after my mother." He glanced her way. "I'm an only child. In addition, I had to keep the captain's business running in order to support his wife, children, and mother."

"Goodness, Richard! You were responsible for a great many souls during the war."

"True. But I was prepared to defend the Union if called to duty."

"Quite honorable." Sarah felt impressed by his capabilities and commitment to others. Suddenly she felt his stare, and slowly she met his gaze. "Just what are you looking at? I'm sure I don't have a wart on the end of my nose."

"I'll say you don't."

Sarah clucked her tongue and turned her head.

Richard cleared his throat. "I realize it's none of my business, but you, Sarah, are much too pretty to be twenty and without a husband."

"Oh, you think I need a husband, do you? Are you proposing?"

At that he inhaled sharply and sent himself into a coughing fit. Sarah gave him a few good whacks between the shoulder blades.

"Touché, Sarah."

She laughed.

Heading toward the Sinclair residence, Richard had to marvel at what had just transpired. *Bested.* Most young ladies with whom he was acquainted grew insulted rather than dishing back his tart remarks. But not Sarah. "I suppose that's what I get for prying into your affairs."

"Oh, that's all right." Her gaze lingered on the buildings they passed. "Actually, I'm rather used to it. I guess it's not very natural for a woman to *choose* to remain unmarried. However, I do. I like my independence."

"Independence, huh?" Richard cocked a brow. "You're not one of those woman suffragettes, are you?"

"Hardly, although..."

He inclined his head, curious.

"My parents have a ministry to the, um, *working girls* in Jericho Junction."

Richard guessed she meant prostitutes.

"We share the love of God and help them discover their self-worth. Then we assist them in finding respectable work in other towns and cities."

"Commendable."

"The saloon's owner doesn't think so. He accuses my father of hindering his business. But Pa considers it a compliment."

"And it is."

"But getting back to the point about women's suffrage..."

"I understand now." Richard felt impressed. "Allow me to show you a building of significance, one I think you'll appreciate." Taking a slight detour, he slowed the buggy once the tall brick building came into view. "This is Milwaukee Female Seminary, founded in the 1840s. Later a famed educator named Catherine Beecher became associated with the school."

"It's a college for women?" Sarah seemed awed. "I always wanted to attend college. All I managed to do was get my teaching certificate; I made the trip to St. Louis three times to meet with my overseeing instructor. It wasn't at all like a *real* college where a girl lives away from home."

"Well, this is a real college. Also noteworthy is that Miss Beecher's sister is Harriett Beecher Stowe, who wrote the novel *Uncle Tom's Cabin*."

"Really?" Sarah swung her head around to face him. Her shapely brows slanted inward. "You're not teasing me again? I'd certainly look silly if I wrote home about this only to discover you made the entire thing up."

"I kid you not, my dearest Sarah McCabe." Richard was delighted that he'd impressed her.

"I'm going to write to my folks as soon as I settle in tonight. I've had quite the adventure today."

Richard grinned. He wondered if she'd include his name in her letter home. Did he want her to?

They rode the rest of the way to the captain's home in amicable silence. When they reached their destination, Richard halted the buggy.

"Thank you for a most pleasant evening." Sarah gave him a smile.

"It was entirely my pleasure—especially since the captain paid for all of it." Chuckling, Richard hopped down. He reached for Sarah's hand and helped her alight. When she lost her footing, he put his hand on her waist and steadied her, liking the feeling of her nearness. "Are you all right?"

"Yes, thank you."

He heard a note of embarrassment in her tone. He stepped back, but Sarah didn't move.

"Richard, what's that noise?"

"What noise?"

"That...that roaring. Can't you hear it?"

He listened, realizing what she referred to. "That's the lake." He reached for her hand, glad for the excuse to touch her again. "Come with me. I'll show you."

Crossing the paved street and a grassy yard, he led her near the edge of the cliff. The captain had erected a wooden guardrail years ago to deter the children away from the rocky shoreline below.

Sarah's gloved hand gripped his palm tightly, and Richard couldn't help but enjoy it. But he could understand it might seem frightening out here in the dark with the wind whipping. Above, clouds shadowed the moonlight.

He put her hand on the wooden rail so she'd feel safe.

"It looks like a dark abyss out there...and the noise."

Richard smiled. "You'll grow accustomed to it."

The moon suddenly shone its nearly full face, illuminating the choppy waves beyond the cliff. Richard thought it a good thing for Captain Sinclair that he'd had smoother sailing earlier today. The clouds blew over the moon's glow again, and darkness surrounded them.

"I can't wait to see this lake in the morning." Sarah reached for his arm.

Richard secured her hand around his elbow and led her back across the street.

"I'll bet it's a magnificent sight. Where I grew up, we had rivers close by, and I crossed the Mississippi by ferry. But I've not seen a great body of water like Lake Michigan."

"Not even in Chicago?"

"I was near the music academy, which was miles from the lake, and I didn't venture out by myself. So I've only had glimpses of it, really."

"Well, you'll see it enough beginning tomorrow morning."

They made their way up to the porch, where Richard banged the large brass knocker against the front door. Beneath the faint lamplight, he saw her curious expression.

"With no governess, where have the children been all day? Who has been taking care of them?"

"Captain Sinclair's mother, Mrs. Aurora Reil, cares for the children on Wednesdays. She'll return them in the morning. I trust you'll meet everyone tomorrow." Richard hoped Sarah wouldn't be put off by Aurora's eccentric ways.

"Oh. Then I take it Wednesdays are to be my day off?"

"Yes, or at least that's how it's been in the past."

"Richard, how many governesses have there been?"

"Six or seven since Mrs. Sinclair passed away last December."

Sarah gasped. "I had no idea she had passed so recently."

He nodded. "It was a trying winter for the captain and his children—for the entire household, really."

"How sad..." A few moments ticked by before Sarah straightened. "And they've gone through six or seven governesses? It's only June!"

"Now, don't be discouraged. One governess lasted almost two months." Richard figured she was liable to hear all about the women who had attempted to fill the position and failed at it. He might as well be truthful from the start. "But I sense you'll have an easier time." He concealed a smile, thinking she'd win over the captain's two boys just like she'd all but stolen his heart today.

The front door suddenly swung open, and Mrs. Schlyterhaus met them with a frowning countenance.

"Good evening. I'm returning the captain's new governess."

The housekeeper replied with an indignant toss of her graying hair, and he saw Sarah shift uncomfortably.

"I trust Sarah's trunk of belongings has arrived by now." Richard ignored the older woman's scowl and prayed Sarah would learn to do the same. "I sent it on earlier."

"Yes, it arrived." Mrs. Schlyterhaus sounded none too pleased.

"Well, good." Richard wasn't about to let her get away with what she pulled this afternoon. He took a step forward and Mrs. Schlyterhaus opened the door, albeit reluctantly. Taking hold of Sarah's elbow, Richard ushered her into the foyer.

Sarah felt as though she were stepping into another world. "What a lovely hallway." She took in the floor made up of various shades of

brown terrazzo. Next she glanced at the goldenrod papered walls. "How absolutely lovely."

Mrs. Schlyterhaus donned a bored expression as she lit another lamp and set it upon a marble-top table. "Your room is on the second floor." Her voice sounded strained. "It is next to the nursery, vhich is in the far hallvay, first door to the right vhen you come up the back stairs...and that's another thing." She wagged a finger at Sarah. "Be sure you use the servants' stairvell and not this front vun." She inclined her head, indicating the grand, curving staircase at the end of the foyer.

Then she strode off into the darkness.

When Gretchen was out of earshot, Richard leaned closer. "Listen, Sarah, if something doesn't seem right..." He paused as if groping for words. "Well, please let me know if you're uncomfortable in any way."

"Thank you, Richard, but—"

"Anything at all, Sarah, I mean it."

She knew by now that he did. "All right. And thank you again, Richard, for everything. You've been so kind, and I don't know what I would have done without you."

"My pleasure. But, um..." He strained to see the hour on the grandfather clock in the next room. "I need to take my leave."

"Of course." Again she sensed she'd kept him from something important.

He reached for her gloved hand, giving it a squeeze before leaving the house.

From where she stood in the center of the foyer, Sarah watched him close the massive front door after him. She expelled a weary breath. Now to get settled.

Taking the lamp that Gretchen had set on the table, Sarah walked through the foyer to the kitchen. It was a large room, tiled in white and yellow and scrubbed clean for the night. There appeared to be a breakfast nook at one end of the room, and Sarah noted the children's chairs pushed in neatly around the table.

So this is where the children dined. Sarah found herself counting the hours until their meeting. And she absolutely loved this house. Why, it seemed like the house of her dreams, with beautiful rooms and beautiful things. This house was nothing like the small, wood-framed parsonage in which she'd spent her early years. Even the "big house," which the church had built for her family later, couldn't compare to a home of this magnitude. One would never feel crowded here.

Beyond the kitchen Sarah found another hallway, dark and imposing. She realized this was the "servants' stairwell" Mrs. Schlyterhaus mentioned. Climbing the steps, she reached the second floor and found her bedroom. As she stepped inside, she gaped at her surroundings. Had she made a mistake? This seemed too grand a chamber for a governess. But it must be her room. Sarah had entered the first door to her right, just as Mrs. Schlyterhaus had said. This was it.

Setting the lamp upon a desk in the far corner, she did as much exploring as possible, given the poor lighting. Afterward she felt one thing was sure. She'd enjoy living here for the summer.

And yet she wondered why governesses came and went so frequently. Why hadn't they stayed?

"Good heavens, Richard! Where have you been? I've been worried sick!"

Standing in the kitchen of the farmhouse that his father had built some fifteen years ago, Richard grinned at the sight of his mother. Her thick auburn hair was tied in rags for the night, and traces of cold cream looked like patches on her face. Her white cotton nightgown billowed around her ankles as she moved forward.

"Mama, you're a vision of loveliness."

Beatrice Navis stopped short as though she sensed she was about to be the object of a joke. "The Lord commands that you respect your mother—even when she's not looking her best!"

Richard chuckled nevertheless as Mama smoothed the cream on her face and patted her hair. "Well, I suppose I do look a sight, don't I?"

"A sight for sore eyes, Mama."

"Oh, you just hush!"

Richard laughed while she shook her head at him. "You are so much like your father. Always finding the humor in every situation. Sometimes I truly wonder if I'm the only one in this house with any lick of sense."

"Oh, now, Mama..." Walking to the counter, Richard uncovered a loaf of bread and cut off a thick slice. "I know you love Pops and me anyhow."

"I do. So where were you tonight? You never answered my question, and I've been concerned."

"I'm sorry." Richard turned serious. "Captain Sinclair's newest governess arrived today, and of course, he forgot about her."

"Is the governess for him or the children?"

Richard smiled at the tart question. His mother was fully aware of the captain's absentmindedness. "As far as I know, she came for the children."

"That man needs a wife."

"Well, all he's got is a governess at this point—and quite a pretty one, I might add."

His mother's ears perked up. "Oh? Is that so? She's pretty?"

Richard nodded. "And I took her to dinner on the captain's orders. We had a very nice time."

He knew his mother hung on his every word. She'd love nothing better than for her only son to settle down with a pretty wife and produce some grandchildren. So he decided to have a little fun with her.

"We get along very well, Mama. Did I say she was pretty?"

"Yes... yes, you did."

"And she's a believer."

"Is that right?"

"Her father is a preacher in Missouri, and Sarah hopes to teach music in Chicago come fall. She's only in Milwaukee for the summer."

"And you like her, huh?"

"Oh, yes." Richard fought to keep a straight face. "Such a pity she's as wide as a house, though." He shook his head, feigning a look of remorse. In truth, Sarah had a very comely figure, but he couldn't resist the prank on his mother. "Mama, you should have seen her putting the food away at the dinner table tonight. She would have shamed any lumberjack."

She paled beneath her cold cream. "Heaven above!"

"Yes, it is." Richard sent his mother a grin before kissing her petal-soft cheek. "And I'm teasing you. Sarah isn't really as wide as a house."

"Richard Andrew Navis!"

"But she is ninety-four. I don't know how she'll ever keep up with those children. However, she uses a cane. I suppose it'll come in handy."

Mama gave him a leveled look. "You have five seconds to get up to your bedroom before I thrash you within an inch of your life!"

Richard's eyes widened in mock terror, and after grabbing another hunk of his mother's fresh bread, he took the steps up, two by two.

# Four

PALE STREAMS OF EARLY SUNLIGHT TRICKLED IN FROM beyond the thick, lilac-colored draperies, awaking Sarah. She cast aside the thick quilt and crawled out of bed. Then, after washing, she dressed in a blue-and-white striped dress with white pinafore. For working, she thought the apron was perfect, whether for a governess or a music teacher alike as it sported two large pockets in the front and it fit nicely over the crinoline underneath her skirt. Moreover, the apron protected her dress. How glad she was that her mother had suggested sewing several of them.

With a final pat of inspection to her braided and coiled blonde hair, Sarah picked up her Bible. She read from the Proverbs, and the third verse in chapter sixteen struck a chord in her. *Commit thy works unto the Lord…*

Closing her eyes, Sarah gave this new position to God, praying that the children would like her.

She left her room and ventured downstairs. Everything looked different in the daylight, and she admired the handsome wainscoting along the walls of the servants' stairwell. Nearing the kitchen, she inhaled, fearing she'd encounter the stern housekeeper. Instead, she found a plump, smiling woman standing at the stove.

"I'm Isabelle." She scooped scrambled eggs along with a couple of flapjacks onto a plate, then handed it to Sarah. "I take care of the cooking here, but I leave for my own home at seven o'clock. Don't board here in the house like Gretchen. I have dinner prepared. Just needs to be served, and Gretchen takes care of that."

"I see." Seating herself at the table, Sarah prayed over her food. Then she poured syrup over the pancakes. They practically melted in her mouth. "This is delicious, Isabelle."

The cook smiled with satisfaction and went back to her work at the stove.

Sarah ate alone, remembering that the children were with their grandmother. She imagined the kitchen would be much livelier in the next days, more of what she was accustomed to. Back in Jericho Junction she never dined in silence. Jake and Luke were usually around—at least they were until about a year ago. Then they left for an expedition of the Arizona Territory with the intent to start a church where one was needed. Ben and Valerie and their little ones, Maggie and Daniel, came for frequent visits. Maggie never stopped chattering. Ma said that's how Sarah was as a little girl too.

A sorrowful feeling filled her as she realized she wouldn't be home to help celebrate Daniel's first birthday next month. She most likely wouldn't be home in the fall when Valerie gave birth to her third baby, either.

But Sarah determined to stick to her plans. Big plans. God willing, there'd be an opening for a teacher at the music academy in Chicago this fall. Only then would she have arrived at the doorstep of true independence.

Once she finished eating, Isabelle took her plate. After thanking the pleasant cook, Sarah strode from the kitchen and bided her time by meandering through the house as she waited for Captain Sinclair. He said they'd get acquainted this morning. She admired the expensive-looking artifacts in the display cabinets and the oil paintings on the walls, particularly the portrait that hung above the hearth in the parlor. Sarah wondered if the subject was the late Mrs. Sinclair. If so, she'd been beautiful. Flaxen hair swept regally upward and a sophisticated light shone in her tawny eyes. With those features, she'd fit into the McCabe clan, except for a couple very different details: the ivory silk gown and a stunning emerald necklace. No McCabe woman ever enjoyed such finery, except for maybe Valerie before she'd married into the family. No, Sarah's mother and grandmothers on both sides hailed from simpler lots in life. Country women, all of them.

Sarah, however, refused to carry on the legacy. She wanted to be a city girl.

The sound of children's voices reached her ears. Sarah peered out the front windows and saw what had to be the Sinclair brood making their way up the walkway. The two boys sauntered, kicking stones from their path, one little girl skipped, and the littlest, another girl, pumped her little legs and did her best to keep up with the others. A woman wearing a fashionable olive-colored skirt and jacket over a white ruffled blouse trailed them. A beautiful felt hat with a ring of dried flowers sat on her carefully coiffured, dark-brown hair.

The kids spilled into the foyer but stopped short when they spotted Sarah. The regal-looking lady stepped into the house next.

"Well, well, well, who have we here?" Her dark gaze roamed over Sarah, and except for the fairer complexion, she bore a decided resemblance to the captain.

"I'm Sarah McCabe, the new governess. You must be the captain's"—Sarah frowned—"sister?"

"Oh..." The woman laughed. "You and I are going to get along famously." She held out a gloved hand. "I'm Aurora Reil, and these urchins"—she gestured to the children—"are my...my—"

"Grandchildren," put in the tallest boy. He was obviously the oldest. Turning to Sarah, he grudgingly explained, "Aurora hates the words *grandmother* and *grandchildren*."

"Gabriel, really! I don't *hate* those words." She lifted her chin. "At least not always. Just only when they apply to me."

"You're...you're the captain's mother?" Sarah blinked. "But you look so young."

"And you must be brilliant. Just don't ever refer to me as a...well, you know."

"*Grandmother!*" the children declared in unison. Giggles immediately followed.

The woman ignored them. "Please call me Aurora."

Sarah covered her shock. Every grandmother she had ever known wore the title proudly, feeling truly blessed by her grandchildren. How could it be that Aurora Reil was so different?

"I must be off." Aurora lay the back of her hand across her forehead. "I'm exhausted after my duty day."

Sarah smiled at the dramatics.

"Ta-ta, my darlings." Aurora bent slightly, allowing each child to place a perfunctory kiss on her powdery cheek. "Be kind to your new governess, and I shall see you next duty day."

With that she was gone. No introductions. No explanations.

Sarah surveyed the children. Oddly, they didn't look the least bit intimidated to have been left in the company of a complete stranger. Not even the youngest, who didn't look any older than three years old.

They stared up at her curiously.

"Come with me." Sarah led the way into the magnificent reception parlor. "Let's get acquainted."

The children followed. Gabriel held his baby sister's hand.

Sarah sat down and smoothed out her skirts. They continued to stand, and Sarah wondered why. "All right, let's start with you." She pointed to the oldest. "Gabriel, isn't it? How about telling me how old you are?"

He wore a stony expression. "I'm almost twelve, and I don't need any dumb governess."

The older of the two girls gasped. "You said 'dumb.' Daddy's gonna give you a licking!"

"Oh, quiet, Libby. You don't know anything."

Sarah wasn't put off by the boy's behavior. She had contended with big brothers and wasn't fazed in the least. "Fortunately for you, Gabriel, I'm highly intelligent. I can talk, see, and hear. So I don't fit the description of 'dumb.'"

He rolled a shoulder and looked like he might be mentally searching for another adjective.

"Sit down. All of you."

"We're not allowed to sit on the furniture in here." Gabriel folded his arms. Freed from his grasp, the little one came closer to Sarah to get a better look at her.

"Not allowed?" Sarah wondered if the rule applied to her as well.

"But sometimes we sit on it anyway," Libby said. "If Mrs. Schlyterhaus doesn't catch us."

"We sat on it lots when our mama was alive," said the younger of the two boys.

Sarah's heart filled with pity. So young to have lost their mother. Clearly, these children must be hurting. "I'm truly sorry for your loss, but please believe me when I say that in time God will heal your heart."

"How do you know?" Gabriel puffed out his chest.

"The Bible says so. Joy cometh in the morning." She grinned. "Besides, my pa is a pastor, and my brothers and sister and I have grown up helping others. I've seen the Lord heal sadness plenty of times."

The youngest girl, a little blondie, suddenly climbed into Sarah's lap, watching with wide, curious hazel eyes.

"What's your name?"

"Rachel."

"Nice to meet you, Rachel. I'm Sarah."

The girl smiled.

"She's three," Gabriel offered.

Rachel worked to hold up three fingers.

"Very good." Sarah hugged her, missing her little niece Maggie, who was about the same age.

Turning back to the other girl, Sarah searched her eyes. They were like her father's, black as coal. Her features resembled his as well, especially the color of her ebony hair that hung in one fat braid down her back. So like the captain's, so black the hair looked blue.

"So you're Libby?"

She nodded.

"Her given name is Elizabeth."

Sarah looked at Gabriel, nodding her thanks for his input.

"And this is Michael, my brother." As if to prove the point, the older gave the younger a brotherly shove.

Michael returned the gesture.

"Now, now, I'll have no roughhousing in here. Surely if you can't sit on the furniture, you can't roughhouse either."

The boys ceased their antics.

Sarah's gaze rested on Gabriel. He was fairer than his father. His eyes were bluish-green and his hair dark brown. "You know, eleven years old is quite mature. I'm thinking that because I've never been to Milwaukee before, I'm going to need you, Gabriel, to show me around the city. Why, I'm also going to need you to let me know how things are done around here at home. Would you help me?"

He appeared stunned before shrugging again. "I guess..."

"I'll help you too, Miss Sarah."

Sarah looked at Michael. "Well, thank you."

He inclined his head, and a lock of walnut-brown hair lopped over his forehead. Then he sent her a charming grin, and there was no doubt which parent he took after. "I just turned ten, but I know more than Gabe does."

"You do not!"

"Do so!"

"Do not!"

"Boys!" Sarah exclaimed while trying to hide a smile. "I'm quite sure I'll need both of you," she added diplomatically. "Gabriel? Michael? Is the matter settled?"

Gabriel replied with the shrug that now seemed habitual, and Michael nodded.

"I want to help you too, Miss Sarah." Libby stared up at her and leaned against her knee.

"Aw, you're just a baby," Gabriel groused.

"I am not! I'm six!" Libby retorted. "Rachel is the baby; Aurora even said so."

*Aurora?* "Really, Libby." A frown settled on Sarah's brow. "You don't actually call your grandmother by her given name, do you?"

"Well, you heard her," Gabe spouted. "She hates the word *grandmother*. She said she'll take the switch to us if we call her that."

"I'm sure she was joking." Sarah could hardly believe her ears, although Michael, Libby, and Rachel nodded vigorously.

"Do you have a grandmother?" Libby's voice was soft.

"No, but I have a niece and nephew who call my mother Granny."

The kids replied with a collective gasp.

Then Gabe smirked. "I wonder what Aurora would do if we called her Granny." He snickered together with Michael over the idea.

Sarah just shook her head at the both of them before placing a kiss on Rachel's head.

A masculine voice suddenly interrupted from the entryway. "Well, kids, I see you children are getting along with your new governess."

Sarah turned to find Richard standing in the entryway, wearing a wide grin.

"Mr. Navis!" At least three of the four children cried his name happily. Little Rachel squirmed off Sarah's lap to greet him. Gabriel strode toward him, his hands shoved into his pants pockets.

Richard rewarded them all with a striped candy stick. "I brought one for you too." He handed a pink-and-white one to Sarah.

"Thank you, Mr. Navis." She glanced at the children in silent reminder of their manners, and they thanked Richard as well.

"How 'bout we sit outside?" Richard motioned toward the door. "No telling what Mrs. Schlyterhaus will do to us if she finds sticky fingerprints on the polished furniture."

The threat was enough to move them along. Sarah followed them out to the front porch, where they sat and ate their sweet treat. Sarah pocketed hers for later.

"Captain Sinclair left a note and told me to stop over." Richard leaned against a pillar. "He had an early appointment this morning, but he'll be home at lunchtime to give you a bit of orientation. He sends his apologies."

"I'm sure it couldn't be helped." Sarah's feelings teetered between disappointment and frustration. She was on her own with these children and ignorant of what their father expected of her.

"It would seem you have everything under control."

Sarah sent Richard a smile, then watched the children enjoying their candy. She looked past them then and up into the sunshine, now well above the lake. The roar of the water had ceased, although the water looked choppy. Nonetheless it made an inspiring sight.

"Beautiful day." Richard folded his arms. "A bit cooler than yesterday."

"Yes, and it would seem you've gotten away from your books and out-of-doors once more." She couldn't resist the jab.

"Hmmm..." He pretended to think about it. "Well, what do you know? I did get away, didn't I?"

He laughed while Sarah smiled again, although it wasn't as if he were slacking. He was doing his employer's bidding.

"Say, there's a concert tomorrow night at the Shubert Theater. It opened last year, and it's quite a popular place. Would you like to go?"

"Well, um..." The offer caught Sarah off guard. "I don't know."

"We will be properly chaperoned," he added quickly, "in the company of several of my friends."

"*You* have friends?"

He narrowed his gaze.

Removing her eyes from his, she looked back toward the lake. Sarah couldn't decide whether to accept his offer. It would be wrong to give Richard false hopes of there being anything more than a friendship between them. Even so she had to admit that in the last twenty-four hours he'd been one of the most valuable friends she'd ever had.

"The concert will be an enjoyable evening out. You'll see." He straightened and stepped forward. "Say you'll come. I'll pick you up at precisely seven o'clock tomorrow evening."

"But I might still be on duty."

He gave a wag of his blond head. "The hours of your position are from seven to seven."

"Oh." Sarah smoothed the folds of her pinafore. "I'm glad at least one of us is aware of that."

"Then it's a date." With a chuckle, Richard bounded down the brick stairs.

"Wait..."

"Bye, kids. Behave, or else no more candy from me."

"Oh, we'll be good, Mr. Navis," Libby promised. "Honest we will."

He tousled the girl's inky-colored hair before unhitching his horse.

Sarah watched him mount. She caught his smile and decided her brothers would like him. One part man's man and three-quarters part stinker.

As a grand farewell, Richard gave the children a dramatic salute. Then he cantered off down the street. The younger children laughed, Sarah smiled, and even Gabriel grinned.

# Five

Captain Brian Sinclair arrived just before noon. Sarah and the children joined him in the dining room for lunch. Isabelle had prepared plates of sliced beef and cheese, which were served on chunks of freshly baked bread. For dessert she brought out a jar of her canned pears. Sarah observed the boys eating fast and furiously while the girls were more interested in talking and getting their father's attention.

"Papa, my toof is loose." Libby pulled out her bottom lip. "See?"

"Not at the table, darling." Despite the endearment, the captain's tone was terse.

The little girl promptly remembered her manners.

Rachel attempted to stand up on her chair.

The captain reached over and paddled her backside before reseating her. "We do not stand at the table. Understand?"

Rachel began to cry, and Sarah fought the urge to take the child in her arms and comfort her. Surely the captain didn't have to be so hard on the little one.

"Papa, will you throw the ball with me and Gabe after lunch?"

"I don't know, Michael, I'm a very busy man."

The boy's features dropped in disappointment. He tucked his chin and lowered his gaze.

Sarah felt frustration taking root with the captain's insensitivity.

The man finished the last of his meal. "Why don't you children tell me and your new governess what you did at Aurora's house yesterday?"

"Same ol' boring stuff," Gabe groused.

"Hmm..." Captain Sinclair peered at his eldest from beneath one arched brow. "Shopping?"

"Uh-huh. One stupid store after another."

Michael moaned. "All day long."

"Me an' Rachel got new dresses." Libby obviously hadn't minded the outing.

Rachel stopped crying and sniffed.

The children said nothing more. Once they'd all finished eating, the captain ordered Gabriel and Michael to watch the girls in the backyard so he and Sarah could discuss her position. She observed that Michael was quick to obey. He seemed to adore his father in spite of his harsh treatment. Gabriel, on the other hand, acted like he had a chip on his shoulder that he dared his father to knock off.

"Did you hear what I said, Gabe?"

The boy muttered.

"What's that?" The captain took him by the upper arm, forcing Gabe to look him in the eye. "I gave you an instruction, son."

"Yes, sir." Gabe ground out the reply.

"All right, then." Captain Sinclair released him. "I don't want those girls straying into the front yard and anywhere near the cliffs. Understood?"

"I said, yes, sir." Gabriel jerked backward. "Did you want me to salute you or something, like one of your Navy soldiers?"

Sarah glanced at the captain, wondering if he'd discipline the boy for such back talk.

But he ignored it and turned to her. "Miss McCabe, why don't you follow me to my study where we can talk privately?"

"All right."

As she trailed him through the house, she passed the housekeeper. Mrs. Schlyterhaus sent her a scathing look. Again Sarah wondered why she was the recipient of such contempt. Was the older woman unhappy in her position? And what did she, Sarah, have to do with it?

"Sit down, Miss McCabe," the captain told her after they'd entered his study. "May I call you Sarah?"

"You may." She chose one of the two black leather chairs situated in front of the captain's large oak desk. The captain closed the heavy paneled door and crossed the room in a few easy strides. Then he surprised her by taking the chair beside her instead of sitting behind his desk as she'd expected.

He smiled, and little crinkle lines appeared at the sides of his black eyes. "I'm so sorry about all the misunderstanding yesterday. It's really not the way I had intended to greet you and introduce my children."

"Apology accepted." She glanced at her folded hands in her lap.

"Now, about the children and the household situation as a whole..." He stretched out his long legs. Tapered black pants were tucked snugly into black boots. His tall frame looked as though it had been poured into the chair, for he seemed so relaxed. Meanwhile Sarah felt somewhat timid in his presence. "I'll start with some background information. My wife, Louisa, was sick for a long time and passed away about six months ago. This may sound awful, but her death came as almost a relief. I hated seeing her suffer."

"I understand." Sarah thought of her cousin Catherine Elliot who had died of burns she'd suffered when the barn caught fire. Catherine experienced terrible pain right up until her death. "Is your wife's portrait hanging above the mantel in the reception parlor?"

"Yes."

"She must have been a beautiful woman."

"Indeed. She was." Wistfulness stole over his expression.

Sarah sensed he grieved in spite of his earlier claim.

"The children seldom saw Louisa. During the years that she enjoyed good health, she busied herself with her social schedule. I did my duty for the United States Navy and only came home on short leaves, but we basically lived separate lives. I returned home from the war just over a year ago to find an ailing wife, an inconvenienced mother, an aging nanny, and four very undisciplined children." His voice had an edge to it when he referred to the children. Then he took a breath and paused. "Pardon all my candidness, but perhaps it will help you in your new position within my household."

"It will, sir, and I'm so sorry to hear about your wife's untimely death." Sarah's heart went out to him.

"Thank you." He drew himself up, seeming to steel himself. "Now, getting back to your position, I'll expect you to care for the children every day of the week but Wednesday."

Sarah nodded. "Richard informed me of that much."

"Good. My mother calls it her 'duty day.'"

"Yes, so I heard." Again, Sarah found the situation odd. "Did your mother remarry? I noticed her last name isn't Sinclair."

"Yes, she's gone through two husbands and is currently a widow." The captain shot her a look. "Did you meet Aurora this morning?"

"Yes. But I must admit I'm surprised the children address their grandmother by her first name. It seems..." She caught herself before she used the word *disrespectful*. That might be too strong. Clearing her throat, she began again. "Well, I guess it doesn't seem conventional."

Captain Sinclair chuckled. "There isn't anything *conventional* about Aurora. And Louisa was the same way. The two were the best of friends."

Sarah tipped her head. "Did the children call their mother by her first name also?"

"No, no. Only Aurora gets away with that offense, as it were." Again he paused, and it seemed as if he contemplated whether to continue—as if he were debating whether to let Sarah in on some great secret. Finally he said, "It's my intent that my children have some sense of family unity. I never did. Aurora acted more like my sibling than my mother, a fact that she freely admits. A fact she's actually quite proud of. I came to accept it a long time ago. But I don't want the same for my children."

"Yes, Captain." Sarah found it commendable. She lowered her gaze once more, this time staring at the plush imported carpet. "I'll do my best."

He brought his legs in and sat forward. "I don't want you to be deterred either by the fact that my children haven't been properly mothered or their odd relationship with Aurora. We have had governesses come and go in the past months, ever since Nanny Beckman resigned because her rheumatism got the best of her. She could no longer chase after the children. The females I hired…well, none of them worked out. I can't understand it, either." He rolled a broad shoulder, reminding Sarah of Gabriel. "Perhaps they weren't qualified. But you, on the other hand…" He sounded confident. "I sense you're different from all the rest, Sarah. You're compassionate, accepting…loving."

He studied her in a way that caused her to blush.

"Children need those sorts of things."

"I think so too."

The captain sat back in his chair. He pursed his lips and seemed deep in thought as he regarded her.

"Captain?" Sarah grew uncomfortable. "You were saying?"

"What was I saying?"

"Your household? Governesses come and go?"

"Oh, yes…and household staff too, for that matter. The only one of my staff who has stayed on is Gretchen. She and her husband had been in service with my in-laws—both of whom are dead now, along with Gretchen's husband. But back fifteen years ago, upon my marriage to Louisa, I acquired both Gretchen and Ernest as household help. Gretchen has been faithful ever since." The captain's mouth curved into a sardonic grin. "Of course, I do pay her very well."

Sarah pushed out a polite smile, although she wondered if the housekeeper's hostile disposition had scared away the other governesses. Gretchen's coldness bothered Sarah more than Aurora's unconventional ways and the children's behavior.

"Now, your hours are from seven in the morning to seven at night. Evenings are your own. I'll pay you five dollars a week, and—"

Sarah lifted her hand to her mouth, stifling a surprised gasp. The coveted teaching position in Chicago paid less.

"I know the amount is more than we agreed upon." He leaned

toward her and reached for her hand. "But I'm hoping to convince you to stay longer than the summer."

Sarah had to admit it was tempting.

"Is everything to your satisfaction? Your accommodations? Are they adequate?"

"Oh, yes, thank you." She'd only dreamed of sleeping in such an elegant bedroom.

A knock sounded. "Come in." Dropping her hand, the captain twisted his upper body around.

The door opened and the ornery housekeeper appeared. "Mr. Navis has sent a message. You are late for your two o'clock appointment."

Sarah glimpsed the confused expression on his suntanned face.

"Did I have a two o'clock appointment?"

Mrs. Schlyterhaus lifted her hands, palm side up. "Apparently."

After a sigh, the captain's dark gaze fixed on Sarah. "It's a good thing I have Richard and Gretchen, Isabelle…and now you also. Together we'll make a fine family."

With that he rose and strode from the room, but not before giving the housekeeper's shoulder an affectionate pat. The woman bestowed him a grin, then scowled at Sarah before spinning on her heel and hurrying off.

Sitting in the captain's study alone, Sarah found it incredibly sad that Captain Sinclair thought he could purchase a family for himself and his children. Those special ties that bound folks together couldn't be bought. Even Sarah knew that. But the real question remained. Did she want to be any part of this odd acquisition?

After the captain left for his meeting, Sarah went upstairs with the children. The girls were heated up and whiney when she'd called them in from playing outside. Sarah figured they were in need of a short rest time.

"Boys, you can read a book or play quietly in your rooms," she told Gabriel and Michael while directing Libby and Rachel into the bedroom referred to as the nursery. "Libby, you may take a nap or look at a book, but you must not disturb your sister. She needs to sleep."

"Yes, Miss Sarah." Libby pulled several children's stories from the white bookshelf at the far end of the room. Then she climbed onto the bed.

Sarah lifted Rachel into her bed. The little girl's whines and complaints became a full-fledged temper tantrum. Rachel screamed so loudly that the boys ran in to see if she'd been hurt.

"Rachel, honey, you are overtired." Sarah managed to unlace the child's ankle-high leather shoes despite the kicking. "Sleep awhile and you'll feel better."

"No! No! No!"

Sarah glanced at all three pairs of eyes watching her. "I see I shall have to plan our afternoons around Rachel's naps."

"Are you going to hit her?" Gabriel tipped his head. "The other governesses did."

"I can't see how hitting Rachel would help matters." Sarah knelt beside the bed and held on to Rachel's arm so she wouldn't get up. Then Sarah began to sing Psalm 23.

The Lord's my Shepherd
I shall not want.
He makes me lie down in green pastures.
In pastures green he leadeth me,
Beside the still waters so calm.

Gabriel and Michael walked farther into the room and sat down to listen to Sarah sing.

Yea, though I walk
Through the valley of the shadow of death,
I will fear no evil—
Fear no evil.
For thou art with me.
Thy rod and thy staff they comfort me.

Before Sarah finished, Rachel was sleeping soundly. Sarah smoothed the little girl's hair off her perspiring forehead and gave her a gentle kiss. Turning, she noticed Libby's eyelids growing heavy. Meanwhile, Gabriel and Michael had stretched out on the floor.

Sarah crossed the distance between the two beds and rubbed Libby's back as she continued to sing.

Surely goodness and mercy shall follow me,
All the days, all the days, of my life.

Libby fell asleep, and as she did for Rachel, Sarah removed her leather shoes. She kissed Libby's forehead.

Next she shooed the boys out of the room and closed the door.

"Is that true?"

"Is what true, Gabriel?" Sarah guided him toward his own bedroom.

"Is it true about the shadow of death?"

"It's called the 'valley of the shadow of death,' and yes, it's real. It sounds like a scary place, I know, but I feel sure the Lord Jesus will walk me through it. The psalm says, 'For thou art with me.' That's why believers don't have to be afraid."

"We're believers," Gabe said. "Mike an' me."

"Yeah, Mr. Navis told us about Jesus," Michael informed Sarah. "We asked Jesus into our hearts."

"I'm so glad to hear it." Sarah felt more impressed with Richard now. And Pa would be thrilled to hear how he'd led these precious children to Christ.

"But our mom didn't want to hear about God." Gabe sounded so very downcast. "Neither does our dad."

"That's a shame. But maybe one day your father will see his need for the Lord."

"I doubt it," Gabe muttered.

Sarah gave his shoulder a gentle squeeze to encourage him. "All right, now you two have a bit of quiet time in your rooms while I unpack the last of my belongings. Then we'll figure out something fun to do before dinner."

The boys didn't argue but did as she bid them.

Inside her own room Sarah closed the door and leaned against it. She sensed much anger and hurt emanating from those two boys. Didn't Captain Sinclair see that his harsh treatment of them caused such feelings? But he said he wanted a sense of family for his children. It all seemed quite puzzling to Sarah. And why didn't the past governesses last in their positions here? The children were absolutely lovable.

She glanced around her tastefully decorated bedroom, admiring the light purplish-blue satin draperies and coordinating bedspread. The furniture was oak, and a large chifforobe stood against the far wall. Who could complain about these accommodations? Certainly not Sarah.

With a sigh she moved to unpack the remainder of her things. Perhaps the captain was right. The other governesses simply hadn't been qualified enough for the job, and it took its toll on them. To Sarah, however, her new position in the Sinclair household promised to be the easiest work she'd ever had!

# Six

Richard awoke with a start. Morning light filled his bedroom. Quickly he tossed aside his bedcovers, dressed, and ran downstairs. He found his mother in the kitchen cooking breakfast.

"Your father couldn't wait for you." She stirred a pot on the stove. It looked and smelled like oatmeal. "He's already out in the barn."

"I woke up late." Richard combed his fingers through his hair.

"Well, it wouldn't have mattered if you got up at dawn anyway. Your father didn't sleep."

"His legs?"

Mama nodded. Her auburn hair hung down her back in a fat braid. Later, when she dressed, she'd wind it up into its usual bun.

Richard decided he'd better not tarry a moment more. Chores awaited him. "I'll be back in a while."

Opening the back door, he left the large kitchen and walked down the wooden ramp, which had been built after his father's return from the war. A Rebel's bullet caught Pops in the lower back. The damage caused by removing it had rendered his legs useless. Since then he got around the house and property in a wooden chair that had two large wheels on each side. Richard was only too glad that he'd been able to purchase the special chair at a good price, thanks to Captain Sinclair and all his contacts. And although Pops was confined to the thing, his disposition remained as good-natured as the day he'd marched off to enlist in the Army.

"G' mornin'!" Richard called the greeting as he entered the barn. Hay particles tickled his nose. He grabbed a pail and proceeded to milk Lyla, one of the family's Guernsey cows.

Pops wheeled up beside him. "I've milked two cows already."

"Sorry. I overslept."

"Been keeping late hours there, haven't you, son?"

Richard grinned, then shrugged. "Business is booming."

"Right-o," his father replied, albeit on a sarcastic note. "'Course I don't imagine your coming in after dark the past two nights has anything to do with this new governess your mother told me about."

Embarrassment got a hold of Richard's tongue. The first day Sarah arrived he'd taken her to dinner as the captain had asked. Then yesterday after he finished working at the store, he'd ridden over to the Sinclair home. He ended up playing a game of catch with Gabriel and Michael and talking to Sarah a while. Tonight he would take her to the theater. "Seeing as Sarah is new in Milwaukee, Pops, I've felt the need to—"

"Look to her comfort?"

"Yes. That is...no. I mean..." Richard groped for the right words. "What I mean is...the captain asked me to help her, seeing as he's been busy." Richard slid a glance his father's way and smirked. "All right, so I like her just fine. But don't worry. I haven't been making a pest of myself."

Pops replied with his usual lopsided grin. "Listen, I'm proud of you for taking care of things for the captain like you do. You're a good man."

Richard's heart warmed. "Thanks." He appreciated the fact that his father noted how hard he worked here and at Sinclair and Company.

Pops wheeled off and went about his early morning chores. Richard worked quickly to keep up. Then, being so tardy, he entered the house, ran upstairs, washed, and changed into a fresh shirt. He donned his tie, grabbed his suit coat, and barreled back down the steps. In the kitchen, he gobbled a few bites of breakfast, much to his mother's consternation. Next it was back out to the barn again, where he saddled his horse, Poco.

"I'm staying with Aunt Ruth and Uncle Jesse tonight," he told his father as he put his foot into the stirrup. "I won't see you until late tomorrow."

"Ah, yes, it's Friday." Pops gave him a nod of understanding. "Don't suppose you've invited that new governess to the theater with your friends."

Richard couldn't quite conceal a grin. "Pops, you've got it over on me."

"Well, I was young once too, you know."

"You sure about that?" Richard laughed at his father's feigned scowl. He pressed his heels into Poco's sides but halted when his mother beckoned to him from the back door.

"Ask Sarah to church on Sunday...and Sunday dinner too. The Staffords are joining us."

Richard looked from Mama's hopeful expression to Pops's amused grin and wondered if the two people he loved the most in this world were getting more serious about Sarah than he was.

But the truth in his heart ran contrary to the notion. He was more interested in Sarah than he'd been in any young lady he'd ever known. Her manner differed in a refreshing sort of way—familiar and fun with a hint of vulnerability. He couldn't stop thinking about her.

Little wonder that his parents noticed.

"Sarah will most likely have the captain's brood with her on Sunday," he warned his mother. "Four pistols, you know."

"Oh, I just love those kids." A sparkle entered Mama's eyes. "Tell her it's OK to bring them. They're invited too."

"Orders from headquarters." Pops guffawed.

Richard smiled. "You two have a good day." Spurring his roan forward into a gallop, he rode the five miles into the city. Reaching Sinclair and Company on Water Street, he dismounted.

*Another day of bookwork.* The thought threatened to rip the joy of living right out of him. He'd rather milk cows, slop pigs, muck out stalls, and plow and plant fields. Anything on the farm suited him just fine.

Still, he'd make the best of his position with the captain. Just as he did every day.

Sarah decided on a walk along Milwaukee's magnificent lakefront while the children ate breakfast with their father. His sternness with them made Sarah feel somewhat tense—and confused. A stroll would clear her head.

She found the well-worn path that led down the cliffs to the beach. A cool wind swept off the water, blowing locks of her blonde hair into her face. She brushed them back with one hand as she thought about Captain Sinclair. How could she help him?

Sarah bent to pluck an interesting-looking stone out of the sand, thinking she admired the captain's desire to give his children more of a sense of family than he knew as a child. But it didn't take a genius to see that Gabriel craved his father's approval but only received reprimands. Michael looked up to his father and wanted to emulate him but went ignored. The little girls needed their father's affection, although their basic longings went unnoticed too.

Tossing the small rock into the water, Sarah thought Captain Sinclair seemed quite capable of loving. So why didn't he?

Picking up her pace, Sarah walked for over a half hour. She used the time to plot and plan the day ahead.

When she finally arrived back at the Sinclair residence, the captain was just getting ready to leave for the day. "Excellent timing." He sent her a grin. "Are you refreshed from your walk?"

"Yes. It seemed to get my blood moving."

"The lake breezes do that for a body." His smile grew. "So what are your plans for today?"

"We're going fishing, right, Miss Sarah?" Michael sidled up to her, looking at his father. "Miss Sarah says she knows how to bait a hook just the way the fish like it."

Sarah felt her face flame with embarrassment. While the boy

meant it as a compliment, she didn't want the captain to think she wasn't ladylike.

He, however, didn't seem to notice. "I take it we'll have fish for dinner this evening."

"Oh, you bet we will!" The tilt of Michael's chin reflected his determination.

Gabriel stood by, looking interested.

Libby wrinkled her little nose. "I hate fish. They smell."

"I wholeheartedly agree." Sarah sat down in a nearby chair and pulled Libby onto her lap. "But I thought you and Rachel could collect stones while the boys fish. I have an idea for a special project, and it will take lots of beautiful stones and paste. Then later we'll begin your piano lessons."

"Goody!" Libby happily jumped up and down.

A dark frown shadowed Captain Sinclair's face. "Stop that noise, Libby."

She did, albeit with a large pout.

He straightened his frock coat and sent each of his children a pointed look. "You all behave yourselves. I want a good report from Miss Sarah when I get home this evening. Understood?"

Michael straightened like a soldier.

The girls bobbed their heads, Libby less enthusiastically,

Gabriel turned and ran up the stairs without so much as a backward glance at his father.

An hour later Sarah found herself back down at the beach. Libby and Rachel had taken off their shoes and stockings and with one hand hiked their skirts to their knees as they searched for "diamond rocks." Each girl carried a pail with the other hand as they walked through the wet sand at the water's edge, looking quite serious about their work. Sarah kept a close eye on them as she sat on the long brick pier.

"So show us how to bait the hook like you said." Michael looked eager.

"All right, well…you've got to fold up the worm onto the hook…like so." She plucked a pink, wiggly worm from the boys' tin, impaled it, and wrapped it around the hook.

Gabriel squinted, watching her closely. "I never knew a lady that wasn't ascared of worms."

"Afraid, Gabriel," Sarah corrected. "And, no, I'm not afraid of worms."

"How 'bout snakes?" Michael asked with a tip of his chin.

"What kind of snakes?" She stifled a grin.

"All kinds…but mostly really slimy, slithery ones."

"Oh, those are the best kind." Sarah fought the urge to giggle. No doubt these two were up to something, what with all their questions.

"Our last governess didn't like any kind of snakes," Michael blurted. "She especially didn't like them in her bed."

"Oh, mercy! You little rascal! You didn't really put a snake in your last governess's bed, did you?"

"Nope. Gabe did it."

Sarah clucked her tongue at him.

"We didn't like her," he said simply, as if that was all the reason he needed to do such a dastardly deed.

"For shame." Sarah thought it over. "Why didn't you like her?"

"She was mean." Gabe took the fishing pole from her.

"But don't worry," Michael added with his heart in his eyes, "we like you, Miss Sarah. You're not mean. Right, Gabe?"

"I guess."

High praise, coming from Gabe. "Well, I'm very fond of both you boys." Sarah gave each one a smile. "Now, let's get busy and catch some fish!"

Richard couldn't resist. When Captain Sinclair announced that Sarah had taken the boys fishing, he just had to see it for himself. So when the captain sent him on his daily errands, he promised to check on his children and their new governess.

And there she was... bare feet dangling in the water, her blonde hair tousled by the lake breeze, her bonnet blown backward, and a fishing pole in hand. He chuckled. What a sight she made.

Still smiling, he walked toward the pier.

"Hi, Mr. Navis," Libby shouted from several feet away.

"Good morning, girls." Richard waved to her and little Rachel.

"Hey, look, it's Mr. Navis!" Gabriel called.

Sarah gasped and spun around. "What are you doing here?" Her blue eyes widened. She appeared embarrassed.

He hiked a brow. "I came to see the refined music teacher fishing like an old seaman."

Sarah gave him a quelling look. "Oh, fine. Well, now you've seen me, barefoot and all. So go on back to your books where you belong."

Richard laughed. She was fun to goad.

"And I'm hardly an 'old seaman.'"

"I'll say. But if you're not careful, you'll have a fine sunburn."

Sarah inhaled sharply again and nearly lost her pole to Lake Michigan as her hands leapt to secure her bonnet on top of her head. Richard chuckled all the while.

"Why can't Miss Sarah get a sunburn?" Michael wanted to know.

"Because it will smart," Richard replied.

"More so because it will tan, and then I'll look like the farmer's daughter." She released an exasperated sigh. "I just hope my face and hands aren't already pink from this outing."

"What's so bad about looking like the farmer's daughter?" Gabriel turned away from his fishing pole to peer up at Sarah.

"Yeah, what's so bad about it?" Richard folded his arms. After all, he had been born and raised on a farm. His mother never complained about the sun tanning her skin, and she looked healthy with that little bit of brown.

"A *real* lady," Sarah began, "shades her skin from the sun. I learned in Chicago that all the women whiten their skin with powder. It's stylish."

"Hmm..." Richard pursed his lips. "So, what you're saying is that sophisticated city women think it's stylish to look sickly."

"Like Aurora," Michael remarked.

"And Mrs. Kingsley," Gabriel interjected.

"Who is Mrs. Kingsley?" Sarah asked.

"She's one of the ladies who visits Dad sometimes. She has powder-white skin like you said and wears her dresses so low you can see clear down to her—"

"That's quite enough, Gabriel, thank you!" Sarah turned a shocked expression on Richard, who had the good sense not to even grin but changed the subject instead.

"How many fish have ye caught, men?" He imitated a rugged seafaring man.

Sarah glared at him for including her as one of them.

"We caught three, mate," said Michael, playing his part. "But Miss Sarah is the one who caught 'em, so I guess they don't count."

"Now, see here!" Sarah frowned.

"Besides, they're puny," Gabriel added.

An indignant grunt escaped her. "That does it! I'm going to help Libby and Rachel collect diamond rocks!"

Richard laughed and laughed. What fun she was!

"You're not *really* angry, are you, Miss Sarah?" A worried little frown stretched across Michael's brow.

"You bet I am!" A second later, she turned and gave the boy a look to say she teased him.

He grasped the meaning with a nod and turned his attention back to his fishing line.

Gabriel sat by, smiling broadly. It appeared Sarah was winning him over. But how could she not with her sweet spirit and fun-loving nature.

"I wish you were my governess," Richard teased as they walked side by side along the pier.

"You, sir, *need* a governess... to keep you at your books!"

Richard chuckled at the comeback while Sarah sat down beneath the sunshade she'd brought along.

"I thought you were going to help Libby and Rachel."

"I changed my mind." She sounded tired. "I need a rest."

Richard dropped down beside her while Sarah removed her bonnet. She smelled of fresh air, and her feet were covered with sand—so was the hem of her skirts, but she didn't seem to care. In fact, she looked comfortable, completely natural, in this environment.

"Is everything going well at the captain's home?" Richard leaned back on his hand. "I mean, with Mrs. Schlyterhaus?"

"Everything is fine, although I try to stay out of that woman's way."

"That's probably wise. At least until she gets used to having you around."

"I just don't understand why she doesn't like me. I've been nothing but kind and respectful to her."

"It's not you, Sarah." Richard wished he could quell her misgivings. Maybe by bringing up Mama's offer…

He cleared his throat. "My parents asked me to invite you and the children to church on Sunday and then back to the farm for dinner afterwards. Would you come?"

Sarah's jaw dropped slightly and a curious light entered her blue eyes. "Your parents? You told them about me?"

He felt like a besotted fool. "I mentioned the captain had another new governess." He gazed out over the teal-blue water. "Since they know the children, it's only natural they inquired about you."

"I'm glad for the invitation."

"You are?" He glanced at her.

"Yes, I've been wondering what to do about church and the children on Sunday." She paused a few seconds, seeming deep in thought, and Richard wondered if she'd refuse his offer.

He held his breath.

"Richard, I get the impression that Captain Sinclair is not a man of faith. The boys practically said so."

"It's true. By his own admission he's not a Christian."

"Will he mind me taking his children to church?"

"I doubt it. On Sundays past, while in between governesses, I've picked up the children for the day. The captain thinks it's good that his kids are exposed to 'religion.' He just doesn't believe God and church are meaningful for him."

"Perhaps the captain will have a change of heart soon."

"That's our prayer."

"And I understand you shared Christ with Gabe and Michael."

"They told you?"

Sarah nodded.

"Praise God! For months now I've been wondering if they understood."

"Seems like they did." Sarah gave him a smile that rivaled the sunshine. "With the captain's permission, I'd love to come on Sunday."

"I'm glad." He thought she had to be the prettiest young lady he'd ever met. *Lord, is it possible for a man to fall in love in less than three days? If it is, then I believe I've succumbed!*

Richard had never been interested in any one woman, not seriously, anyway. Then again, no one he'd met was like Sarah McCabe.

"Well, I'd best get back to work." He couldn't put off the inevitable for much longer. "But I'll see you this evening." He got to his feet and brushed the sand from his trousers. "Unless, of course, you're too *sunburned*!"

"I will not be sunburned!" She quickly arranged her skirts so they covered her feet and fixed the sunshade so it protected her arms and face.

Richard chuckled as he left the beach.

# SEVEN

"SO, WHAT DO YOU THINK OF THE SHUBERT THEATER?"

"It's a fine place." Sarah watched as Richard's cousin Lina took her fiancé's arm. "The concert was delightful."

"Being a music teacher, Sarah ought to know." Richard stepped in beside her as they strolled toward the ice cream parlor up the block.

"I don't know how expert I am, but I thought the ensemble played without a flaw."

"I thought so too." Walking just ahead, Lina turned and sent a smile to Sarah. The hem of her salmon-colored dress swirled around her ankles.

Sarah liked Lina. Outgoing and bubbly with apple-dumpling cheeks, she taught at a local elementary school and had the summer months off. Their interest in teaching and children bonded Sarah and Lina immediately. Lina's betrothed, a plump fellow named Timothy Barnes, worked as an expressman, delivering packages, parcels, and mail. Sarah thought the two made a sweet couple.

"Bethany? Lionel?" Lina whirled around. "How did you both enjoy the concert?"

Sarah glanced over her shoulder to view the pair walking behind her and Richard. Mr. Lionel Barnes was Tim's brother, and Bethany Stafford lived next door to the Navis family.

"I thought the clarinets played off key." Lionel sounded bored as he stared across the street.

*Clarinets?* Sarah hid a grin. They were oboes.

"I enjoyed the violin solos," Bethany offered. She hadn't said much all night.

"Oh, yes, those were lovely." Lina turned forward again.

They finished their trek to the ice cream parlor and stepped inside.

Other theatergoers pressed into the quaint shop. Richard, Lina, and the Barneses knew a number of people, and as they greeted each other Sarah found herself pushed back toward the corner next to Bethany.

"My, but it's crowded in here tonight." Sarah pulled in the skirt of her dress to make more room.

"Exceedingly." Bethany folded her arms across the bodice of her lilac dress, and her kitten-gray eyes seemed fixed on someone in particular.

Following her line of vision, Sarah suspected she watched Lionel. He chatted with two other blushing females. "Is he your, um, beau?" She hoped not. The man flirted shamelessly.

"No." Bethany shook her head. Locks of her fine, light-brown hair fell over her shoulder. "I can only hope."

*For him?* Sarah bent her head close to Bethany's. "You're interested in Mr. Lionel Barnes?"

Again, Bethany shook her head. Her gaze fell on Sarah and narrowed slightly. "Mr. Richard Navis."

Sarah was embarrassed. "Oh, I...I'm sorry, Bethany. I didn't realize that you and Richard—"

Bethany looked away, her cheeks turning pink. "No need to apologize. It's a childhood crush. Nothing more. I laugh about it, really."

Bethany lowered her head and didn't say another word.

"You really didn't have to walk me back to the captain's residence."

"Of course I did. I couldn't let you walk home alone." Richard took her hand and tucked it into his elbow.

Sarah probably shouldn't have insisted on walking, but she wanted the air. "In Jericho Junction I walked everywhere alone." She smiled. "Of course when I was growing up, it wasn't much of a town. One long main street. Saloon on one end, hotel and railroad station in the middle, and my pa's church at the other end. It's expanded much more now. Like a real town. But up until the day I left I walked unescorted to the general store all the time."

"This isn't Jericho Junction, Sarah."

She bristled at his gentle chastening. "In Chicago I was on my own. I did just fine."

"I'd say God protected you."

"Well, yes…I'm sure He did."

Richard stuffed his hands into his jacket pockets. "Like Chicago, Milwaukee is a big city. The shipping industry brings in sailors, and many of them are out after dark, looking for trouble. There are taverns on most of the street corners, and intoxicated individuals cannot be trusted."

Across the street she glimpsed a brightly lit establishment. No signs of rowdiness on the walk yet, but lively strains of piano music wafted on the night air. She inhaled deeply. The lake breezes smelled as fresh as line-dried linen.

"And how will you get home now that Lina, Bethany, and the Barnes brothers took the buggy?"

"I'll take one of the captain's horses. He won't mind—especially since I'm walking his stubborn governess home."

Sarah averted her gaze and quickened her step.

"I sense something is amiss. Have you been offended?"

"No…" She thought about telling him what Bethany said earlier then decided against it. What did she care if Bethany hoped for Richard's attention? Except she'd noticed Richard's solicitations and felt sure that Bethany had also.

"Must be your sunburn then." His tone was a cross of concern and amusement. "How does it feel?"

She stifled a groan. "It smarts, all right." Her forearms were pink where she'd rolled up her sleeves. The bridge of her nose was cherry-red, along with her cheeks and the back of her neck. Sarah had applied a good amount of cold cream on the areas in hopes they wouldn't tan.

"So much for the fashionable pasty look." Richard chuckled.

The tart remark made her grin. "Well, I suppose getting sunburned was worth it. The boys caught a couple of fish. Brown trout, we're guessing. One was a beastly thing." Sarah wasn't accustomed to lake fishing. "I think they wanted to impress their father."

"And? Was the captain impressed?"

Sarah's heart sank as she recalled the disappointment on Gabriel's face. "The captain didn't come home when he promised, and before we could stop her, Isabelle cooked up their fine catches."

"Captain Sinclair is a hard one to keep on a schedule." Weariness hung on Richard's tone. "It's miraculous when he's on time."

They reached the Sinclair residence. Richard steered her toward the porch, but she halted him.

"Mrs. Schlyterhaus scolded me about using the front door. I need to enter through the side."

"Ah..." He walked her around the stately manse. "I guess you're officially part of the household staff."

Sarah didn't feel so positive about it. She'd been reprimanded twice for not using the servants' stairwell. Talk about mixed signals. Captain Sinclair wanted that family feeling in his home, while his housekeeper wanted to maintain a strict distinction between staff and family.

"I had a very nice evening, Richard. Thank you for inviting me out."

"It was entirely my pleasure." He bowed slightly.

Sarah suppressed a giggle. Even when he wasn't trying to be funny, he amused her.

"I'll come for you after breakfast on Sunday," he stated on a more serious note. "About eight."

"That'll be fine. Captain Sinclair has given his approval, so the children and I will be waiting." She touched his sleeve. "Good night."

"G'night, Sarah."

There was no mistaking the tender note in his voice.

A loud clap of thunder awoke Sarah early Saturday morning. By the time she'd dressed and walked downstairs, the captain and his children already sat at the kitchen table.

"Am I late?" Sarah pulled out the dainty watch pinned to the bodice of her chambray dress. The time read six forty-five.

The captain stood. "The storm has us all up earlier than usual." He pulled a chair out for Sarah, and she sat down.

"Yeah, who could sleep with Libby and Rachel crying like babies," Gabriel said.

"I'm not a baby!" Libby stuck out her tongue.

"No bickering at the table, children." The captain reclaimed his place at the head of the table.

"I'm sorry I didn't hear the girls, Captain." Sarah usually didn't sleep so soundly.

"You weren't on duty."

But her bedroom was next to the girls'. Turning, Sarah touched Rachel's blonde hair. "Are you sick?" She glanced at Libby. "Why were you crying?"

"They're ascared of a little storm."

"Gabriel, that's enough." Captain Sinclair eyed his son in warning.

Thunder reverberated over the house. Rachel covered her ears. "I don't yike dat noise!"

"Thunder can't hurt you." The captain lifted the silver coffee pot and refilled his cup. "Don't be afraid." He glanced her way. "Miss Sarah isn't afraid of the storm." A frown puckered his brows. "Is she?"

"No, I'm not afraid." She pulled Rachel onto her lap, holding her close. "I actually enjoy a good thunderstorm. Clears the air."

Lightning flashed and another rumble sounded, low and ominous. Libby slipped off her chair and ran around the table, burying her head in Sarah's lap.

"Everyone in their places at mealtime." Gabe was forever spouting the rules whenever Sarah inadvertently broke them.

"Could we make an exception?" She glanced at the captain with pleading eyes. "The girls are still young and need affection."

He seemed to struggle with his decision. Finally he said, "Well, maybe just this time."

"Goody!" Libby climbed up on Sarah's left leg while Rachel still sat on her right.

"How are the piano lessons coming along?" The captain wisely changed the subject.

"Oh, Daddy, I can play good now!" Now that she felt secure, the fear was gone from Libby's tone.

"You can't play that good," Gabe groused.

"I'd rather go fishing than play piano," Michael remarked.

"Tell you what..." The captain sipped his coffee. "If you learn to play a whole piece on the piano by the end of the summer and if I can *recognize* the piece," he added with a grin, "then I'll throw a party for you—a recital. And I'll invite all my friends to come and hear you play."

"Really, Daddy? A party? For us?" Libby clapped her hands together.

"For us, Daddy?" Rachel mimicked her older sister.

"Who cares about a dumb ol' party," Gabe said.

Michael just rolled his shoulders.

Sarah grinned. "Don't let the boys fool you, Captain. They're actually quick learners and caught on to the concept of reading music after just one lesson on Thursday afternoon. The girls also show much talent."

Captain Sinclair seemed impressed. "Then we'll have that, um, 'dumb ol' party'"—he sent Gabe a pointed stare—"come the fall. Right before school begins."

Sarah looked down at her plate, wondering if she'd still be here in Milwaukee.

After breakfast, the captain went about his business while Sarah situated the children in the music room. It was located at the end of the hallway between the ladies' parlor and the men's parlor—not to be confused with the reception parlor. And Sarah was again amazed at the home's enormity.

Opening up several sheets of music, Sarah began the piano lessons. Good day for it. The storm had blown over, but the rain continued.

She went over reading notes, showing them how each one sounded on the piano. She hadn't fibbed when she'd told the captain his children learned quickly. They did! Sarah was delighted. By lunchtime Gabriel, Michael, and Libby could play one of the primary tunes.

"Can we have the party now?" Libby asked, her black eyes wide.

"Not quite yet." Sarah felt sure the captain expected to hear more than a basic four-note piece.

The day progressed indoors because of the inclement weather. Mrs. Schlyterhaus lectured Sarah about the children straying into other parts of the house and making messes, so she confined them. *How sad to live in this great big house and be unable to fully enjoy it.*

Upstairs, Gabriel and Michael occupied themselves in their separate bedrooms while Sarah read to the girls and watched them play with their dolls. Every so often she checked on the boys to make sure they weren't up to any mischief. Michael had made a fort with blankets and read a book beneath it, and Gabe appeared busy at his desk, writing or drawing.

Captain Sinclair arrived around eight o'clock. Late as usual. But Sarah didn't have anywhere to go, and she didn't mind being with the children. She supervised their baths and saw to it they were all ready for bed when their father got home.

"Daddy, Daddy!" Libby ran down the front stairs before Sarah could catch her.

Sarah followed, only to meet Mrs. Schlyterhaus at the bottom.

"You use the servants' stairwell, Irish. You're a servant." She spoke with a heavy German accent and through a clenched jaw. "Understand?"

Sarah pulled herself back.

"Gretchen, it's all right." Scooping the little girl into his arms, the captain strode across the foyer. "Sarah followed Libby downstairs. It couldn't be helped. Wherever my children are, that's where I want

Sarah too." He patted the older woman's shoulder. "Now, take the night off and relax, will you? I know you've worked hard today."

Chagrin reddened Mrs. Schlyterhaus's face, but her expression said she'd been disarmed. She marched off without a reply.

Sarah expelled a breath she hadn't been aware she'd held. All day long she'd avoided the crusty housekeeper with success.

"Sorry about that, Captain."

"No need to apologize." He hugged Libby before setting her slippered feet onto the tile floor.

Sarah noted the hug and quietly rejoiced. Perhaps he'd taken the hint at breakfast. Nevertheless, the child was clad in her nightgown, and Sarah felt embarrassed that she hadn't been able to contain her upstairs.

"Daddy, listen to what I can play!" Libby grabbed his hand and pulled him toward the music room.

As Sarah stood at the doorway, Libby played her little song. When she finished, the captain applauded with vigor.

"Such talent!" he exclaimed, with a wink at Sarah. "I'm so proud of you, Libby!"

The little girl beamed and ran into her father's lap. Sarah recalled the days when, as a little girl, she found love and security in her daddy's lap.

She smiled at the sight before her. *Maybe the captain really does love his children.*

"Sarah, why don't you call the other children and then you can play for us?" Captain Sinclair suggested. "A bedtime melody."

"Yes, yes!" cried Libby.

Sarah felt embarrassed but agreed. Exiting the music room, she collected the boys. Rachel was already asleep for the night. Returning, she made her way to the piano. Under the tutelage of her sister-in-law, Valerie, she'd become quite accomplished.

She began to play. Her long, slender fingers danced above the ivory keys in practiced motions. First a piece from Chopin. Then Mozart.

A Brahms lullaby next. And, finally, one of her favorite hymns: "Be Still, My Soul."

When Sarah finished, she closed her eyes for a moment. That last piece never failed to stir her heart. In the next moment, however, she remembered her audience. Turning around, her gaze met the captain's.

"That was beautiful, Sarah," he said quietly. His black eyes shone beneath the pale glow of the lamplight.

"Thank you, sir."

The admiration in his eyes turned to amusement. "But now look what you've done."

Noticing all of the children had fallen fast asleep, Sarah smiled. What a touching photograph they'd make—a father and his children. Three of the four anyway. Such a pity her brother Ben wasn't here with his camera.

Captain Sinclair stood and scooped Libby into his arms. "I'll carry her, if you'll wake the boys. They're old enough to stumble up to bed."

Sarah set to the task, gently shaking Michael first, then Gabriel. They moaned and groaned and stomped up the front staircase, angry to have been awakened.

With the children all in their beds, Sarah met the captain in the hallway.

"I've made a decision tonight." He leaned back against the staircase's railing.

"A decision?" Sarah tipped her head. "And what might that be?" She had a hunch a new rule was about to be instated—something, perhaps, about the children being down in the music room, dressed in their nightclothes well after their bedtime.

"I've decided," the captain said softly, "that I'm going to do whatever it takes to keep you here, Sarah McCabe. You're good for my children, I can see that already. And tonight, for the first time ever, I felt like a family man instead of a businessman. I have you to thank for it."

"Oh..." She smoothed down the skirt of her smock. She wasn't sure how to reply.

But the captain didn't seem to expect one. He reached out and set his hand on her upper arm. "Good night, Sarah." He moved forward then headed down the steps.

Alone in the long, wide hallway, Sarah experienced a tumult of emotions. She would love to live in this house forever, and she couldn't help but wonder at the look in the captain's eyes when he said he had decided to "keep her here." Could that have been a romantic gleam shining from their dark depths?

*I'm imagining things.* Leah always said she had a runaway imagination. She sighed heavily. *I never should have read the Brontë sisters' books!*

# Eight

"What do you think about it, Richard?" To serve as something of a reality check, Sarah decided to mention the incident the following day after church. Richard had already proved himself trustworthy—and he knew the captain well.

"He said that? That he's going to do 'whatever it takes'?"

Sarah nodded, wishing Richard didn't look so amused. She glanced down at Rachel in her lap. The little girl's eyelids fluttered closed. It had been a long morning. Gabriel, Michael, and Libby were in the back of the wagon, singing as they rode to the Navises' home. "So what do you think?" Sarah certainly couldn't guess.

"I think maybe I'll help him...keep you here, that is."

"Oh, Richard, be serious."

"I am."

Sarah rolled her eyes, but she took note of Richard's pensiveness. "What is it? What are you thinking?"

"Well, as you know, Captain Sinclair has hired many governesses in the last few years. Personally, I think Mrs. Schlyterhaus scares them away."

*Or it could be the snakes.* Sarah recalled how Gabriel and Michael had confessed to the prank.

"I suppose the captain has seen how well you manage the children, and he doesn't want to lose you. That only seems logical." Turning to Sarah, he raised his brows expectantly.

"Yes, so it does." And of course she had imagined that look in the captain's eyes last night. It wasn't a romantic gleam at all, but a look of...of desperation. The poor man. He couldn't afford to lose another governess.

Richard continued to drive the wagon west on Lisbon Plank toll road.

"How much farther?" Sarah wanted to know.

"Less than a mile."

Farm fields now stretched out as far as the eye could see. They had left the city behind, although they were still in Milwaukee.

"Out here near Western Avenue, it's rural. What's more, as you'll notice, the temperature is a good ten degrees warmer than it is closer to Lake Michigan."

"Why is that?"

"Once you cross the river, it's hotter. And in the winter, it's colder. However, nearer to the lake, you never can escape the humidity."

"Yes, it's that way in Jericho Junction too. Except we have both during the summer months—the heat *and* the humidity. It's ghastly."

"I imagine so."

Minutes later Richard turned onto a neat gravel driveway that split in half to form a large circle that passed in front of his house. There he halted the wagon and jumped down.

He reached for Rachel, who stirred while being transferred. Then, holding the little one over his shoulder, Richard helped Sarah alight. She noticed this section of the driveway was all brick, like the house. Once her feet touched the ground, she surveyed the rest of her surroundings. To her right was an apple orchard next to a small pond. To her left was another orchard, but it stood behind rows of flowers.

"What a lovely place."

"Glad you like it." Richard smiled as he easily lifted Libby out of the wagon. The boys hopped down on their own. "The house is quite unique, although we're just average folks and this is a typical farm."

"But it doesn't look typical. This house looks like a country mansion. Why, it's much larger than any farmhouse I've ever seen."

A pleased expression crossed Richard's face. "My father inherited money and used it to build this house. His dream house, you might say. He patterned it after his aunt's villa in Germany, where he had spent some time as a child. He loved it there, so when my great-aunt bequeathed to him the sum, he decided to honor her in this way. With this." He made a great sweeping gesture toward the house. "My father finished building it in 1851."

"Fascinating." Sarah had never been to another country before, and she was in awe of anyone who had.

"The actual farm is out back," Richard continued. "We've got hogs, cows, sheep, chickens, a vegetable garden, a cornfield, a wheat field, and a grove of pear trees."

"How nice for you and your family." Sarah hid her disinterest. She'd grown up around farms and fields. What appealed to her now was the bustling city life.

Richard's parents' buggy pulled into the circle drive, drawing their attention. Sarah gathered the captain's children while Richard helped his father down and into his wheelchair. Sarah had already met Mr. and Mrs. Navis at church, and the children were well acquainted with them from previous visits.

"Sarah, dear, let's go inside," Mrs. Navis suggested. She was a sturdy-looking woman and wore a light-blue checked dress with a wide lace collar. "Richard and Marty will take the children out back to the barn to see the kittens."

Sarah followed the woman up the front porch steps.

"The Staffords should be arriving soon." Mrs. Navis removed her bonnet, revealing auburn hair. "Richard told us you met Bethany on Friday evening."

"Yes, I did." And she hadn't forgotten their strange conversation either.

"And I invited my sister Ruth, her husband, my niece Lina, and Mr. Tim Barnes, my niece's fiancé."

"Oh, how lovely. I met Lina and Mr. Barnes on Friday night also."

"I'm so glad. Some of my favorite people, they are." With a glance around the room, Mrs. Navis heaved a sigh. Then she glanced at Sarah. "There's much to do, but can I show you around before I get busy?"

Sarah nodded and followed her through one room after another. The furnishings in the Navis home weren't elegant like the captain's. Small braided rugs, not imported carpets, were scattered upon the hardwood floors. Homespun quilts instead of satin coverlets blanketed all the beds, and a brown knitted afghan had been spread across the divan in the parlor as if to conceal worn upholstery. Sarah was reminded of her parents' home in Missouri.

Once the tour ended, Sarah turned to Mrs. Navis. "Can I help you make dinner?"

"Sure can. I'm roasting three large chickens."

*In this heat?* Sarah began rolling up the sleeves of her dress.

"Then I'll bake up some biscuits and set out some of the pickles I canned last year. How does that sound?"

"Sounds hot," Sarah replied in all honesty. "Except for the pickles."

Mrs. Navis laughed at the comment and waved her into the cellar. "I've got a summer kitchen down here."

A wave of cool air met Sarah after she'd descended the stairs. She glanced around at the whitewashed walls, cupboards, and large wood-burning stove and oven. It was nearly fifteen degrees cooler down here. Then Mrs. Navis led her into the fruit cellar, where numerous glass jars stood on paper-lined shelves.

"We'll have some applesauce too," she stated, grabbing a few jars.

Upstairs, Sarah helped Mrs. Navis with preliminary meal preparations. Richard came in sometime later, carrying three freshly butchered chickens.

"I had the boys help me pluck and clean 'em, and would you believe Gabe and Michael squawked louder than the hens?" He shook his head. "Such complaining!"

Sarah laughed.

"What a good job for those boys," Mrs. Navis replied.

Richard must have divined Sarah's thoughts. "Not to worry. We all put on aprons. The boys haven't ruined their good clothes." He chuckled. "But give them time."

Sarah could well imagine the grass and food stains on their good shirts. She chided herself for not thinking to pack play clothes. "Where are Libby and Rachel?"

"They're with Pops on the back porch, holding the kittens."

"Pops?" Sarah found the word humorous. "You don't really call your father Pops, do you?"

"Sure, I do."

Mrs. Navis nodded.

Richard glanced at Sarah, and she saw a gleam in his blue eyes. "He's Pops and she's... Mops. Mops and Pops."

The comment didn't go over well. Mrs. Navis raised an annoyed brow. "Mops, you say?"

Sarah shook her head. "You poor, poor woman," she teased, "having to put up with your son's bad jokes."

Richard brought his chin back, as if insulted. "That wasn't a bad joke, Sarah."

"The worst I've heard." She folded her arms and shook her head. "Mops? Please."

He shrugged.

Meanwhile, Mrs. Navis put an arm around Sarah. "An ally. At last I have an ally!"

Shortly after Mrs. Navis got the chickens into the oven, the Staffords arrived with their eight children. Bethany was the oldest, and there was a wide gap between herself and her siblings. The younger ones were the same ages as the Sinclairs. So the girls played nicely while the boys chased each other around the yard. Bethany busied herself in the kitchen. She said little as she worked and seemed at home in both of Mrs. Navis's kitchens.

Feeling in the way, Sarah stepped onto the porch and watched the children. She saw Richard a ways off, near the barn. His shirtsleeves were rolled to the elbow as he emptied a bucket of water over the fence and into the horse trough. She recalled his expressing his passion for being outdoors and his disdain for accounting.

She looked away, unable to comprehend his reasoning. Didn't Richard realize how fortunate he was to hold such an impressive position with Captain Sinclair?

Harnesses jangled as another wagon pulled into the driveway. A middle-aged couple disembarked, as did Richard's cousin Lina and her fiancé, Tim Barnes.

"Good to see you again." Lina gave Sarah a hug and introduced her parents, Ruth and Jesse Johnson.

When dinner was ready, they ate out on the lawn with their plates in their laps. It reminded Sarah of picnics back home in Jericho Junction. She fought against missing her family and instead focused on her charges. Sitting between Libby and Rachel, Sarah made sure the girls ate enough nourishment despite their pleas to get up and run. But she had no trouble coaxing the boys to eat. Richard sat several feet away. He had little problem engaging Gabriel in conversation. Sarah tried to listen in, but she couldn't hear over the girls' constant chattering.

"Do we have to take a nap this afternoon?" Libby gazed up at Sarah. "I don't want to."

"I don' wanna either," said Rachel. Perspiration had curled her blonde hair.

"Maybe a short rest, then. I wouldn't want to have to tell your father you got heatstroke running around in the sun all day."

They finished eating, and Richard carried dishes into the kitchen. The kids took off with laughs and giggles, so Sarah followed him into the house.

"I promised all the children cow rides," he said with a grin.

"Cow rides?"

Richard sent her a sheepish look. "Last time the captain's children were here, I gave them a ride on Lyla's back. She's one of our Guernsey cows, and the children had so much fun that they have requested to do it again."

Sarah smiled. "How fast does Lyla go?"

"About as fast as I can pull her."

She gave a laugh, and once the dishes were deposited into the wash bin, she watched from the back porch as first Libby, then Rachel took a ride on poor Lyla. When their turns came, Gabriel and Michael bounced and shouted, "Giddyup!" The cow, however, wasn't very cooperative.

From her place near the kitchen door, Sarah could hear the rattling of pans and dishes. She decided to help with cleanup. Stepping into the yard, she put her fingers in her mouth and blew a high-pitched whistle that garnered more than Richard's attention. Embarrassed, she motioned she was going inside. He nodded, but Sarah could see he harbored a good chuckle over her rather unladylike gesture. Well, it seemed better than hollering.

Entering the house, Sarah was surprised to find only Bethany in the kitchen washing dishes. "Here, let me help you." Sarah grabbed a dishtowel.

Bethany didn't reply for a long while. "Miss McCabe, I'm quite embarrassed about my comment on Friday night."

Roasting pan in hand, Sarah began drying it off. "I must admit, you took me by surprise."

"Did you tell him or Lina?" Bethany stared at the basin, but lifted a chin.

"No, I didn't share our conversation with anyone."

She whipped her gaze to Sarah. Then a grateful expression fell over her features. "Thank you."

Sarah inclined her head. "Between the two of us, you have nothing to worry about regarding my friendship with Richard."

Bethany stopped washing the plate in her hands. "Your *friendship* with Richard?" Her lips curved upward into a cynical smile. "Is that what you call it? *A friendship*?"

"Well, I've only been in town five days." Setting down the towel, Sarah put her hands on her hips and lifted a defiant chin. "Yes.

*Friendship* is most exactly the word I would use. Richard has been very good to me since I arrived in Milwaukee. We both work for Captain Sinclair. He's provided helpful insight on my employer, which is important since I care for the captain's children."

Bethany considered it several moments and then said, "Richard is not that gallant. Trust me. I've known him practically all my life. Besides, Captain Sinclair has had dozens of governesses, and Richard never took one of them to the theater or home to meet his family."

Sarah paused to think about this. She'd sensed Richard's interest but hadn't thought it was anything serious. "I'm only here for the summer. Then I hope to teach music in Chicago. That's my plan. I want to live in a big city with theaters and restaurants and shops on every corner."

Bethany regarded her. "So you're not interested in Richard?"

"Not romantically. I mean it wouldn't be wise to begin a relationship I couldn't continue. Come the end of August, I'll be packing for Chicago."

Once the dishes were washed and put away, Sarah and Bethany joined everyone else in the yard. Cool evening breezes began to blow, rustling the branches of the fruit trees overhead. Gabriel and Michael were at the pond, trying to catch a frog or two, and the little girls were playing hide-and-seek in the orchard. Bethany no longer ignored Sarah and struck up a friendly conversation. She pointed out their neighboring farm and talked of the concert they had heard two nights ago.

A while later Mrs. Navis discovered the kitchen had been cleaned when she went inside to make coffee. And when she learned Sarah and Bethany had cleaned it, she chided them, saying, "No guests of mine clean up the kitchen!"

"But we wanted to help," Sarah told her.

"Nonsense! Now you'll both have to come back next week so I can be a proper hostess."

"Yes, ma'am," Bethany replied with a tiny smile that almost reached her sad gray eyes.

Sarah only smiled. She didn't want to intertwine herself with the Navis family. She had one of her own back in Jericho Junction.

Once Mrs. Navis strode off, Bethany leaned over and whispered to Sarah, "Mrs. Navis says the same thing every Sunday because every Sunday I clean up for her."

"That's kind of you, Bethany."

She looked both pleased and embarrassed. "I feel like Mrs. Navis has so much else to do since Mr. Navis was maimed in the war."

"I suppose that's true." Sarah nodded her understanding and sensed Bethany had a real heart for this family. She and Richard would make a nice couple.

*But where is Richard's heart?* Sarah wondered, but deemed it none of her business.

They talked awhile longer, then Richard appeared from around the side of the house. His gaze fixed on Sarah.

"My aunt and uncle have offered to take you and the children home."

She regarded him. The sun began to set as he stood on the lawn, near the front porch. Sarah couldn't fight the notion that he made an impressive figure against the orange sky with his broad shoulders, muscled forearms, and hands resting on narrow hips.

*And I shouldn't even care!* she told herself.

"Are you listening to me?" Richard grinned.

"Yes, of course I am." Sarah lowered her gaze, certain that her cheeks now flamed like the sunset.

"I said my aunt and uncle—"

"I heard you. Thank you." She looked up at him again. "And that's very nice of them."

"Well, they don't live far from the captain, so it's no trouble." He nodded to where the children now played. They had moved from the backyard to the front, where a small fountain stood. Gabriel and Michael splashed each other while the girls dipped their hands in the water. "The 'trouble' will be rounding up those four rascals."

"Hmm, yes, I believe you're right."

Bethany laughed softly. "My folks had trouble getting my brothers and sisters to go home too."

Sarah stood.

"Try that whistle of yours, Sarah." A smile played across Richard's mouth. "I'll admit to being impressed."

She sent him a quelling glance and still regretted the action earlier. Highly unsophisticated, that's for certain. She stepped off the porch.

He walked toward her. "Did your older brothers teach you to whistle like that?"

"No, I taught myself because I wanted to blow a shrill louder than theirs."

"I believe you succeeded." He rubbed his ear for effect.

She passed him by and began collecting kids. "Time to go." At the announcement, the two boys took off, and it took a bit of doing to catch and subdue them. But finally the four Sinclair children were loaded into the Johnsons' large buggy.

"Thank you for everything. I had a splendid day, and I know the kids enjoyed themselves. They'll sleep well tonight."

"I'm sure they will." Richard helped Sarah up. His hand held hers moments longer than necessary. "I'll see you tomorrow." A light of promise glinted in his blue eyes.

Sarah gave him a nod in reply and pulled her gaze from his. She straightened the skirt of her yellow-and-green printed dress. Then she glimpsed Bethany standing off to the distance. Sarah smiled and waved. Bethany returned the gesture.

On the way to the Sinclairs', Sarah wondered whether Richard was truly interested in her romantically, as Bethany presumed, or if his intentions, like the captain's last night, were all in her girlish imaginings.

# Nine

STANDING AT THE FRONT DOORWAY, HER ARMS FOLDED, Sarah watched the children drag their feet as they walked to their grandmother's waiting carriage. None of them looked happy to be going to Aurora's house. Gabriel begged to stay home. Rachel fussed when Aurora took her hand and led her away from Sarah. But it was Wednesday, Sarah's first day off, and she had much to do. Among other tasks, her clothes needed washing. While she'd been diligent about rinsing her undergarments, several dresses needed a more thorough laundering.

She waved good-bye to the children. Their unhappy faces stared back at her, and she felt like telling the captain she didn't need a day off. But, in truth, she did. The children weren't any trouble really, but it was healthy to have a break from time to time. Besides, Hamlin's Department Store had been calling her name for days. She'd seen several colorful silk scarves in the window as she happened by and thought they'd make special gifts for Ma, Valerie, and Leah.

Sarah made her way through the house, remembering to take the servants' stairwell to her bedroom upstairs. There she packed the items she needed washed. Then, back on the first floor again, she met Mrs. Schlyterhaus in the kitchen.

"I see you are leaving?" She arched one brow while her eyes took in Sarah's traveling suit and valise. "I didn't think you'd make it here more than a veek."

Sarah grinned and shook her head. "I have no intention of vacating my governess post, if that's what you mean. But I'm afraid I don't have a basket and I didn't want to walk downtown with my arms full of soiled clothes. As for wearing my traveling dress, it's the nicest thing I own, and I plan to go shopping today."

The housekeeper seemed momentarily speechless. Sarah asked, "I don't suppose you could recommend a launderer close by?"

"Van Donn's on Knapp Street is the one I use."

"Is it far from here?"

"No." Mrs. Schlyterhaus shrugged but didn't offer any directions.

Sarah didn't press her. She would ask about it as soon as she reached the downtown area. She knew the way to the street where she could climb aboard the horse-drawn trolley.

"You might be vise and take some time to rest. You'll be no good to anyone if you don't have someting of a rest."

"Yes, I'll be sure to do that." Was the woman actually being nice?

"Even God took a rest after He made the vorld."

The remark caused Sarah to smile. "Are you a believer, Mrs. Schlyterhaus?"

A heavy frown settled on her brow. "It is none of your business vhat I am or vhat I am not."

Sarah inhaled sharply. "I'm sorry. I didn't mean…what I meant was…"

Mrs. Schlyterhaus scowled. "*Irish.*" She spat the word at Sarah before walking away.

"What?" Sarah felt stunned, but before she could say another word, Mrs. Schlyterhaus hurried from the kitchen.

Sarah took her leave. Why aggravate the housekeeper further? However, the woman's sudden bout of anger just didn't make sense. As a pastor's daughter, Sarah was accustomed to openly discussing her faith and forgot that on occasion the topic offended people. Was that why Mrs. Schlyterhaus had become barking mad?

"Sarah! Sarah!"

Hearing a man calling her name, she turned to find Richard driving a small black buggy. As he neared, he reined in his horse.

"May I give you ride?"

"Yes, thank you." Sarah dropped her valise into the back and then reached for Richard's hand. He helped her into the carriage. The bench and backboard were padded and upholstered with soft red leather, and Sarah had no difficulty making herself comfortable.

"Where are you off to?" Richard leaned toward her. "Not the train station, I hope."

Sarah laughed. "No. And you're the second person to make that assumption. But the truth is, I'm on my way to find a launderer before shopping at Hamlin's."

"I take it the captain remembered to pay you." Richard spoke in a hushed tone.

Sarah nodded. She still couldn't believe the amount of money she earned weekly. The sum was more than three month's salary for some folks in Jericho Junction.

"I'm glad to hear it... and relieved that you're not headed for Union Depot." He smiled and slapped the reins. "What's more, I believe I can accommodate you."

"Thank you." Sarah glanced at Richard, noting how fine he looked in his pepper-gray trousers, matching short-waist coat, and white shirt. His black tie was even straight, and he wore a handsome black hat. "You must be seeing to some important business today."

"I had to pick up some documents at the captain's home office. He'd forgotten them, and they must be signed and in the attorney's hands by noon."

"Ah. Then it's no wonder you look so dapper today."

"Dapper?" Richard tucked his chin in surprise. "Why, thank you, Sarah."

She lowered her gaze, feeling a warm blush slide up her neck and pink her cheeks.

Richard chuckled.

"So you were in the captain's house just now? Did you hear my conversation with Mrs. Schlyterhaus?"

"No, but I saw her march out of the kitchen. I assumed she and Isabelle had a disagreement." He considered her askance. "But it was you?"

Sarah inclined her head. "Although we didn't have a disagreement, really. I must have offended her, and then she called me 'Irish,' as if the name was a slur. I can't understand it."

After giving the matter some thought, Richard replied, "It's not you, personally, Sarah. It's just that... well, it seems Mrs. Schlyterhaus isn't a very forgiving person, and your being Irish just gives her an excuse not to be friendly. I believe the woman knows the Lord, but she obviously refuses to exercise forgiveness toward others."

"I still don't understand."

Richard steered the buggy to the left and turned a street corner. "About ten or fifteen years ago, the Germans and the Irish were at war with each other here in Milwaukee. Each side had claimed its own section of the city, and if one wandered into the other's area, there was a bloody fight—or sometimes a riot. Gretchen's husband was killed in one of those riots."

Sarah grimaced. "How awful."

"Yes. And later, when a law was proposed to ban alcohol here in Milwaukee, the Germans and the Irish—both known to like their beer—joined forces and rallied, or perhaps I should say *rioted*, against the proposed law."

"They must have won too," Sarah murmured, "for I've noticed that there's a tavern on practically every corner of this city."

Richard chuckled. "That there is, my dear Sarah McCabe. However, sometimes I wonder if Mrs. Schlyterhaus still believes she's at war with the Irish." He smiled. "But please don't be too concerned about it. You're perfectly safe. I'll make sure of it."

Richard searched her face in a way that gave Sarah yet another indication he might be interested in her. Again she felt herself blush and quickly lowered her gaze.

"Will you allow me to take you to lunch today? There's a delightful sandwich shop right down the street from Hamlin's. I'll meet you there around twelve-thirty."

Sarah smiled. "I'd enjoy that very much."

"All right, then." He slowed the buggy and stopped in front of the large, four-story, red-brick building. "Have fun."

"But my laundry—"

"I'll drop it off for you. It'll be done by Friday."

Uncertainty filled her being. She hated to make her soiled clothes Richard's responsibility.

He changed the subject. "King's Sandwich Emporium is right down there." He pointed. "See it?"

Sarah strained to look around the many people coming and going on Grand Avenue. But she managed to glimpse the sign. "Yes, I see it."

"Good." Jumping down from the buggy, Richard walked around and helped her onto the plank sidewalk. "Have fun shopping."

Sarah glanced at the store's windows, noting the array of women's fashions. "Oh, I'm afraid I will."

Richard climbed into the buggy and tipped his hat in such a mannerly way that Sarah felt impressed. If she were completely honest, she'd have to admit she was attracted to him in his present state. With a wave, she watched as he steered his horse back into the busy thoroughfare.

*Richard Navis.* She thought of how he'd become her best and only friend here in Milwaukee. He was dependable and charming and...well, quite amusing.

Sarah glanced at the enameled timepiece pinned to her bodice. She had two hours to shop before meeting Richard for lunch. That wasn't much time.

She strode with purpose to the front doors of the department store. Inside, the scent of expensive perfume tickled her nostrils. Beyond the fragrance display, glass jewelry cases trimmed in mahogany lined the center of the store. The men's apparel was on her left and the ladies' apparel on her right.

Sarah stepped in the direction of the lovely gowns. One in particular caught her eye—a gray silk with blue ribbon bands edged with black lace. Almost in reverence, she reached out a gloved hand to touch it.

"May I help you?"

The stern voice caused her to jump. Turning slightly, she glimpsed a prim-looking brunette with spectacles on her long nose. "I was just admiring this dress."

She smiled without her lips ever parting. Her eyes roamed over Sarah. "Yes, and with a few slight alterations, I think it would fit you nicely."

"Oh, well..." Sarah didn't think she could ever afford to purchase a gown this beautiful.

The clerk seemed to read her thoughts. "The dress was designed from last year's Godey's fashion plates and has been marked down considerably." She quoted the price.

Sarah forced herself not to gasp. The sum was still beyond her means.

"You could open an account with Hamlin's, and a small down payment today will hold the dress until the end of the month."

"Hmm..." Sarah figured she could probably afford the dress on those terms. She fingered the skirt's blue silk inset.

"Why don't you try it on?" The clerk slipped it off the hanger and set the gown in Sarah's arms. "Private fitting rooms are over there, behind the counter."

"Thank you." Sarah couldn't resist.

Within the hour, she stood in front of the wood-framed mirror while the seamstress marked the nips and tucks. She stared at her reflection, wondering who the lovely young woman in the exquisite dress looking back at her could be.

"You must have the matching cap," the clerk said, placing it on Sarah's head. Silk ribbons of gray, blue, and black made up the edging and cascaded down the back. "When I opened your account, Mr. Hamlin said I could offer it to you at half price."

Sarah knew she had to have it. What was a gorgeous gown like this without a coordinating cap? "Yes, I'll take it. Thank you."

Smiling, Sarah ran her hands down the soft gray bodice. Wait until

Ma and Leah saw this creation. They'd be awestruck. Valerie had grown up with such finery, but Sarah was sure even her dear sister-in-law would be impressed.

Once the alterations were measured and pinned, Sarah changed back into her own clothes and strode to the counter. The clerk who had been assisting her stood beside a stout gentleman in a black suit.

"Miss McCabe," he said, "I'm Arthur Hamlin, owner of the store, and I need to ask you a few more questions before I can authorize your account with my store."

"Yes, sir."

He pursed his lips smugly and glanced down his squat little nose. "Who is your employer, and what is your occupation?"

"I work for Captain Brian Sinclair. I'm his children's governess."

The man leaned forward and arched a brow. "Another one?"

Sarah didn't know how to respond.

Drawing in a deep breath, Mr. Hamlin squared his shoulders. "Miss Dowers," he began, referring to his clerk, "I am not convinced this customer has stable employment. I'm afraid I cannot authorize her credit."

"But Mr. Hamlin, she's making a down payment today."

"No matter. We have no guarantee this young woman won't abandon her governess position tomorrow, and then we've held the dress for nothing." He eyed Sarah as if she were some kind of pesky amphibian. "No credit." With a click of his heels, the man strode off.

From out of the corner of her eye, Sarah spied an elderly customer standing within earshot. Embarrassment nibbled at her. "Perhaps if I come back next week..."

The clerk put her nose in the air and walked off without saying a word.

Now Sarah's cheeks flamed with humiliation. She turned and hurried toward the front doors. She couldn't leave this store fast enough. And she wouldn't spend a nickel in this place. Not ever. She'd have to find scarves for Ma, Leah, and Valerie somewhere else.

Outside on the walk, Sarah felt conspicuous, like she wore a sign on her forehead saying NO CREDIT. Head down, she made her way down Grand Avenue. At the corner she glimpsed the tall street clock and realized she was ten minutes late for lunch with Richard. Quickening her steps, she hurried the rest of the way to King's Sandwich Emporium. She found Richard waiting for her near the entrance.

"I hoped you didn't forget." He flashed her a sunny grin.

"I'm sorry I'm late, Richard." She managed to give him a smile, although she still felt shaken by what took place at Hamlin's. Her integrity had been questioned and found lacking. Nothing like that had ever happened to her.

"Sarah?" Richard touched her elbow. "Are you all right?"

She nodded, staring at the black-and-white tiled flooring.

"Let's be seated, and you can tell me about your morning."

Richard found a table in a secluded corner, and when the waiter came by, he ordered two iced teas. "So...did you have fun shopping at Hamlin's?"

Sarah felt like crying, but she fought off the urge. After all, she was an independent woman. She had to learn to deal with situations such as this on her own.

With as much dignity as she could muster, she told Richard what had happened. "But I have no intentions of quitting my job. I'll just shop elsewhere from now on. I don't need that pompous old goat's credit anyway." Except Sarah mourned the fact she wouldn't own the most beautiful gown she'd ever set eyes on.

Well, no matter...

"I can't believe Mr. Hamlin treated you with such rudeness. And you're certain it was Mr. Hamlin?"

"Positive. He introduced himself."

"Hmm...well, I'm sure he'll soon regret losing such a good customer as yourself."

Sarah tamped down her vengeful feelings.

The teas arrived, served in tall frosted glasses. Richard ordered for both of them the chicken salad special, made with cubed apples and chopped walnuts and served on a freshly baked roll.

"You'll love it, Sarah. I promise."

"I can't wait to taste it." She was glad to have the subject changed. "Did you get your errands done this morning?"

"Every last one." He sighed. "A good thing too, because I need to get home at a decent hour tonight. The captain's had me working some late nights."

"Oh? Do you have an appointment tonight, Richard?"

He smiled and shook his head. "No. Only chores."

"Chores? You mean that after working all day for the captain, you go home and work on the farm?"

Richard bobbed his head in the affirmative. "My father can't manage many tasks anymore, so I do most of the work. But we hired planters this year, and that helped enormously."

"Even so... you must be exhausted."

He tipped his head and gave her a charming grin. "Not too exhausted to take you to dinner before I head for home. Will you come?"

Sarah felt a blush coming on as she thought over his offer. She wondered too if she should encourage Richard this way. She didn't want to give him false hopes, and yet she liked his company. He made her lonesome for her brothers.

"What do you say, Sarah?"

"Well, I don't know..."

"We can ask Lina and Tim to join us if that will make you feel more comfortable."

"That's not necessary."

Richard lifted a teasing brow. "You're not afraid of me?"

Sarah swallowed a giggle. "Not in the least!"

Richard shrugged, indicating that perhaps she ought to be, and this time Sarah laughed aloud. Oh, how he could make her laugh with a mere facial expression or a simple shrug of his broad shoulders.

"Will you dine with me or not?" He took a swallow of his tea.

"Yes, thank you, I will." She smiled. "But will you come for me at the captain's home? I'm going back there this afternoon for a rest and to write a few letters."

"It would be my pleasure,"

"I'm sure it would." She laughed.

The afternoon passed quickly for Sarah, and she never did get that rest she'd been determined to take. She did, however, change her clothes and finish her letter writing before Richard arrived for her.

"Ready?" He met her in the foyer under Mrs. Schlyterhaus's scowling countenance.

"Ready." Sarah chanced a look at the housekeeper. "Good night, Mrs. Schlyterhaus."

"I lock the doors at eight o'clock on Vednesdays." Her tone was stern. "If you're not home by then, I vill lock you out!"

Sarah felt intimidated by the woman's vehemence and stepped back, bumping into Richard.

He gave her elbow a squeeze. "I have a key for emergencies," he whispered. "Don't worry." Next he bestowed a broad smile on Mrs. Schlyterhaus before wishing her a good night.

Feeling relieved by Richard's cleverness, Sarah left Captain Sinclair's residence with him for a riverside cafe. As they entered the establishment, several businessmen greeted Richard by name, and likewise, Richard seemed to know practically everyone in the place.

"Did you take me here to impress me?" Sarah asked impishly when the proprietor seated them at one of his best tables. White linen cloths and candlelight graced each one.

"Sure I did." A grin stretched across his tanned face, and a rebellious lock of his blond hair fell onto his forehead.

Sarah deduced that at least Richard was honest, and in an amusing way. He was obviously a hard worker—Sarah saw the telltale signs worn into his rough hands. They were the hands of a workingman.

A farmer. And yet, there was an air of sophistication about Richard Navis too, a manner that came from education.

But his generosity impressed Sarah the most. Not only with his money, for the meal surely cost him plenty, but how he gave of himself. Like the way he helped his father and the captain, and the way he managed Mrs. Schlyterhaus by not getting in her way, but around her instead. He seemed to strive to appease and accommodate, but never to the extent of compromising his integrity.

*Pa would like him,* Sarah found herself thinking. So would her brothers—especially Jake, that rascal…

"What are you thinking about?" Richard lifted his water goblet. "You're smiling."

Sarah's smile broadened. "I was thinking of my brother Jake. You remind me of him."

Richard arched a brow. "If I remember correctly, that's not always good."

"It's only *not* good when I'm in trouble." Sarah had to laugh, hearing Richard's chuckle.

After supper they boarded the horse car and took it as far north as it ran. They walked the rest of the way back to the captain's home. The evening temperature was mild, even with the Lake Michigan breezes, so their stroll proved an enjoyable one.

"I'll have to take you roller skating some time," Richard remarked. "It's quite the rage in Milwaukee right now. We have several brand new rinks, in fact."

"Really?" Sarah had heard of roller skates. The wooden-wheeled toys had been invented in New York several years ago. "That would be fun, Richard."

Finally they reached the captain's house. At the side entrance, Richard turned the knob. The door opened.

"Not quite eight o'clock." A sheepish expression crossed his face.

Then suddenly, he became serious. Taking her hand, he placed a gentle kiss on the backs of her fingers. His expression told Sarah that he meant business. The courtship sort of business. The whole business Sarah wanted to avoid. Why couldn't she and Richard just be friends?

"I trust I'll see you tomorrow."

"The children will be back from their grandmother's, and I'm sure I'll be awfully busy."

"Well, then, I'll see you sometime soon." He gave a tiny bow. "Good night, Sarah."

"Good night, Richard, and thank you for a lovely evening."

As he walked away, he waved.

Sarah entered the house. *Oh, Lord, I like Richard so much…*

She thought of how his blue eyes twinkled with amusement, how they darkened with earnestness—and interest.

Forgetting herself, Sarah climbed the front stairwell. *Now what do I do, Lord? Now what do I do?*

# TEN

SARAH! COME DOWN HERE, PLEASE!"

Sarah heard the captain bellow up the stairwell. Her name echoed against the plastered walls. She immediately sensed that she'd done something wrong. The tone of his voice seemed edged with displeasure. Entering the foyer, she glimpsed the muscle working in his jaw and knew something was amiss.

"What is it, Captain?"

"Follow me into the parlor, please."

She did as he asked, but stopped short when she saw Mr. Hamlin standing near the cold hearth and clutching his hat.

Captain Sinclair put his hands behind his back and glared at the other man. "Mr. Hamlin has something to say to you, Sarah."

She gulped, unsure of what it might be.

"Miss McCabe," he began on a shaky note, "I fear there's been a dreadful misunderstanding. You see, when I spoke with you a few days ago, I presumed incorrectly that your position with the captain wouldn't last."

"You're not the only one, Mr. Hamlin." Sarah slid a quick look at the captain. "However, I have no intention of quitting."

"There, you see, Hamlin?"

"Yes, Captain." The man's gaze flitted from him back to Sarah. "Please accept my apology for the misunderstanding."

"Of course."

"Your credit is good at my department store. I'll see to it an account is opened in your name."

The captain interrupted. "No need."

Mr. Hamlin appeared stunned. "But sir, I thought you had summoned me here for that purpose."

"No, no, not at all." The captain rocked on his soles. "I hereby authorize Sarah to use my account."

She gasped. "No, Captain, I couldn't—" She took a step toward him.

His dark, adamant gaze silenced her.

"Even the dress Miss McCabe intended to buy?" Mr. Hamlin looked from Sarah to the captain, as if trying to understand their relationship. Sarah shook her head, suddenly embarrassed.

"Everything she wishes to purchase, Hamlin, for the children and herself. Don't be so dense. I just authorized Sarah to use my account. Aurora uses it all the time."

"Yes, I'm aware of that." The man's round face reddened. "I'll add Miss McCabe's name to your account also."

"Captain, please..." Sarah preferred managing her own account.

But he held up a forestalling hand, although his eyes never left the store owner. "Now, unless there's anything else, I believe our business is finished."

"Yes, thank you, Captain Sinclair." He inclined his head toward Sarah. "Good day, Miss McCabe."

"Good day to you too, Mr. Hamlin."

She frowned as Mr. Hamlin strode from the reception parlor, followed by the captain, who saw him out the front door.

Sarah met him in the foyer. "Captain, I can't use your account. I don't feel right about it."

"I noticed that the boys need new shoes." He tipped his dark head. "Aurora enjoys shopping for the girls, but she frequently neglects the boys in that area."

"I'm happy to take them for shoes."

"And use my account at Hamlin's."

"Yes, sir. But about the dress I wanted..."

"Oh, Sarah, I can buy you a new dress." He crossed the foyer in two easy strides and reached for her hand. "It's the least I can do for you. My children seem so happy. I heard the girls giggling in the backyard yesterday, and the sound gave me great pleasure."

"Thank you, but you see the dress... it's not for everyday. I wouldn't feel right about you purchasing it for me. Please deduct the amount from my salary."

"Don't be silly."

She opened her mouth to reply, but he held up one finger to quiet her. "I'll hear nothing more about this matter. Is that clear?"

"Yes."

He dropped her hand and headed for his office.

Sarah followed. "But I do have one question, sir."

Captain Sinclair paused and regarded her.

"How did you know about what happened at Hamlin's?"

"Richard told me."

"Oh." Now it made sense.

"As I said when I hired you, we're a family here. I'll not tolerate a slight from an outsider."

Sarah suddenly felt rather special and that Captain Brian Sinclair was the noblest of all men. Of course, it was also gallant of Richard to inform the captain of the incident.

Richard. She'd thought a lot about him lately and simply couldn't see courtship on her horizon. While she'd managed to avoid him yesterday, she knew he'd probably be along any minute, running errands and stopping by or coming to fetch the captain for a meeting or reminding him of one thing or another. Putting distance between herself and Richard seemed the only logical solution, and that meant leaving the house early in the morning.

"Captain, I've been thinking..." She followed him into his office. "May I enroll the children in swimming lessons?" Perhaps this way she'd even make some friends of her own.

"Swimming lessons?" He lifted his dark gaze from the papers on his messy desk. "My children already know how to swim—well, the boys do anyway."

"Yes, I know. I've seen them at the lake when I've taken them fishing. But the boys are so energetic that I thought—"

"You're seeking to take the, uh, wind out of their sails, are you?" The captain chuckled.

Sarah smiled. "Yes, exactly." But she sought something else with this plan too—namely avoiding Richard. "The swimming lessons will be a perfect way for Gabe and Michael to expend some energy. The lessons begin at eight o'clock every weekday morning and go until noon. The swimming school is right on the river."

"Yes. I know the one. It's north of here."

"That's it, Captain. With your permission, the lessons will begin on Monday morning."

He nodded. "All right. Go ahead."

"Thank you."

Exiting the captain's office, Sarah congratulated herself on contriving the perfect end to the boys' over-exuberance and Richard's midmorning visits. Maybe now Richard would tamp down that spark of ardor in his eyes.

Hours later, Sarah enrolled the children at the swimming school. They stayed at the river and played, and Sarah didn't see Richard all day. That night, when he came to the captain's residence to see her, Sarah claimed to be unavailable and asked Mrs. Schlyterhaus to send him on his way. Amazingly, the housekeeper complied. She felt a twinge of guilt later when she discovered he'd dropped off her clean laundry.

The next day, Saturday, passed uneventfully. On Sunday Sarah and the children attended a local church. Large and ornate, the sanctuary looked impressive. The pastor's voice echoed as he delivered his message. Gabriel and Michael fidgeted in the pew and the girls whined. Sarah barely heard a word from the pulpit and actually felt relieved when they left for home.

"I liked the other church," Michael complained as they made the trek home. "It's smaller, and Pastor Higgins smiles more than the man today did."

"Yeah, and I liked spending the day on the farm afterwards...like last week." Gabriel put his hands in his pockets and kicked a stone.

"I yiked the kitties." Rachel bobbed alongside Sarah.

"I'm hungry, Miss Sarah," Libby whined.

"All right. We'll fix some lunch when we get home, and then we'll think of something fun to do this afternoon."

Inwardly, Sarah felt defeated. How could she compete with good food, kittens, and cow rides? Worse, she found that she missed Richard's company.

"This Sabbath was certainly quieter than last week's, what without the Staffords' brood and the Sinclair children."

Sitting at the dining room table, a slice of rhubarb pie in front of him, Richard glanced at his mother. "Mmm, yes, it was quieter at that."

"Where were the Staffords today?" Pops wanted to know.

"They all have the croup." Mama shook her auburn head. "The kids are barking like dogs. Which reminds me...I told Maribel I'd bring some dinner over later this afternoon. Since Bethany came down with the virus, no one's preparing meals over there."

"They work that girl too hard," Pops muttered. "I lost my legs so human beings could be free. Seems a shame to have slavery going on right over on the next farm."

"Bethany's not a slave, Pops." Richard shook his head at the hyperbole. "She came to the theater with Lina, Tim, Lionel, and me just last week."

"Had to have all her chores done before that stepmother of hers would let her go." Pops gave an indignant wag of his head. "And when I say 'chores,' I'm referring to every single task in that home, milking cows not excluded."

Richard was surprised by the news. He'd never known anything was amiss over at the Staffords' place. "I've never heard Bethany complain."

"Hmm...well..." Mama sipped her coffee. "She's waiting for her

Prince Charming to come along and rescue her. Maribel says she's a dreamer."

"Only way to get through a stage of life you detest," Pops said. "Dream about the blessings to come."

"Amen to that, Pops." Richard couldn't wait until he completed his indentureship.

"You know, after his first wife died, I told Josh not to marry a city woman." Pops lowered his voice and a light of concern entered his eyes. "But he married that Maribel, and she refuses to lift a finger to help around that farm. And all those kids she has—she makes Bethany take care of 'em."

Richard shook his head. "I had no idea any of this was going on."

"No one's advertised the trouble, son." Mama smirked. "One has to be close enough to the family to spot it. Like your father and I. And we're praying for each and every one of the Staffords."

"Prayer is everything."

"Amen, son!" Pops took a swallow of his coffee. "I might hire Tommy Stafford to do chores in the evening, seeing as you've been somewhat preoccupied and come home too late at night to be of any help."

Guilt assailed him. "I'm sorry, Pops."

He just chuckled. "Listen, I was young once too, you know." He reached for Mama's hand and gave it a squeeze.

She smiled back lovingly.

Richard sat back in his chair. "I take it you think I'm 'preoccupied' by something other than the captain's business."

"Well—" Mama exchanged a glance with Pops—"I guess a new governess is part of the captain's business."

They shared a laugh.

"Very funny." Richard shook his head at his folks. "There's nothing between Sarah and me." The remark came out harsher than he intended. But it stung that she'd refused to see him on Friday night.

"Didn't Sarah want to bring the kids to the farm today?" Pops wore a curious frown.

"I never got a chance to ask her." Richard set down his fork. "After work on Friday, I stopped by the captain's home, and Mrs. Schlyterhaus told me Sarah was unavailable, whatever *that* means."

"Perhaps she didn't feel well," Mama pointed out.

"Perhaps."

"Could be that grouchy housekeeper fibbed," Pops suggested.

Richard rolled his shoulders. "It wouldn't be like Mrs. Schlyterhaus to lie."

"Don't give up on Sarah, son." A grin spread across Pops's face.

"We'll be praying." Mama smiled.

Richard's glance bounced between the two of them. He had to chuckle. "Now why do I suddenly feel doomed?"

"Miss Sarah!" Gabriel waved his arms. "Watch what I can do!"

Smiling, Sarah watched Gabriel jump off the long board overhanging the river. He made a splash as he hit the water.

Day four of swimming school, and it was a success so far. The boys were having fun, and Gabriel seemed to be less moody. Libby and Rachel liked their mornings at the river too. They had lessons in a nearby wading pool.

Now Michael's turn. He waved vigorously and jumped up and down. Sarah suddenly felt a presence behind her. She turned and found Richard standing less than a foot away.

He waved back to Michael. As usual, he'd shed his jacket and wore the sleeves of his white shirt to his elbows. He'd loosened his black cravat and appeared quite cavalier as he went about Captain Sinclair's business.

His blue eyes came to rest on her. "Hello, Sarah."

"What are you doing here?" She stepped back, feeling surprised to see him.

Before he could answer, several stones beneath Sarah's feet loosened the earth. She moved to gain ground. Her ankle twisted, and she lost her balance. A little cry escaped her as she felt herself falling downward.

Richard caught her fall. "Careful there!"

Sarah found herself in his arms.

"Are you all right?"

She felt his breath on her cheek and the beat of his heart under her palm. For several seconds her mind went blank. Another few moments later pain zinged through her. "I–I think I may have hurt my ankle."

"Come and sit down over here." Richard helped her to the tiered wooden benches on which other swimming school spectators sat.

"I guess I stood too close to the edge."

"At least you didn't take a tumble."

"Thanks to you." Gratefulness spread through her.

He released her. "Glad to be of service." There was no mistaking the humorous note in his voice. He knelt and inspected her injury. Sarah's leather boot encased her ankle, but he gently moved her foot. "Any pain?"

"Yes." She winced.

"I'll fetch a cold compress."

"No." She put a hand on his shoulder to halt him. "It'll be fine in a minute or two." She didn't want to make a spectacle of herself. *Lord, please...heal my ankle quickly.* She needed to be able to care for the Sinclair children.

He eyed her with skepticism. Then at last he took a seat beside her. For several moments they didn't speak. Sunshine dappled the river, and the air smelled sweet with the last of the lilac blooms.

"I had hoped to see you this past weekend."

Sarah kept her gaze averted.

"But it's nice to see you today."

"Nice to see you too, Richard." She looked up. His flash of a smile displayed his dimples before he gazed toward where Gabe and Michael were about to take another turn off the diving board. Perhaps she'd been silly to try and create distance between them. He didn't seem like much of a threat right now. Quite the opposite really.

"Richard, do you remember when I told you that I plan to return to Chicago and teach music in the fall?"

He nodded. "What about it?"

She felt more the fool that he asked. Maybe he wasn't interested in her romantically after all. "I'm looking forward to it, that's all."

"Ah, I guess that means your first two weeks in Milwaukee have been less than desirable."

"No, I didn't mean it that way and with no insult to you. I'm still getting acclimated to my new job."

"Understandable."

"I have learned that I prefer your country church to the more formal city one we attended on Sunday," she admitted. "And the children missed the day on the farm."

"You're invited anytime. I wanted to tell you that last week Friday evening, but Mrs. Schlyterhaus said you were unavailable."

"I was out of sorts and wouldn't have been good company." She'd spoken the truth right there. Humility enveloped her. How prideful she'd been. Richard had been polite and friendly, his parents opened their home to her, and she'd been nothing but arrogant.

She sent him a timid smile. "So what are you doing here this morning?"

"I made some deliveries for Captain Sinclair. He told me about his children's swimming lessons, and seeing as I was driving by, I thought I'd stop and see if you and the captain's brood would like a lift home."

"That would be a blessing, thank you." She could feel her boot growing tighter around her ankle by the minute. Walking home could prove difficult. "I'm so glad you stopped."

"Are you?" He nudged her playfully. "Are you really glad?"

She did her best not to laugh. "Why, Richard Navis, I would be lying on the muddy riverbank if not for you."

"Are you saying—" he leaned toward her—"that I'm your hero?"

"Hero? That's a bit of a stretch, don't you think?" She couldn't help giggling, seeing his sportive grin.

Suddenly she felt guilty for dodging him this past week. Except she had sensed his interest and didn't want to encourage it.

But now she reconsidered. Maybe they could be friends.

"There's a play at the theater downtown tomorrow night. Would you like to go? Lina and Tim will be with us."

"I'd like to, Richard, but…"

"What is it, Sarah?" For the first time since she'd met him, he looked altogether serious. "Is there a reason you've been rather elusive lately?"

"No, not at all." She bent to loosen the laces of her boot. A sense of dread knotted inside of her. "It's my ankle. I believe it's injured worse than I first assumed."

Richard took another look at it and grimaced. "I'll fetch that cold compress and round up the children." He stood. "We need to get you back to the captain's home and off your feet."

Brian Sinclair looked up just as Richard and his two eldest boys entered the store. His gut twisted. Something wasn't right. Had the new governess quit already?

"What's this all about, Richard?" He strode to the door and flicked glances at his sons. Had they been misbehaving? "Where's Sarah?"

Before his steward could reply, Michael chimed in. "She hurt her ankle, Dad. It's all fat and purple." He wrinkled his nose.

"How in the world did that happen?" Brian set his hands on his hips. His gaze slid from Michael to Richard.

"She slipped and injured it this morning at swimming school, sir. But she's at your home now, and the girls are with her. Rachel is napping. Dr. Feathermayer should be there any minute. I sent for him."

"Good." He wanted a word with Richard in private, so he fished in his pocket and pulled out two nickels. "How 'bout running up the block and buying an ice cream?" He handed each boy a coin.

"Sure!" Gabe snatched it and took off. Michael followed.

Richard closed the door behind them.

"Do you think Sarah will want to quit now?" Brian couldn't stand the thought of searching for a new governess—especially since this one seemed so perfect.

"I doubt it. She's worried you're going to terminate her position."

Brian waved a hand in the air. "Nonsense."

"That's what I told her, sir." A wry grin curved his mouth. "On the other hand, Sarah probably won't be able to be much of a governess for a while."

"How long of a while?" Brian narrowed his gaze.

"I suppose that's up to the doctor." Richard shifted slightly. "But I do have an idea as to what you might do in the meantime."

"I figured you'd come up with something." It always amazed Brian the way his steward could read him and guess correctly at his preferences.

Richard Navis kept Brian on track and on time. Brian didn't know what he'd do without him. For those reasons, he wished December would never come. That's when Richard's indentureship ended. It didn't seem Richard wanted to stay on either. He talked about working on his farm. Brian couldn't understand it. He offered Richard a means to escape such a menial existence and the rigorous labor that went with it. He was handing Richard the opportunity to do something important. Have a career in business. Work himself into Milwaukee's more prominent social sector. Wasn't that what all ambitious young men wanted? Brian had wanted it—and he'd achieved it too.

Now if he could only keep the people he trusted, the ones he cared about, the ones who served him and his family faithfully, within his employ. If there was one thing Brian had learned in life, it was that money and influence had the power to make people stay while admiration, even love, could not.

Well, he couldn't allow Richard to quit. That was all there was to it. Everyone had a price. He'd have to find Richard's.

"The wagon's out front, Captain, and ready to go once we round up your boys. I suggest we go to your home for lunch. Dr. Feathermayer should be there. You can speak with him there."

Brian nodded. "Excellent idea. Thank you."

"You're welcome, sir. Once we learn Sarah's prognosis, I can propose some options."

Again, Brian inclined his head. "I'll fetch the boys."

He left the store. Thoughts of his new governess filled his head. Pretty. Sweet. Talented. Sarah was even winning Gabe's respect. Past governesses hadn't gotten beyond the boy's dislike. But in a week's time, Sarah had Brian's oldest grinning and enthusiastic.

Like Richard, Brian knew he couldn't let her leave. She'd brought a sense of stability into his home unlike any he'd ever known. Fortunately, Sarah's situation wasn't as complicated as his steward's.

Determination enveloped him. A letter to Elliot Withers in Chicago would fix things easily enough.

# Eleven

RICHARD GLIMPSED THE LOOK OF CONSTERNATION IN Sarah's eyes as Dr. Feathermayer arrived at a diagnosis.

"You've got a terrible sprain, my dear." The spindly physician straightened to his full height, equal to Richard's shoulder. He regarded the captain. "I insist your children's governess stay off that ankle for at least a few days."

"But I must be able to care for the children."

"No walking on that ankle until the swelling is down, and if there's no pain when you step down on it, you can begin walking again. Gingerly."

"Yes, Doctor." Sitting longwise on the settee, she modestly straightened the sheet around the lower half of her legs.

"Isabelle, please make Miss McCabe a vinegar poultice."

"Comin' right up, Doctor."

"Thank you, Isabelle." Sarah sent her an appreciative grin.

Mrs. Schlyterhaus pulled her shoulders back "I vill not vatch the children, Captain. Zat is not my job. I have my hands full vith zis house."

Captain Sinclair held up a hand to forestall further complaint. "Now, Gretchen, I realize you're a busy woman. My house is always immaculate, thanks to you. I have no intention of saddling you with yet another task."

His soft-spoken reply deflated her instantly. "Thank you, sir." With that Mrs. Schlyterhaus slipped away.

Sarah appeared apprehensive as she gazed at Captain Sinclair. "I'll find a way to take care of the children, Captain. I'm a fast healer."

"Now, you heard me, young lady." Dr. Feathermayer wagged a finger. "Brian, I trust you'll see my instructions are carried out."

"I will. You have my word."

The doctor gave him a nod. "I'll see myself out."

Captain Sinclair put his hands on his hips. "Sarah, we don't disobey doctor's orders in this house. As for the children, my steward has a plan." He clapped Richard between his shoulder blades and grinned. "Let's hear it."

"I'll take them out to the farm for a long weekend." He sent the captain a winning smile. "Sarah can convalesce there too. It'll work out perfectly. My father will keep Gabe and Michael busy. God knows he can use a couple of able-bodied boys around the place. My mother will occupy the girls, and she'll be glad for Sarah's company."

The captain pursed his lips, thinking it over. "I don't like the thought of an empty house."

"You're going to be very busy, sir. Tomorrow night is the Maritime Ball, and you'll be escorting Mrs. Kingsley. On Saturday you've got a wedding and reception to attend. On Sunday it's the garden party at the Thurmans." Richard had checked the man's schedule before he'd left the shop. "You won't even know Sarah and the children are gone."

"Hmm, I suppose you're right." His gaze fell on Sarah. "You picked a good weekend to injure your ankle."

"You're not angry with me?"

"Now, why would I be angry? Do I look angry?"

"No, sir." Relief spread across her delicate features, followed by a lovely blush.

The captain watched her for several seconds. A mix of admiration and amusement seemed to play across his mouth, and Richard felt the seeds of jealousy begin to root. He shook his head to clear his thoughts. Good grief, the captain was fifteen years Sarah's senior and lived a worldly lifestyle. Sarah was a pastor's daughter and naïve when it came to men like Brian Sinclair.

So why was she looking back?

Richard purposely cleared his throat.

Captain Sinclair glanced his way. "Yes, well...I guess the matter is settled. I'll pack the boys' things, and—" he lowered his voice—"I'll charm Gretchen into packing the girls' clothes."

"Good luck, sir." Richard's tart reply made Sarah laugh, so it was worth the captain's momentary glower.

He left the room. Richard gazed at Sarah and hoped he'd imagined her interest in the captain.

"Thank you for everything, Richard." The sound of her voice was so pure and her expression so demure that he felt a twinge of guilt for arriving at his earlier assumption.

"You're entirely welcome." He glimpsed the little frown puckering her brows. "Is something else troubling you?"

She pressed her lips together as if she didn't want to say.

Richard thought it over, playing back in his mind everything that just occurred until the captain exited.

Then it hit him. Who'd pack her things for the weekend? Perhaps that's what she'd been thinking as she stared at the captain. It made sense now.

A few more moments of contemplation, and Richard came up with a solution for that problem too.

"Come on, Sarah." Bending, he scooped her up. "Hang on to that sheet just in case." But he managed to get his arm under her knees so her skirts remained in modest decorum.

"What are you doing?"

"Stop your wiggling. I'm taking you upstairs so you can pack. I'll ask Isabelle to help you."

Sarah ceased her protests. Their eyes met, and Richard felt himself pause to savor this up-close look. Her skin was a flawless peach and her lips strawberry-ripe.

"You're so kind to help me." She pecked his cheek gratefully.

A surge of energy coursed through him. Amazing what a man could accomplish with a mere kiss. He headed for the stairs.

"Please be careful of my ankle."

"I will, Sarah." He began the ascent.

"Don't let me fall." She clung tighter to his neck. "Once my brother Luke accidentally dropped me when he tried to carry me upstairs like a sack of potatoes."

"I've got a good hold on you."

She whimpered like she didn't believe him and pressed her nose into his shoulder. Richard couldn't say he minded. He could smell the pretty lavender scent she wore. "I can't look down. I'm getting dizzy."

"Close your eyes, Sarah." He chuckled.

He reached the top of the steps only to be greeted by Captain Sinclair's frowning face.

"What's going on here?"

"Carrying her over the threshold, sir." Richard could only wish.

Sarah's head came up sharply, and she squinted a warning at him.

Smiling, Richard passed the captain, who looked to have appreciated his jest as much as she did. Reaching the room between the girls' bedroom and Michael's, Richard paused. He gave a nod and Sarah reached her one arm back to open the door. Inside, Richard set her gently down in an armchair. He dragged over the stool from the vanity and carefully set her ankle on it.

"There." He straightened and stood with arms akimbo. "You survived too."

She smiled. "So I did. Thank you."

"You're welcome. Now to find Isabelle." He dipped his head in parting and left the room.

"Er, Richard..."

Halfway back down the hallway, he spun around at the sound of the captain's voice.

Captain Sinclair motioned him out into the main corridor. "I'd like a quick word with you."

Near the stairwell, he leaned against the oak balustrade and folded his arms expectantly. "Yes, sir?"

"This hasn't yet come up since you've been in my employ, but..." He lowered his voice to a whisper and stood near Richard's shoulder.

"Just for the record, I don't allow domestic help and apprentices to see each other romantically. Do I make myself clear?"

"Perfectly." Richard worked his jaw and looked into the captain's face. "Is that all, sir?"

His gaze darkened. "That's all."

Turning, Richard headed down the stairs.

"Unless you'd like to sign on with me permanently."

He paused and looked up to see Captain Sinclair leaning over the rail.

"The way Gretchen and her husband did."

Richard couldn't help grinning at the ploy. Nice attempt on the captain's part. "I appreciate the offer, sir." He continued his way down to the first floor to find Isabelle.

The wagon rattled its way out of the city. Sarah tightly hung on to Rachel while Libby sat between her and Richard on the bench. The boys traveled in the back with the luggage.

"It won't be long now." Reins in hand, Richard sent them a smile.

Libby and Rachel chattered about what they liked best on the farm. The animals won hands down.

Stroking Rachel's blonde, wispy curls, Sarah listened to her describing the kitty she loved. "It's pink."

"A pink kitty?" Sarah laughed softly and heard Richard chuckle.

"Yes, pink!" Rachel nodded vigorously.

Sarah decided she'd best help the three-year-old learn her colors.

"No, Rachel..." Libby leaned over, her arm resting on her sister's knees. "Your kitty is gray and white and mine is all gray."

"Oh..." She stuck a finger in her mouth as she mulled over her big sister's correction.

"Who's your favorite, Miss Sarah?"

"Hmm..." She thought about the kittens she'd seen a week and a half ago. "Well, my favorite kitty isn't on the Navis farm. My favorite is an orange-and-white tabby that I left back home. Her name is Sunny."

"You miss her something terrible, right?" Libby's dark head bobbed up and down.

"Yes, I do." Sarah fought down pangs of homesickeness. She was a grown woman now. On her own. Independent. "But when a person becomes an adult, they have to put away childish things."

"Doesn't mean you still can't enjoy a kitty...or laugh when the pitchfork goes flyin' out of your grip and lands in the hay loft."

Sarah looked at Richard and laughed just imagining it. "Did that happen to you?"

"Just this morning."

Wearing a wide grin, Richard steered the team of horses onto the gravel drive and up alongside the house. He halted near the barn. Mr. Navis wheeled his chair to the entrance and raised a hand in greeting while Mrs. Navis came out the back door. It banged as it closed behind her.

"Hi, Mama, got some company for you." Richard lifted Libby down first, then Sarah handed him Rachel. Gabriel and Michael hopped out of the wagon bed.

"And, look here, Pops, I've got some strong boys to help you out."

"Well..." He gave a guffaw. "That's all right by me."

"To what do we owe this unexpected visit?" Mrs. Navis wiped her hands on her apron.

"Sarah injured her ankle," Richard told her. "She can't walk on it for a few days, per Dr. Feathermayer's strict orders."

"Oh, you poor thing." Mrs. Navis appeared genuinely concerned.

"It's really not that bad," Sarah demurred.

"Yes, it is. And it looks even worse, all dark purple and pink." Richard gave a little laugh. "Even Gabe and Michael found it impressive."

With a sigh Sarah recalled how the boys gazed at her ankle with enthused expressions. That meant it couldn't be good.

Richard came around the wagon and reached for her. But instead of assisting her to the ground, he scooped her into his arms. Her right arm slid around his neck. Their gazes met, and he grinned.

"You didn't think I'd allow you to hobble into the house, did you?"

It seemed he'd read her mind. "I reckon not."

"You *reckon*?" He chuckled. "I like that."

Sarah chided herself for allowing a little of her country upbringing to slip out. Every now and then she forgot herself.

Quite effortlessly Richard carried her up the steps to the back porch. He'd been the one to transport her from the captain's residence to the wagon too. Sarah admired his strength and appreciated his solicitousness, but there was this small part of her that had wished the captain would have gathered her into his arms…

With a mental shake, she willed away the notion. Captain Sinclair was her employer, and she needed to have the utmost respect for him. Fanciful thinking did not fall under that category.

Richard deposited her on a large swing. Sarah sat sideways on it and arranged her skirts.

"Comfortable?"

"Yes, very. Thank you."

"What on Earth happened?" Mrs. Navis came to stand over Sarah. A worried frown creased her brows.

"I was watching the boys swim, and I slipped off the riverbank. Thankfully, Richard caught me."

"She said I was her hero." He flashed an eyebrow and his smile dimpled his cheeks.

Sarah resisted the urge to roll her eyes. "Such lies…and in front of your mother, yet."

Mrs. Navis snorted a laugh.

"Seriously," she amended, "Richard has been my champion since I arrived in Milwaukee." She sent him a grateful glance.

He gave her a smile.

"Let me take look at this ankle of yours." Mrs. Navis shooed Richard away.

He went into the house. After he'd gone, Sarah lifted her skirts, and Mrs. Navis gently pulled off her stocking. Sarah bit her bottom lip and tried not to moan in pain.

Mrs. Navis winced. "Well, now, I've got some toad ointment. I'll get it and carefully smear some on that ankle."

"Toad ointment?" Sarah thought it sounded like one of her sister-in-law Valerie's concoctions. Valerie made herbal teas, poultices, creams, and of course her Psalm 55 soap, which smelled as heavenly as its name. But Sarah had never heard of toad ointment before. "It's not made with real toads, is it?"

"Why, yes it is, although I'll spare you the details of the recipe. As repulsive as it may sound, you just can't beat the mixture for healing up sprains."

Sarah was all for anything that would help get her back on her feet. "All right. Thank you." Even for *toad ointment.*

After a light supper, Richard supervised the boys as they washed and changed into their nightclothes. Mrs. Navis helped the girls. Sarah could hear the giggling and whoops from where she sat on the stuffed chair in the large parlor. Her left ankle rested on an ottoman.

"Looks like it's just the two of us helpless creatures left down here." Mr. Navis rolled his chair to the large parlor.

"Yes, it looks like it." Sarah hated feeling so incapacitated. She could only imagine how hard it must have been for Mr. Navis to adjust. "May I inquire as to how you were injured?"

"You may." With a broad grin on his grizzled jaw, he rolled farther into the room. His expression told Sarah he didn't mind discussing the matter. "I was with the Eighteenth Wisconsin and took a bullet in Vicksburg, Mississippi. A buddy pulled me to safety, and I could walk and feel my legs at first. But after the surgery to remove the bullet from my back, my legs went numb. Funny thing—bullet's still in there."

"In your back?"

"Uh-huh."

"Oh, my…so the surgery made it worse." Sarah shook her head.

"Aw, now, don't look so glum. I get out of doing a lot of work around here." He chuckled facetiously. "And just look at the fancy chair I get to sit around in all day. I'm living the lazy man's dream."

"I'd admire you for seeing the rainbow through the rain. My brother Jake was so bitter and angry when he first came home injured. But then God turned his heart around, and now he...he..." Sarah bristled as she thought of her older brother. "Well, God healed his heart, but he's as bossy as ever. That's on account of the fact he wanted to be a lawman until he got hurt."

"Is that right?" A grin tugged at the corner of Mr. Navis's mouth.

Sarah nodded. "And my brother Luke...he was grazed by a bullet or something across the head during the battle of Bull Run. Knocked him silly. He still can't remember everywhere he was during an entire six-month time. My brother Ben searched the country for him." She smiled just as she always did when she thought of how Ben met Valerie. "The Lord led him to find his wife...and then Luke too."

"Well, what do you know. Your family sounds like an exciting bunch."

"They do?" Lowering her gaze, Sarah picked at a thread on her dress. "Well, I miss them sometimes, but I knew I had to get away and learn to live on my own and be independent."

Thundering footfalls rumbled down the stairs, and then the boys burst into the parlor. They were breathless.

Sarah sat forward, concerned. "What have you been doing to cause such exertion?"

"We had a—" Michael inhaled—"pillow fight with Mr. Navis upstairs." He glanced at Richard's father. "The other Mr. Navis."

"Yes, I figured it out." The senior Navis smiled.

"I think it's time to settle down now," Sarah warned.

"Mrs. Navis said we can have some berries and cream and eat 'em on the back porch." Gabe wiped the perspiration off his forehead with the back of his hand. Then he plopped down on the gold upholstered sofa. "We just gotta wait here for her."

Sarah sat back, feeling helpless once more. She would have liked to corral these two before the pillow fight. Two weeks of experience taught her that Gabe and Michael took awhile to settle in at night. If they didn't get proper sleep, they were ornery the next day. "Where are Libby and Rachel?"

"Mrs. Navis is tucking them into bed," Gabe said. "She's telling them stories."

Sarah had been singing the girls to sleep these past nights—even though she was supposedly off duty at seven o'clock. The captain was rarely home at that time. More often than not, she put the girls to bed. Now she felt rather sorry that she didn't get to at least tell them good night.

Richard bounded downstairs next, followed by his mother, whose steps weren't as exuberant.

"All right, on the porch with you." Throwing his thumb over one shoulder, he motioned Gabe and Michael to the back of the house.

The boys were quick to obey, although they each attempted to sock Richard on the way out. He successfully dodged them and made like he was fighting back. Sarah had to admit Richard had a way with those two.

She considered him. Dressed in overalls and a light-blue shirt with sleeves rolled high above his elbows, he'd done his chores tonight—and somehow convinced Gabe and Michael to work right alongside him.

He rubbed his palms together and grinned. "I always wanted little brothers to boss." He spoke loud enough for the boys to hear him. "And I just might tell them to go jump in the pond."

"Yeah, tell us to do that!" Gabe said.

"Good way to get them clean for the night." She smiled at Richard.

He whispered, "You read my thoughts exactly."

"C'mon, Mr. Navis, tell us to jump in the pond." Michael's voice reached Sarah's ears.

"All right. You asked for it."

Richard left the room, and Sarah laughed in his wake. Then she closed her eyes and suddenly felt like she was home.

# Twelve

Sarah spent a fitful first night in the Navises' house. Not because of the room. Not at all. The pretty blue-flowered papered walls were soothing as she lay down in the soft bed. After extinguishing the lamp, her ankle began to throb. She tried not to think about it. She tried reciting Bible verses, even singing to herself. Nothing worked. When the early pinks of dawn appeared on the horizon, Sarah was exhausted and her ankle no better.

Scooting herself into a sitting position, she carefully moved her injured limb over the side of the bed. Using her good leg, she hopped to the chair, just a few feet away. Sitting by the window, she saw Richard walk to the barn, pail in hand. It amazed her how hard he worked, both here at the farm and for Captain Sinclair. He was handsome, funny, good with children . . . no wonder Bethany Stafford had an interest in him.

But Sarah wasn't in the market for a husband. Not yet. She had too much independent living to do before she got married.

Now if this ankle would heal up, she could continue with her life.

A knock sounded.

"Come in."

The door opened, and Mrs. Navis poked her head inside the room. "I heard some movement up here and came to check on you. Did you sleep well?"

Sarah shook her head. "The pain from my sprained ankle kept me up all night."

"Oh, dear . . ." Mrs. Navis walked in and carefully took a look at the injury. "Let's take off this tight support stocking. Then I'll give you some medicine to help you sleep."

"But it's daytime, and the children will be waking up soon."

"I plan to feed them breakfast, and then Marty will keep those boys busy while the girls and I pick berries this morning."

"Oh, they'll like that."

"Yes, and it's better you get your sleep."

The stocking came off, and Sarah felt relief at once. Next Mrs. Navis helped Sarah back into bed. She fetched some extra pillows and used them to elevate the bruised ankle.

"I can't say I ever saw a twisted ankle this bad." Mrs. Navis shook her head. "I hope that doctor knew a sprain from a break."

"A break? Perish the thought!"

"Hmm, well, if there's no improvement tonight, then I suggest we have another expert examine it."

Sarah prayed God would heal her…and fast.

"All right, now stick out your tongue. Just a few drops of laudanum should help you sleep."

"Only a few drops? We used to give my Cousin Catherine whole spoonfuls after she'd been burned in the barn fire. She never recovered."

"How tragic."

"Yes, it was."

"Well, I think in your case, Sarah, a few drops will work wonders."

"Good." She closed her eyes and felt Mrs. Navis smooth her hair off her forehead—sort of like the way Ma used to do…

Darkness shrouded him as Richard led Poco into the barn. His bones felt heavy, and his muscles ached from the long day. Why the captain required a complete inventory today, he'd never know.

In the stall, he lit a lamp before removing the animal's bridle and saddle. After a quick rubdown, he promised the gelding he'd do a better job next time. For now, Richard's mind was on getting some sleep.

With saddlebags slung over one shoulder, Richard extinguished the lantern and left the barn. In the yard he paused to appreciate the quiet sounds of nature. Overhead the stars sparkled in the sky, and he couldn't help but appreciate God's handiwork. Inhaling deeply of the cool night air, he continued with his trek to the darkened house. He'd wash up, grab a midnight snack, and then head for the bunkhouse where he'd slept last night. Gabe and Michael occupied his bedroom.

"Hello, Richard."

He'd just placed a boot on the step when he heard Sarah's voice. Turning, he barely made out her form on the swing. "What are you doing out here?"

"I slept practically all day after your mother gave me some medicine. Now I'm wide awake."

And in her nightclothes. "How'd you get outside?" Richard stepped toward her. "You didn't walk on that ankle, did you?"

"No." She didn't offer more.

So Richard persisted. "You got out here...how?"

"Well, I sort of scooted down the steps on my backside. That was the easy part, actually. I hopped the rest of the way on one leg."

He chuckled softly, careful not to wake the household.

"I couldn't help it, Richard. I felt stir-crazy being upstairs all day."

Setting down his bags he walked the rest of the way to the swing. She sat at one end, and beneath the slivers of moonlight he saw her golden tresses cascading past her shoulders.

"Would you like to sit with me awhile? It's a beautiful night."

How could he refuse? "It sure is." The wooden swing creaked beneath his weight.

"You're home awfully late. Did the captain keep you busy overtime?"

"I'm indentured until December, and I imagine the captain plans to run me ragged." *At least while you're here on the farm,* he added silently.

Richard could tell Captain Sinclair had something up his sleeve, something concerning Sarah, although the notion he wanted her for anything other than a governess evaporated tonight when he got wind of the captain's intentions to pursue Mrs. Elise Kingsley, a wealthy widow.

Even so, that didn't stop Captain Sinclair from trying to use Sarah as bait to hook Richard into accepting his employment offer. Obviously he'd detected Richard's attraction to her.

"Do you have the weekend off?"

"Only Sunday." Richard's shoulders felt constrained, so he moved to sit sideways. In addition to giving him more room, he had a better view of Sarah. "You said your ankle is better? I'm glad to hear it."

"The swelling is down, and the pain is almost completely gone. It's certainly bruised, though." A weighty silence suddenly developed between them. "Richard, I had a lot of time to think this evening and... well, this feels awkward to say and I hope I won't seem ungrateful..."

"What is it?"

"I like you very much, but I don't want a serious relationship. Is that all right? On the other hand, I do need a friend here in Milwaukee, so I hope you'll—"

"It's my pleasure to be your friend, Sarah." So she'd sensed his interest too and "liked him very much" anyway. How encouraging. Fortunately, Richard wasn't in any sort of hurry—especially since the captain had dashed his hopes of courtship this summer. But obviously Sarah wasn't ready for such things anyway.

"You're not insulted, are you?" Vulnerability laced her tone.

"To be your friend? Naw, I can deign to such a position."

A heavy sigh in reply.

He quelled a laugh. He enjoyed giving her a hard time. "Would you like me to help you upstairs, Your Highness?"

"Can't you ever be serious?"

"I'm very serious." Richard felt a yawn coming on. "I can't very well go to sleep and leave you out here in the yard. There are wolves about. And bears."

"Hmph! They might prove better company."

He found the fact that she didn't scare easily quite entertaining. "Come on, Sarah." He stood and offered his hand. "Let's go inside."

She set her palm in his and stood, balancing so she wouldn't put weight on her injured ankle. "How does my royal subject plan to help me into the house?"

Beneath the moonlight he saw her lift her chin, silently goading him.

"Hmm... let's see." He wanted to kiss those pretty pink lips of hers but tamped down the notion. "There are many ways of transporting a princess. But I think the most efficient, in your case, is—" In one fluid movement, Richard stooped, gathering her nightgown and robe around her legs, then stood, bringing Sarah up over his shoulder.

"Whh—ooo—aaa!"

"Quiet, Princess, or you'll wake the entire kingdom." Her body was lightweight, and he knew he'd easily manage to carry her upstairs.

"Put me down, Richard. I feel more like a sack of potatoes than a princess."

He laughed, not heeding her request, and headed for the house. "Watch your head, royal one." He felt her duck as he walked through the door.

"Richard, this is most unladylike. Put me down." She squirmed.

He chuckled. "I have your modesty in mind, oh, fair princess."

"I'm serious. Put me down."

He didn't. Reaching the stairs, he began climbing. "Watch yourself." She did, and they cleared the bulkhead. He felt her hands on the small of his back as she tried to support herself.

"Ooohhh!" An indignant sigh to be sure.

Richard grinned and noted her reservation for the next two steps.

"I don't suppose you're ticklish." Her fingers worked both sides of his waist.

"Stop that!" He laughed and grabbed onto the banister, steeling himself against her revenging assault on that sensitive area beneath his ribs. "We're both likely to take a fall. Quit it, will you?"

"Not until you put me down."

Ignoring her tickling took all his efforts, but at last he set her feet on the top stair.

"Finally!"

Richard still had a few steps to go. Reaching her, he watched through the darkness as she pushed her hair from her face before straightening her nightclothes.

"I can hop to my room from here," she whispered.

"Am I being dismissed, m'lady?"

"You absolutely are!"

Richard grinned and watched her take a hop. "Here now, don't chance re-injuring your ankle. Take my arm."

"And then you'll do what? Fling me down the hallway?"

He chuckled. "Sarah..."

"Shh! You're going to wake the children."

In spite of her protest, Richard helped her the rest of the way to her room.

"I don't know if you're a dashing knight or a miscreant." She stood in the doorway.

"Perhaps I'm both." He loved to tease her.

"More the latter, I think."

"Hmm..." Richard folded his arms. "Perhaps in time you'll find out."

In reply, Sarah closed the door on him.

With a hearty chuckle, Richard leaned one shoulder against the wall, consumed with thoughts of her.

"Mr. Navis?"

A child's voice shook him back to the present. Turning, he saw Gabriel stumble from the bedroom across the hall.

"What's going on?"

"Nothing." Richard directed the boy back to bed. "Go to sleep or your princess-governess will have our heads."

"Our heads? Oh..." It took a moment, but then Gabriel played along. "Never fear, we'll escape on the back of our fire-breathing dragons." Laughter rang in his voice. He jumped into bed.

"A good plan. You're a wise knight." Richard made sure the lad settled in. On a serious note he added, "See you in the morning."

"Okay." Gabriel yawned.

Leaving the room, Richard headed downstairs. In the kitchen, he grabbed a light snack before making his way to the bunkhouse.

His thoughts came back around to Sarah. In all honesty she never really left his mind. Just thinking about her made Richard smile. *Lord, what is Your plan? Will Sarah ever be mine? Is it possible she'll ever come to love me? I want to be more than just her friend.*

Those questions and more swirled around his head as he sank into his bunk. The long day took its toll on his body. At last he slept.

Sarah didn't see much of Richard until Sunday, and even then they were mostly surrounded by other people. She noticed the long hours he worked for the captain and marveled at the way he never seemed ill tempered. What's more, Richard's good-humoredness with the boys amazed her, his gentleness with the girls touched her heart, and the deep love and respect he showed for his parents made Sarah feel quite impressed with him. Even his interactions with people at church showed his character, as he patiently listened to a garrulous old woman and earnestly spoke with the pastor about some church issues. He was always unfailingly polite to their Sunday dinner guests, the Staffords. She knew her pa and her brothers would like him, which was high praise considering they ran off every eligible young man who showed the slightest interest in her.

But she and Richard were just friends. Sarah wanted to remember that—and the fact she didn't want to live in the country on a farm. She could have that kind of life in Jericho Junction, but now that she'd tasted city life, she felt that she desired something more. Her feelings were confirmed Sunday night when she found herself back at the Sinclair residence. Although she'd been comfortable at the farmhouse, she was glad to be back at the mansion.

Sarah tucked in the girls for the night and got the boys settled down.

"Swimming lessons tomorrow, so don't stay up too late."

"Yes, Miss Sarah," Michael called from his room.

Gabe sauntered out into the hallway. "I didn't think we were going back again."

"Why wouldn't we?"

He replied with his usual shrug. "'Cause you got hurt. I figured you wouldn't want to go back."

"Nonsense. It was a little accident—and entirely my fault." Sarah gave Gabe a quick hug. "Now get some sleep, young man. You've had a busy weekend."

"It was fun too."

"I'm sure it was." Sarah didn't think Gabriel grumbled once. She pointed over his shoulder, into his room. "Now scoot."

"All right…"

"Excuse me?" She put her hands on her hips.

"Yes, Miss Sarah." A little grin hooked the side of his mouth.

She tousled the boy's hair before he entered his bedroom and closed the door.

Still hobbling slightly, she made her way into her own room. At the writing desk she penned a letter to her parents. She'd been away from home now nearly an entire month. She'd succeeded in obtaining a well-paying position, overcame a sprained ankle, and thwarted a courtship. Not bad.

But would her family be impressed?

# Thirteen

"This is the most beautiful room I've ever seen!"

Sarah glanced at the sculptured plasterwork on the ceiling, the two crystal chandeliers that hung from it, and finally the matching wall sconces. This was the first time she'd been up on the third floor of this house and inside the formal ballroom.

Captain Sinclair turned from the bank of windows that faced Lake Michigan. "I gather you like it, Sarah, huh?"

She heard the facetious note in his voice. "It truly is beautiful, Captain."

He looked pleased.

Her eyes continued to wander around the room. The hardwood parquet floor gleamed beneath its new coat of wax, and the tables lining the walls were covered with freshly washed and starched linen cloths and set with polished silver utensils.

He must have followed her line of vision. "I see Gretchen has already begun to prepare for the party on Friday night."

Sarah glanced at him and met his dark gaze.

"I'd like the children dressed formally so they can make an appearance." A spark of pride entered his eyes and a grin played on his mouth. "I enjoy showing off my children."

"As you should."

"And you too."

Sarah raised questioning brows.

He looked chagrined. "Plan on making an appearance. I didn't mean to imply that I'd enjoy showing you off, although—" the captain raised a dark brow as he considered Sarah in two sweeping glances— "I may enjoy it at that."

Sarah felt a deep blush creeping up her neck and face, but she chose to laugh off the remark. Surely he was teasing. But in truth, at times his flip remarks and scrutiny caused her to wonder.

She strolled to the end of the ballroom where a stage had been prepared for musicians. And a piano…

Her eyes grew wide. Two pianos in one household? Incredible! Wait until she wrote and told her family.

She dabbed at the sudden perspiration on her temples. "It's awfully hot up here, Captain. I can't imagine a ballroom full of people in this heat."

"The wind will soon shift, bringing cooler breezes off the lake." He smiled. "The ladies will need their shawls by Friday evening."

"How do you know?" She tipped her head, regarding him.

"Come here." He waved her over to the windows.

Sarah crossed the room.

"Notice the color of the sky."

"It's blue."

"Ah, but it's not the typical blue. And it might seem clear enough, but watch tonight as the sun sets. You'll see halos. It's a sign rain is on the way—probably tomorrow night. The front will come through, and then milder temperatures will prevail."

"That's amazing…if it's true." Sarah couldn't help throwing out the challenge. She believed only God knew what the weather would be like.

The captain chuckled. "You just wait and see. This room—" he stretched out his hand, indicating their surroundings—"will feel delightfully cool come party time."

Sarah turned and faced him. "Is Richard coming?"

"Yes. He'll be here in case I need him to explain my books." Captain Sinclair rubbed his palms together. "Hopefully Friday night we will secure several new shipping deals." A wry grin curved his lips. "Elise Kingsley will be here."

"Elise?"

"Her late husband owned Great Lakes Shipping. The poor woman has no idea how to run the business, which has led me to make an important decision."

Sarah wondered if she should ask.

In the end she didn't need to. "I want Elise's business—at any price, and that's why Richard's attendance is required."

"You're going to buy Mrs. Kingsley's business?"

"Yes, except she doesn't know it's for sale yet." He laughed, a deep, rich sound.

Sarah ran her finger along the edge of the piano. "So Friday's dinner is more business than pleasure?"

"It's both. On Friday night this room will be filled with Milwaukee's biggest beer barons. Frederick Miller and Jacob Best's son, Phillip. Captain Fred Pabst and Valentine Blatz, just to name a few. A reporter from the newspaper will be here as well. It ought to be very interesting."

"And all those men you mentioned make beer?"

"They do. And they're rich, Sarah." The captain folded his arms across his broad chest. "Very, very rich." He looked at her askance. "Have you ever tasted beer?"

She shook her head. Her father preached against partaking in strong drink.

"Well, perhaps you can have a small glass on Friday night after the children are asleep. Just to taste it."

"Kind of you to offer, sir." She already knew she'd refuse it.

"Do you know how to waltz?" The captain's arms dropped to his sides.

Sarah gave a nod in answer to his question. "Jericho Junction isn't that backwards. We have barn dances and..." Realizing what she just said, she laughed. "I guess it is somewhat behind the times compared to this." Her gaze roamed about the ballroom again, imagining ladies in grand attire sweeping across the polished floor.

"Let's practice, shall we?" The captain took a step forward and bowed. "May I have this dance?"

Sarah squelched her urge to giggle at his game.

He put his hand alongside his mouth, arched a brow, and whispered, "This is the part where you curtsy and accept."

"Oh…of course." Sarah made a graceful dip and then held her hand out to him.

The captain took it and gently pulled her in his arms. He held her with confidence and smelled of an expensive, department-store fragrance—something men back home never wore.

They began to waltz, and she had no problem following his lead. He hummed a tune she wasn't familiar with as they danced to the other side of the room and then around, making a full circle. At last the captain spun her in a pirouette.

Sarah laughed. But he didn't release her. Instead he brought her close to him again.

They didn't move. Sarah's heart hammered as he gazed down at her. An intensity she'd never seen before shone from his black eyes.

Her smile slipped away.

"You're a lovely young lady, Sarah."

"Thank you, sir," she eked out.

He bent his head close, his lips seeking hers. Suddenly Sarah's knees grew weak, and the room began to spin.

She turned her head away. "Captain Sinclair!" She pushed at his chest, trying to escape.

"Forgive me. For a moment I could have sworn you were Louisa." A wistful look shadowed his face. "You remind me of her when she was young and vibrant—the days before I left for the war." He gently released her.

Sarah's senses calmed. She could hardly blame him for the lapse in judgment. The war had taken its toll on a great number of men. Suddenly she even pitied him.

Still, he had no right. "Back where I come from a man kisses a woman only if he's got serious intentions."

The captain laughed. "How very provincial."

Confusion engulfed her. Did he think a kiss meant nothing? So a woman who kissed a man for pleasure was sophisticated and broad-minded?

He exhaled audibly and changed the subject, further puzzling Sarah. "Now, then…the reason I requested you to come up here is that I have a favor to ask."

"And that is?"

"I know tomorrow is your day off. But it's the Fourth of July, and I have plans with friends to take my schooner *The Adventuress* out on the lake. Will you watch the children for me? Aurora insists on coming with me instead of fulfilling her duty day, as she calls it."

"Of course…" Sarah planned to picnic with Richard and his cousin, but she could either take the children with her or find another way to spend the holiday. "Yes, I'll watch them."

"I knew I could count on you." He placed his hands on her upper arms. "You are the most valuable governess I've ever hired, Sarah McCabe."

The compliment warmed her heart.

Strains of laughter and footfalls on the steps alerted them to the children's arrival. Captain Sinclair hurried to forestall them from entering the ballroom. His long, muscled arms spanned across the doorway.

"Gretchen has already set things up for our company Friday night. Turn around now. Back downstairs."

He followed them out.

Alone in the ballroom she walked to the windows and gazed out over the lake. Teal melded into dark blue and ships looked like white specks on the horizon. She relived the memory of waltzing with Captain Sinclair. In her mind's eye she envisioned dancing in his arms at his party on Friday night. She'd wear her brand-new dress from Hamlin's Department Store. She'd smile and mingle with all his important friends…

"Sarah?"

She whirled around to find Richard standing behind her. She wondered how long she'd been staring.

"I called to you, but you must not have heard me. When I didn't see you with the children downstairs, I started looking for you."

"Oh?" Embarrassed to be caught daydreaming, she straightened her dress then pushed several hairpins back into place.

Richard sat on a wide sill and folded his arms. "Are you all right? You look sort of...dazed."

"Yes, I'm fine." She grappled for a way to change the subject. "By the way, I'm watching the children tomorrow."

"Ah..." A smile entered Richard's voice. "So the captain charmed you into sacrificing your day off, huh? Not that I mind his children one bit."

"Charmed?" Sarah tipped her head.

Richard raised his brows and inclined his head toward her. "He's quite good at it, isn't he?"

"The captain didn't charm me." Sarah jutted her chin. "I'm not such a little fool. He asked and I accepted."

The glint in Richard's blue eyes told her he didn't buy it. "Well, charmed or not, bring the children tomorrow. They're more than welcome."

"Thank you." Sarah felt her cheeks flame. Had Captain Sinclair used her? Tried to kiss her only to weaken her senses? How incorrigible!

Worse, she'd fallen for it—

Or maybe she'd fallen for him!

# Fourteen

The Fourth of July dawned sunny and bright with a cloudless sky. Sarah washed and dressed, then read from her Bible. Psalm 119:45 seemed to fit the holiday. *And I will walk at liberty: for I seek thy precepts.* She recalled how Pa once preached on Christ's freeing power over sin and death. Christ had won that victory when He went to the cross. With that same sense of liberty burning in her heart, America won her freedom over tyranny during the Revolutionary War. Today celebrated that victory. Sarah felt suddenly very blessed to be enjoying freedom on both accounts. She bowed her head. *Thank You, Jesus.*

Closing her Bible, Sarah left her room and made her way downstairs. As usual she ate breakfast with the captain and the children. Afterward she helped Isabelle in the kitchen, preparing the picnic lunch. Richard had said everyone brought food to share in the park.

"Well, well, what's going on here?"

Sarah whirled around to find Aurora entering the kitchen. Taste and sophistication described her white-and-black striped organdy muslin dress edged with scarlet braid. The white chip hat with red ribbons completed the outfit, and in her hand Aurora held a matching parasol.

Sarah couldn't stop gaping. "Why, Aurora, you're stunning. Will you really wear that beautiful gown on your lake excursion?"

"Thank you, my dear…and yes, of course I'll wear it."

Sarah had not realized boating was such a grand affair.

"Has my escort, John St. Martin, or Elise Kingsley arrived yet?"

"No, ma'am." Sarah continued with her packing.

The captain walked in next, dressed in a dark blue frock and gold brocade waistcoat. He rubbed his palms together as if readying himself for the day's events. "Where are the children, Sarah?"

"Outside playing."

"Children? Why, Brian, they're monsters." Aurora fingered a ruffle on her sleeve. "Those boys called me 'granny' when I stepped out of the carriage. Then they ran off laughing."

Sarah pressed her lips together and tried not to smile.

"Boys will be boys." The captain stepped in beside Sarah and sampled a rhubarb cake, cut into bite-sized squares. "Mmm...delicious, Isabelle."

"Really, Brian," Aurora continued, "those boys need more discipline."

"Sarah hasn't complained." He nudged her with his elbow. "Have you?"

"No, sir."

Isabelle piped in. "Captain, it was Sarah and the children who made up that treat you're tasting. Made it last night. I merely operated the oven."

"The boys too?" He reached for another.

Sarah nodded. "Yes, sir."

"See, Aurora, they're no more monsters than you are a granny." He chuckled.

The woman harrumphed. "Really, Brian, this isn't amusing. I think you should take Elise's advice and send those boys to boarding school. The girls should have a strict nanny. No more of this fishing and beach-combing all day."

Sarah cringed, sensing the remark had been pointed at her. She and the kids had the freckles to prove it.

"Aurora, my children are my business." The captain snitched a cookie. One would think the man hadn't eaten breakfast.

"Oh, why are we conversing in the kitchen anyway?" Aurora turned with a flare of skirts and headed for the doorway. "I'll be in the reception parlor, waiting for John and Elise."

Sarah gave the captain a hooded glance, curious as to his reaction. He resembled Michael as he munched on the sugary treat.

"Don't mind Aurora. She'll be fine once we're out on the lake and she's sipping rum punch."

The captain's boyish charm had her smiling at him.

He caught her eye. "I'll have to take you on an excursion next. Where would you like to go? Up to Green Bay? Or perhaps you'd like to sail to Chicago so you can see what the city looks like from out in Lake Michigan."

"That would be marvelous. I'm sure I'd enjoy the sightseeing." She saw Isabelle's frowning disapproval and realized how inappropriate the offer might sound. She quickly amended her reply. "That is . . . the children and I would enjoy it."

"You don't get seasick, do you?"

"I've never sailed before, so I don't know."

With a little rumble of a laugh, he chucked her under the chin. "I guess we'll soon find out, won't we?"

He strode from the room, and Sarah watched him go. His charm and broad-shouldered confidence made Sarah's heart beat faster while his promise hung in his wake.

Just then the Sinclair boys burst into the room. Sarah shook herself.

"When are we leaving?" Gabe reached for a cookie.

Sarah slapped at his dirty hand. "Go wash first. Both of you."

The pair grumbled but headed back outside to the pump. Sarah glanced at her timepiece. She'd have to hurry now and finish packing the picnic basket. The Navises would be by to collect them soon.

"Look over there." Richard pointed to north, where several tall-masted schooners were sailing across the smooth, glassy surface of the lake. "I think that's your father's boat."

"Oh, who cares?" Gabe's voice resonated with discontent. "If he cared about us, he would have taken us with him today. His friends are always more important. Same with Aurora."

"That's not true." Sarah still couldn't get over the fact the kids called their grandmother by her first name. And she felt compelled to defend

Captain Sinclair. "Your father cares a great deal about you—about all of us." She remembered his smile this morning when he promised to take them on a lake excursion someday soon.

Richard nudged her and Sarah jumped. Covering her embarrassment she shielded her eyes and strained to see the captain's ship from where they stood overlooking a bluff. Then she turned to look for Gabriel. He was long gone, back in the park.

"Sarah, what's the matter with you today?" Richard took her elbow. "Is the heat bothering you?"

She faced him, noticing that the cobalt-blue of his eyes rivaled the deep end of Lake Michigan.

"Sarah?" He gave her a mild shake.

"I'm so sorry. I don't know what's gotten into me lately."

"Come on. Let's go sit in the shade awhile."

He wound her hand around his elbow and led her across Lake Park's wide lawn. They stepped onto the paved road, littered with confetti from the parade earlier. Off to the left, in a large white gazebo, a band played "The Battle Cry of Freedom." Hearing the banjo made her lonesome for her brother Luke.

"What are you thinking about?" Richard peered at her.

She adjusted her bonnet. "I was recalling how my brother Luke liked to play the banjo." She laughed. "I never thought I'd miss the likes of him." She rolled her eyes, thinking of his bossing and teasing.

"Are you homesick, Sarah?"

"No." A half-truth, she supposed. "I like being on my own."

"Hmm…" He paused at the lemonade stand and purchased two glasses.

Sarah sipped from hers. It tasted tart and refreshing. She drank more. "Thank you, Richard. I didn't realize how thirsty I was."

"I suspected. Your cheeks are a bit pink."

"It's a hot day, to be sure."

They walked back to the area where the Johnsons, Navises, and Staffords had laid out their picnic blankets. Sarah's gaze quickly found all four Sinclair children. The girls were playing nicely on a nearby blanket, and the boys threw a ball to each other. With the children accounted for, Sarah sat down near Lina. Richard planted himself across from her and next to Tim Barnes.

"What a lovely day for a picnic, isn't it?" Lina adjusted the skirt of her dark blue organdy dress with its white ruffles.

Likewise Sarah tucked the folds of her pale yellow, dotted swiss dress beneath her knees lest a breeze off the lake blow them over her head. What a ladylike sight that would make.

Lina bent toward her and spoke in low voice. "Sarah, you probably don't know this, but Richard's birthday is coming up in a few weeks. Tim and I are planning a surprise party for him. Would you like to help?"

Sarah glanced at Richard. He caught her eye. "So what are you two ladies whispering about?"

A grin pulled at her mouth. "I'll thank you to mind your own business." A laugh escaped her before she cut her eyes toward Lina.

Lina patted her hand. "We'll talk about it later," she promised. "Lunch next week?"

"Yes. Lunch followed by shopping. I'd love it."

"Then it's a date."

Smiling, Sarah gazed in the direction of Lake Michigan. She took another sip of her lemonade. For the umpteenth time today she imagined how tall, handsome, and commanding Captain Brian Sinclair must appear as he sailed on the lake.

"Lunch and shopping? Sure, I'd be happy to join you." Richard joked.

"You're not invited, silly." Lina clucked her tongue at him.

"Why in the world would you *want* to be invited, Richard?" Tim quipped. "Wouldn't catch me shopping with a couple of ladies. *Ugh*!"

"Oh, hush!" Lina swiped at his arm.

Sarah barely heard the banter. Her thoughts were still consumed with the captain. She recalled the feeling of being in his arms yesterday.

The expert way he held her. Would he dance with her at his party on Friday night?

"Sarah?" Richard reached across the distance between them and took her hand. "Are you feeling all right? Your eyes look a bit glassy."

"Maybe it's the heat." Worry lines etched Lina's brow.

"What?" Sarah blinked and gave herself a mental shake. Reality set in. "Oh, I apologize." Embarrassment over having been fantasizing about her employer put a blush in her cheeks. "I'm fine, really."

"Are you certain, Sarah? Your face is so flushed."

"Really, I'm fine." She pulled her hand free and sent Richard, Lina, and Tim each a polite smile. She forced herself to concentrate and kept her gaze from wandering toward Lake Michigan.

But there was no denying it. Her present company paled in comparison to her imagination. How she wished she could be out on *The Adventuress* instead, clipping across the cool water with a certain magnificent-looking captain at the helm.

THE NIGHT OF THE PARTY ARRIVED, AND SARAH WAS GLAD the weather turned. The captain's prediction had been correct. Now cool breezes wafted in through the bank of windows on the eastern side of the ballroom.

"How long do we have to stand here?" Gabriel groused.

Sarah smiled at the boy. He looked so handsome, all dressed up, except he'd made it clear that he'd rather be fishing. And he had been making his feelings known for the last half hour.

"Your father said he'd let us know when it's time to go. He wants to show us off to his friends."

"He probably forgot all about us." Gabriel shifted. "He always forgets. Can't we just leave?"

"No. And let's remember to be respectful at all times. He is your father, whether he forgets or not."

Gabe shrugged and let out a sigh.

Libby tugged on Sarah's skirt. "Miss Sarah! Miss Sarah!"

"What is it, dear?" She bent to give the girl her full attention.

"There's Mrs. Kingsley—the one who came to Aurora's house when we were there. Look!"

Glancing across the crowded ballroom, Sarah spied the woman. "Don't point your finger that way, Libby. It's not polite." But Sarah had to will herself not to openly gape. The elegantly clad woman was, by far, the belle of the ball. Tall and slim, Mrs. Kingsley wore a red silk gown trimmed with black lace. Her brunette hair had been expertly curled and pinned.

Something knotted in Sarah's insides as she watched the way she swayed intimately in Captain Sinclair's arms. There wasn't anything innocent about it. She lowered her gaze. No one in Jericho Junction would dare dance that way.

Peeking up, she saw the captain glide across the dance floor. He never so much as glanced her way. His black eyes were fastened to the woman he held close.

Finally tearing her gaze completely away, she considered the other attendees. Well dressed and holding their heads at proud angles, they looked as rich and important as Captain Sinclair had stated. Sarah felt like her new dress from Hamlin's was mere peasants' garb compared to the beautiful silk gowns swishing around her.

But her scrutiny didn't miss the way both men and women alike consumed beer, wine, and champagne. She gasped as a female guest lost her balance and knocked over several stemmed glasses on the buffet table. Waiters were quick to clean up the mess. Another man stumbled toward the small musical ensemble, bumping into couples on the dance floor. Sarah shook her head. She was familiar with that sort of stumbling—she'd seen it enough near Jericho Junction's saloon.

A half hour passed, and Gabriel began to complain again. "Can't we go now? I hate this dumb party."

Michael slouched against the wall. "I'm hungry and tired."

"And I'm hungry too, Miss Sarah," Libby said with a pout.

Rachel stood on a chair and Sarah quickly scooped her off before she fell. The little one began to whine and squirm.

"Dad forgot us. As usual," said Gabriel. "So let's go."

At that precise moment, Captain Sinclair strode over with Mrs. Kingsley on his arm. The woman's plunging neckline caused Sarah to blush. Then she noticed another man with bushy brown whiskers walking alongside the captain too.

Sarah quickly positioned the children and warned Gabe to stand up straight.

"Gerald, Elise...meet my family. My sons, Gabriel and Michael, and my two daughters, Libby and Rachel."

Sarah waited, but he didn't mention her.

Rachel wiggled out of Sarah's grasp. "Daddy!"

When she reached him, the captain turned her right around and sent her back to Sarah. Looking up, he sent Sarah a dark frown to say she should have kept a better hold on his daughter.

Sarah felt herself wither slightly.

"You have a fine collection of children, Brian." Mrs. Kingsley's gaze flitted over them. "So well mannered."

"How old are you two fellas?" Hands behind his back, the whiskered gentleman rocked on his heels.

Michael replied, "I'm ten, and Gabe's almost twelve."

"Well, you'll soon be working for your father, won't you?"

"Not me." Gabe puffed out his chest and glared at the captain.

Sarah cringed inwardly seeing the shadowed expression on Captain Sinclair's face. He was none too pleased.

*Oh, Lord, please help Gabe behave…*

"What? You're joking, lad." The male guest chuckled. "Your father has an impressive business that's widely known and respected."

"I don't care about his business."

Sarah took Gabe's arm and applied a small amount of pressure. "He didn't mean that. I'm afraid he and all the children are tired and hungry."

"Make no excuses for my children, Miss McCabe."

She swallowed. The captain had certainly put her in her place.

"How appalling that you have to reprimand your hired help in public, Brian." Mrs. Kingsley raised a gloved hand to her lips while clinging to his arm.

Sarah overheard the comment, and feelings of humiliation and hurt fell over her. Hired help or not, didn't she warrant some courtesy?

She glimpsed the captain's meaningful stare, pointed directly at Gabe. No doubt the two of them would finish the matter of his impertinence later. Then the captain's features brightened.

He smiled. "How about more champagne? Elise? Gerald? Follow me." He led his friends away without a flick of a glance in their direction.

*How utterly rude.* Sarah didn't know if she felt more angry or confused.

"You're in big trouble," Michael muttered to his older brother. An element of glee tinged his tone.

"Yeah, Gabe." Libby clung to Sarah's hand. "I hope you get a licking."

"That's enough." Tamping down the tumult inside of her, Sarah eyed her four charges. They needed her now. Their father certainly had no use for her—or for them. How foolish she felt for thinking otherwise. For the first time, she fully understood the cause of Gabriel's sullen behavior. He was angry and disappointed in his father.

So was she.

The captain's talk of having a strong sense of family seemed more like hypocritical charm intended to manipulate her into taking his children off his hands.

Sarah motioned them toward the doorway. "Come on, children. Let's go."

Sarah fed the children in the kitchen. Then, after tucking Libby and Rachel into bed and seeing that Gabe and Michael were quietly reading in their rooms, she decided on a stroll. She wished for a chance to feel pretty in her new gown before she hung it up for the night. She wondered when she'd wear it next…perhaps to a recital at the music academy. But one thing was sure. She would pay that blackheart, the captain, back every cent he'd spent on the dress.

In the hallway Sarah could hear strains of a violin and grand piano mixed with laughter coming from upstairs in the ballroom. She hoped the captain and his friends wouldn't disturb the children.

She took to the stairs, meeting Richard at the bottom. He appeared casually dapper in brown trousers, matching waistcoat, a crisp rust-colored shirt, and dark necktie. She smiled when she saw his gaze drink in her attire.

"Sarah, you look…" He seemed awestruck. "You look beautiful."

"Why, thank you." A blush worked its way into her cheeks, but it was the reaction she'd longed for all night. A pity the captain hadn't noticed.

Sarah considered Richard as he stood by the balustrade. "Where have you been all night? Why haven't I seen you until now?"

He sighed and loosened his necktie. "I've been holed up in the captain's office, minding his books."

"Oh, yes, that's right." Sarah recalled how Captain Sinclair planned to purchase Mrs. Kingsley's shipping business.

"I've been keeping company with bankers." He stifled a yawn. "You're a welcome—and lovely—reprieve."

"What a charmer you can be, Richard Navis."

He chuckled.

"Well, I'd like to stay and chat, but I'm going out for a stroll. You see, I'm in need of some refreshment myself."

"Hmm, do you mind if I join you? My work is finished for the night."

Sarah smiled. "I'd like that." Perhaps Richard's wit would pull her out of the funk in which she found herself due to the captain's boorishness.

Outside, the stars looked sharp in the inky-black sky. The easterly wind off the lake felt cool, and Sarah hugged her shawl more closely around her shoulders.

"Pretty night," Richard remarked. He offered his arm.

Sarah took it. "Yes."

"I'm sure the captain and his guests are glad the oppressive heat is gone. That third-floor ballroom would be miserable if the higher temperatures persisted."

"When the children and I were upstairs, the ballroom was quite comfortable." Sarah sent a glance Richard's way. "Did you know that the captain predicted the weather would shift?"

"I believe it. He has a keen barometrical sense. Most nautical men do, I suppose."

"Yes, well, speaking of the captain's ways..." Sarah searched her mind for the right words. Finally, she just came out with it. "Richard, the captain treated the children and me very badly tonight."

"I'm sorry to hear that. What happened?"

She hugged Richard's arm. "He ignored the children after they'd put on their best clothes. Little Rachel ran over to him, and he sent her right back to me as if her excitement over seeing her father was naughty. Then Gabriel smarted off, and perhaps I was wrong, but I defended him by explaining that he and the other children were tired and hungry. The captain reprimanded me in front of Mrs. Kingsley and another guest."

"Hmm."

"I've never seen that side of him before, and I didn't like it. He made me feel like a lowly servant when I had the impression that the captain considered his employees part of his...family."

"Family?"

"Yes. When I was hired, the captain told me he wanted the children to have a sense of family, something he never had."

"So you felt you were his equal, so to speak."

"I *am* his equal."

"In certain situations, perhaps. Around his friends and in public, however, you're the governess, a position deemed by the captain as being beneath me, his assistant, but above his housekeeper and cook."

"Another reason why Mrs. Schlyterhaus might resent me." Sarah breathed in a slow breath. "The captain certainly put me in my place tonight."

Richard covered her hand with his palm. His touch felt warm.

"So here we are—two underlings out for a stroll." He chuckled.

"It's not funny."

"Sarah, you're really upset, aren't you?"

She nodded even though Richard probably couldn't see it.

"Would you like me to speak to the captain about it?"

"If you'd like. Heaven knows I won't be speaking to him anytime soon."

Richard pulled away slightly. "You're not thinking of quitting, are you?"

"No. I'm just miffed." As they turned a corner, a gust of wind swept several strands of hair onto her cheek. "And I feel badly for the children. The captain had a complete disregard for them after he claimed to want to 'show them off' to his friends."

"I'll speak with him tomorrow."

"And the dress Mrs. Kingsley wore...it was so immodest that I wanted to put my hands over Gabe's and Michael's eyes when she approached."

"Unfortunately those boys are used to it."

"It's not right that the captain exposes them to women in such revealing attire."

Richard steered her across the street and toward the steep bluff overlooking Lake Michigan. Moonlight glimmered off the water. The view was inspiring. Sarah leaned her head on Richard's arm, realizing how exhausted she felt. It had been a long day, and as usual, she'd put in more hours than her position required.

"Let's pray, Sarah."

"All right."

Richard stepped back and took her hands in his. "Lord God, we come boldly to Your throne of grace. We ask for Captain Sinclair...Lord, please continue to work in his heart so he'll come to know You one day."

Chagrin shot through Sarah. Her anger dissolved and a forgiving spirit enveloped her.

"Help Sarah and me to be godly examples so the captain and his friends see the difference You, Lord, have made in our lives. We praise You for our salvation and ask for Your guidance and protection. In Christ's name...amen."

"Amen." Sarah looked up at Richard. She could barely make out his features. "Thank you. I feel so much better. Suddenly my perspective has changed."

"You're welcome."

"You're a good friend, Richard."

"Well—" there was a grin in his voice—"as the Bible says, iron sharpeneth iron." He gave her hands a gentle squeeze before turning and offering his other arm to her.

Sarah threaded her hand around his elbow.

"Shall we head back and see what tasty leftovers from the party are back down in the kitchen?"

"Good idea." A vision of the cream cakes and other delectable desserts she'd seen in the ballroom came to mind. "I reckon there's an advantage to being an underling after all."

He chuckled. "Yep, I reckon so, you country girl, you."

Sarah gave his arm a good yank for the teasing. Yet, in spite of it, she enjoyed hanging on to him as they walked slowly back to the captain's house. Handsome and strong, Richard made her laugh, and she trusted him. She felt certain that with any more of these moonlight strolls she could actually fall in love with him.

But she had to remember…they were only friends.

The next morning the captain was late to the breakfast table. When he finally arrived, Sarah thought he looked a bit rough.

He raked one hand through his coal-black hair. "Good morning, everyone."

Mutters came from the boys, Libby said nothing and stared at her oatmeal, and Rachel eyed the captain as if he were a stranger.

"Good morning, sir." Sarah kept her tone stiff and formal. She was, after all, only the governess.

She caught his speculative gaze. She usually wasn't so stiff with her replies.

"Why is everyone so quiet?" He glanced around the table.

Sarah didn't answer but sipped her tea.

Isabelle walked in and set a pot of coffee in front of the captain.

"Thank you."

"Your eggs will be ready shortly."

"Good." The captain poured himself a cup of the steaming dark brew.

Isabelle left the room, and Sarah thought she'd seemed short with her employer today. Perhaps she shared a bit of Sarah's sentiment.

"How did you like the party last night, children? Wasn't the orchestra divine?" He smiled at his sons first, then his eyes rested on the girls. "No one enjoyed the music?"

The boys' gazes were fixed on their plates. Rachel, however, wasn't listening and struggled to stand on her chair.

"I wanna play with my dollies."

Sitting beside her, Sarah kept the little girl in her chair. Rachel fussed.

"Oh, let her go," the captain said. "I'm not in the mood for disciplining this morning."

"Children need consistency, sir." Sarah tried to interest Rachel in a blueberry muffin. "And you desire an orderly mealtime…correct?"

He replied with a series of short nods and narrowed his gaze.

Sarah spied the boys elbowing each other. "Stop that, Gabe…Michael. Finish your breakfast."

"Are we going cave exploring after that?" Michael spooned in a bite of his hot cereal.

Sarah nodded.

"Cave exploring…sounds exciting." The captain took a swallow of his coffee and looked at Sarah. "Are they the caves north of here?"

"Yes, sir." She didn't expound and say that Richard had told her about them. But he did. Richard said the caves were hidden in the bluffs.

Libby pushed her plate away and put her head down on her arms. Sarah reached over and rubbed her back. She'd crawled into bed with Sarah sometime during the night and this morning stated the noise from the party above had scared her. Consequently the girl hadn't slept well.

"I'm done!" Gabe slid his chair back. "Can I be excused?"

The captain rubbed his shadowy jaw. "Yes, I suppose so."

Michael perched on the edge of his seat. "Me too?"

Libby's dark head sprang up. "And me too?"

"I wanna play with my dollies." Rachel stood and Sarah lifted her down to the carpeted floor.

"Yes, you may all go."

Sarah stood and prepared to follow the children, who bolted from the dining room. The captain's low, strong voice halted her when she reached the doorway.

"Perhaps I should come along on the cave expedition today."

"Not necessary, sir." She turned to face Captain Sinclair. She remembered how Richard prayed that they would be godly examples and softened her stance. "We'll be fine."

"I insist. Those caves can be perilous. I explored them as a boy and know them well." Lifting his coffee cup, he took a long drink.

Watching him, Sarah wished he'd change his mind. His presence would spoil the entire day for her and the kids.

"I'll tell Isabelle to parboil some wieners, and the kids can cook them the rest of the way over a campfire. I'll tell pirate stories to the children. The boys especially like my pirate stories."

"Yes, sir."

He arched a brow. "Are you going to 'yes, sir' me all day long? That's rather unlike you."

"It's only fitting, sir." She lowered her gaze and tucked her hands into the pockets of her pinafore.

"Now, Sarah, I sense you're angry with me over something. Come out with it already. Your mood affects my children—and me."

"No, Captain." Her gaze flew to his. "Your behavior affects your children, and it's high time you start taking some responsibility for their upbringing."

"I beg your pardon." He tipped his head.

"Can't you see how Gabriel resents you for all your broken promises to him? And Michael—he adores you and just wants your attention. And the girls only desire your affection. It's not really very difficult...*sir.*"

For a minute Sarah thought she was about to get the reprimanding of her life. Would he terminate her employment? Well, so be it. And as long as she was on a roll...

"As for me, I am insulted by your actions of disdain last night. You asked me to attend your party. I should think you'd treat me with some respect. After all, you've entrusted me with your most valuable possession—your children."

Captain Sinclair sat back in his chair. His stare never wavered, although his features softened.

"Go ahead and end my employment if that's your intention. But at least I'll leave here with my integrity."

"What are you talking about? Are you mad? I'm not about to lose another governess." He sighed. "I suppose I deserved that dressing-down."

Sarah felt a tad guilty at his admission.

"Please accept my apology. I'll make it up to you and the children today. Cave exploring followed by cooking over a campfire." He smiled in an ever-so-charming way.

But before Sarah could answer, Isabelle entered the room, carrying his breakfast.

"Thank you."

She nodded and curtseyed at the same time. "And a messenger just arrived with this note." She handed him a piece of paper. "It's from Mr. Navis."

Sarah watched the captain unfold and read the missive as Isabelle left the room. Sarah would have gone too, but the captain's throaty groan held her in place.

"Is anything wrong?"

"Yes." He stood. "I forgot about a meeting this morning. You'll have to excuse me."

"Of course."

The captain headed out but paused when he neared Sarah. Taking her by the shoulders, he brought his face close to hers. "I hope you believe me when I said I'm sorry about my bad manners last night." His voice was as smooth as velvet. "Forgive me?"

"Yes." How could she not?

"Good. I promise it'll never happen again."

"Thank you."

The captain's dark eyes held hers while his hands slid slowly down her arms. Seconds seemed like hours before he turned and strode from the dining room. Sarah let out the breath she'd been holding and rubbed the places on her sleeves where his touch seemed to linger.

*Don't be charmed, you goose!* She gave herself a mental shake. Then she went to gather up the children. So much for their father's presence today as they explored caves.

Now, why did she feel a stab of disappointment?

RICHARD GLANCED AT SARAH AS THEY RODE HOME AFTER church. She stared down at her gloved hands, resting on the printed fabric of her dress.

"You're unusually quiet this fine morning."

"Forgive me, Richard."

"Nothing to forgive. I'm just stating an observation. That's all."

No reply.

Richard sucked in a deep breath. "Pastor Higgins preached a good sermon this morning." He adjusted the leather reins in his hands.

"Yes." That's all the reply he got.

But little Rachel had more to say. She began babbling from her perch. Mama sat in the backseat with Libby, and Richard could tell she enjoyed the little girl's banter. But Sarah didn't join in, which seemed odd.

Finally he halted the wagon near the barn. He crossed in front of Sarah and jumped down. Next he lifted Sarah down.

"Are you all right?"

She bobbed her head.

Meanwhile the girls squealed to get down. Richard took hold of Rachel by the waist, swinging her so she giggled. He lowered Libby the same way, which produced the same result. Smiling, he helped his mother. The Sinclair boys had already hopped out and were running for the house.

Walking to the back of the wagon, he slid out the ramp for Pops. He made sure the wide, thick board didn't rest at too steep of an angle. Then he jumped onto the flatbed and carefully rolled his father down to the ground. Mama pushed his chair into the house.

Richard tended to the horses. Since Sarah and the kids would ride home with his aunt and uncle and Lina this evening, he removed the animals' harnesses and turned them out to pasture. By that time he was ready for a cool drink of water.

Sarah met him by the pump in the yard. She'd shed her gloves and bonnet.

"Dinner ready?" Splashing water onto his face, he figured Mama sent her to fetch him.

"Well, um..."

He paused, looking at her. Wiping his face, he straightened.

"I need to talk to someone. Someone I can trust." She worked her lips together. "Can I talk to you?"

"Of course." Taking her elbow, he steered her outside and around to a shady thatch. They'd be able to talk in private here.

They sat down on the grass.

"What's this all about, Sarah?"

She broke off a piece of long grass and twirled it around her fingers. "Well, the captain has been...his behavior has me puzzled. I told you how he said he wants a sense of family for his children, but he treats them like framed artwork. Objects to be appreciated from afar. And he's treated me...well, you know."

"Yes. We discussed it Friday night."

"Right. Then yesterday at breakfast the captain and I had something of a heated exchange, and I..." She lowered her gaze. "I told him exactly what I thought of his parenting skills."

Richard laughed. "I know. The captain told me all about that conversation when he arrived at the store."

"Was he angry?" Her gaze darkened.

"No, I'd say he was more surprised than anything. I believe he respects you for spouting off to him the way you did. No one else has been able to point out his shortcomings as a parent without consequence."

"My intent was mostly to point out the needs of the children. My heart breaks when I see how much the boys want his attention and how much the girls want his love. But there's something else. Something I don't know quite how to handle. I think it's an act of persuasion, but . . . well, it's difficult to go into detail."

Richard's hackles went up. He knew of his employer's persuasive manner. "Sarah?"

She fixed her gaze on the blade of grass in her hand.

"Has Captain Sinclair been trifling with you?" When she wouldn't look at him, Richard reached over and cupped her chin. "Has he?"

Wide eyes stared back at him in the affirmative. But did he read guilt in their depths also?

"What's he done? What's happened?"

Discomfort laced her features before Sarah stood and walked out a few paces. "Yesterday after breakfast he touched me in a way that was almost paralyzing, and . . . and last week he tried to kiss me."

"Kiss you?" Richard wrestled with a jolt of jealousy. "I'll speak to him about it." He couldn't help flexing his fists.

"No, Richard. I can handle myself with the captain. It's what he might be thinking that has me confused. Since Pa and my brothers aren't here, I thought I'd ask you. After all, you're a man."

*So she'd noticed.* Richard continued to fight the mounting resentment he felt toward his employer. Paralyzing touches? Near kisses?

"Richard, please help me make sense of all this."

The pleading note in her voice touched him. "All right. But first let me make sure I understand. You wonder if the captain cares for you. Is that it?"

Sarah rolled her shoulders.

"You're joking."

She gave him a hard stare. "Well, what's a girl supposed to think when a man shows her such interest?"

Richard clenched his jaw. The thought of the captain seducing Sarah sent molten-hot anger coursing through his veins. He pushed to his feet. "I can tell you he doesn't care, Sarah—not in the way you're thinking. I suspect the captain has kissed a good number of ladies."

Sarah sucked in a breath. "No!"

Richard responded with a helpless gesture. "Pure speculation on my part."

"But how could he?" A shadow of disappointment wafted across her face.

*Disappointment*? Richard stood stock-still. What was she thinking?

She dallied around in a circle. "I'd never kiss a man I didn't truly love."

"Glad to hear it." Richard forced himself to breathe, hoping it'd be him when the time came.

But did she want to give her first kiss to him—or to Captain Sinclair?

He moved forward. "Where did the captain take such liberties the first time?"

"In the ballroom. The day before the Fourth."

Richard thought it over, recalling that day. "Was it before or after the captain asked you to watch the children on your day off?"

She paled. "Before. And you don't have to say it. He attempted to charm me, all right. But the truth is all he would have had to do is ask. I adore the children."

"I know." A question burned on his tongue. "Do you have feelings for the captain, Sarah?"

"A great many. But they're all tangled, and I can't sort them out. I've been trying. That's why I came to you. You know the captain. You've worked for him longer than I have."

"Sarah, if you want my opinion, I'll tell you that the captain takes advantage of a person's good nature. Obviously he's preyed on your naiveté."

"But he said I reminded him of his deceased wife, Louisa, when she was young, before he left for the war. I felt sorry for him."

"Exactly." Richard arched a brow. "What do you know of their relationship?"

Sarah shrugged. "Just that she was beautiful and something of a socialite."

Richard took her hand and led her back into the shade. He lowered himself onto the grass and tugged her so she sat down beside him. "Let me begin by saying the captain is basically a good man. Honest…" Richard sighed. "Well, he's honest if his back is to the wall. He fibs about the small things. But that's the way of the world, isn't it?"

She nodded.

"He's been generous to me and my folks. In general I respect him, although I'll admit to falling victim to his manipulation too. I learned to stand my ground…to a point. There are certain things he won't tolerate from me." Richard couldn't conceal a small grin. "Like a quip when other employees or customers are around."

"I can understand why." Her blue eyes sparkled.

Richard grew serious once again. "I think it's important to remember that the captain is not a Christian, Sarah. He thinks of himself as a self-made man and told me that he doesn't see why he should humble himself before God. In many ways, he purchased his mother's love and continues to do so."

"I wondered about that…" Sarah looked pensive.

"Mm-hmm…" Richard nodded. "He treated his wife, Louisa, much the same way, bought her whatever her heart desired, although for several years the captain served in the Civil War and they were apart."

"Yes, the captain told me."

"I think it's how he approaches relationships in general. Captain Sinclair uses his money and his charm to buy people's friendship and devotion. He's afraid the elite, like Mr. Miller, Mr. Blatz, and Mrs. Kingsley, would have nothing to do with him if he weren't wealthy."

"That's so sad. How can he ever know who's a true friend?"

Richard didn't have an answer for that one.

"He trusts you, Richard."

"But he pays me to be trustworthy, Sarah. Besides, I don't really have a choice right now."

She nodded. "I see your point."

Richard's gaze roamed over her sweet face. That certain spark he admired had returned to her eyes. "Feeling better?"

"Yes." She rewarded him with a grateful smile. "You've helped me keep the situation with the captain in proper perspective."

"Good." Richard prayed God would guard her heart as well as her mind.

The cowbell hanging on the back porch clanged, and Richard knew his mother meant business. Dinner was on the table.

Standing, he helped Sarah up.

"You know what?" She tipped her head. Her eyes searched his. "I consider you a true friend—one of the best I've ever had." She threw her arms around his neck and hugged him.

"Glad I could help." His arms encircled her waist, and he added a meaningful squeeze. *Sarah, I wish I was more than your friend.*

# Seventeen

Sarah read the message that Mrs. Schlyterhaus just handed her. It had arrived by courier.

"What does it say, Miss Sarah?"

She turned and saw the curious light in Gabriel's eyes.

"You've got a big frown on your face," he said.

A sigh escaped her. "Your grandmother can't come to pick you children up until later this afternoon."

"Hooray!" Gabe jumped in the air.

"No, not 'hooray.'" Sarah set her hands on her hips. "It's Wednesday, my day off, and I'm meeting my friend Lina for lunch and to go shopping afterwards." Richard's birthday was Friday, and she and Lina planned to discuss the details of a surprise party for him on Sunday after church. In addition, Sarah wanted to buy Richard a gift. She also had laundry to drop off, and that task would come before meeting Lina.

"We'll come with you. We'll behave. Honest."

"I don't believe you." She narrowed her gaze. "You hate shopping, Gabe."

"I know. But I hate going to Aurora's house even more."

Sarah sent a glance upward. "Oh, dear…" She strode into the music room and plopped down on a velvet armchair. She was only half aware that Gabriel stood in the doorway. "I guess I'll have to contact your father."

"No, Miss Sarah, take us with you. Michael and I can ride on the trolley cars all afternoon while you shop."

She sent him a quelling stare. "I don't think your father would approve of that activity."

"He doesn't care."

"Yes, he does, Gabe. He just doesn't show it much." Sarah hoped she wasn't fibbing, although she couldn't bear the thought of breaking the boy's heart. A little attention from his father would go a long ways.

Gabriel walked to the piano and banged on a few ivory keys.

"At least strike the chords I've taught you."

He grumbled. "If our mom was still alive we wouldn't have to go to Aurora's house... ever."

A wave of sorrow crashed over Sarah. She hadn't ever discussed Mrs. Sinclair's passing with the children. Occasionally they mentioned her, but conversations never ensued. Now Sarah regarded herself as rather thoughtless in this matter—thoughtless and, today, selfish.

She stood. "You know what, Gabe? I've reconsidered. You children are never any trouble for me. We'll all go downtown and have lunch with Lina—and, yes, we'll even ride the trolleys."

The boy's countenance brightened at once. "I'll tell Mike that we can't complain if you look at ladies' stuff."

"It's a deal." Sarah stuck out her right hand, and Gabe pumped it several times. "Now, go get your brother and sisters. I'll collect my laundry and reticule and we'll be off." She smiled as Gabe sprinted from the room.

Within thirty minutes she and the children had reached the corner where the horse-drawn trolleys made scheduled stops. They only had to wait a few minutes before a car came along. They boarded, and as they rode toward Grand Avenue, Sarah found her mind wandering. Would she make a good mother someday? What if the Sinclair kids one day became her own? But that would mean she and the captain—

Libby patted her arm and jerked Sarah back to reality. "Look at that man's furry lip, Miss Sarah."

"Shhh..." Sarah whispered close to the girl's ear. "It's not polite to talk about the way people look." However, the gentleman in the adjacent seat did sport an interesting-looking mustache.

Their destination neared, and Gabriel and Michael took turns ringing the bell to alert the driver to stop. The conductor glowered at their persistence.

"That's enough, boys." Sarah shook her head at the pair.

The car slowed to a halt, and Gabriel and Michael were quick to jump off. Sarah took the girls' hands in hers, and they descended the trolley car with the conductor's polite assistance.

As they strolled down the busy avenue, a flash of silver in a jeweler's storefront window caught Sarah's eye. She backed up a few paces, taking Libby and Rachel with her.

"What do you see, Miss Sarah?" Libby asked.

"Why, it's a set of writing pens. More handsome than I've ever seen." She lifted Libby, then Rachel, so the girls could glimpse the shiny pair. In doing so, she viewed the price tag. Quite expensive, but she'd manage it.

She worked her lower lip between her teeth and wondered. *Hmm…*

Gabriel and Michael began hollering to them from down at the end of the block. Their boyish voices echoed between the tall brick buildings and caused more than a few heads to turn. Sarah could see where the Sinclair children might get the best of her today.

But at least she'd found the perfect birthday present for Richard!

Richard slowed the carriage when he saw Sarah and the children parading up the block. It was Wednesday. What was she doing with the kids today? He noticed then the packages she carried.

Pulling up alongside them, he reined in the gelding. "Would you like a ride?"

The boys smiled and ran to the road to greet him.

Richard gave each one a nod. "Gabe. Michael."

They climbed into the back of the carriage.

Sarah and the girls approached him next.

"Hi, Mr. Navis!"

"Hi, Libby." He smiled. "Hello, Rachel." Then looking at Sarah, he raised his brows in question.

"Aurora can't pick up the children until later. So we all went shopping."

"Well"—he chuckled—"you look no worse for wear."

"Actually, it's been a fun day." Sarah deposited her brown paper-wrapped purchases into the backseat between the boys. Next she helped Libby climb in. "Here, Gabe, hold your sister on your lap."

Richard held out his arms for Rachel and set her beside him. Then he reached for Sarah's hand. She took it. The skirt of her blue-and-white dress fell across his knees as she made her way to the place on the other side of Rachel. She righted the cap tied beneath her chin, and once situated, she pulled the little girl onto her lap.

"I presume you're headed for home," Richard said.

"Yes." Sarah expelled a weary sigh. "Oh, I'm so grateful for the ride back. Thank you for stopping. We missed the trolley car and decided to walk until we saw the next one."

"You're welcome. I had hoped I'd run into you today."

"Running errands for the captain?"

"I am." He watched as Rachel snuggled against Sarah with droopy lids. In the back, all was quiet as well. "Nothing like a shopping trip to expend some energy."

"I'll say." Sarah looked exhausted also. "I dropped off my laundry, and we met Lina for lunch at Pershing's Eatery. Lina said to give you her regards if I saw you today. I reckoned I would."

Richard shook his head, sorry that Sarah had to juggle the children, laundry, lunch, and shopping on what was to have been her day off. "I wish you would have sent me a message. I would have come to pick you up. I'm sure that, under the circumstances, the captain wouldn't have minded."

"Oh, Richard, now how could I pull you away from your books?" Sarcasm laced her tone and a teasing gleam entered her blue eyes. "I know how much you're attached to them, especially on beautiful days such as this."

He couldn't contain his smile.

When they reached the Sinclair manse, Richard jumped from the buggy and helped Sarah and the kids alight. He thought it odd when she wouldn't allow him to carry her purchases for her. Empty-handed, he followed her into the side entrance of the house. Inside he removed his hat. The boys took off for the backyard while the girls went upstairs with Sarah.

Minutes later, she returned alone and without her packages. Richard trailed her into the kitchen.

"Libby and Rachel are going to rest for a while. Would you like some refreshment? I'll fix us some tea with fresh mint."

"No, thanks. I'd best be on my way. But before I go..."

Sarah turned to him. In spite of her busy day she looked so pretty that Richard's heart skipped.

"Would you care to go to the concert in the park on Friday night? I begged off early." He paused, before adding, "It's my birthday."

"Oh..." Sarah seemed both happy and slightly flustered. "I'd love to, really, but I can't. You see, I have a...a..."—she wetted her lips—"a previous commitment."

"Previous commitment?"

"Yes, I promised someone...well, let's just leave it at that, all right?" She whirled around. "Now about that tea..."

"Sarah?" *What previous commitment?* Richard longed to question her.

She brushed him off and went about her business.

Irked beyond imagination, Richard donned his hat and left. *She promised someone? What did she promise—and to whom did she promise it?*

Back in the buggy, he pulled on his driving gloves. His shoulders tensed. Something wasn't right. Sarah was usually candid with him.

His fists tightened around the leather reins. Did Sarah's reticence just now have anything to do with Captain Sinclair? Richard felt himself glower. What had the man charmed her into doing this time?

Well, he'd certainly do his best to find out.

"I see we've got a little art project going on." Captain Sinclair walked around the cluttered kitchen table on which Sarah and the children had been cutting out and pasting colored paper.

"It's birfday cards for Mr. Navis!" Rachel's voice rang loudly with excitement.

"I forgot all about Richard's birthday." Captain Sinclair folded his arms.

Sarah rolled her eyes. The man would forget his head if it weren't attached.

The captain pulled at his chin. "He's been acting strangely the last few days. I wonder if his birthday had something to do with his dark mood. He even gave me something of a tongue lashing because Aurora didn't show up on Wednesday."

Sarah grimaced. "I'm sure the birthday celebration did—and does—affect Richard. You see, he doesn't know about it. He thinks we forgot." She knew she'd hurt Richard's feelings by turning down his concert invitation, but hopefully the surprise would make it all worthwhile.

"Hmm...then perhaps I'll make like I was in on it."

The back of Sarah's kitchen chair creaked under the captain's weight as he leaned on it.

"His birthday was really yesterday, Daddy," Libby said, "but his party is tomorrow, right after church." She looked to Sarah for confirmation.

"That's right." Sarah glanced at the captain. "I didn't think you'd mind my taking the children, since they've accompanied me to church and then the Navises' farm every week except one so far."

"I don't mind at all," he said graciously. "I only wish I would have remembered that Richard's birthday was yesterday." The captain narrowed his gaze at Sarah, feigning irritation. "You should have reminded me."

Sarah tamped down the urge to retort, but she feared she'd already overstepped her bounds in her tirade last week. The captain, however, hadn't said another word about the incident.

"Take a look at my card, Dad," Michael said.

"Well, it's a fine-looking creation."

"How 'bout mine, Daddy?" Libby asked. "Do you like it?"

"Very good, darling."

Sarah's senses went on alert. Was the captain trying to mend his ways with his children?

"Look at mine! Look at mine!" Rachel grabbed her card and stood, climbing over Sarah's lap to reach her father. Her motions were so swift that the scissors slipped, cutting Sarah's palm.

Captain Sinclair caught Rachel as she toppled sideways.

"Young lady, how many times must I tell you not to stand on chairs—or, in this case, Miss Sarah's lap?"

The little girl pouted.

The captain jostled her in his arms then kissed her cheek.

Sarah blinked. He'd just kissed his daughter!

"As for your birthday card, Mr. Navis will enjoy it."

Sarah reached for her hankie and tied it around her wound. She'd tend to it properly later and hoped the captain hadn't seen the mishap. It might shed a poor light on her governing abilities.

"What about yours, Gabriel?" The captain set Rachel back down in her chair. "Can I see it?"

He shrugged before grudgingly handing it to his father.

"Say, this is very good."

Sarah turned in time to see the look of approval in Captain Sinclair's dark eyes.

"I should say you're a talented young man."

"You've seen the pictures in his bedroom, haven't you, Captain?" Sarah asked.

He frowned. "No, I haven't."

Sarah looked across the table at Gabriel. "You'll have to show your father your *gallery*."

"You really want to see my pictures?" Doubt clouded Gabe's light-green eyes.

"Of course I want to see them!" The captain cleared his throat while his hand encircled Sarah's wrist. "Right after I see your governess."

"Oh?" Confusion weighed on her brow.

His strong hold uprooted her from the chair. "Gabe, you're in charge here. Guard those scissors from your sisters."

"Aye, aye, sir."

Michael snickered.

"What did I tell you about that back talk, son?" The captain's tone sounded ominous at best. "And Michael?"

The boy sat up straighter.

"Gabe?"

"*Yes, sir.*"

Sarah fought a grin at the unison reply.

"It would help if you didn't look so amused," he muttered near her ear.

"Yes, Captain." Sarah willed any remaining humor away.

The captain's voice lightened. "Follow me."

She did. They left the kitchen.

"Gretchen, I want some antiseptic and a bandage."

"Yes, Captain." The housekeeper seemed to appear out of nowhere, but Sarah learned that wherever the captain went in the house, Mrs. Schlyterhaus hovered nearby.

Sarah expelled a long breath. So he'd seen the accident with the scissors. Her insides knotted. Entering his study, she figured a reprimand was coming.

Captain Sinclair closed the door behind him and took a seat on the edge of his wide, cluttered desk. "Let me see." He held out his hand.

"It's nothing."

"Sarah..."

That commanding tone of his left no room for argument. She slowly stepped forward, unwrapping her hand.

He inspected her palm. "A good-sized gash, but it doesn't require a stitch." He met her gaze. "I'm no doctor, but I've seen enough wounds in my day."

Sarah couldn't argue the point. As a captain in the United States Navy during the war, he probably saw more than a man ought to see.

A knock sounded and the captain called admittance. Gretchen marched in with the items he'd requested. She tossed Sarah a look of disdain before exiting.

After the woman had gone, the captain tore away a small piece of the gauzy bandage and soaked it with antiseptic. "Has Gretchen been bothering you?"

"No. I just can't figure out why she doesn't like me."

A grin hiked up the corner of his mouth. "Take heart. I don't think she likes me either."

The comment made Sarah smile. But when the captain applied astringent to her wound, it stung so badly that the room began to swim. Next thing she knew her head had sunk onto Captain Sinclair's broad shoulder and she all but sat on his knee.

"Oh..."

He held her securely around the waist. "I'm sorry to have hurt you, Sarah, but it's impossible to know where those scissors have been."

She caught her breath and struggled to put distance between them.

"Relax." He bandaged her hand.

But she didn't want to be so close and within his embrace. Worse, she felt like Libby or Rachel who might perch on his lap. "I'm not a child. Let me go."

"I'm almost done, Sarah. Stop fighting me."

Against her better judgment, she acquiesced.

He turned slightly. Suddenly his lips were so close they shared a breath. "I hardly think of you as a child."

Her gaze traveled up his shadowed jaw. *Don't look into his eyes*, her heart seemed to scream.

He leaned closer, and for a millisecond Sarah thought about it—about kissing him, lingering in his arms…

*But no!*

She brought her arm up and pushed back against his chest. "Captain Sinclair, your behavior is quite inappropriate!"

He sighed in resignation. "You're right. I apologize." He reached for her injured hand. "Here, let me finish. You can stand an arm's length away from me if you wish."

She allowed him that much.

He tied off the bandage. "Sarah, I must say that I'm very attracted to you."

"You shouldn't talk to me that way."

"But it's true. What's more, I think you're attracted to me too."

"I'm not." She yanked her hand free. What would Pa say if he knew the captain spoke to her in this manner? Why, he'd come fetch her and take her home immediately.

"Don't fight it." The captain stood and reached for her. His arms encircled her waist.

She pushed him away again. "Captain, please…stop this nonsense at once!"

He put his hands on his hips. "All right. You win." He smiled. "This time."

She swallowed hard. Had that been a threat or promise?

"But I'll break your resolve eventually."

"No, Captain, you won't."

She pushed past him and left the study, closing the heavy paneled door behind her. She sagged against it, thinking she'd never met a man like the captain. He could cast a kind of spell, one that tempted her to skew her principles.

She closed her eyes. *Lord, help me…*

Suddenly September couldn't come fast enough.

# Eighteen

Sarah crumpled another piece of stationery and tossed it in the brass wastepaper basket beside the writing desk in her room. She slumped back in the chair. She'd begun a letter to Ma, telling her about the children and the grand home in which the Sinclairs resided. Then somehow she wrote about the captain too. Knowing Ma would make her come home at once if she guessed at the improprieties going on, Sarah tore that letter to shreds. Same thing happened when she started writing to Leah. And now Valerie as well. They all loved her, she knew. But she also suspected they would doubt that she could handle the situation with the captain.

Except she could!

And she'd prove it.

She began another letter, this time addressed to her entire family. The more generic the better. She'd almost finished it when a knock sounded on her bedroom door, causing Sarah to jump. "W-who's there?"

"Gretchen Schlyterhaus."

Puzzled, Sarah crossed the room and opened it.

"Give this to Mr. Navis." She thrust a basket covered with a checkered linen cloth into Sarah's arms.

"Whatever it is, it smells delicious."

"It's apple kuchen." Mrs. Schlyterhaus wiped her hands on her white apron. "Mr. Navis loves my apple kuchen, so I made him a dish for his birthday."

Sarah smiled. "That was very thoughtful."

She bobbed out a curt reply. "You vill give it to Mr. Navis, then?"

The question sounded more like a command, but Sarah nodded anyway. Then she had a question of her own to ask. "Why don't you address Richard by his first name instead of calling him Mr. Navis? I heard him specifically tell you to call him Richard."

"It is not my place, Irish!"

"My name is Sarah." She tipped her head. "Why do you call me Irish? Is it supposed to be an insult? I'm proud of my heritage."

"I'm sure you are." Mrs. Schlyterhaus gave a toss of her head. "As for Mr. Navis, he holds a higher position than I do. Higher than yours too."

"But we're friends. He asked me to call him Richard."

"Vhat you do is none of my concern. The children address their grandmother as Aurora. Is that proper? I should say not! But the captain allows it anyhow, and it is hardly my place to tell the captain his business."

Sarah lifted a shoulder, thinking maybe somebody ought to!

"If a better housekeeper came along, I vould be gone in a minute." Mrs. Schlyterhaus snapped her fingers. "Ve are guaranteed nussing in this lifetime. In minutes, life can change and that vhich ve love can instantly be gone."

Sarah frowned, trying to understand the rant. But then the pieces of what Richard had told her of Gretchen's past fell into line. Did Mrs. Schlyterhaus feel angry and bitter because of her husband's death? If so, perhaps she tried desperately to hold on to the only thing she thought she had left—her position with Captain Sinclair.

Sarah's heart began to ache for the older woman.

"Just make sure to give the apple kuchen to Mr. Navis."

"Yes, of course, I will."

As the housekeeper turned toward the door, an idea formed. "Mrs. Schlyterhaus, would you like to come with us tomorrow?" She felt certain the Navises wouldn't mind. Just like her family back in Jericho Junction, they thought the more the merrier. "We'll attend church and then Richard's birthday party."

"Sunday is my day off," she replied gruffly over her shoulder.

"I know. That's why I wondered—"

"Of course I vould like to come!" Whirling around, Mrs. Schlyterhaus snatched back the apple kuchen. "I vill give this to Mr. Navis myself!"

With that she stomped away, leaving Sarah gaping. Then, on an afterthought, she called, "Be ready by eight o'clock. Richard's cousin Lina is coming for us."

No response. But somehow Sarah knew the crusty German woman had heard—and she'd be ready right on time.

"Miss Johnson and Mr. Barnes are here!" The boys burst into the foyer with the news.

Sarah collected Libby and Rachel, making sure she'd tucked away Richard's birthday cards, and headed for the carriage. After introducing Mrs. Schlyterhaus, she climbed in after the girls with the help of Mr. Barnes.

"Look, there's Daddy!" Libby stood and waved.

With a hold on Rachel, who emulated her big sister, Sarah glanced up and saw the captain standing tall on the second-floor balcony. He waved, and she sent him a parting smile.

"Bring me back a piece of birthday cake, mates," he called out to them.

"OK, we sure will!" Michael returned.

"It's supposed to be a surprise," Gabe groused. "The whole city's gonna hear your big mouth."

From the corner of her eye, Sarah saw Michael raise his fist. Gabe raised his in reply.

"Boys, your father is watching."

"Heavenly Father included." Smiling, Mr. Barnes gave a flick of the reins, and the horses set off.

When they arrived at the little country church, Mrs. Schlyterhaus walked in with the children as Lina held Sarah back by the elbow.

"What happened on Friday?" she whispered.

Sarah smiled conspiratorially. "Just as you suspected, Richard asked me to dinner and the theater, but I told him I couldn't go because of a...a *previous commitment*."

Lina giggled. "Oh, that's just grand. Richard probably stewed all weekend!"

Sarah's own smile waned when she thought of his expression two days ago. The usual shine in Richard's bright blue eyes had disappeared like the sun behind thunderclouds. "Lina, I think I hurt his feelings, turning him down on his birthday."

"Never mind. You can make it up to him today. And Richard will laugh about it when he finds out why you turned him down. He loves a good prank. Here he thinks all his family members and friends forgot his birthday, when we've really been planning a party all along."

They entered the sanctuary and found their places. Richard and his parents were seated in the pew in front of them. After she had sat down and settled the children between herself and Lina, with Mrs. Schlyterhaus at the other end, Richard turned around. He narrowed his gaze speculatively, first at Lina, then at Sarah.

"What are you two ladies up to? I saw you whispering outside."

"None of your business," Lina answered.

Sarah rolled her shoulders innocently. Then, after giving her an I-know-that-you're-up-to-something look, he turned back around. Sarah and Lina exchanged grins.

The service began with hymns of praise. Sarah watched curiously as Mrs. Schlyterhaus opened the hymnal and followed along. She didn't sing, although she seemed to be looking at the words. It occurred to Sarah that perhaps Mrs. Schlyterhaus couldn't read English. She was, after all, from Germany.

After church, Sarah ushered the Sinclair children outside. Mrs. Schlyterhaus suggested that she keep the two little girls with her and ride with Lina and Timothy while Sarah take the boys and ride with Richard and his parents in the wagon. The offer surprised Sarah.

"Ve vill not be so cramped." She fanned herself with her white gloves.

"You've got a point there." Sarah looked into the azure sky from which the sun relentlessly beat down.

Richard helped Sarah up into the wagon, after which he boosted the two boys into the back. He had already helped his father aboard.

"So tell me. How did you manage to get Mrs. Schlyterhaus to church this morning, Sarah?" Richard gave a slap of the reins, and the wagon jerked forward. His arm bumped against hers.

"I just invited her."

"I've been inviting her for years." Richard shook his head. "So has my mother."

"Seriously? And here I figured I would be the last person she'd accept an invitation from. Maybe Mrs. Schlyterhaus doesn't dislike me after all."

Richard flashed a charming grin. "I'd wager that it's impossible to dislike you." He chuckled. "Why, you've even managed to win over Gabriel and Michael, and they disliked every governess the captain ever hired."

"Yes, so I've heard in great detail. Grass snakes in beds. Frogs and toads jumping out from just about everywhere. They tried that prank on me twice now. I admit to a shriek or two, but then I merely captured the creatures and turned them loose outside. I didn't even give them a stern talking-to. I just got even."

Richard chuckled beside her. "What a fun governess you are. What did you do?"

"Threw them into the river when they weren't expecting it." Sarah turned and glanced into the back of the wagon. The boys inspected something in Michael's palm. An insect, no doubt.

"I'm so pleased you're spending Sundays with us," Mrs. Navis said from where she sat behind Sarah.

"Thank you. I look forward to them. Being on the farm gives me a break with the children, and they're happy. What's more, your farm reminds me of home." *It also gets me away from the captain*, she added silently.

When they arrived at the farm, Mrs. Navis urged Sarah to keep Richard preoccupied while they set everything up inside. So she followed him into the barn.

"Mind if I keep you company awhile?"

"Not at all. I wanted to talk to you about something anyway."

He reached for her hand, and Sarah placed her palm in his. He led her out of the barn. They strolled alongside the potato field.

"You said coming here reminds you of your home?"

"Yes, in many ways. Like all the activity after church. Ben and Valerie and Leah and Jon bring their little ones. My brothers are there." Sarah felt pangs of homesickness just talking about it.

They neared the cornfield where stalks stood almost as tall as she did. All the while she felt Richard's warm and protective grip. She wondered what he wanted to discuss with her.

"I thought you were glad to be away from Missouri."

"I am for the most part. I enjoy being on my own. I value my independence, you know. I just miss my family sometimes."

Walking around the property, they ended up on the far side of the apple orchard.

"So, you value your independence, do you?" Richard asked, cocking an eyebrow.

They sat beneath the shade of the large tree.

Sarah nodded to his question and removed her bonnet. Patting several pins back into place, she congratulated herself on keeping Richard occupied this long. Mrs. Navis, Lina, and Bethany Stafford would have plenty of time to decorate and prepare for the big surprise.

However, Richard seemed troubled about something. "Sarah, how independent do you really think you are?"

"Excuse me?"

"Think about it. You don't have to cook, launder clothes, clean house, concern yourself with finances. You have a roof over your head, clothes on your back..."

"I am too concerned about the clothes on my back!"

He grinned. "That's not my point. Sarah, don't you see? Everyone takes care of you. The captain. Mrs. Schlyterhaus. Isabelle. Me."

"You're joking, right?" She shook her head, wondering over his insult. "If you haven't noticed, I work for my living. Taking care of four children isn't exactly complete luxury."

"I'll say! I've done my share of caring for those kids."

"And you resent it?" She tried to understand. "You're sorry I came here when I sprained my ankle?"

"No, that's not it."

"Then perhaps you resent my independence."

Richard was quiet for a long while. "Sarah, you know what I think? I think you're not independent. You're spoiled."

She turned sharply, studying his face. She couldn't tell if Richard was teasing or if he'd meant that last remark. In any case, Sarah thought she deserved to be a little spoiled. Hadn't she worked—and worked hard!—to save her money so she could afford to leave Jericho Junction? She knew very well what it was like to do all those things Richard had mentioned, cooking, cleaning, sewing, and mending. It wasn't until she'd met her sister-in-law, Valerie, that she'd begun to hunger for a different way of life. A glamorous life. The sort of life Valerie had lived in New Orleans before she married Ben. And although Valerie maintained she was happier in love and doing all those mundane household chores, Sarah had grown tired of them and had longed to be on her own.

And now she was.

Richard suddenly stood and held his hand out to Sarah. She refused to take it and pushed to her feet on her own.

"And you're stubborn too."

"Well, I can think of plenty of choice words to describe you, Richard Navis." Sarah whirled around, intending to head for the house, but he caught her elbow.

"Wait."

"I thought you were my friend. I thought—"

Before she could finish, Richard set his hands on either side of her face and kissed her. She tried to push him away, but something about the intimate contact gave her pause. She ceased her struggles.

Slowly he collected her in his arms. His kiss deepened and a spark ignited deep within her. Her arms slipped around his neck.

"I love you, Sarah." He brushed the words against her lips.

Her eyes fluttered opened, and she glimpsed the sincerity in his eyes.

"I love everything about you—your talents and your faults. Can't you see that?" He moved back slightly. "I'm sorry I said you're spoiled and stubborn. It's just that…well…I've been smarting all weekend because you chose a 'previous commitment' over me on my birthday." He released her and stepped back. "I hope I don't know him."

"Him?" It suddenly dawned on her. He suspected her of spending Friday evening with some other gentleman. Perhaps even with Captain Sinclair. "No, you don't know *him*. And where do you think I'd meet *him*? Oh, but I suppose with my lollygagging around all day—"

"Sarah…" He took her in his arms again. "Tell me I have nothing —no one—to be jealous about."

"I'll do no such thing." Except she hoped he'd kiss her again. Her gaze slid up, from his strong jaw to his blue eyes, and she thought maybe she loved Richard right back. Only…weren't these the same feelings she had for the captain? The same fluttering…the same desire?

Confused and disgusted with herself, she pushed away.

"Sarah, forgive me. Don't be angry with me, please. All these emotions are new to me. I never suspected I had a single jealous bone in my body. But I confess I do."

The clamor of the cowbell suddenly wafted to her ears on the heavy July breeze. Sarah took another step back. She'd think all this through later. Right now there was a surprise party waiting for Richard—and he'd be surprised, all right.

Lifting her bonnet off the grass, she whacked him across the chest with it.

He appeared sufficiently contrite. "I suppose I deserved that."

"Yes, you did, you beast!" With that, Sarah spun around so he wouldn't see her confusion. Then she ran from the apple orchard and away from her dizzying thoughts.

First the captain, now Richard. Who did she love?

Who *should* she love?

# NINETEEN

SURPRISE!"

Richard tucked his chin and took in the sight before him. Family and friends packed the dining room. Paper streamers hung from the ceiling. Wrapped gifts were piled in the center of the table. He was speechless.

Raucous laughter exploded from the men. The ladies giggled. And one particular lady seemed most amused. He narrowed his gaze at Sarah. The light in her eyes danced with merriment.

"We got you this year, son." Pops wheeled his chair forward.

"Sure did," Richard agreed.

Lina clapped her hands in glee.

Even Gabe Sinclair laughed.

Richard shook his head.

"We pulled a prank on the prankster." Sarah gave him a sly smile.

Hands on hips, Richard grinned back. "So you were in on it too, huh?"

A pretty shade of pink crept into her cheeks, and he figured he owed her an apology. But it didn't seem that she'd hold his jealous behavior against him.

"Let's all pray," Pops said. "I, for one, am starving."

"Me too!" one of the Stafford kids added.

Pops said grace, and then Mama shooed everyone into the kitchen, where an array of foods awaited them. Everyone brought a dish to pass, and Mama made her famous smoked chicken pastry puffs that contained a bit of her apricot jam and a touch of sage. One of his favorite meals.

All the while Richard helped himself to the bountiful spread, he kept reliving his encounter with Sarah in the apple orchard. He felt like a lovesick sap. But her response to his kiss, her yielding, and the warmth in her eyes afterward made him think she might care deeply about him too.

Did he dare to even hope?

After lunch Richard opened his gifts. The first was Mrs. Schlyterhaus's apple kuchen.

"My favorite!" He glanced at the usually cross housekeeper, feeling rather amazed that she was in attendance today. "*Danke schoen.*" He knew at least that much German.

She inclined her head and actually smiled. "*Bitte.*"

The next present came from Bethany—a handkerchief on which she'd embroidered his initials.

"Thanks, Beth." Richard tucked it into his pocket. "I'll put it to use immediately."

He opened Tim and Lina's generous gift of two theater tickets. "Much appreciated."

"If you're lucky, you'll even find a date for the second ticket," Tim joked.

"Very funny." Richard sent a smile in Sarah's direction.

Lina came over to give him a hug. "I finally pulled a joke on you, dear cousin."

Richard grinned. "With a lot of help, I might add." His gaze remained on Sarah and her oh-so-innocent expression.

He opened her gift next. His breath left him when he saw the twin black and silver pens inside the velvet box. "Sarah? I…I don't know what to say."

"Do you like them? I thought they might help you enjoy your work for the captain a bit more."

"They're incredible." But what was she thinking? Her birthday present to him outshone all the others and must have cost her plenty. He felt blessed and troubled all the same. Would a farmer have any use for such magnificent writing tools?

"Richard, you have a strange look on your face."

He shook himself. “Forgive me. Thank you, Sarah.” He stared meaningfully into her eyes. “I’ll cherish them forever.”

Pops rolled his chair in beside Richard. “Hmm…almost be a shame to use those fancy pens.”

Richard had to wonder if he’d use them at all once his indentureship was over.

The evening sun cast long shadows across the lawn. Richard watched as the last of the carriages pulled out of the circle drive, heading toward Lisbon Plank Road. He waved to Sarah, who returned the gesture with a smile.

Inhaling the fragrant summer air, Richard turned and walked to the front porch. He took the steps two at a time, deciding he would treasure this afternoon’s memory for a long, long while.

“Did you have a good birthday, son?” Pops wheeled his chair forward.

“Can’t remember one better.”

Pops chuckled. “I didn’t think your cousin Lina would pull it off, but she managed to surprise you.”

“With a little help from Sarah.” His father’s laughter made him smile. A niggling of shame followed. “To think I was all inside out, assuming the worst when Sarah refused to go to the concert with me on Friday night.” He sat down in one of the white wooden chairs on the porch.

“I can tell you’ve set your cap for that girl, son.”

“From the very first day she arrived.”

“She seems to like living in the city.” Pops expelled a long sigh. “Well, if you want to change your mind about the farm—”

“I don’t. I won’t.” Richard’s resolve was firm. “I’m called to be a farmer, Pops. I want to work the land, marry Sarah, and live here…and raise my family here.”

His father guffawed. “Well, I know you’ve always loved this place,

Richard." He paused. "I hope your mother and me aren't becoming too much of a burden."

"What?" He shook his head. "No. Never."

"You're my only son, and I've got a permanent war injury. Being saddled with in-laws might not appeal to Sarah."

"I can tell she's very fond of both of you, and she comes from a large, closely knit family herself. One of her brothers has a war injury too. She's very sympathetic."

"I know." Pops bobbed his head, then smiled. "But to hear you talk about marriage..." He chuckled again. "Until you met that pretty little gal from Missouri, you were singing a bachelor-for-life tune."

Richard grinned. "I guess that's true."

"Your mother and I always prayed you'd find the right girl."

"I believe I have."

Pops squinted speculatively. "Do you think Miss Sarah will want the same—living on a farm and sharing a home with her in-laws? What if she wants her own house?"

"We've got plenty of land, Pops. If Sarah wants her own house, I'll build her one."

Pops laughed. "You always have everything figured out—just like the captain's books."

Richard leaned his head back and closed his eyes. He might have things all planned out, but Sarah had become a huge part of his life's equation. He prayed she'd come to love him enough to live anywhere on God's green Earth...including his farm!

"It may be, son, that you'll have to choose between this farm or Sarah, in which case your mother and I'll work something out for ourselves. The Johnsons have already said they'd take us in."

"Don't talk like that, Pops." Richard looked over at his father's gaunt and weathered face. "I'll never abandon you and Mama."

"But what if it comes down to one or the other?" Pops stared back at him. "Then what?"

Richard didn't answer right away, thinking the question through.

Finally he said, “Pops, I refuse to make that sort of decision. I want Sarah for my wife, and I want this farm and you and Mama to live here with us. I believe, because I’ve taken this matter to God, that He intends to bless me with both.” Looking across the acreage, Richard’s gaze stopped at the small pond. “A good amount of my sweat and an equal amount of my tears may have to be shed, Pops, but, with God as my witness, I’m going to work this land as best I’m able—and I’m going to marry Sarah McCabe.”

# Twenty

THE MONTH OF JULY SAILED ON LIKE A SLEEK SHIP ON THE water. The hot and humid days reminded Sarah of summers in Jericho Junction. She felt homesick, especially when she received letters from her family. But at least here in Milwaukee she could exercise her independence. She enjoyed living in the captain's beautiful home and savored her early morning strolls. While the heat of the day was sometimes oppressive, the lakefront always provided a cool reprieve. Each day after swimming school, Sarah took the children to the beach for picnic lunches. The boys liked to fish on the pier, and the girls played in the sand while Sarah watched them from a copse of trees that lined the foot of the cliffs. Occasionally the girls napped on the blanket in the shade as Sarah practiced her guitar or read a book. Then around three o'clock when Richard ran his errands, he came by and picked them up, giving them a lift home.

On one such a day—the last day of the month—she entered through the side door with Richard and the children, only to find complete mayhem.

"I didn't get a chance to tell you," Richard said.

"Tell me what?"

Sarah gaped at the crowd in the kitchen. Isabelle was flanked by assistants and utilized every pot and pan in the kitchen. Mrs. Schlyterhaus ran hither and yon, and a hired maitre d' wearing a black suit and white shirt and gloves roamed about, giving orders to the uniformed maids.

"What's all this?" Standing in the spacious foyer now, Sarah sent the four children upstairs.

"Preparation for the engagement party."

Sarah turned to Richard. "What engagement party?"

"That's what I wanted to tell you. I just learned about it this afternoon myself. The captain and Mrs. Kingsley are getting married and plan to make the announcement tonight. The captain forgot to inform us—and his household staff—of the event. Now everyone has to scurry."

"He forgot? How does one forget...?" Sarah shook her head. "Oh, never mind."

Richard grinned. "That's the captain for you." Taking hold of her elbow, he steered her clear of a maid carrying a tray of deviled eggs. He quickly grabbed one as the woman passed. "Mmm...delicious."

Meanwhile Sarah worked to overcome her shock. "He's marrying Mrs. Kingsley? But...but..."

She recalled how just weeks ago the captain admitted being attracted to her—not Elise Kingsley. Physical attraction didn't constitute love, she knew that, but...

"Does he love her?"

Richard shrugged. "Who knows?"

And wasn't it just the Fourth of July when Aurora said that Mrs. Kingsley suggested sending the boys to boarding school? "Richard, that woman doesn't even know the children. How can the captain marry her?"

Richard leaned close and whispered in her ear. "She's rich and he wants her shipping company."

"I thought he was going to buy it," Sarah whispered back.

"He was—is."

The truth dawned on her. "But this way he doesn't have to pay for it. That is, he does, initially. But once they marry, all the Kingsley assets will belong to him too."

"I'd say that about sums it up."

Sarah's jaw slacked. *Outrageous!*

Richard set a calming hand on her shoulder.

Just then the groom-to-be strode into the foyer. "Good. You're both here." He looked at Sarah. "Scrub up the children. I'd like them to make a brief appearance tonight." His tone was calm but to the point. "Can one of them play a little ditty on the piano?"

"Well, I'm sure I can arrange something."

"Good. And Richard?"

"Yes, sir?"

"Stick around tonight in case I need you. Lillian LaMonde will be here from the newspaper. Try to see that she gets at least a few of her facts straight."

Sarah tucked her hands into her apron pockets when she heard Richard's throaty groan. She didn't read the woman's column, but she knew it contained the latest gossip and scandals.

"I want everything perfect tonight." The captain glanced from Richard to Sarah and back to Richard again. "Is that clear?"

"It is, sir."

Sarah nodded.

Watching him head for the maitre d', Sarah found it difficult to contain her swell of emotions. She had that feeling of being a mere underling again when the captain had spoken to her, but his tone was always quite different when they were alone. A nib of jealousy struck her heart. The captain couldn't possibly be in love with Mrs. Kingsley.

She felt Richard's hand on her arm.

"Are you all right?"

Sarah touched her forehead, hiding the tears that clouded her vision. "I think I must have gotten too much sun today. If you'll excuse me..."

She bolted for the front staircase. Halfway up, she realized her mistake of not using the servants' staircase.

Oh, well. Too late now.

Dear Ma and Pa,

How true God's words are. Money is the root of all evil. The captain is marrying a woman solely for her wealth. I know this because I watched his expression tonight when

> he looked at the Widow Kingsley. She's a very beautiful and sophisticated lady. Tonight she wore a sleeveless green silk gown that matched her eyes and white gloves. I dare say she revealed more than just her bare upper arms. Her plunging neckline was disgraceful. I found myself blushing just looking at her. By contrast, I wore my ivory dress with the high neckline and a matching rose-on-the-vine, button-up wrapper. But as lovely as I looked tonight, I couldn't hold a candle to Mrs. Kingsley's worldly finery. As for Captain Sinclair, I saw no light in his eyes as he regarded her. But then his gaze fell upon me where I stood at the opposite end of the reception line with his children at my side. He smiled in a way that warmed my insides and he sent me a wink. I quickly turned away and thought how dare he bestow such a look of affection on me, his children's governess, when he's engaged to another woman! I call that sheer evil.

Sarah sat back in the desk chair and reread her letter. Moments later she tore it into shreds. She couldn't send such a missive. Pa would come for her in a second. Except she knew she owed her parents an update. However, she knew it impossible to describe the tumultuous state of affairs here in Captain Sinclair's home—and in her own heart.

Suddenly she thought of Gabriel. He'd threatened to run away from home when he learned of his father's plans to marry Mrs. Kingsley. Little did he know that he'd likely be *sent* away very soon.

A knock sounded, and Sarah crossed her bedroom. "Who's there?"

"It's me, Irish. Open z'door."

Sarah turned the knob and pulled. The lamp in the hallway revealed Mrs. Schlyterhaus's tired features. From behind her, music and laughter wafted up the stairs along with the rich smell of tobacco.

"Mr. Navis would like a vord vis you before he leaves."

"All right. Thank you." Sarah walked back to the desk and replaced the cap on the inkwell. Exiting her room, she closed the door behind her.

Richard waited in the kitchen, nibbling on leftovers. "It's a beautiful night," he said. "How about we get some air?"

Nodding, Sarah followed him outside.

"I wanted to make sure you're all right before I headed for home. I noticed that you've seemed troubled."

"You're right. I must confess. I am troubled." She ambled toward the well-tended garden. Lanterns glowed throughout, and Sarah noticed several guests mingling nearby.

Richard took her hand and led her toward the street. "Let's stroll on the walk so we can talk without disturbing the captain's party."

"My dress isn't made for strolls, I'm afraid."

"It's lovely... you're lovely. I wanted to tell you all evening."

A smile pulled at her mouth. "Thank you."

"I won't take you far. I promise." A ways away, he wrapped her hand around his elbow. "Now tell me what's bothering you."

"The captain's engagement, of course." She wished her voice hadn't sounded so harsh. "Forgive me, Richard."

"Of course." He remained silent for several long seconds. "Just what is it about the captain's engagement that's bothering you?" His voice sounded strained.

"The lack of love between the marrying couple for one thing."

"From what I understand, Mrs. Kingsley is crazy about the captain."

Sarah knew in her heart that he didn't love the woman back. But then who did he love? What caused him to feel passionate? Her brother Jake once said some men loved the thrill of the chase. Now that the captain had ensnared Mrs. Kingsley, would he be happy?

"And what about the children?" She didn't realize until moments later that she'd spoken the question aloud.

"Yes, I too am concerned about their welfare after the marriage takes place."

"How vicious the cycle. The captain grew up without love, and now his children will too."

"Ah, but Sarah, you forget. Our God still reigns on His throne of grace. He loves the Sinclair kids more than we can imagine."

"I haven't forgotten. There is always hope." Her world seemed back on its axis again. She had to grin. "Perspective is everything, isn't it?"

"Mm-hmm." Richard paused, turned, and set his hands on her shoulders. "Sarah, with all this talk of engagements and weddings…well, do you think about marriage sometimes?" Darkness shrouded his features.

"Sometimes…yes."

He cleared his throat. "I do too…sometimes." He let his arms fall away. "I think about the day my indentureship is over and I'm free to go back to my planting and plowing." A smile lifted his tone. "I see myself raising a family on my farm while peace and contentment fill all the corners of my days."

Sarah couldn't help a fond smile, although she didn't share the same vision. "I dream of living in the city."

"Could you ever be a…a farmer's wife?"

She gave a laugh of disbelief. "Why, Richard Navis, are you proposing?"

"No! I mean…" He seemed flustered. "Well, not yet."

Sarah wasn't amused. "You're fishing, then? This is hardly the time or the place. We haven't even properly courted."

"Sarah, you know how I feel about you."

"You're supposed to be my friend." She'd all but pushed the memories of his kiss and words of love from her mind. She didn't want to think about them—or her own feelings for Richard. It all seemed so very complicated.

"I *am* your friend, Sarah." He reached for her.

She gathered her skirts and took a step back.

"But maybe it's not right that a man and a woman be such good friends." A hint of a challenge edged his tone.

Should she take the bait?

She held her breath. One moment. Two. Three. Four.

Finally she blew out a breath of exasperation. “Oh, Richard, why are you speaking to me like this when you know my head is already filled with other problems?”

“You’re saying our relationship is a problem for you, Sarah?”

“No, that’s not what I’m saying.” She whirled around and headed for the captain’s house.

Richard stepped in beside her. “Is it wrong for me to want to know where I stand with you after I’ve made my feelings perfectly clear?”

“I don’t wish to discuss this matter.” She picked up her pace.

“Why, Sarah? Because it might mean reexamining your heart? Rethinking your future? Seeking God’s will and not your own?”

“No, Richard.” She stopped short, and he went a step ahead of her before pausing too. “Furthering this discussion might mean I lose my best friend.” Her words split the night like a slap across the face.

Richard didn’t move, didn’t reply.

Her throat ached with unshed emotion. “But it seems I’ve already done that, doesn’t it?”

When no further comment came forth, Sarah lifted her hems and ran the rest of the way to the captain’s house.

# Twenty-One

"Why on Earth are you frowning so hard?"

Sarah blinked and swung away from the front door. She'd been watching as Richard mounted his horse then rode away after delivering the captain's mail.

"You're lucky Aurora didn't see you. She'd give you an hour's lecture on how a frown ages a young lady's face." The captain chuckled as he sorted through the envelopes in his hand. "And tell me why you've been so terse with Richard the last few days."

"I don't know what you mean." Sarah crossed the polished floor of the foyer. She didn't wish to discuss the matter either. "I'd best check on the children and make sure they're eating their lunch."

Captain Sinclair caught her arm as she tried to pass. "Don't lie to me, Sarah." A warning glint flashed in his dark gaze.

She drew back, freeing her arm. "Richard and I have come to an impasse. He wants a life on his farm, and I want—"

"A different life." The captain's dark gaze roved over her face. "And you deserve it."

"I don't know about deserving it, Captain, but it's what I most desire. A life in a large city where I can surround myself with culture and be happy and busy."

"I know," he said gently. "I could tell the day we met. What's more, I could have saved you time and heartache. You are hardly a match for Richard, given his chosen profession." A smile curved his lips. "If you weren't quite so young, I'd be tempted to marry you myself."

"Captain, don't speak to me that way!" Sarah clenched her jaw.

He looked amused.

"You're marrying Mrs. Kingsley, and... well, I hope the two of you are very happy together."

He chuckled. "I'll be happy, all right. Marrying Elise means I don't have to purchase Great Lakes Shipping. It'll be mine through matrimony."

Sarah tensed. So her presumptions had been correct. "That's the only reason you're marrying her? For her business?"

"Of course." He sent her a speculative glance. "Did you think I was in love with her?"

"Where I come from love is the reason for marriage."

"And where I come from marriage is a fabulous business arrangement."

"How sad."

"Sarah, I admire your innocence and your courage. In fact, I'm captivated by it."

She didn't feel so brave at the moment. Not when she spied that certain glimmer in his black eyes. She looked away and steeled herself against his oncoming charm. *Be strong and of good courage...fear not nor be dismayed...God is with thee and will not fail thee...* Words she'd long ago committed to memory flitted through her mind.

The captain strode toward her and paused only a foot away. He glanced at the correspondence in his hand and held an envelope out to her. "You have a letter. From the music academy in Chicago, I see."

Hope surged inside of Sarah. "News of my position." Smiling, she took the proffered envelope and tore into it.

> Dear Miss McCabe,
>
> Based upon the referral we have received, we cannot add you to our staff here at the Academy. Consequently, we have filled our open position...

"Based upon the referral they received?" She glared up at the captain.

"Did I mention that I know Elliot Withers?" He folded his arms across his broad chest.

"The dean of the music academy." Sarah slowly wagged her head from side to side in disbelief.

"I told him you were a far better governess than music teacher."

"You did…what?" A cold wave of shock rushed through her, numbing her to the core. "You told him…how could you?"

"Sarah, it's obvious my children aren't indoors practicing piano. They're too busy at swimming school or picnicking on the beach. They're as brown as nuts."

She lowered her head, aware of her own freckled skin.

"When they're with my mother on your days off, she says all they do is talk about you and the fun they're having. 'Miss Sarah does this' and 'Miss Sarah does that.' It drives her crazy." The deep rich sound of the captain's chuckle filled the entryway. "That pleases me to no end."

"Sir?" For a moment she thought he sounded unhappy with her service.

"I'd be a fool to let you go."

"But—" Sarah's dream shattered before her eyes.

"You'll be far more satisfied working for me. My children adore you. I need you. I'll give you whatever you want, and of course, I pay you better than the academy ever would."

She turned her back to him, clutching the letter from Mr. Withers to her heart. Shards of the vision she'd held for her future cut to the quick of her soul.

A heartbeat later, she felt Captain Sinclair's hands on her shoulders. "I've made up a contract for you to sign when you're ready. All right?"

Did she have a choice? What were her options? A farmer's wife. A governess. Or…going home.

"No!" She shook off his hold and stepped back. "I refuse to sign your contract."

"Don't be silly, Sarah. I'm handing you a perfect opportunity. You only have to accept it."

"I won't. You had no right to manipulate my life the way you did!"

"Lower your voice, Sarah. The entire household will hear you."

She didn't care. "How could you do this?" She closed her eyes. Her teaching career in Chicago. Gone.

"I only did what I thought was best for you." His tone took on a custodial note.

She glared at him. "You're not my brothers or my pa. And if you'd start thinking about what's best for your own children for a change—"

"Sarah..." A warning hung on each syllable.

"What? Will you send me packing? Terminate my position?" She couldn't keep the sarcasm from her voice. She ran her fingertips over the mahogany side table in the foyer. "Well, go ahead."

Her goading caused the captain to come swiftly toward her. Sarah refused to shrink even when she spied the anger in his eyes.

Grasping her elbow, he propelled her into his study and closed the doors. Slowly he turned and faced her. "I think that's quite enough now, Sarah."

Her entire body shook with the anger and disappointment she felt inside. She clutched the envelope from Chicago, then glared at the captain. He had single-handedly ruined her plans for her future. "How could you?" The question bore repeating.

The captain slowly lowered himself onto the edge of his wide desk. "Sarah, you're part of my family and—"

"You have a very twisted view of what a family is... *sir.*"

Captain Sinclair arched a brow.

"Family members aren't showpieces that you acquire. They don't appear and disappear at your whim. They cannot be ignored or treated like annoying objects when you're in the company of your snobby friends."

He folded his arms and donned a bored expression.

But Sarah had to speak her piece. "I am not part of your family, Captain, because you can't buy me."

"We'll see about that." He stood and came toward her. "Everyone has a price, dear Sarah."

He cupped her chin, and she slapped his hand away.

"You're a feisty little thing, aren't you?" Merriment entered his eyes. But suddenly all humor fled his features. "Oh, how can I be so callous? You're hurt. And it's my fault. I admit it. Now, come on..."

He pulled her close, and with one hand behind her head he urged her ear to his chest. "There, now, let me comfort you."

For the next passing seconds, she did. Her eyes fluttered closed as he kissed her forehead, her nose, her—

"Captain, no." She pushed him away.

"You're so pretty, Sarah, and when I look into your eyes I see a perfect summer day." He gathered her in his arms again.

With her fingers splayed across the brocade of his maroon waistcoat, she held him at bay. "But you and Mrs. Kingsley...we shouldn't. We mustn't!"

"Ah, Sarah, sometimes the taste of forbidden fruit is the sweetest." His voice was husky close to her ear and sent shivers down her neck and spine. "Let me show you."

With the last ounce of willpower, she struggled out of his embrace. In doing so, her elbow struck the crystal vase on a nearby shelf, sending it crashing to the floor.

Her senses returned. "Captain, I–I'm so sorry." She knelt to collect the broken pieces, when he caught her wrist.

"I'll ask Gretchen to clean it up later." He pulled her to her feet. Desire still pooled in his dark gaze.

She twisted her arm from his grasp. Walking a few paces, she retrieved the letter that lay on the carpet. "I'm going to find it very difficult to ever forgive you for this." She held up the missive. "And I'll leave the first of September, just as we agreed."

"Now, Sarah, don't be so unreasonable. I'll make it up to you. I promise."

"You can't. It's impossible." Tears threatened as she traipsed to the study door and yanked on the polished brass knob. Out in the foyer, she ran headlong into Richard.

He caught and steadied her.

"Wh–what are you doing here?" Sarah suddenly realized she'd lost several hairpins during the tussle with the captain. Blinking away her tears, she worked to tuck the strands back into her chignon. "I thought you left." She tried to collect herself.

"I forgot to give the captain another message."

Sarah saw his brow furrow as he took in her mussed hair and flaming cheeks. Then he glanced over her head at the captain. She could practically see the accusations forming in Richard's jealous mind. But couldn't he see she was hurt beyond belief? Her future had been irreparably ruined.

Whirling on her heel, Sarah hastened up the front staircase as fast as her feet would carry her. She scurried passed Mrs. Schlyterhaus in the hallway.

"Irish! Vill you ever learn to use the servants' stairvell?"

The reprimand only served to further her grief. Her throat ached with an oncoming sob. When she reached her bedroom, she entered and gave the door a good, hard slam.

*WHAT IN HEAVEN'S NAME IS GOING ON IN THIS HOUSE?* Every muscle in Richard's body tensed as he strode across the foyer. Had the captain accosted Sarah? It certainly appeared that way. Her hair hadn't slipped from its pins for no reason.

The boys came running in, skidding to a halt in front of him.

"We heard a huge bang!" Gabriel sounded breathless. His eyes were wide and full of worry.

The captain stepped from his study. "The wind blew a door shut. Nothing to worry about. Now run along back outside—and mind your little sisters. Miss Sarah will be out soon."

Gabe looked from his father to Richard. "OK."

Richard pulled several candy sticks from his coat pocket. He hadn't seen the kids earlier. All he could think about was Sarah and how upset she'd looked. He'd happened into the middle of a quarrel, that's for sure.

"Thanks, Mr. Navis." Michael grinned as he snatched the candy sticks. He gave one to his brother and then took off toward the back of the house.

"Share with Libby and Rachel," Richard called after him.

"I will."

Gabe sauntered off as well.

Taking a deep breath, Richard faced the captain. "Sir? What just occurred here?" The boys' appearance had drained some of his anger. "What I witnessed is most disturbing."

Mrs. Schlyterhaus came down the steps wearing a shocked expression. "Vhat is wrong vis that girl? She almost knocked me over."

"You mean Sarah?" The captain spoke in a lazy drawl. "Oh, she received bad news in the mail today." With hands clasped behind his back, he shook his dark head. "She's taking it badly, I'm afraid."

"What sort of bad news, sir?" Anger turned to genuine disquiet inside of Richard. "Has it anything to do with her family?"

"In a manner of speaking." He inclined his head toward his housekeeper. "Go about your business, Gretchen."

"Yes, sir."

"Richard, follow me into my study."

He did, closing the door behind him. "I've never seen Sarah so upset."

"She'll get over it." The captain sat down in his desk chair and motioned for Richard to take a seat.

He shook his head. "I prefer to stand." He suddenly spied the toppled vase. "What happened here?" Richard hated to even guess.

"Just a clumsy accident. Gretchen will clean it up later."

Richard stepped farther into the room. "What sort of bad news did Sarah get today?"

"She'll have to tell you herself." He smirked. "Oh, but wait...she isn't speaking to you, is she?"

Richard narrowed his gaze.

"But perhaps if you'd accept my offer and forget farming for a living, Sarah might reconsider you as a suitor."

Richard stiffened. "My decision is final."

"She certainly has pretty blue eyes. When she looks up at a man, so wide-eyed and innocent, it's almost his undoing."

"That does it, sir." In two quick strides, Richard reached the captain's desk. He slapped his hands down on the cluttered surface. "Leave her alone." He stared hard into the captain's dark eyes, caring little that the man was his employer.

A long moment passed, and then another.

"Now, Richard..." The captain sat forward, his gaze never wavering. "I'm only having a bit of fun with you. Sarah's my children's governess. She means nothing more to me than that, although I greatly value her services. It's obvious she loves my kids. In fact, I think she'll be staying on with me come September."

Richard eased up. "She's not taking the teaching position in Chicago?"

"No." The captain grinned easily. "Doesn't that work out nicely for you? Long-distance romances seldom succeed."

Richard had to admit that he'd been wondering what to do once Sarah left for Chicago. He figured they'd correspond by mail and make an occasional visit whenever they could arrange it.

Without a word, he walked to the windows and stared out over the front lawn.

Captain Sinclair came up behind him. "Remember when you first came to me? You were sixteen years old and in need of employment through the winter. It's my slow season, but something made me want to hire you. It didn't take long for me to see that you were competent and trustworthy. Then the war came. I was called into service, as was your father. We both depended on you, Richard, and you didn't disappoint either of us."

"I appreciate your saying so." It wasn't the first time the captain had expressed his gratitude.

Richard expelled a long breath. His anger abated. He relaxed his shoulders.

"I paid for your education at the business college," the captain continued. "You agreed to a five-year indentureship and...well, here we are." He sighed. "I dare say I can't do without you now, Richard. I've even decided to give you a different position. Instead of bookkeeper and steward, you'll be promoted to my assistant."

Richard didn't think it sounded much different from his current position. "I'm a farmer, Captain." He turned and faced the man. "It's in my blood, my soul."

"And what will you do if your father needs further medical treatment?"

"I suppose my parents and I will deal with the issue when the time comes."

"Hmm...Well, if you continue to work for me, Richard, you won't have to worry about finances." He made a helpless gesture. "I mean, what happens if your crops fail one year and your father needs a doctor? If you agree to be my assistant, I'll take care of your father's medical expenses. We'll see that he gets the best of care."

Richard shifted, wondering if he'd been selfish all this time. He'd been so dead-set on working his family's farm, being outdoors, being unconstrained and free, that he hadn't considered the downside of leaving his position with the captain. *Lord, what do You want me to do?*

"Keep your farm. You'll make enough working for me to pay hired hands." The captain took hold of one of Richard's shoulders. His expression was one of sincerity. "What do you say?"

"I don't know..."

"Richard." The captain gave him a mild shake. "Think about it." He smiled rather rakishly. "You'll win Sarah's heart. She's awfully fond of you. I'll see to it a small efficiency is made for the two of you right here in this house, just like I did for the Schlyterhauses. Sarah will enjoy that. She adores my home."

A knot of angst tightened in Richard's chest. He wished Sarah would love the farm—and him—just as much.

"Visit your farm and your parents whenever you like. I'll marry Elise and take over Great Lakes Shipping. You'll help me with the merger. Sarah will govern the children. We'll all be one happy family."

"That's quite an offer. The best you've come up with to date, sir."

"Yes, I know." The captain looked quite pleased with himself as he crossed the room and sat back down at his desk. "For now—" he glanced at the mess of papers in front of him— "perhaps you can help me sort this mess out."

It was then that Richard recalled his message for the captain. He pulled out his pocket watch and glanced at the time. "Captain, you're expected at a luncheon for Mr. Saunders, the retiring bank president."

"Oh, that's right." He stood. "I'll go get ready while you straighten up my desk. Then go back to the store. I'll meet you there later this afternoon."

"Fine, but there's just one more thing."

The captain gave him a curious look.

"It's about Sarah. I can hardly consider your offer if you continue to trifle with the woman I...well, I love her, sir."

"Yes, it's quite obvious." The captain rounded his desk. His eyes narrowed. "What say we make a deal? You agree to sign on with me, and I'll be a perfect gentleman where Sarah is concerned from now until...forever."

Richard felt like a man up against a corner with a blade at his throat. "In all the years I've known you, sir, whenever you've given your word, you've stuck by it."

The captain offered his right hand. "And so it shall be."

Richard knew he was licked. But his future affected more than just himself. At least now his parents would be taken care of, and Sarah—

He clasped the captain's hand. "You've got a deal."

Now Sarah would be safe.

BUT WHY?" GABRIEL STOMPED HIS FOOT. "WHY CAN'T WE GO to the Navises' farm after church?"

"Yeah, Miss Sarah," Michael complained next. "This is the second week we can't go."

"I have explained this to you already." Sarah pulled on her gloves with a vengeance. "We no longer have a standing invitation there."

"But the other day Mr. Navis said we're invited if you'd say yes." Gabe's remark sounded like an accusation.

She gave him a pointed stare. "No."

The four Sinclair children looked up at her with pleading gazes. Sarah tried to harden her heart. "I will not accept Mr. Navis's offer." She wasn't that naïve. She knew the *offer* went well beyond a visit to the farm. Richard hoped to change her mind.

Well, she wouldn't. For the last two weeks she'd held both Richard and Captain Sinclair at arm's length, doing everything she could to avoid being alone with either one of them. She simply couldn't handle the confusion and tumult of feelings each man aroused in her, and she had nowhere to turn for advice. She dared not tell her parents, lest they order her home. Nor could she confide in Lina, who would probably side with her cousin Richard. And for all she knew, Bethany Stafford still had feelings for Richard. So as much as possible she kept her days and her thoughts busy with the children.

And yet she would miss another Sunday afternoon with the Navis family—and yes, with Richard too! *If only he weren't so intent upon being a farmer,* she mused. *And he once called me stubborn! Ha!* She was only too grateful to be getting a ride to church and back from the Schmidts, friends of Mrs. Schlyterhaus. Richard needn't feel obligated to come and fetch them.

"Please, Sarah," Gabe continued, "it's the only thing that makes me happy—going to that farm on Sunday afternoons."

Sarah swung around from where she had been examining her appearance in the foyer's looking glass. "Why, Gabriel, we do plenty of fun things."

"But they're not like being on the farm."

Considering the boy, Sarah tilted her head. "Why not?"

"'Cuz I'm free there," Gabriel replied simply. "It's not like here, or at Aurora's house. I'm not free here or there. I have to sit up straight and not slurp my soup and I have to wear fancy jackets that make me feel sweaty. But on the farm, I can just be me, and if I accidentally slurp my soup, nobody cares."

Sarah sighed, thinking the matter quite trivial. "Nobody cares here either, Gabe, if you accidentally slurp your soup—"

"You don't understand!" he shouted. "You're just like them! My father...and Aurora!"

The outburst took Sarah aback.

"I thought you were different!" Gabe bolted up the front staircase just as the captain entered the foyer.

"What's going on here?" He sent Sarah a quizzical look.

Quickly she scooted Michael, Libby, and Rachel onto the front porch. "It was nothing, Captain. Really." She turned to Michael. "Watch your sisters for me."

He nodded.

"But the shouting." The captain stood with arms on his narrow hips. "Was that Gabriel?"

Sarah hesitated in her reply. She didn't want to get the boy in trouble.

"Sarah? Was Gabriel shouting at you?"

"Actually, we were discussing something that Gabriel feels very strongly about, sir. But I'll fetch him now, and everything will be fine."

Forgetting herself, as she often did, Sarah ran up the front stairs. She passed Mrs. Schlyterhaus in the upstairs hallway.

"Vill you ever learn?"

"Yes, ma'am, I will," Sarah promised over her shoulder. "I'll try not to forget again."

The housekeeper clucked her tongue. "My friends vill be here soon."

"We're almost ready." Ever since Richard's birthday party, it seemed the crusty old housekeeper was softening.

Sarah reached Gabriel's bedroom and knocked on the door. "Come on, Gabe," she called, "open up. Everyone is ready for church. Even Mrs. Schlyterhaus."

Slowly, the door opened, and Sarah had to force herself not to react when she saw Gabriel's tear-streaked face. The sight was enough to bring tears to her own eyes. Gabriel Sinclair was not a boy easily moved to emotion.

"It's that important to you, Gabe? Visiting the farm?"

He just stood there, staring back at her.

Sarah gave the matter more thought. "You know, freedom really starts in the heart of a person. It's not a place. And only Jesus can make us completely free."

Gabriel shook his head. "You don't understand. I can't explain it. It's like I'm happy there at the farm, helping Mr. Navis with the animals. But I'm not happy here."

"Perhaps that's because the Navises are people with a strong faith, and you can sense it." Sarah smiled, thinking of how Richard and his folks lived out their faith. Pa would be proud.

Gabriel appeared to be taking in her explanation. "The older Mr. Navis said that if I ask Jesus into my heart, then I'd be happy anywhere."

"And that's true." Sarah leaned against the doorframe.

Gabriel regarded her askance. "Have you asked Jesus into your heart?"

Sarah nodded. "When I was a little girl."

"Then how come you can't be happy anywhere? How come you can't be happy on a farm?"

Sarah tapered her gaze. "Has Richard been talking to you?"

"No, I heard you talking to Miss Lina the day we all went to lunch. You said you could never be happy on a farm."

Sarah drew back her chin. "I was speaking of a different kind of happiness." She sounded defensive to her own ears. "Besides, you can't understand such things because you're a child. Now, come along, Gabriel."

Sarah marched through the hallway and then down the front staircase. At the bottom, she found Captain Sinclair leaning against the banister, smiling.

She blew out a breath. "I forgot. The stairs."

The captain chuckled. "It's a good thing Gretchen didn't see you. I escorted her out to the carriage and saved you another tongue lashing."

Sarah sent him a diminutive grin. "I'm grateful, Captain." She still felt pangs of anger when in his presence for the poor reference he'd given her. But she could apply elsewhere. There were other music academies.

"And what about Gabriel?"

"He's coming, sir."

"Very good."

Sarah suddenly felt bold. "And what about you, Captain? Will you come to church with us today?"

"I think not, but I appreciate the offer. I am not interested in hearing anything a long-winded preacher has to say." Looping Sarah's gloved hand around his elbow, Captain Sinclair ushered her toward the front door. "Besides, I won't hear anything at your church that Richard hasn't already told me. Sitting in a pew won't do me a bit of good."

"My pa and brothers—my entire family—would disagree."

"Now, Sarah," he chided her gently, "I'll hear no more of it. The fact is I can't go to church even if I wanted to. I have an engagement. I'm taking Elise, Aurora, and her escort, John St. Martin, on a lake excursion today. We set sail midmorning. Aurora has already sent a messenger so I won't forget."

Captain Sinclair suddenly grinned. "Why don't you and the children join us? Come sailing with me out on beautiful Lake Michigan instead of perspiring in a stuffy chapel. It'll be so refreshing. Sailing does a body wonders. And Aurora is very fond of you. She says you have 'possibilities.' And the boys can fish. What do you say?"

Sarah faltered, but only momentarily. She wouldn't feel right about skipping church to go sailing. Her parents taught her that one misses church only if one is at death's door.

"Thank you, Captain, but I think it would please God more if I went to church."

"Are you certain, Sarah? You look like you might be persuaded—"

She hesitated, wondering what it would be like to go on a lake excursion with a man like Brian Sinclair and his affluent friends.

But Jesus sacrificed His life for her—couldn't she spare one day a week for Him?

"Sarah?"

"No, thank you, sir." Determination marked her words

"Very well." He exhaled a sigh of resignation. "You and the children go to church. I suppose it's good that the children get some religion. I never did."

Sarah nodded as Gabriel trudged down the stairs. His eyes were dry, and he seemed ready to go.

The captain walked Sarah out to the awaiting carriage. Suddenly she felt burdened for him. He was marrying a woman solely for her shipping business. As Richard had once said, the captain tried to buy his relationships, so they were all based on expediency. How utterly sad.

"I'm going to pray for you, Captain Sinclair."

"You do that." Lifting her hand, he pressed a kiss to her fingertips.

She yanked her hand away. "You're incorrigible."

"Thank you." He smiled—or was he laughing at her? Kissing Rachel's cheek, he set his daughter next to Michael in the outer bed of the carriage.

Stepping back, the captain waved to Mr. and Mrs. Schmidt. The stoic couple replied with stiff grins before sending a curious glance in Sarah's direction.

The carriage jerked forward, and the Schmidts began speaking to Mrs. Schlyterhaus in their native tongue. Mrs. Schlyterhaus replied before turning to Sarah.

"They vant to know if you are more than z'captain's governess. They ask vhy you are coming to church today."

"Mrs. Schlyterhaus!" Sarah swallowed her horror and indignation. It occurred to her then that the captain's bold actions as he helped her into the conveyance might have given them the wrong idea about her. "What did you tell them?"

"I said I didn't know." The housekeeper narrowed her gaze and lowered her voice. "After all, Captain Sinclair affords you great privilege in his home. Isabelle and I do not get z'same treatment."

"Only because I'm the children's governess. And that's all I am. First and foremost I am a decent, Christian young lady."

"Maybe...but maybe not. You have gone into z'captain's study, behind closed doors, to...*talk*."

"We talk about the children!" Sarah hissed the retort, although their last meeting still caused her to blush.

"You and z'captain are frequent topics of gossip."

"No!"

"Everyone has seen how he treats you even though he plans to marry Mrs. Kingsley. I have been asked if you will be his...*mistress*."

"That's ridiculous." Sarah's jaw slacked at the implication. In truth, the captain had been inappropriate with her. But Sarah thought she had successfully managed each situation. "Please tell the gossips the captain is my employer. Nothing more."

"As you say, Irish."

"And stop calling me that! Milwaukee's Bridge Wars are long over. The German folks and Irish people are no longer at odds."

The housekeeper jutted out her chin in a proud angle.

Meanwhile a sense of dread rained down on Sarah like the sunshine spilled from the blue August sky. "Am I really the topic of gossip?"

"*Ja*. I vould not lie."

Consternation spiraled deep within her. She had written to her parents about the situation in Chicago. She told them she didn't want to stay on as the captain's governess and had begun looking for a position as a music teacher locally. But what if the captain had sullied her reputation in Milwaukee? If that were the case, then there would be no career for her in teaching music.

With her dreams of independence already threatened by the captain and now her reputation at stake, Sarah realized she might be left with only one option.

The very one she'd feared from the beginning. Going home.

Sunshine drenched the churchyard, and the breeze felt like little waves of heat against Sarah's face as she watched the children chase each other around. Didn't they know the temperature soared near ninety degrees? She loosed her bonnet and peeled off her gloves as she waited for the stoic German couple to emerge from the church building. They'd not said a word to her since leaving the captain's house.

Glancing to her right, she saw Mrs. Schlyterhaus approaching. She appeared uneasy.

"Is something wrong?"

"The Schmidts told me they vill not drive you home." She lowered her voice. "They are ashamed to be seen vis you."

"Me? But—"

"I do not agree vis them, but it is not my carriage."

Tears stung. "Fine." Thoughts whirred in her head. How would she get the children back home?

"So I told the Schmidts I vould not ride vis them because I did not vant to be seen vis gossips."

Sarah blinked and stared at the housekeeper. "You did that for me? You stuck up for me?"

"Of course." The woman arched a dusty-brown brow and stepped in beside her. "Ve are family, so to speak." She patted Sarah's arm. "Vatch yourself around the captain, *ja*?"

"Yes, I will. I promise." She sighed and glanced around the

churchyard. "In the meantime, we have to find some way to get home."

"I vill vait here."

*So much for help.*

Sarah stepped around Mrs. Schlyterhaus in hopes of finding either Lina or Tim. Perhaps they'd take her and the children home. However, she didn't see them anywhere on the front walkway where clusters of people gathered to fellowship.

Or were they gossiping...about *her*?

In that very moment, Sarah felt conspicuous and just a tad frantic. She was responsible for the Sinclair children, and the Schmidts had left them and now also Mrs. Schlyterhaus fairly stranded on the hottest day of the year.

*They are ashamed to be seen with me.* Sarah couldn't shake those words from her mind. How could the Schmidts call themselves Christian and not extend to her the benefit of the doubt?

She pressed onward, finally spying Richard. His gaze briefly touched hers before he leaned to hear something Bethany Stafford said. In spite of the fact they hadn't spoken at length to each other in almost two weeks, Sarah knew he was her only hope.

She tried to catch his eye again. He looked her way, and she motioned to him. Excusing himself, he strode toward her.

"Hello, Sarah."

"Richard." She dipped her head. Of all days why did he have to look so handsome today? Wearing a crisp white dress shirt, he'd loosened his tie and rolled his sleeves a few turns. His face and forearms were suntanned. "I need a favor...and I'm asking as a fellow employee. Nothing more."

Hardness glinted in his blue eyes. "What can I do for you?" He may have well been talking to one of Captain Sinclair's customers.

Sarah took a no-nonsense approach. "The children and I need a ride back home. The Schmidts decided they couldn't, um, accommodate me—us."

"What a shame."

Was he teasing her?

Richard jutted out his bottom lip in momentary thought and then looked toward his wagon. "I'm happy to assist you—as a fellow employee. Nothing more."

His mockery stung like a horsewhip, and Sarah couldn't help wondering if part of his churlishness stemmed from having heard the gossip too. She didn't think he'd believe it—except she'd confided in him about the captain's advances.

Humiliation pressed down on her harder than the heat of the day. Her eyes fluttered closed for a breath, then two. She steadied herself and gazed back at Richard. His expression seemed to soften.

"I have to drive my parents home. Mama cooks for the usual folks who come for Sunday noon dinner. Why don't you come along? We'll get the kids fed, you and Mrs. Schlyterhaus can have some lunch, and I'll drive you all home afterwards."

"Thank you." Sarah wanted to refuse the offer to come to the farm. But how could she? "I'm very grateful."

He inclined his head. "Why don't you round up the children and meet us at the wagon?"

"All right."

When Richard walked away, Sarah's heart plummeted. Something was different. He'd changed.

Maybe with the distance she'd put between them coupled with the gossip, Richard realized he didn't love her anymore.

Sadness, like none other she'd ever felt, gripped her heart.

"I don't know why you brought her here today."

Standing in the sunny kitchen, Richard helped his mother snap green beans. He sensed her hurt. "Mama, Sarah and the children had nowhere to go, no way back home."

"So she doesn't mind being our friends when she needs something."

"Now, Mama..." Richard sort of felt the same way.

He inhaled slowly. Last week he'd had to give his folks some explanation as to why Sarah refused to come to the farm after church. His broken heart got the best of him, however, and he ended up spilling the entire tale. Sarah didn't love him enough to be a farmer's wife.

Although it didn't appear as if Richard would be a farmer after all.

It was then that Richard told his folks how he'd signed on with Captain Sinclair indefinitely. Neither Pops nor Mama could argue with the benefits the captain offered, but Mama continued to worry over Richard's happiness—or lack thereof—and blamed Sarah for it.

"I thought she and I had become good friends when she sprained her ankle. I took care of her. We talked a lot."

"Mama, we *are* her friends." He leaned closer to his mother and whispered, "That's the problem. I want to be more than Sarah's friend."

"But she thinks becoming a farmer's wife is beneath her." Mama sniffed. "I am a farmer's wife."

Richard set a hand on her thick shoulder. "Mama, she only meant the vocation isn't for her, and I knew that from the start. It's my fault to have thought I could change her mind. But maybe when she discovers I'll have a career with the captain—"

"She should love you regardless," Mama sniffed.

"I know, Mama, I feel the same." He wanted Sarah to fall in love with him whether a farmer or the captain's assistant.

"Oh, Richard, she shouldn't have come here today. That's all."

A golden flash caught his eye, and Richard turned to see Sarah's bright blonde hair as she stepped into the kitchen. She paled, and he sensed she overhead Mama's remark.

"What can I help you with, Sarah?" He strode toward her, shielding his mother. He set his hands on his hips.

She moved her mouth to speak, but no words came out. Then she shook her head and waved a hand in the air as if erasing a blackboard. She spun on her heel so quickly her skirts brushed against Richard's ankles.

He resisted the urge to go after her. He'd finish helping his mother here, and then he'd talk to Sarah later—when they could be alone.

SARAH RAN AS FAST AS HER FEET WOULD CARRY HER. SHE didn't stop until she reached the end of the cornfield. At long last she released the sob she'd been holding in after hearing Mrs. Navis say Richard shouldn't have brought her here today. So she felt like the Schmidts did. The sheer mortification of her situation doubled her over. She thought she might even be sick.

"Sarah! Sarah!"

The female voice penetrated her consciousness. Suddenly she felt an arm around her shoulders.

"Sarah, are you all right?"

She looked up and through her tears saw Bethany Stafford.

"Sarah..." Her voice sounded thick with compassion. "What's wrong?"

"It's too horrible...to even say."

"Come on and sit down over here." Bethany steered her into the shade of an apple tree. "Come on. That's it. Now sit down."

Sarah crumpled onto the grass. As her senses returned, she realized she shouldn't have left the children. Rachel had asked for more milk. She'd never been able to fulfill her request. She'd been too much in shock over Mrs. Navis's remark to utter a word.

*She shouldn't have come here today...*

Sarah hated the thought that her presence shamed the Navises.

"Did you and Richard have an argument, Sarah?"

"No. Not exactly." She turned and regarded Bethany. She looked pretty in the yellow gingham checked dress that hugged her slender frame. She appeared cool. Comfortable. Strands of her brown hair were streaked with sunshine-gold, and her wide-brimmed straw hat couldn't hide the smattering of freckles on her face.

"Don't worry. You can talk to me. I no longer see Richard as anything more than the friend who lives on the neighboring farm." A sad little smile played across her mouth. "I realize now I mistook his kindness for something more. The truth is, Richard is kind to everyone."

"Yes, he is."

"I fantasized about him because I wanted to feel special. My life consists of nothing but taking care of my brothers and sisters and doing chores. But then I thought Richard might rescue me from the drudgery."

"Wouldn't you be trading one drudgery for another?"

"Of course not!" Bethany pulled back, looking surprised. "Being a wife and mother is a blessing. And I've seen how Mr. Navis and Richard treat Mrs. Navis. Like a queen. They reverence her." A blush made its way through her suntanned face. "I wouldn't mind having a taste of it."

Sarah had been treated like a princess all her life. "You're not cherished at home?"

"Hardly." Bethany kept her gaze lowered. "But I shouldn't say more. My parents try their best. It's me who's restless. In a way I'm afraid that if I don't leave home soon, it'll never happen. My mother, stepmother actually, grows more and more dependent on me and less responsible. Does that make sense?"

"I think so."

"But I'm talking about myself too much. Tell me about your trouble, Sarah."

She toyed with a long blade of grass, debating whether to confide in Bethany. Moments later, she figured it might be beneficial if Bethany heard her side of things. "I learned today that there's some gossip floating around about me and..."—she could hardly say it—"...and Captain Sinclair."

"How dreadful. Well, it's not true. Ignore it."

"I wish I could, but I fear it's done permanent damage to my reputation here in Milwaukee as well as with the Schmidts at church and…even the Navises." Sarah swallowed the sorrowful lump in her throat. "I'm sick about it."

"I don't blame you." Bethany reached over and grasped Sarah's hand. She bowed her head and closed her eyes. "Heavenly Father, please look down upon my friend Sarah with favor and clear her good name. Grant her Your peace which passes all understanding. Fill her with hope—just as You've done for me. I ask this in Jesus's name. Amen."

"Thank you for that prayer." Perhaps it was her imagination, but Sarah thought she felt better already. She'd noticed too that Bethany referred to her as a "friend." That's exactly what she needed right now. A friend.

"Come on." Bethany stood. "I have to take those lemon bars to Mrs. Navis." She nodded to the pan resting in the shade several feet away. "Let's walk back to the house together, shall we?"

"Yes." Sarah knew she needed to get back—back to the children. Despite her troubles she had four children in her care. They needed her, and she had a job to do.

Later as they rode back to the captain's house, Sarah sat in silence beside Richard. The girls and Mrs. Schlyterhaus rode in the backseat, while the boys, as usual, found places in the wagon bed. Libby and Rachel chattered like magpies, and Richard replied, although Sarah couldn't detect the usual smile in his tone, and he never chuckled. Not even once.

They arrived at the captain's home, and Richard reined in the team of horses. Next he stepped over Sarah and jumped down, helping her alight before Mrs. Schlyterhaus. The children ran to the door, and Richard followed them all inside.

"Sarah, may I have a word with you please?" Richard asked.

She paused at the servants' stairwell. "I have to get the children ready for bed."

"I'll wait."

"Fine." Her terse reply was in response to the sound of his voice.

Upstairs she washed up Rachel and Libby, lending the younger girl the more help. She supervised the boys, reminding them of their swimming lessons in the morning.

At last Sarah made her way back downstairs. The August heat and long day had taken its toll. She felt exhausted. She walked outside to the pump and washed her hands and face, taking several gulps of the cool water. Next she repinned a few pieces of hair before stepping back into the house and meeting Richard in the front foyer.

He motioned her into the reception parlor. Sarah hoped he'd be quick about whatever he had to say. She didn't feel like talking.

"I wanted to apologize for earlier. I think you may have overheard some of my conversation with my mother."

She didn't have the energy to fib politely and say she hadn't. She nodded.

"Please forgive Mama. She's hurt. You see, she's very fond of you and had hoped for a match between us."

Sarah noted the past tense. She lowered her gaze. "I'm sorry I've disappointed her." She sent him a glance. "And you."

Richard gazed heavily at a vase filled with freshly cut flowers. His mouth seemed frozen in a frown.

"I don't know if the captain told you, but I agreed to work for him indefinitely. He's promoting me to his assistant." Richard's eyes slid to hers.

"What?" Sarah moved slowly toward him. "But you were looking forward to the day when your indentureship was over so you could work on your farm."

"I've tossed those ambitions aside."

"How could you?" Sarah's mind groped for words. "But…why? When?"

"Over a week ago." Richard rolled a shoulder. "He made me an offer I couldn't refuse."

"Hmm, yes…" Disappointment flooded Sarah's being. "Well, the captain did say once that everyone has his price. I reckon he found yours."

"Sarah—" Richard's eyebrows drew inward—"I thought you'd be pleased by the news."

"Pleased? Pleased that you succumbed to the captain's manipulation...and after warning me all summer not to fall into that very trap?" She lost a few points of respect for Richard.

He cocked his head. "But you've decided to stay on as his governess."

"Who told you that?" Sarah squared her shoulders. "Why should I?"

"Because the children need you, and..." He shook his head and made a gesture of resignation. "Oh, it doesn't matter..."

*It doesn't matter what I do?* As far as Sarah was concerned, Richard's personality had done a one-eighty-degree turn from the day she first met him.

Pieces of her heart smashed. He had been her bulwark and friend since the day she stepped off the train in Milwaukee. He said he loved her. But now he didn't care whether she stayed or left. He must believe that scandalous talk—like the Schmidts.

Tears threatened, but Sarah blinked them back. "I wish you all the happiness and success in the world." She walked purposely to the doorway. "Good night, Richard."

Three days later, preparations were underway in the Sinclair household. Service people of every kind traipsed in and out: painters, carpenters, and bricklayers. The Kingsley-Sinclair wedding ceremony and reception, slated for the Saturday before Christmas, was being held at the mansion, which was to be completely refurbished for the event. Sarah was only too glad that she wouldn't be around to witness the travesty.

Standing by the side doorway, she pulled on her gloves, happy to have the day off. Aurora had come to collect the children, who'd arrived with Mrs. Kingsley.

"Miss Sarah?"

She glanced up to see Gabriel and Michael peering around the corner.

"Can we come with you today?"

She hesitated, taking in their forlorn expressions. "But you're supposed to spend time with Aurora today."

"We don't want to." Michael came forward.

"Well, life is filled with things we don't want to do, so you'd best get used to it. Besides, I have errands, and then I plan to spend the rest of my time off shopping." Sarah grinned, knowing the last word would cause the boys to cringe.

"We'd rather shop with you than Aurora and that snippy ol' Mrs. Kingsley."

"Yeah."

"I heard that!"

Sarah grimaced as the regal brunette entered the room and eyed the boys with a piercing stare. "I want to see you both in your father's study," Mrs. Kingsley commanded. "Now."

The boys took off.

"And you..." She sashayed toward Sarah with narrowed almond-shaped eyes. "I recognize you now. You're the children's governess."

Sarah had to admit the woman was beautiful even with anger creasing her unblemished brow. She wore a clingy white dress dotted with tiny strawberries and edged with lace.

She nodded. "I'm Sarah McCabe, ma'am." She glimpsed Mrs. Kingsley's maid, hovering in the shadows. She appeared to be the same age as Mrs. Schlyterhaus.

"I remember you from the ball earlier this summer. You're a pert little thing, aren't you?"

Sarah didn't reply, but she painfully recalled how the captain had reprimanded her for defending Gabriel that night.

"I'll have you know that my maid, Lizzie here, is very good with children. Once Brian and I are married, your services will no longer be needed."

"It's just as well. I plan to leave at the end of the month anyway." Sarah tried not to smile at Mrs. Kingsley's dismayed expression.

"End of the month? But Brian said—"

"I'm afraid there's been some misunderstanding." Sarah lifted her laundry bag.

The captain's broad shoulders suddenly filled the doorway that led down the long hallway toward the kitchen and foyer. "What's amiss now, Elise? My sons came bolting into my study like a pair of wild horses. They startled Aurora, and she spilled tea on her skirt. She's quite upset." He sighed audibly and caught sight of Sarah.

She saw the exasperation pooled in the depths of his dark eyes. "I'm just leaving for the day, sir." She'd be out of the way, at least.

"Lucky you. And the boys are chattering about going with you?"

"They asked me, but—"

"It's your day off."

Sarah bestowed on him a grateful smile.

Mrs. Kingsley cleared her throat. "I was just telling Miss…McCabe, is it?"

Sarah nodded.

"That her services won't be required once we're married." Mrs. Kingsley sidled up to the captain and put her hand on his arm.

"Sarah is indispensable to me, Elise." He leaned one shoulder casually against the doorframe. He made an impressive figure in his white sleeves and apricot-colored waistcoat.

"But the girl just said—"

"Sir, I'm leaving come the first of September." Sarah didn't like feeling as if she were an object to be quarreled over. "You must have forgotten."

"I'm sure I didn't. In fact, as I recall, you and I settled this matter earlier this month. In my study. We had a very intimate discussion."

Sarah's face flamed as she recalled the day he last attempted to kiss her. It was the same day she learned he'd ruined her chances for a position at the music academy in Chicago. "I didn't agree to anything."

"Oh, but you did, Sarah." His eyes seemed to darken, if such a thing were possible.

"Brian, you're a devil." Mrs. Kingsley's voice was a mix of amusement and anger. "But I must put my foot down. Any trysts will have to cease once we're married."

The implication broadsided Sarah and left her reeling. She wanted to defend herself but couldn't quite manage to utter a sound. What could she say? He never touched her, never whispered in her ear?

It was true. The captain had behaved inappropriately with her. She'd even enjoyed it to a degree. She'd been curious, infatuated. However, in that moment all those whirling, wayward emotions seemed to come to a screeching halt.

*God forgive me.*

Sarah made a hasty exit from the house. She hurried down the block, heading for the trolley stop. What had she agreed to? Pa always taught her that when a person gave her word, she had to stick by it.

Had she really told the captain that she'd sign on at the end of August? Had she promised him? Surely he'd misunderstood.

She'd have to wire back home when she was downtown today. She needed her pa to help her sort all this out. Her circumstances suddenly overwhelmed her. No one had ever told her that being independent had a downside. No one ever warned her she'd feel so unprotected, vulnerable, and alone.

Sarah realized then that she didn't know a great many things, but one particular truth she knew for sure. She wasn't in love—no, far from it—with Captain Brian Sinclair.

# TWENTY-FIVE

THE TINY BELL ABOVE THE DOOR JANGLED, SIGNALING customers. Richard glanced up and saw two strapping men saunter in. Something about them rang with familiarity, although he felt certain he'd never met either. They removed their wide-brimmed hats, and Richard noticed both had hair the color of chestnuts. As they came forward, one man walked with a limp and used a cane.

Richard peeled off his wire specs. "May I help you?"

"We're looking for Captain Sinclair," the second man said. His blue eyes roamed the store before settling on Richard. "We were told at the train station that we'd likely find him here."

He'd seen those blue eyes before.

"I'm sorry, but the captain is gone for the day." Richard stepped around the counter and stuck out his right hand. "I'm Richard Navis, the captain's steward."

"Luke McCabe." He clasped Richard's hand in a firm grip.

*Sarah's brothers.*

Richard turned to the man with the cane. "You must be Jake McCabe."

"I am." The brown-eyed man with the cane stepped up and offered his hand.

Richard shook it. "A pleasure."

"Likewise. But I see our reputation has preceded us. You must be acquainted with our baby sister."

Richard smiled. "Sarah speaks of her big brothers quite often."

"Hmm...now why does that have me more than a little concerned?" Jake moved his cane and shifted his weight.

Luke replied with a chuckle. "I don't suppose you'd know where we can find Sarah right about now? We failed to get directions to the captain's place of residence."

Richard pulled out his pocket watch. Six o'clock. "She most likely has finished supervising the children's dinner hour and has them out for a final stroll. Either that, or she's watching them play in the yard. When I happened by days ago the boys were attempting to build a tree house."

"Sounds like something boys would do." Jake narrowed his brown eyes. "Seems like you know Sarah's schedule quite well."

"Sarah and I are—" Richard paused. What could he say? At this point he and Sarah weren't even friends. In the last two weeks he'd only spoken a few words to her in passing. Ever since he'd revealed his plan to stay on with the captain, she'd been even cooler toward him, if that were possible. He could understand why she avoided him when she thought he was going to be a farmer, but why now? He could only conclude that her heart was engaged elsewhere.

"Sarah and I," he began again, "are great acquaintances, as we both work for Captain Sinclair."

Both men replied with a slight inclination of their heads.

"I'm just finishing up here for the day. If you'd like to have a seat for a bit, I'll close the store and take you over to the captain's house. Sarah's off duty in an hour anyway—that is, if Captain Sinclair makes it home by then."

"Appreciate the offer." Jake nodded. "Thanks."

While the two McCabe brothers settled into chairs by the window, Richard entered the last of today's receipts and locked up the accounting books. Then he went around to the livery and had one of the captain's buggies brought around. It was after seven by the time he'd locked up the store.

Finally they boarded the conveyance and headed for the captain's house. They rode across one of the city's many bridges, then up Wisconsin Avenue. Tall structures loomed on either side, with many others under construction. Richard pointed out the usual sights, a theater, department stores. They passed Riverside Printing House and Lager Beer Hall.

"I'm seeing an awful lot of watering holes." Cynicism edged Jake's tone.

"Yes. Milwaukee is the beer capital of the world. Of course, that presents its own set of problems."

"I imagine so," Jake said.

Richard added a couple more positive tidbits. "Before the Civil War, we were the largest shipper of wheat in the world. Once the war ended, the city began excelling in manufacturing. There's an influx of people from all around the country, seeking jobs and finding them here in Milwaukee."

"Interesting."

Richard smiled sadly to himself, remembering how Sarah had called him something of a walking textbook on the first day she'd met him.

Luke piped up from the backseat. "One large city looks just like another. But in the Arizona Territory—"

"That's right. Sarah said you're both missionaries, starting a church out West."

"I first got burdened for the Territory when I rode with McCulloch during the war," Jake said. "I talked Luke into an expeditionary visit, and while in the town of Silverstone, God burdened him—the both of us—for the people there."

"We came back for supplies and to recruit," Luke said. "It's rather primitive in the Southwest. We need professionals, doctors, teachers..."

Richard's gut knotted. The captain had informed him that Sarah had declined the position in Chicago and was staying on as the children's governess. So why were her brothers here? Had they come to take Sarah to be a teacher in Arizona Territory?

Arriving at the captain's home, they climbed from the buggy. Richard knocked at the massive front door. If he didn't have guests with him, he'd walk in. But the captain demanded formal proprieties be upheld when visitors were present. As always, Mrs. Schlyterhaus peeked at them from behind the grillwork.

"Good evening," Richard said. "I have Sarah's two brothers here. They wish to see her."

The lead glass panel slid shut and the housekeeper opened the door. Richard sighed with relief. At least Mrs. Schlyterhaus was in a cooperative mood.

Stepping into the foyer, the men removed their hats.

"She is upstairs with the children. I vill get her."

"Thank you." Richard led Jake and Luke into the reception parlor. "Make yourselves comfortable."

Luke let out a long, slow whistle. "Will you get a load of this room, Jake?"

"I'm seeing it. The word *fancy* doesn't even come close."

Richard smiled. "That's the general reaction." He had to admit, the room was something to behold with its walnut-carved mantelpiece and moldings. The wall covering was of a rich brown print, and gold-plated wall sconces with iridescent glass prisms added a handsome touch. An oriental rug covered the darkly polished floor.

The usual polite small talk ensued, and then suddenly Sarah stood beside him. Richard thought she seemed breathless, as if she'd dropped whatever she'd been doing and ran to the reception parlor. Her blue eyes were wide with shock.

"What are you two doing here?"

Richard didn't miss the accusation in her voice. He bit back a grin.

"Ma and Pa couldn't come, Sarah," Jake said. "They sent us to fetch you."

"Oh." Disappointment weighted her tone.

"What kind of greeting is that?" Luke opened his arms.

Sarah seemed to shake herself and ran to him, hugging him around the waist. Next Jake got a hug. When she stepped back, tears glistened in her eyes.

"What's going on, baby sister?" Luke slung an arm around her. "What sort of trouble did you get yourself into this time?"

Sarah's bottom lip quivered. She sent Richard a glance that didn't reach his eyes before lowering her gaze. Then all of a sudden a sob wracked her body. Then another.

"Sarah..." Richard stepped forward, hand outstretched, but was halted by her brothers' stare. He had no place here. He rubbed the back of his neck. "I'll leave and give you some privacy."

Surprisingly, Jake followed him out of the parlor. Richard slid closed the heavy mahogany doors.

"I'm afraid I have no patience when it comes to a woman's tears," Jake groused.

Richard, on the other hand, felt quite unnerved. Why was Sarah so upset? Was it him?

His back to Jake, Richard scoured his mind. He loved Sarah, wanted to be more than just her friend. She chose to put distance between them. He thought it was because of her confusion over her feelings for the captain—and perhaps him too. He'd been waiting, hoping, praying, she'd sort through her heart and reach out to him. But had he done something wrong?

Or was the captain up to his old tricks? No doubt that would bring Sarah's brothers from Missouri.

When Jake cleared his throat, Richard snapped to attention. "Allow me to show you into the men's parlor. We can wait there."

"Another parlor?"

"One of three. There's a lady's parlor too."

"You don't say?" Jake sounded awed.

They entered the room, and large masculine furniture upholstered in red velvet greeted them.

Jake sat down in an armchair, setting his cane on the floor beside him. "I can see where Sarah would enjoy living in this place for the summer. The description of this house in her letters didn't do it a bit of justice."

Richard wondered if Sarah ever mentioned him. But why was she crying? She'd looked so broken a few minutes ago.

A huge *boom*, followed by another, sounded from directly overhead. The antler chandelier swayed slightly. Richard stood. "Excuse me while I check on the boys."

"The captain's not home, huh?" Jake glanced toward the ornate mantel clock. "You said she got off at seven? Sarah should have been off work a half hour ago."

"Right, but she usually cares for the kids until they're either sleeping or the captain comes home."

"So let me get this straight. Captain Sinclair disregards those seven-to-seven hours he contracted her to work?"

"Not intentionally, and Sarah never complains. She loves the children."

"Hmm."

Richard left and took the front stairs two at a time. Mrs. Schlyterhaus was already standing outside Michael's room, wagging her finger and scolding them.

"I vill not clean up the plaster you shake loose vhen you jump off your bed like zat."

"And who's gonna stop us?" came Michael's sassy reply.

The housekeeper stepped back to allow Richard to lean around the corner of the doorframe.

Both Gabriel and Michael straightened.

Richard noted the tent made of blankets, the play gun, and arrows. "What are you two doing up here?"

"I'm the cavalry," Gabe said, "and Mike's an Indian."

"Ah...well, it's time for a peace treaty. I expect your father home any minute."

Gabriel groaned but gathered his blankets and pushed out the doorway. He traipsed to his own room with a trail of bedcovers following in his wake.

"Those boys need a firm hand," Mrs. Schlyterhaus said before walking away.

"Indeed." Richard gave Michael a wide-eyed stare.

The boy grinned.

"G'night."

"'Night, Mr. Navis." Michael's eyes lit up. "Come back soon with candy sticks. Or maybe next time you can pretend with me and Gabe."

"We'll see. Behave now." He checked on Rachel. She slept soundly in her bed. In the next bed, Libby leafed through a book.

Back downstairs, Richard passed by the main reception parlor. The doors were still closed. He could hear the sound of Luke's voice but couldn't make out the words, not that he was trying to eavesdrop, of course. Jake still sat alone in the men's parlor.

"I hope Sarah's all right."

"She'll talk to Luke, and then we'll figure things out."

Richard faced the mantel and stared at a decorative bronze ship. He recalled how on his birthday he called Sarah spoiled. He regretted that now. He'd spoken out of jealousy, not love. He sighed. He had a lot of regrets these days. He still couldn't figure out if signing with the captain was one of them. His dream of farming had vaporized. Had his notion of marrying Sarah disappeared too?

*Lord, please make Your will clear. I felt so sure Sarah would be mine.*

He turned to meet Jake's speculative gaze. But before any words could be spoken, Luke entered the room.

Looking at his brother, he shook his head. "It's worse than we imagined."

Jake sat on the edge of his chair, his head tipped. "Worse?"

Luke glanced at Richard, obviously not willing to discuss the matter in front of him.

Richard spoke up. "I'm sure you're both as thirsty as I am. I'll go see about some refreshments."

As he strode from the parlor, Richard felt compelled to check on Sarah first. What could have possibly upset her so? He found her on the settee, drying her eyes with a hankie. He approached her carefully.

"Sarah?"

She didn't look his way.

He inched closer. Reaching her, he knelt by her side. "Sarah, what's wrong?"

She didn't reply but buried her face in her hankie.

"I know we've been at odds, but I hope you know you still could have come to me."

"H–how could I–I know that?"

Icy remorse ran through him. "Oh, Sarah, I'm sorry." He touched several strands of her bright blonde hair that had come lose from her chignon and tucked them behind her ear. "Don't cry." Her hankie looked like it needed a good wringing. Richard offered his clean one.

She accepted it, but when she glanced at him his heart twisted. Her eyes were red-rimmed and puffy.

Richard couldn't help assuming the worst. And yet he couldn't believe that the captain would break his part of the bargain.

Booted footfalls sounded on the tile floor in the foyer. A man cleared his voice. Richard glanced over his shoulder to find both Jake and Luke McCabe at the doorway. Slowly he pushed to his feet.

"Sarah, you go on and pack your things." Jake's voice sounded constrained with unshed emotion. Anger? "At least enough for a day or two."

"Until we can talk to Captain Sinclair," Luke added.

Richard's mind raced through the week ahead. Tomorrow was Sarah's day off, and if she hadn't renewed her contract with the captain, her last scheduled day was Friday. After that she'd walk out of his life forever.

Sarah rose. "I'll go pack, but I can't leave the children."

Luke walked to an armchair and sat down. "Then I reckon we'll wait right here until Captain Sinclair comes home."

Up in her bedroom, Sarah packed her valise. She hadn't been expecting her brothers. It was a shock to see them at first. She had hoped Pa would come. Pa and Ma. Sarah felt like she needed her mother. But when she hugged first Luke then Jake, she realized how much she'd missed them. And then she'd poured out her heart to Luke. He'd listened with a patient ear and promised to help her resolve things before he and Jake took her home.

*Home.*

A lead weight seemed to drop inside of Sarah. She felt defeated at the very thought of going back to Jericho Junction. She always imagined she'd return as a successful music teacher who lived on her own in Chicago. But now she'd return as... nothing. Not even as a woman destined to be a farmer's wife.

She thought of Richard's show of concern downstairs. Ever since he'd signed on to stay with the captain, she'd feared going to him with her problems, thinking that he would talk her into staying on as governess. But knowing what she did about the captain's character, she couldn't continue working for him, nor respect Richard for doing so either, even if he'd done so in an effort to win her hand.

Sarah shuddered, recalling Luke's reaction when she'd told him of the captain's romantic advances and insinuations. Luke had balled his large hand into a fist, and Sarah sensed he longed to drive it into the captain's handsome, shadowed jaw. Although an ordained minister like Pa, Luke wasn't afraid to defend a loved one's honor.

Except the captain didn't deserve all the blame. Sarah made that fact plain to Luke. True, the captain behaved inappropriately, but she felt responsible, guilty, and ashamed. The captain had been correct when he said that she'd been attracted to him. His large, tastefully decorated house impressed her. His children won her heart. And his affluence and romantic words fed her illusion of someday marrying a wealthy, handsome man, living happily ever after in a stately home, and raising intelligent, sensitive children.

Luke had just held her while she cried it all out. She had wanted to be so grown up and independent, but in the end she'd been such a naïve fool!

And now she felt trapped by her illusions.

Valise in hand, she looked in on the children. All sleeping. Taking a deep breath, she made her way downstairs, using the servants' stairwell. Through the kitchen, down the long hallway, she heard male voices coming from Captain Sinclair's study. It appeared he'd come home to find Jake and Luke waiting for him. In the parlor, she found Richard sitting alone. He stood when he noticed her in the doorway.

"Feeling better?"

She nodded, although she couldn't get herself to look him in the eye. "I didn't think you'd still be here."

"Of course I wouldn't leave your brothers. In fact, I promised to see them—and you—settled into a hotel." He crossed the room and set his hands on her upper arms. "Sarah, can you tell me what this is all about?"

She shook her head. "I can't. Please don't make me."

"No, of course I won't." Richard lowered his arms, then took her hand.

She pulled it away. His attempts to comfort her only made her feel worse. Where was he weeks ago when she desperately needed him? Signing on with her nemesis, Captain Sinclair.

She strode to the windows to put some distance between them. Dusk had settled over the neighborhood. The hot summer air cooled rapidly now, thanks to a breeze off the lake. She wondered what her brothers were saying to Captain Sinclair. She felt confident they'd use caution when confronting him, but there was always a chance the captain would take offense.

The moment the thought took root, her brothers burst from the study. Glimpsing the grim line that was Jake's mouth and the tight knit of his brows, Sarah knew the meeting couldn't have gone well. The captain, on the contrary, seemed well composed.

"Time to go, Sarah." Jake limped toward her.

"I must insist that Sarah finish her term with me." Folding his arms across his broad chest, the captain leaned his shoulder against the wall and crossed his booted feet. He looked handsome and debonair, standing there in the darkened hallway, like a hero who'd just stepped from the pages of a novel. In spite of herself, Sarah felt transfixed.

He sent her a wink.

Reality claimed her, and she quickly lowered her head. How shameful to stare and more so to feel enamored by a man who'd dashed her dreams and sullied her reputation. She should despise Captain Brian Sinclair.

But she didn't.

"As I told you gentlemen in my study, I don't have a replacement for Sarah, and my children need a governess." His voice sounded calm, his words even. "What's more, Sarah intimated that she'd sign on with me permanently, so I didn't bother advertising her position."

Her head shot up. "Captain, I never did any such thing!"

"Sarah..." Luke held up a hand to forestall further argument. "Under the circumstances, Captain," he ground out, "the original date of August 31 will suffice. That gives you a few days to make plans for your children."

"I beg to differ. What you're not understanding is"—the captain stepped out of the shadows—"Sarah has become more than a governess to me."

Her heartbeat quickened.

"She's like one of the family."

Sarah let go of the anxious breath she'd been holding.

"So you see, taking Sarah from us would be extremely detrimental to my children."

"Don't listen to him." Sarah recognized the strains of his persuasive charm. "I'm not part of his family. I never agreed to anything more than governing his children until the end of the month."

"Calm down, Sarah." Jake looked from her to the captain. "I'll afford you the weekend, Sinclair. That's it."

"How very kind of you." The captain gave him a mocking little bow.

Sarah saw Luke's jaw flex. "Come Monday morning we're on the

8:15 to St. Louis." He raised his chin. "Meanwhile, Sarah stays in a hotel with us."

"Which is ridiculous. I've got plenty of room here, and it won't cost you a cent." The captain set his hands on his hips.

Sarah thought her brothers seemed to consider the offer…

Until the captain sent her one of his captivating grins.

Sarah looked away.

"I think not." Luke took hold of Sarah's upper arm. "You wait outside," he told her in a low, unyielding tone. Next he took hold of her valise.

Sarah walked through the foyer.

"Mr. Navis, are you willing to help me carry out my sister's trunk of belongings?"

"Certainly, but—"

Sarah whirled around. "Tomorrow morning is soon enough for me to pack the rest of my things, Luke."

"No. You'll do it now. My mind's made up." He sounded determined as he eyed the captain. "My sister stays with us from here on out."

# Twenty-Six

I KNEW WE SHOULDN'T HAVE LET YOU LOOSE IN THE WORLD ALL by yourself. I still don't know what Ma and Pa were thinking!"

Sarah watched her brother Jake pace the plank floor of their hotel suite's breezeway. Thanks to Richard, they'd secured adjoining rooms at the Newhall House. But now that they were settled in, her brothers had a lot to say—especially after Sarah told Jake what she'd said earlier to Luke.

She sunk inside herself at Jake's scolding, knowing she deserved it.

"Ease up, Jake," Luke said. "She feels bad enough as it is."

"I'm not so sure about that." Jake squared his broad shoulders and stared at Sarah. "All those winks and smiles from Sinclair. Frankly, I'm shocked and more than disappointed in you. You know better. You were raised in a Christian home with Bible-based values."

"I didn't wink or smile back. I can promise you that!"

"But you could have left long before now!" Jake accused.

Luke intervened. "Jake, you know full well how the world works. Let's be fair. The captain had all the power here—his age and experience, his position, his money, his personality—and Sarah had next to none. Add to that the fact he knows he's a very—" he cleared his throat, embarrassed—"physically attractive man who is well versed in using all his charms to his own advantage." Luke's features tightened. "Are you going to blame Sarah for *his* evil? I'd say our baby sister did amazingly well considering the circumstances." He stared down his brother, who finally shifted his gaze and shrugged.

"I reckon you're right."

Luke's words fell like balm on Sarah's soul. For the last month she'd struggled alone, trying to do the right thing, to care for the children and finish out her contract. Maybe she shouldn't blame herself as much as she did.

"Why didn't Ma and Pa come?" She turned to Luke with tears clouding her vision.

"A fever swept through the Morrison family." Typical Luke to break the news gently. "Little Billy got it the worst. He went to be with the Lord Saturday afternoon."

Sarah moaned. She'd taught Billy in Sunday school. He'd been about Michael's age. "How horrible."

"Of course our folks couldn't leave."

"Of course." Putting her hands over her face, Sarah sobbed all over again. For little Billy. For herself.

Jake put a heavy hand on her shoulder. "Sinclair has taken sore advantage of you, baby sister," he conceded.

Sarah straightened, wiping her eyes. "I know it, but you're right. I could have left sooner or at least told Ma and Pa. I thought I could handle it myself. But I couldn't, and rumors began to fly. It was Mrs. Schlyterhaus, the housekeeper, who told me about the gossip."

Luke hugged her around the shoulders. "Rumors and gossip will abate, Sarah. Don't focus on it. What's important is for you to learn from this and move on. Forgive the captain. And yourself."

Looking down, Sarah nodded weakly. For so long she didn't know if she could forgive herself so easily. But because Luke's nuggets of wisdom had suddenly clicked in her mind, she could. And did. What's more, they helped her make sense of Richard's actions.

She wondered. Perhaps Richard really hadn't wanted to sign on to stay with Sinclair. Perhaps Richard was as much a victim of the captain as she was.

She caught her breath at the next thought. *Perhaps the captain used me as bait!*

The following day, Richard found it difficult to keep his mind on his work. He hadn't slept well last night, fretting over Sarah, and now as noontime approached, he felt exhausted. He hadn't seen the captain yet, so his suspicions had neither been confirmed nor alleviated. Had Captain Sinclair behaved as less than a gentleman where she was concerned? But why would she allow such a thing…unless she harbored amorous feelings for the man?

Steeped in his troubled thoughts, he barely heard the tiny bell above the door when it jangled.

"Richard?"

*Sarah?* He glanced up from the ledger in front of him. "Over here." Moments later the very subject of his thoughts strolled toward him. She appeared to be feeling better, although she barely afforded him a grin.

"It's another hot morning."

"Indeed." Seeing her made his heart ache. "What brings you here?"

She lowered her lashes. "I've been showing my brothers around town, and they've stalled in Miller's Gun Shop. So I thought I'd drop by and properly thank you again, Richard, for your assistance last night."

"You're welcome." He couldn't think of more to say.

"Well…"

"Well…" Was that regret in her eyes? Richard suddenly longed to pull her into his arms.

"I had a chance to do some soul searching last night."

"Glad to hear it." He rounded the counter, wondering what she discovered.

"But I reckon I shouldn't take up more of your time."

He had to smile at that country drawl of hers. "I'm not terribly busy." He moved closer to where she stood.

"I really just came by to say hello and to thank you once more."

"Again, I was glad to help."

She turned, heading for the door.

Richard followed and caught her hand as she reached for the brass handle. He gently pulled her back a few feet. "Sarah, about what you said last night…about not feeling as though you could come to me with your troubles." He drank in her every feature. "At the beginning of the summer I promised to be your friend, but I haven't lived up to it, have I?"

"I wouldn't say that. For the most part you've been like a brother."

Richard hated the comparison at once.

"You're about the sweetest man I know, save for my brother Luke."

*Sweet?* He bit down hard as dark waves of helplessness, anger, and jealousy rolled over him. Brotherly friendship and sweetness hadn't won the battle for Sarah's heart, and even his decision to stay on with the captain had backfired in his face, losing him Sarah's respect. And then there was the captain, wielding his peculiar powers, keeping him close while poisoning his relationship with Sarah. Richard suddenly saw things for what they were. He'd been manipulated into impotence.

*No more*, he told himself. *Never again.*

The door opened, jangling the bell as well as Richard's nerves.

"Sarah?"

She whirled around, and Luke McCabe entered the store. He removed his hat and gave Richard a nod. Then he extended his right hand.

Richard gave it a shake.

Luke turned to Sarah. "Jake and I are waiting on you."

"All right." She glanced at Richard and smiled. "Thank you…for everything."

"Of course." He inclined his head, keeping his tone casual and careful to not hint at his new resolve. The last thing he wanted was to run off Sarah and her brothers. "It's almost lunchtime." His gaze alighted on Sarah. "What say I take you and your brothers to Piper's for a sandwich? Since the café is below ground, it'll be nice and cool there."

"Really, Richard? You'd want to take us to lunch?"

"Why wouldn't I?"

"Well, because…" She suddenly seemed at a loss for words.

"Your offer for lunch is quite tempting," Luke said.

Sarah flicked a glance at him. "My brothers are never ones to turn down a meal."

"I thought so. Give me an hour to wrap things up here, and I'll meet you at Piper's. You know how to get there?"

"Yes." Her blue eyes glimmered with a show of gratefulness, and then she smiled.

*Smiled.*

Hope soared within him. It was a start.

He showed them out, and by the time he'd returned to the counter, an idea began to form.

The captain walked in just minutes before Richard planned to leave to meet the McCabes.

"Minding my business, eh, Richard?" With an easy smile, he strode to the counter and stood beside him. He set a hand on Richard's shoulder. "Anything I should know about?"

"Can I speak with you privately, sir?"

The spark of curiosity in his eyes preceded a curt nod. "Of course."

Richard prayed for wisdom as he followed the captain to his office. He closed the door. When the captain faced him, he figured there was no point in hedging.

"I want to ask Sarah and her brothers to stay at the farm until Monday morning. Of course, this means the children will come too. They enjoy the country, and this might be their last time to visit before school begins." He paced a short distance before meeting the captain's gaze again. "I think Sarah needs the break, and being at the farm will keep her brothers out of your way."

"Hmm, yes." Captain Sinclair shrugged out of his jacket and hung it up. "You've got a point. I'm up to my ears in Elise's list of demands." He wagged his dark head. "Acquiring Great Lakes Shipping is costing me plenty."

Richard couldn't muster an ounce of sympathy. "Back to Sarah—"

"Yes, that's fine. Ask her. And I hope you plan to convince her to stay."

"Yes, I do." But not the way the captain thought. While Richard cared deeply for the Sinclair children and knew they loved Sarah, he felt just as certain that working for the captain wasn't in her best interest.

"I won't be able to afford you extra time off what with the merger and the wedding both looming on the horizon."

"Well, I can't convince Sarah to stay if I never get a chance to see her."

The captain sighed. "I suppose that's true enough." He put his hands on his hips. "We'll try to work something out, but I can't promise."

"Very good. Thank you, sir." He moved to leave, but something deep and instinctive gripped him and kept him rooted to the floor. Then, before he could think better of it, he brought his right arm back and smashed his fist into Captain Sinclair's jaw.

The captain staggered backward a pace. Shock filled his gaze. His hand rubbed the bruised spot to the side of his chin. "What in blazes was that for?" A scowl crept across his face.

"I told you to stay away from Sarah, and I meant it."

The captain didn't reply, but something akin to respect settled over his features.

Richard turned on his heels and exited the office.

The cool air in Piper's restaurant flooded over Sarah the moment she and her brothers entered the establishment. She sighed a breath of relief. Jake and Luke removed their hats and wiped their perspiring brows with colorful bandanas.

"Don't know how hot it is outside till you come into a place like this." Luke glanced around. He squinted, adjusting to the dimmer lighting.

Sarah had passed this place from time to time but never stopped. Long-stemmed glasses hung upside down in wooden slats above the bar. Beyond it stood rows of tables covered with white linen cloths, and every one of them appeared to be occupied.

A gentleman approached them wearing a casual brown suit. "You wouldn't happen to be Mr. Navis's guests, would you?"

Sarah replied, "Yes, we are."

The greeter smiled. "He'll be here shortly. I have instructions to seat you. Come right this way."

Luke took her arm, and they followed the man through the upscale bar. Jake used his cane and limped behind them. They walked by other diners until they came to a spacious area and a round table that was large enough to seat more than four.

"Our best table." The greeter held out a chair for Sarah.

Almost at once, the waiter appeared, balancing a round, wooden tray, and deposited glasses of iced tea and water in front of them. Sarah hid a grin. Her brothers looked impressed. Leave it to Richard to go out of his way.

He arrived minutes later, and Sarah saw him nodding greetings to several other patrons as he made his way to their table.

"Your friend must be an important man, Sarah." Jake murmured the remark as he raised his glass of tea to his lips.

"Richard's position with the captain allows him to become friendly with many of Milwaukee's upper echelons. He has a reputation for being trustworthy and dependable."

"Well, my, my," Luke said with a grin.

Richard made it to their table, and as he shook Luke and Jake's hands, he winced. It wasn't obvious, but Sarah saw it and wondered if he'd injured his hand.

He claimed his place beside her. "I hope you don't mind, but I took the liberty of ordering for us. Beer-stewed bratwurst in onions and sauerkraut with a side of German potato salad."

Sarah laughed at her brothers' wary expressions. "It's a German sausage, cooked in beer. But don't worry. The alcohol in the beer evaporates during the cooking process. Sauerkraut is a kind of cabbage and…you'll enjoy this type of potato salad. It's made with a hot bacon dressing, vinegar, and mustard, so it's got a bit of a tang to it."

"Well, now, baby sister—" Jake smiled. "You've become quite the connoisseur of German cuisine."

She glanced at Richard. "I've gotten to sample different dishes each time Richard takes me to lunch. I'd say we've eaten at most of the establishments along Grand Avenue."

Richard agreed. "I'd say so." A spark of amusement entered his eyes, and Sarah didn't realize why until she glimpsed Jake's curious frown.

"I don't believe you mentioned all these luncheons in your letters to Ma and Pa, Sarah."

Her conscience pricked. "Oh, I'm sure I did." She thought over the many letters she'd written and destroyed. It was hard to recall which ones she actually mailed. "Didn't I?"

"I don't think so."

Their meals arrived, and Sarah exhaled in relief. Richard asked the blessing, and then they began eating.

"Sarah tells us you live on a farm west of the city." Luke sliced his bratwurst with his knife.

"That's right. I commute, and my father oversees the hired hands."

"Mr. Navis was wounded during the war." Sarah looked Jake's way. "Fought with a Wisconsin regiment at Vicksburg."

"Is that right?"

"I already told Mr. Navis about how our family had members on both sides of the battle lines, North and South."

"I'm just glad the war's over with," Jake said.

"Amen to that!" Luke took a drink of his tea. "So tell me, Richard, does your family raise livestock?"

"Yes." Richard took a swallow of water. "We grow corn and wheat primarily, but we harvest seasonal vegetables too."

"And speaking of food, Richard's mother is a marvelous cook," Sarah declared. "She has two kitchens—one in the basement so it's cool, like this restaurant. Every Sunday after church she prepares a large meal for neighbors and cousins. Made me feel right at home."

"Sarah, I *know* you didn't mention this in your letters." Jake narrowed his gaze.

"I meant to." She had a sinking feeling that she'd hear more about this later.

"Sounds like you're a man of faith, Richard." Luke's tone was easy.

"Yes, sir. I invited the Lord into my heart as a boy."

Sarah was pleased to see how her brothers approved. She'd known from the start that they'd like Richard.

"I also get the feeling that you've looked out for our baby sister this summer, and Jake and I are mighty obliged to you."

"That's right. We are." Jake sent Sarah a hint of a scowl. "It's practically a full-time job watching over her."

She rolled a shoulder and ignored him.

"It's been my pleasure."

"So much for being great acquaintances like you told us yesterday." Jake sat forward.

Bewildered, Sarah gazed at Richard.

"Actually, we've been good friends for most of the summer. But Sarah and I had a disagreement earlier in the month, and—"

Underneath the table, she tapped his boot with her foot. Her brothers didn't need to know the details.

But too late. Luke and Jake stared at her. Suddenly she didn't know what to say.

"It's entirely my fault," Richard began.

"A misunderstanding," Sarah added.

Dropping her gaze, she recalled how he said he loved her. Did he still? Or had he changed his mind once the gossip about her and the captain began to circulate?

"Sarah told us about the rumors flying around." Luke spoke just above a whisper. "I can tell you're not a man to believe hearsay."

"What rumors?" Richard seemed genuinely surprised.

Sarah jerked her gaze to Richard.

He looked into her eyes and shrugged.

"You really haven't heard?"

"Sarah, have I ever lied to you?"

"Well, no."

"Reckon you two need to have a conversation." Luke took the last bite of his lunch, cleaning his plate. "Now, that meal was some kind of good." He pushed his chair back and stood. "We'll be waiting outside."

Jake took the cue but didn't seem too enthused.

Alone at the table, silence hung between them.

Finally Sarah spoke up. "That day I got stranded after church. It was because the Schmidts said they didn't want to be seen in my company."

"Why would they say that?"

Sarah's cheeks flamed. "They saw Captain Sinclair kiss my hand that morning. He was trying to be amusing. But his actions caused the Schmidts to believe the gossip they'd heard about us. Then Mrs. Kingsley made insinuations as well. That's why I wired home. It's the reason I can't stay in Milwaukee."

A muscle worked in his jaw, and he flexed his wrist.

"Did you injure your hand working this morning?"

"I guess you could say that." He shook his head. "It's fine."

Sarah thought it looked a bit swollen, but she didn't press the issue.

A moment passed. "The captain wishes you'd stay and work for him." Richard paused. "I wish you'd stay too."

"I won't. I refuse. Not after the captain purposely sent a poor recommendation to Mr. Withers at the music academy in Chicago." Sarah took several long breaths. "That's why I wasn't offered the teaching position. It's the captain's fault!" She felt her turmoil coming on again.

Richard covered her hand with his. "Why didn't you tell me all this?"

"Would you have listened?"

He drew back as if she'd slapped him.

"I had no one to turn to. I figured everyone, like the Schmidts, who had heard the gossip wanted to disassociate from me—including your mother." Sarah softened her tone. "But then you explained she had reacted out of her own hurt feelings. However, I thought even you—"

"No." Richard shook his head. "Sarah, can you ever forgive me?"

"Yes, of course." She sensed his sincerity. Nevertheless, she pulled her hand free from his warm grasp. She enjoyed the feeling of her hand in his, but the fact remained: both he and the captain wanted her to stay. But the truth was suddenly crystal clear. Until Richard disentangled himself from Captain Sinclair, she could not consider a future with him. She wanted nothing more to do with a man like Sinclair.

"It's all water under the bridge, as the adage goes." Sarah didn't want any regrets. "In a little over four days, my brothers are taking me home for good."

# TWENTY-SEVEN

After lunch Richard walked up the wooden sidewalk with the McCabe brothers while Sarah browsed in a nearby hat shop. The hot sun beat down on them relentlessly, so they found a shaded area in which to continue waiting. Neither Luke nor Jake forged any meaningful conversation, and Richard had a feeling they were waiting for him to explain himself in regard to their sister. He didn't have a problem with it. He felt he owed them that much. What's more, he needed Sarah's brothers' help. It seemed doubtful that she'd accept the invitation to stay on the farm for the next four days unless Luke and Jake were behind the idea.

"About Sarah..."

The brothers leaned forward with interest.

"I think I fell in love with her the day I met her."

"Seems to me that she likes you well enough," Luke said. "But you should have wrote our pa."

"Hear me out." He held up a hand.

The McCabes agreed to that much.

"Sarah said I'm one of the best friends she ever had. The trouble is, I don't want to be Sarah's *friend*." Judging from the brothers' expressions, it seemed they understood. "Had she consented to a courtship, I would have written to your father immediately and asked his permission. On my honor. But our relationship never got to that point." He gave his head one sad wag. "I hold the captain partially responsible. Sarah took his trifling seriously, and I think she's enamored by him—well, at least she was. Weeks ago I had made a deal with the captain, and he promised he'd cease all inappropriate behavior where Sarah was concerned."

"What sort of deal?" Jake asked.

Staring down the block, seeing nothing in particular, Richard replied, "I agreed to continue working for the captain after my indentureship ends. Before that, I had intended to live out my ambition to farm. There's good money in harvesting wheat." He gestured, deciding to spare the McCabes the details. "Anyway, farming is what I love to do."

"You sacrificed your future for Sarah?" Dismay tinged Jake's tone.

"Partly so, yes. I also have my parents to think about. My father's an invalid and will likely need medical attention in the future."

Each McCabe brother nodded in understanding.

"But Sarah told me she could never imagine herself living on a farm. She desires the city life. I figured she'd be glad when I told her my decision to accept the captain's offer, but instead I think she was disappointed in me for caving in to his demands." He momentarily tightened his jaw. "I've been miserable on all accounts since making the decision, and then last night it seemed obvious to me that the captain hadn't kept his part of the bargain." Richard flexed his fist. His right hand was swollen and sore, but socking the captain was worth the pain—especially after learning about the gossip the Schmidts spread. It had devastated Sarah, and it was all Captain Sinclair's fault.

Richard felt like punching the man again.

But he wouldn't.

Luke responded with a long, slow whistle.

"Would you like us to step in to talk to Sarah about this?" Jake asked.

"If you think it's best, although—" he glanced from Jake to Luke— "I do have a plan."

"Let's hear it." A smile split Luke's face.

Richard set his hands on hips. "I figure I have four days in which to win Sarah's heart. It's my last chance. However, the captain is a distraction, and I feel strongly that if she could get away from his home and all the goings-on there, she might reexamine her heart. Deep down I believe she loves me too. She just hasn't realized it yet." He couldn't conceal a confident grin. "So I wondered if you'd accept my invitation to stay on our farm tomorrow through Sunday. I already obtained the captain's permission for Sarah to take the children there for a long weekend. The kids enjoy it there. So does Sarah. And it might be the last time they can all visit, what with Sarah's leaving on Monday and school resuming for Gabe, Michael, and Libby next week."

"Hmm...what do you say, Jake?"

"I don't know." His brown eyes inspected Richard from head to toe. "If things work out and he marries Sarah, he'll take her off our hands," he conceded.

The two chuckled, and Richard shook his head at them both. Then he saw Sarah leave the hat shop. "You'd best decide quickly, 'cause here she comes."

Silence.

Richard couldn't help feeling a mite desperate. "No hotel fees to pay. Home-cooked meals. The bunkhouse will be comfortable enough for us fellows."

Jake set a hand on his shoulder. "We accept."

Once they'd said their thank-yous and good-byes to Richard, Sarah took her brothers for a stroll along the Lake Michigan shoreline. They ambled at a slow pace so Jake could keep up. But after some time, his leg began to ache.

"Let's sit over on that bench a spell." He nodded several feet away.

Claiming the spot between her brothers, Sarah found the view breathtaking. Endless sky and wide water.

She adjusted her skirts, but suddenly she began feeling hemmed in...and she knew the park bench was plenty long enough.

She shifted from side to side. Her brothers wouldn't budge. Finally she pushed her elbows into her their sides, sensing they were up to no good. A game of intimidation. She knew it all too well.

"Move, you big oafs!"

Laughing, they inched over slightly.

She sent a hooded look to Luke, then Jake. They had removed their unstylish jackets so they could enjoy the cool breeze on this torrid August afternoon. Sarah noticed they both could use new dress shirts as well as suits. But they really had no need of good clothes in the dusty town of Silverstone, Arizona.

Pinned between them, their powerful arms blocking any escape, Sarah ceased her struggles. "All right. What do you want?" They couldn't be blackmailing her into doing their chores like they did when they were kids.

"Didn't I tell you this was going to be fun, Jake?"

"You sure did. I just didn't know how much."

They did so enjoy torturing her.

Sarah gazed at the azure sky and followed it to the horizon where the deep blue of Lake Michigan began. "What do you want?" She made her tone sharper this time.

"We want to know about Mr. Richard Navis." Jake settled back. "And don't forget any details, baby sister. Luke and I noticed his interest in you last night. And today at lunch."

"I'm not a baby."

"She's right, Jake." Luke folded his arms. "Start talking, Sissy."

She sighed. Sarah didn't mind telling her brothers about Richard. It simply annoyed her that they took such pleasure in extracting the information.

"As I said at lunch, Richard's been a good friend to me since I arrived in Milwaukee. He's been kind, considerate..." She recalled his kiss—her very first. And his concern last night. "He's sweet, caring..."

"Nice of him to pick up the tab for our lunch today," Jake said, staring out over the lake.

"And he's generous too," Sarah continued.

"A Christian man, open about his faith." Luke bobbed his head. "I like that."

"I knew you would." She smiled in spite of herself. "Richard said he loved me, but I don't know how I feel about him, so I never wrote to our folks about him."

"Pa will probably tell him to get in line behind a dozen other bucks in Jericho Junction." Jake chuckled.

Luke laughed.

"You two make me so mad!" Sarah pushed at them again.

"Simmer down now." Jake still had a smile on his face that slowly began to fade. "Sarah, it's simple. You either love someone or you don't."

"But it's not that easy for me. Sometimes love and hate feel the same." She thought of the captain and how he sparked her emotions, both good and bad. "Richard's a simple man. He wanted to farm, but he let himself get bamboozled, and he signed on with the captain indefinitely."

"Ever think on why he might of done it?"

She had her suspicions, but she could only declare what she knew. "He told me he signed on because the captain made him an offer he couldn't refuse. It irks me that the captain got his way. Richard should have stood up to him." She shrugged. "Now I think Richard hopes to convince me to sign on with the captain too. Except I won't. I love the children, that's true, but I can't get past the captain's trickery and inappropriate behavior." Memories of the times he gathered her in his arms caused her to feel ashamed and angry with herself for allowing such concessions. "I must admit, I've relished living in the captain's house and being surrounded by beautiful things. I like walking downtown. I like the feel of a new store-bought gown, and I enjoy the theater and eating in restaurants."

"Just think how much all that same money spent could fund missionaries."

Luke's remark plucked chords of remorse in Sarah's heart. She'd hoarded the money she'd earned this summer, spending some of it on herself, but sending none back home. "You're right. It could have been better spent on furthering God's kingdom. I've been very selfish." She sighed. "Do you see why I can't even trust myself, much less the captain?"

Her brothers sat silently beside her for several seconds. She didn't sense judgment or disappointment from them. Somehow she sensed they understood.

"We-ell," Jake drawled, "I reckon it doesn't matter anyway, hoity-toity living or a simpler, country life." He stood and stretched. "You're coming home with us, baby sister."

Again, a sense of failure, weighty and dejecting, filled her being.

"In the meantime," Jake continued, "I'm mighty glad for Richard's invite to stay at his farm the next four days."

"What?" Sarah snapped to attention. "What invitation?"

"Oh...guess it came while you were in that fancy hat shop." Luke grinned like a fat cat.

Jake continued. "Richard says the children love the farm, and—"

"And did I mention *sneaky* when I listed Richard's attributes?" Sarah pouted.

Her brothers both chuckled.

"I prefer the city to the Navises' farm, well-maintained as it is. That's part of the trouble between Richard and me."

"We prefer the farm," Jake said.

Sarah folded her arms. She hated the feeling of being tricked and coerced. As an adult, she wanted to make her own decisions.

Both her brothers laughed now.

*They think they are oh-so smart.*

Moments later all traces of teasing quickly melted away from Jake's rugged features. "Seriously, Sarah, considering the rumors flying around this city about you and the captain, I'm glad for Richard's invitation. He's right. There's too much distraction in that household, and he's already obtained the captain's permission for you to take the kids to the farm. It might be the last time you all get to visit there together."

"Yes, I suppose that's true." Sarah would leave come Monday, and the children began school on Wednesday. "The children have so much fun there." And it might serve as the perfect time to tell the Sinclair kids that she was leaving. She had put off telling them for far too long, dreading their reaction, not wanting it to sway her from her decision to leave.

"And that means that while you're on Sinclair's time clock, you'll be safe from his charms and under my watchful eye." Luke arched a decided brow.

"Mine also," Jake declared.

Sarah rolled her eyes and borrowed a word from Libby and Rachel's vocabulary. "Goodie." Except she sounded like a wind-up toy on one of its last turns.

# Twenty-Eight

The next morning Sarah reported for duty at seven o'clock sharp. Her brothers accompanied her. She found the children at the dining room table eating breakfast. Captain Brian Sinclair occupied one end. Sarah introduced her brothers to the children. Gabe and Michael perked up when they heard Luke and Jake had recently come from the Arizona Territory.

"Please, sit down and join us. All of you." The captain swept his arm over the group.

"Thank you, sir." Sarah's stomach growled hungrily as she spied Isabelle's waffles topped with fresh strawberries and whipped cream.

The captain stood and politely held Sarah's chair. She gave him a curt but grateful smile.

"Kind offer." Luke grinned. "Thank you."

"Yes. Much obliged, Captain Sinclair." Jake offered an amicable nod before he and Luke pulled out chairs and sat down.

"You're entirely welcome." A lock of the captain's ebony hair fell across his forehead, giving him a rakish appearance.

Sarah wished she hadn't noticed.

They each silently prayed over their food.

"Daddy, we forgot to pray before eating." Libby quickly squeezed her eyes closed. "Thank You, God, for this food, and for my daddy, and for Miss Sarah, and for Isabelle—"

"Just hurry up and give thanks, Libby." Michael's impatience flattened his tone. "I want to finish eating."

"And for Rachel, and Mrs. Schlyterhaus too. Amen."

The boys heaved a sigh of relief.

"Thank you for that nice prayer, my darling." The captain reached over and gave her small hand an affectionate squeeze. "As for you gentlemen, I mean to show you that there are no hard feelings."

"Likewise," Jake said.

"Are you two cowboys?" Gabe threw the question out to Sarah's brothers.

"Never herded cattle myself." Luke sent the boy a grin. "No."

Sarah smiled. "Luke, I think your checked shirt with that dark blue bandana tied around your neck is more fitting for Silverstone than Milwaukee."

"Well, my apologies for any offense."

"None taken, I assure you." The captain looked at his eldest. "Did you know both these men are not only from the Arizona Territory, but they're reverends—like Sarah's father?"

"Wow." A derisive gleam entered Gabe's eyes. "You get to yell at a whole churchful of people every Sunday."

Michael snickered.

"I look mighty mean, don't I?" Luke lowered his head to cover his grin.

"You had me shaking in my boots Tuesday evening... *Reverend.*"

Sarah grimaced at Captain Sinclair's cynical rebuff.

Luke seemed to take it in stride. "Just pointing out a few erring ways. Can't blame a reverend for that."

"I suppose I can't."

Sarah kept her gaze averted from the captain's. No more being lured by his smiles and manipulations. She'd been such a fool. Why hadn't she seen through him sooner? She set aside her fork. Suddenly she wasn't hungry anymore.

Alone in her hotel room last night, she'd prayed for God's wisdom to touch her heart. She knew now that her feelings for the captain had been a powerful mixture of physical attraction and manipulation. But what of her feelings for Richard?

She thought of his strong arms, his warm blue eyes, his kiss... Yes, she was physically attracted to him too. But was that all? Was that enough?

What was true love, anyway? What did the fabric of it feel like?

Rough? Smooth? Velvety soft? Would she recognize it immediately, or would she have to browse awhile? Would true love fit her perfectly or be like a store-bought gown in need of alterations?

But the main question plaguing her thoughts was—Had true love come along already…and gone?

The sweet smell of long grass and golden wheat wafted on a torrid breeze. Swinging leisurely with Rachel on her lap, Sarah watched the sun sink into patches of pink and gray.

"Been a long, hot day." Mr. Navis wiped his brow, then sipped from the glass of lemonade in his hand. He wore his shirtsleeves rolled up and sat in his wheelchair. His thick white-blond hair was cropped short, and its spiky top reminded Sarah of a harvested cornfield. "I expect Richard will be home soon. The captain must have found something for him to do to keep him out so late."

"I'm sure he did." Sarah figured it would likely get worse too.

Only she and Mr. Navis and a very sleepy Rachel were on the porch. "Tell me, Mr. Navis…why did Richard accept the captain's offer?"

"You don't know?"

"All Richard said was that the captain made him an offer he couldn't pass up. I figured money won out over Richard's desire to farm. Captain Sinclair told me every man has his price." Sarah didn't think she'd ever forget those words. She wished Richard hadn't proved their cunning employer correct.

"Well, it's a little more complicated than that. I'll let Richard be the one to tell you. But I'd say given the alternative, he made the right choice. My son's a smart man with a heart of pure gold."

"Yes, he is that all right." But why had he given in to the captain? Could her suspicions be true—that the captain had used her as bait?

Just then Sarah's brothers stepped out onto the porch.

Rachel yawned, so Sarah decided to carry the little one up to bed. Libby had already fallen asleep for the night. Gabe and Michael, on the other hand, were chasing around the yard with a few of the Stafford boys.

"I'll carry her for you, Sarah." Luke held out his hands and peered at Rachel. "Will you come to me, sweetie?"

She nodded, and Luke swept her up into his arms. He headed for the door, and Sarah followed him into the house and up the staircase. Sarah pointed to the small room on the left. Twin beds with painted white headboards took up most of the space.

"Hugs and kisses! Hugs and kisses!"

"Shh, you'll wake Libby," Sarah whispered.

After a squeeze around Luke's neck and a peck on the cheek, Rachel flung herself at Sarah. "I love you, Miss Sarah."

"Love you too." The words made her heart squeeze. If she loved the Sinclair kids, how could she leave them?

She turned to Luke. "This is our nightly routine." With a glance at Luke, Sarah held Rachel for several long moments, then tucked her into bed.

"Good night, honeybun."

"Honeybun with jam." Rachel giggled.

Sarah smiled and tenderly brushed her wispy bright curls off her forehead. "Sleep tight, honeybun with jam."

A dreamy smile on her face, Rachel turned on her side and closed her eyes. Sarah quickly checked on Libby, kissing the top of her head. When she finally strode toward Luke, she noticed him looking around the room curiously.

"Lots of room in this house for only three people."

"Mr. and Mrs. Navis wanted their quiver full of blessing. God only gave them Richard."

"Maybe Richard will have a brood of his own someday."

Sarah didn't know why the idea caused her to blush. She was only too glad for the long shadows in the stairwell as they made their way back outside.

"I can see that you love the Sinclair children, Sarah."

"I do. I suppose one can't help it. They're terrific children, and the girls are so sweet."

"I'll say."

Downstairs, Sarah saw Luke smile beneath the dim lamplight in the living room.

"Rachel reminds me of Maggie."

Sarah nodded. She missed her niece—and nephews too.

Luke paused. "Speaking of... Valerie's about ready to give birth to that next baby. She hasn't had an easy time of it, either."

"No?" Sarah grew concerned.

"Ma's doubly glad you're comin' home. Valerie could use another set of hands."

Sarah supposed that lessened the shame of returning to Jericho Junction. "Well, if I'm needed—"

"You are."

He guided her to the front door. They'd just set foot on the porch when the sound of drumming hoofbeats suddenly replaced chirping crickets. Soon a lone figure of a man astride a horse came into view.

*Richard.*

The pack of boys sprinted across the front lawn to meet him. Watching them, Sarah smiled. She hadn't see Richard all day, as he'd been busy working for the captain. He'd hitched a team to the two-seated wagon this morning and tethered his gelding, Poco, behind it. All so Luke could drive it back to the farm with all of them packed in comfortably. Richard's thoughtfulness never ceased to amaze Sarah.

*He's a special friend.*

She squinted into the encroaching darkness and saw him rein in near the children. He reached into the pocket of his lightweight suede jacket and removed what appeared to be candy sticks. He had a fistful, enough for each child. Sarah wagged her head. How he spoiled those kids.

"I thought I heard Richard's approach." Mrs. Navis stepped out of the house and onto the porch.

"He's been detained by a pack of urchins."

Mrs. Navis laughed softly. "So I see." She set a hand on Sarah's shoulder. "By the way, I have a bar of soap ready for Gabriel and Michael. They can wash up in the pond before getting into their nightclothes."

"Good idea." She'd seen the dirt on those two boys. "I don't know how they can race around in this hot weather." Looking over her shoulder at her brothers, she asked, "Were you both so active? I can't recall."

"Are you kidding?" Jake chuckled. "Heat didn't bother us."

Luke's rumble of a laugh confirmed the remark. He stood. "Mrs. Navis, would you care to sit down?"

"No, thanks. I need to get Richard's dinner warmed up. I'm sure he's hungry."

"Can I help you?" Sarah asked.

"If you'd like." Sarah figured it was as close to a yes as she'd get.

Following her into the house, Sarah wished she could be of more help. Mrs. Navis hadn't sat down for hours. She'd been busy in the kitchen making dinner, serving the meal, then washing dishes. She insisted no one lend a hand. Afterward she'd gone out to the bunkhouse to ready it for Richard, Luke, and Jake.

"Mrs. Navis, please take a seat here at the kitchen table. I know how to warm Richard's food."

"I'm not tired, Sarah. But you've been chasing after those Sinclair kids all afternoon. You take a seat."

She shook her head. "I'm fine."

Mrs. Navis got busy.

"Thank you for allowing my brothers, the Sinclair children, and me to impose on you like this." Packing the children this morning, Sarah had realized that she did indeed need a break. This country retreat before heading home would do her wonders.

"It's a blessing for me to have guests in my home, Sarah." Mrs. Navis sent her a smile. "So I don't mind fussing one bit. I get lonesome here when it's just Marty and me, not that he's bad company. But he doesn't like me hovering or bending his ear."

Sarah could understand how Mrs. Navis might feel lonely here on the farm. "As the youngest of four, plus a brother-in-law and a sister-in-law, a niece and nephews, and the daughter of a pastor whose congregation feels free to drop in at any time, I can tell you solitude rather appeals to me."

Richard's mother barely grinned, and she kept her gaze from meeting Sarah's. It had been that way all day. A cool distance between them.

Sarah felt the need to set things straight. "Mrs. Navis, I'm sorry I hurt your feelings. I had tried to be honest with Richard, and I know I hurt him...and you...but it's what I hoped to avoid in the first place."

"Of course. I understand." At last her gaze met Sarah's. "I accept your apology. Thank you." She returned to heating Richard's dinner of sliced smoked ham and potato pancakes. "I must confess to hoping you and my son would marry and I'd have a...a daughter. Then grandchildren. Filling up this home with warmth and laughter." She shook her head. "It was wishful thinking and selfish on my part." A smile came from over her shoulder as she sent a glance Sarah's way. "And unrealistic, of course."

"Of course." Compassion mixed with an odd sense of disappointment filled Sarah.

A while later Richard strode in after tending to his horse. Sarah thought he looked no worse for wear, considering his long day.

He sauntered over and kissed his mother's cheek. "Well, now, I could get used to coming home and finding the two of you in the kitchen."

Sarah rolled her eyes. "I always admired your subtlety, Richard." To her surprise, she found herself easily drawn back into the old banter, like when they'd first become friends.

He grinned.

"How about some dinner?"

"No, thanks, Mama. The captain took me to dinner tonight. We had much to discuss. I had some apologizing to do. It's amazing that the captain still holds me in high regard. After how I behaved yesterday, he could have demoted me to a dockworker. But we ironed things out."

"I'm pleased to hear it, son." Mrs. Navis gave him an approving smile.

Sarah grew all the more curious. What had happened?

"Well, if you don't want any supper, I guess I'll put the food away."

"Mrs. Navis, I'll put the food away. I insist. You go out on the porch and put your feet up."

"Mama, I'm in agreement with Sarah. She's insisting, after all."

Taking off her apron, Mrs. Navis crossed the room and hung it up. "Seeing as I'm licked, I guess I have no choice." She sent them each a smile.

Sarah grinned and began the cleaning process. Over the summer she'd become familiar with Mrs. Navis's kitchen and the way the woman liked things done.

Richard leaned back against the counter.

Sarah slid her glance to him. "What happened yesterday? Why did you owe him an apology?"

Richard chewed the side of his lip in thought and then sent her a smile. He reached over and brushed a few strands of her hair off her face. "It's nothing you need to concern yourself with. But, um…I was wondering if you'd like to go to the outdoor theater with me tomorrow night. Lina and Tim will meet us there. Your brothers are welcome to join us. And my mother will be here for the children."

So Richard was going to pour on all his charm in an effort to keep her here. Just like Sinclair. Her back stiffened and she turned away. "I don't think that's a good idea. I'm leaving on Monday, Richard. It's too late."

Tears stung her eyes, and she ran from the room.

# Twenty-Nine

All of Richard's plans to woo Sarah one last time were toppling around him. Not only had she refused his offer to attend the outdoor theater, but also the next morning Captain Sinclair announced that he wanted a full accounting of Great Lakes Shipping's books, and Richard needed to oversee it. There wasn't really a need for it, none that Richard could see—at least not yet. He'd reminded the captain that he had company waiting for him. But that hadn't mattered to that blackheart. Richard was seeing the man for what he was, and yet Richard knew he had to honor his employer's wishes. He'd just rededicated himself to doing so after yesterday's luncheon with the captain.

Seemed the Lord wanted to put that new decision to the test.

Richard hadn't gotten home at all Friday night and bunked in the store's upper chamber. He was up with the dawn and pored over the bookwork all day Saturday. And it wasn't until the late afternoon sun hung in the western sky like a red round ball that Richard finally rode home. He'd lost precious time to win over Sarah—and the captain knew it. Perhaps he'd realized Sarah's resolve to leave and, in a pique, decided to exercise his last bit of power by denying Richard the chance to win her.

As he neared his farm, he heard such hilarity that it forced a smile to his lips in spite of his dark mood and weariness. At the driveway, he dismounted and led the horse up the graveled path. He stared into the direction of the commotion and saw the Sinclair children swimming around in the pond. Luke and Jake were floating on their backs. And his father? Richard blinked. Pops was up to his armpits in water. Chuckling, Richard had to admit it looked like fun. It'd been another scorching August day. Maybe he'd have to jump in with them.

Just then he saw Luke emerging from the pond. Seeing Richard, he waved as he made his way to the front porch. No more than a minute later a scream split the air. Richard tensed, stopping in his tracks.

"Don't you dare, Luke McCabe! Put me down!"

Luke descended from the porch with Sarah slung over one shoulder.

"Luke, I'm warning you. When we get home, I'm telling Pa."

Her protests went ignored. Instead the men guffawed, and Gabe and Michael laughed uproariously. Libby jumped up and down, clapping her hands.

"Don't you dare throw me in that pon—"

A huge splash. Next a shriek of indignation.

Richard chuckled the rest of the way to the barn. Poor Sarah. No wonder she had such spirit. She wouldn't have survived her childhood otherwise.

With Poco rubbed down, watered, and fed, Richard trekked to the house. Halfway there he happened upon Sarah, wringing her skirts in the grass. Looking up, she did a double take when she saw him.

"I didn't hear you come home." She seemed embarrassed.

"I believe you were just entering the pond as I turned in the driveway."

Her expression darkened. "That insufferable brother of mine!"

Richard dared not even grin.

"But I must admit the cool water felt rather good."

He noticed the way her soggy dress clung to her shapely form. He cleared his throat and steered his mind on to other things. "Would you like some towels?"

"Don't bother. I'll get them myself." She turned to leave.

"Sarah."

The tone of his voice stopped her. "The sun and wind will dry you. Won't you stay with me a moment—we were friends. Remember? Why does that have to change?"

She stared at him for a moment, then gave a small nod.

Richard reached for her hand and led her up the wooded hill

behind the house. At the top, the hot wind whipped through the long grass and skipped across the fieldstones. He gestured around, at the view of fields and orchards and his home below. “This is one of my favorite spots in the world.”

Sarah gazed out over the scene. “It's beautiful,” she agreed. “So peaceful. I've really come to love it here.”

Sarah walked to a large granite-like rock and leaned against it. She pulled the pins from her hair and shook her head. Her blonde hair tumbled down past her shoulders. Watching her, Richard felt mesmerized.

Sarah faced him just as he sat on the large fieldstone. Her expression appeared both intent and sincere. “Will you write to me in Jericho Junction?”

“Do you want me to?”

“Yes. I think so.”

“Then, yes. I will.” Richard thought he'd won a milestone victory. At least she didn't want to leave Milwaukee and sever ties with him completely.

Several moments passed. “Will you tell me why you accepted the job with the captain?”

Richard was startled at the question, but he shrugged to put her off. “What does it matter?”

“It's been bothering me, Richard. The captain said everyone can be bought. Everyone has his price.” She stepped closer. “What's your price, Richard?”

He tipped his head, unsure of what she meant.

“At first I thought it was the money. But you're not lured by money. You see it come and go all day long in your ledgers. So what could the captain possibly have used to hook you into signing on after your indentureship?” Sarah stood just inches away. With her eyes narrowed, she searched his face. “He must have hung something over your head. Something sacred, special...”

Richard touched her hair, allowing his fingers to run down its length.

"Or maybe...he used someone...someone you...you love."

Did he tell her that she'd arrived at the correct conclusion?

"Me? Was it me?" She gazed at him, searching his eyes. "Did the captain coerce you by threatening you with me?"

"Now Sarah..." Richard's arms encircled her waist, and he pulled her to him. He could feel the dampness of her clothes as it penetrated his shirt. "I'm a man. I make my own decisions."

She lifted her chin. Questions pooled in her blue eyes.

Richard stroked her petal-soft cheek. "I have more than just myself to think about. My father may need future medical treatment."

"Mm...so your family's financial security was the promise, but what was...*the price*?"

"Are you inquiring over my salary?"

"You know I'm not." Her persistence amazed him.

"All right, if you must know, the captain agreed to be a complete gentleman where you're concerned if I signed on with him."

Tears collected in her eyes—but something else glimmered there too. Was it respect?

"So it *was* me. I had a feeling that was it. Oh, Richard, because of me you're trapped in a position you hate."

"Sarah, it was my choice, and I made my decision based on what the captain presented to me. Can't you understand? His promise of good behavior was merely icing on the cake. Besides, I couldn't allow him to continue trifling with you."

She brought her head up and looked at him. "So you did know about it?"

"I guessed, but I'm so sorry I left you alone to deal with it."

"You have nothing to be sorry about." Her body tensed. "I despise him, Richard."

"Don't." He wished she didn't feel anything for the captain. Although he thought he might despise the man too, especially after this weekend. "You'll only hurt yourself by allowing such negative emotions to take root." He ran his hands through her hair. It felt like spun silk. "I love you, Sarah." Would she ever know just how much?

Leaning forward she touched her lips to his and murmured, "I know."

He couldn't help giving in to the kiss. He pulled her close, desire spreading through him like wildfire. It was several long seconds before sanity returned, then every ounce of his willpower to gently push her away. "Let's not get into trouble here, Sarah. I don't want you to regret giving in to your emotions with me—like you did the captain."

She took a step back. "You're right. I'm sorry."

Richard clasped her wrists. He still battled his own feelings and couldn't completely let her go. "You're a passionate young woman. I've always sensed and admired that quality about you." He meant it as a compliment.

A pretty pink crept into her cheeks.

"I find it encouraging that you enjoy kissing me."

"I confess that I do enjoy it." She lowered her gaze.

At first he felt pleased, but then a blade of jealousy knifed him. He thought of how Sarah had initiated the kiss just now. An open invitation. He'd managed to remain a gentleman, but he didn't think the captain would refuse such an offer. Had Sarah drawn the line at kissing? Had the captain dared to cross it?

Richard clenched his jaw. What had the captain said—when Sarah looked up at a man in such a way it was his undoing? Did he have firsthand experience? Of course he had. Richard glimpsed Sarah's come-hither expression on occasion too, except he'd fooled himself into thinking that she reserved it for him.

"But perhaps it's not me, per se. Perhaps you just enjoy the kissing."

She gasped, and the next thing Richard heard was the slap of her palm connecting with his cheek.

"I reckon it's a good thing I'm leaving Monday morning," she spat out.

"I *reckon* it is." He was so angry he couldn't face her, but from the corner of his eye he saw her spin around.

"And about writing to me... don't bother!"

With that, she ran in the direction of the house.

The church service on Sunday morning did wonders for Sarah. She'd been reminded of what love is. The pastor read from First Corinthians chapter thirteen. Love suffers long and is kind. Love does not envy. Love doesn't vault itself. It is not puffed up. Most of all, *love never fails.*

Sarah repented as she allowed God's words of love to shine through her. She'd been selfish, thinking only of what she wanted from others and not thinking of how God might want to love them through her.

As she prayed, God's peace filled her, and then it wasn't hard to rejoice and worship. She glanced down the pew at Richard. He seemed stoic. By all accounts a different man from the one she'd first met. And how unfortunate that their anger at each other came on the heels of the stirrings of love she felt deep inside when she'd kissed him. Not only was she attracted to him, but also she knew he was in most ways a good and honorable man, a believer, a hard worker, a son who honored his parents and treated the people around him with respect. And most of the summer he'd been a good friend to her.

But how could she love a man who might as well have accused her of living up to the gossip?

The service ended, and as if driving the dagger further into her heart, Richard carefully avoided her as he exited the white clapboard chapel. The Schmidts and others stayed clear of her too. Lina and Tim, however, proved themselves loyal friends, and even Mrs. Schlyterhaus walked across the churchyard to say hello. Sarah introduced them to Luke and Jake.

It was sometime later that she headed for the Navises' wagon. Bethany Stafford caught up to her.

"You just missed meeting my brothers."

"Perhaps later." Bethany sounded breathless. "Do you think there's room for me to ride home with all of you today?"

"Are you sure you want to be seen with me? Some of these people act like I've got the bubonic plague."

"Ignore it."

"I'm trying. But it's not that easy."

"Oh, Sarah..." Bethany looked pained as she lifted the hems of her brown skirt to step over some dung.

"I'm sorry. I shouldn't have snapped at you. It's not your fault." Sarah sighed. "It's a beautiful day." She forced herself to concentrate on the positive.

"I wish we could have gotten to know each other better. You're beautiful, vivacious, talented—everything I wished I could be."

"Please don't idolize me. I'm not worth it."

"You mean you're only human."

"I guess that's a good way of putting it." Sarah picked at her lace gloves. "My sister Leah always says 'pretty is as pretty does.'" Glancing at Bethany, she couldn't help but grin. "You remind me of her, my older sister."

"I'll take that as a compliment."

"Please do." Sarah's smile broadened, and she realized she missed her sister. "As for enough room in the wagon, Bethany, we'll make room."

"I appreciate it. My little brother has a stomachache, so my parents took him and the other children home before church ended. But I'd like to come to your farewell party this afternoon."

"Farewell party?"

"Mrs. Navis and Lina planned it. Did I give away a surprise?"

"Those two." Sarah gave a wag of her head. "One would think they'd have enough to do in preparation for Lina's wedding."

Bethany flashed a shy smile. "Lina and Tim's wedding will be quite the occasion."

"I'm sure." Sarah regretted that she wouldn't be in Milwaukee for the special event, although she knew that Lina had asked Bethany to be a bridesmaid.

Turning, she eyed Bethany curiously. There was much she didn't know about this younger lady. Sarah had been too absorbed in caring for the Sinclair kids and sorting out her tangled feelings for the captain and Richard.

Well, that would change now.

"Pardon my curiosity, but I've noticed there's a lot of years between you and your younger brothers and sisters. And you once mentioned your stepmother."

"Yes, my mother died when I was eight. My father remarried."

"I'm sure losing your mother was very hard for you."

She nodded. "It was. But God sent a lovely woman into my dad's and my life. She's my mother now."

Sarah thought Bethany had more to say so she kept silent.

"But sometimes I feel like the governess." Bethany's cheeks pinked at the admission. "I've been thinking you and I have a lot in common. It's too bad we couldn't have gotten better acquainted."

"I'm not leaving until tomorrow," Sarah quipped.

Bethany laughed in a way that made her gray eyes glimmer. In that moment she looked downright…*beautiful.*

Luke and Jake approached the wagon.

Sarah made the appropriate introductions. "Bethany Stafford, meet my brothers, Jake and Luke McCabe. They're both ministers in the Arizona Territory."

Jake politely removed his hat. "It's a pleasure, Miss Stafford."

Luke did the same. "Pleased to meet you." Then he just stood there grinning. If Sarah didn't know better, she'd say Luke had taken a shine to Bethany.

Suspicion filled her and Sarah folded her arms. Or was he up to something?

"May I be so bold as to inquire over your profession, Miss Stafford?" Luke asked.

"Oh, I don't have one." She kept her gaze lowered. "I help take care of my brothers and sisters. Our farm is next door to the Navises."

"I see. Have you ever thought about teaching?"

*So that's what he's up to. Recruitment.*

"Oh, yes. I think about it often." She lifted her chin. "In fact, I've talked to Richard's cousin Lina, who is a schoolteacher, about obtaining my certificate." Bethany gave a slight shrug and an embarrassed grin. "But…well, the funds just aren't there to send me to school."

"That's a shame. I think you'd make a fine teacher."

The compliment caused Bethany to blush.

"What say we get into the wagon?" Jake threw a thumb over his shoulder. "Richard's rounding up the children, and Mr. and Mrs. Navis are making their way over right now."

"Bethany is riding home with us."

"Well, that's fine." Luke smiled. "Allow me to help you into the wagon, Miss Stafford."

Sarah shook her head, amused. When they weren't being insufferable, her brothers could be quite charming.

# Thirty

Sarah glanced around the Navises' yard. An array of brightly colored summer flowers graced the garden bed near the back porch. A large cut of pork roasted over hot coals, filling the humid air with a smoky, mouthwatering scent. Tables lined with food stood beneath a tarp. Sarah learned her brothers had helped Richard erect it without her knowledge this morning. Sneaky, sneaky, every one of them. But more surprising were the number of friends that had come to say good-bye and wish Sarah well. The Barnes brothers, Lina and her folks, Bethany and two of her sisters, and even Mrs. Schlyterhaus and her friend from church were in attendance. And, of course, the Navises.

Sarah spied Richard near the fire pit. As much as the gathering warmed Sarah's heart, he wounded it. His avoidance pierced it through like a razor-sharp arrow. Time and again she tried to catch his eye in hopes they could settle their differences and enjoy their last afternoon together. But Richard never even glanced her way. He'd said he loved her, although his actions didn't clearly show it, and this wasn't the first time Sarah had questioned his profession.

But at least Jake and Luke seemed to be enjoying themselves. They conversed with Bethany and Mrs. Schlyterhaus near the food table.

"We'll eat soon." Mrs. Navis came up behind Sarah and touched her shoulder.

Sarah turned to her. "I don't know where I would have been these past months if it hadn't been for your kindness. Thank you."

"Oh, now, don't make me cry." She took on a brusque attitude. "Help me tell everyone to grab a plate and make a line near the fire pit. Richard will carve the meat. The other food's ready too."

"Yes, ma'am." Sarah stepped off the porch to do Mrs. Navis's bidding.

She made sure to stay out of Richard's way and managed to make plates for Libby and Rachel without having to traipse to the fire pit.

Later, after she'd eaten, Sarah collected the Sinclair children and directed them into the parlor. Then she told them the news.

"I'm leaving. My brothers are taking me home to Jericho Junction tomorrow morning."

"And me too?" Rachel's eyes lit up.

"No, honey. You can't come."

"But why?" The child wore a confused frown.

"You're leaving us?" Libby's dark eyes searched Sarah's face before tears welled up in them.

"Now, now…" Sarah sat on the floor and gathered the girls into her arms. "I was hired to be your governess for the summer months. It was always the plan that I'd leave come September."

"But our dad said you were staying." Gabe stood from the armchair in which he'd been sitting. "He lied!" Fists clenched, he added. "He lies and he forgets us all the time!"

"Gabe, no…" Why Sarah felt the need to defend the captain she couldn't guess. This mess was his doing. "Your father…well, he misunderstood my circumstances."

"No, he lied."

"Gabe, I'll not have you talking about your father in such a disrespectful manner."

"I hate him."

"Stop it, Gabe!" Sarah noted Michael's silence, although his dark expression matched his brother's.

"Please, don't go, Miss Sarah," Libby sobbed.

Rachel wagged her head. "Don't go."

"I'm sorry, but I must." She looked across the way at the captain's second eldest. "I wish you'd say something, Michael."

Determination weighed on his brow line. "If you leave, I'm stowing away in a ship and sailing all the way to Spain. I know how. My dad told me, and I've read adventure stories."

His adamant tone concerned Sarah. "You will not be a stowaway."

"I'll go with you, Mike," Gabe piped in. "But I'm going to France to become a famous artist."

"Stop this nonsense, both of you."

"If you're leaving, me and Mike are too."

"I don't want my brothers to go away." Libby cried all the harder.

"Don't go, Miss Sarah. Peeeeze, don't go." Rachel sniffed.

Things were getting out of control quickly, in Sarah's estimation.

Libby's breath came in quick successions. "Who will tuck me into bed at nighttime?"

"Rachel, don't cry. Libby, you either. You're big girls now." Sarah hugged them to her.

"What's going on here?"

Sarah recognized Richard's voice at once. She glanced at the doorway where he stood but said nothing. Another arrow of sorrow met its mark.

"Miss Sarah's leaving us." Gabe folded his arms. A hardened glint entered his eyes. In that split second, Sarah saw the captain, and it caused her to wonder if hurt and disappointment were the reasons he manipulated his world and everyone in it. Would Gabe follow in his father's footsteps?

"I know she's leaving." Richard's tone was flat.

"Mr. Navis is actually glad that I'm going." The words were out before she could stop them.

"That's not true, Sarah."

"Oh, so now you deign to speak to me?"

Before he could reply, Libby spoke up again. "Miss Sarah, why can't you marry Daddy instead of Mrs. Kingsley?"

Sarah's eyes darted to Richard, who kept a stony face. "Because I don't love your father, Libby. I believe a woman should love the man she's intending to marry. Like Miss Johnson loves Mr. Barnes."

Gabe snorted. "I heard my dad say that marriage is a business deal."

"Not so," Sarah replied.

"You mean he lied *again*?"

"No, Gabe. Your father is just plain *wrong* about marriage."

"I'm never getting married," Michael said. "My wife might die like Mom did."

Sarah's heart constricted painfully,

"Instead, I'm sailing the high seas."

"Me too." Gabe jerked his chin.

"You two are not running away. Understand?" Sarah sent them both a stern look.

"Why should you care? You're leaving."

"Don't go, Miss Sarah," Libby pleaded. "Don't go."

She glanced at Richard. No help there.

Sarah's gaze moved over the children's faces. She read sorrow, anger, and determination in their expressions. She had sensed they would take it hard and had known that they and they alone had the power to convince her to stay. So why hadn't the captain unleashed them on her before now? Is that why the captain had agreed to this weekend at the farm? Not because he expected Richard to convince her. No, he'd gambled on precisely this: his children talking her into staying.

Well, he'd won his gamble. Their threats, tears, and pleas bent her resolve. "All right." She held up her hands. "If I stay..." She eyed the boys. "Will you both stop this nonsense about running away and never bring up the subject again?"

"Hooray!" Gabe pumped his arms in victory.

"Now, wait...listen. My stay will be on a temporary basis."

"How long is temporary?" Michael wanted to know. Vulnerability shown in his dark eyes.

Richard spoke up. "Sarah, don't make promises you can't keep."

She gave Richard a pointed stare. "I don't have difficulty keeping my promises, unlike some men in this room."

He arched a brow and stepped forward. "Oh?"

"I clearly recall that a certain man promised to always be my friend. It was during the time I sprained my ankle. We sat on the back porch swing." She saw by his expression that he remembered.

Sarah shoved aside her injured feelings and focused on the children. "I'll have to discuss this matter of my staying with my brothers, and my pa will have to approve. But if all goes well, I'll stay until your father marries Mrs. Kingsley." She paused. "Unless your father hired a new governess." She turned to Richard and arched her brow.

He shook his head.

"Will you stay till Christmas?" Hope alighted on Libby's gaze. "And buy us presents?"

Sarah couldn't resist the girl's sweet face. "All right, until Christmas."

"Okay, deal." Gabe shoved Michael. "Next we'll get her to stay 'til Easter. Then forever."

"You're a chip off the old block," Sarah said with a grin. She didn't look at Richard to see if he found the quip amusing.

Gabe glanced at Sarah. "Just get one thing straight. I don't need a governess."

"Me either," Michael said.

Sarah gestured helplessly. "In that case, why do you want me to stay so badly?" She figured the answer had to do with caring for Rachel and Libby.

However, Michael's reply shook her soul.

"We want you to stay 'cause you're like a mom."

The afternoon progressed. Many of the guests, including Mrs. Schlyterhaus, left for their own homes as dark, ominous clouds began to form and a cooler wind blew through. Thunder rumbled off in the distance.

"Storm's comin'," Mrs. Navis said. "Let's get everything picked up and into the house."

Sarah gathered up dishes and walked with Lina into the kitchen.

"Did you know your brother Luke left to walk Bethany and her sisters home?"

"Just now?" Sarah peered at the sky. The clouds were moving fast.

"Yes. They left only minutes ago."

"They're probably running by now." A brilliant flash of lightning made Sarah grimace, but she put on a brave face for the girls who followed her around like puppies. "We'll stay away from the windows and pray that Luke and Bethany are safe from the storm."

Libby closed her eyes and folded her hands. "I pray, Jesus, that Reverend McCabe and Miss Bethany are safe... amen."

"Amen."

"Why, that was very sweet, Libby." Sarah felt proud of her.

Lina hugged the little girl. "Is there more to Luke's seeing Beth home, I wonder?"

"Could be." Sarah had observed him acting solicitous to Bethany all afternoon. Sarah hoped he wouldn't charm and manipulate Bethany just so she'd agree to go out West and become part of his and Jake's ministry. Sarah didn't see how that would be any different from the captain charming and manipulating her into becoming part of his so-called *family*.

Suddenly the space around them grew dark as night, and a strong gust of wind blew through the treetops outside the open bedroom window.

"I'm scared!" Libby cried.

"Me too!" Rachel covered her ears as a loud, deep rumbling rattled the windows. "I don't yike the thunder!"

"Don't worry." Sarah lit the lamp. "Jesus will take care of us."

"That's right." Lina pulled out a chair and sat down. "Let's tell stories while we wait for the storm to pass."

"Story about the free bears." Rachel clapped her hands.

"No, Sleeping Beauty!" Libby countered. "And the prince has to wake her up."

Just then, Mrs. Navis called to them. "Girls, Marty thinks it's a twister coming."

Terror shot through Sarah. She grabbed each child's hand while Lina extinguished the lamp. They hurried into the back hall where they met everyone else. Moving into the basement, they took cover in the summer kitchen under the house. Tim and Richard carried Mr.

Navis down. Jake and Gabriel grabbed each side of his wheelchair and lifted it down the steps.

"What about Luke?" Sarah felt suddenly panicked. "And Bethany?"

"They'll be fine." Jake slung an arm around her shoulders. "Luke's a quick thinker. He'll make sure they take cover."

Richard and Tim lowered Mr. Navis into his chair. Next Richard straightened his father's legs before draping a light blanket around them. Mrs. Navis lit two oil lamps. The room filled with a golden light.

Sarah had enjoyed cooking in the coolness of this room. Now she saw it as blessed shelter from the storm.

Richard dragged over several old barrels that served as seats for the men while the ladies took the chairs around the large, square worktable.

"Let's play some chess," Mr. Navis suggested with a challenging grin. "Who wants to be the first to play me?"

"I do." Gabriel accepted the challenge.

"I get to play next." Michael sidled up to the middle of the board game.

The game commenced. The boys' attention had been captured.

Sarah rocked Rachel while wooden beams overhead creaked from the force of the wind. Occasional thuds upstairs and the tinkling sounds of glass made Sarah wonder how the men could stay so calm. Her heart pounded out a hard, steady rhythm that reached her ears.

*Be still, and know that I am God…*

Words from the familiar psalm came to mind. Sarah whispered them to Rachel as the girl clung to her. Lina held and comforted Libby.

Richard sauntered over and hunkered in front of her. "Are you all right?"

Sarah nodded. She wanted to say more, but she knew Jake was carefully watching.

"Would you like a blanket? It's awfully cool down here."

"No, thank you."

Richard stood and then knelt near his cousin. He asked Lina the same questions. Sarah knew then that he'd only been acting out of kindness.

*Love never fails.*

Sarah held Rachel tighter, wondering if things could ever be normal between Richard and her. So many false starts. So many misunderstandings. Who could untangle it all?

At last the roar of the storm diminished, then ceased altogether. Richard and Tim left to investigate.

"It's all clear," Tim came back and announced.

As they walked out of the basement, Sarah saw that shafts of sunshine lit the entrance. The temperature had cooled at least twenty degrees, and now the angry dark clouds were blowing eastward, over the lake.

Once Mr. Navis had been carried upstairs, Richard, Tim, Gabriel, and Michael walked around the property, looking for damage. They came back nearly an hour later with Luke, reporting a few downed trees. But that was all.

"Nothing damaged at the Staffords' place either," Luke said.

Sarah touched his arm. "Did you make it to their house before the storm?"

"Just made it." Luke's blue eyes widened. "And down in their cellar, I found myself with a captive audience. I told them about Silverstone and shared my burden for the territories. Amazingly, I didn't bore anyone. Even the kids seemed interested in what I had to say."

Jake rapped him on the back and grinned. "Nice work, PB."

He chuckled.

Sarah had to smile over Jake's use of Luke's nickname. At Richard's questioning stare, she explained, "Luke earned the nickname while in a Union army camp. PB stands for Preacher Boy."

Luke waved a hand. "It's a long story."

"But if you want to hear it, he'll be glad to tell you." Jake let go of a guffaw.

Richard set his hands on his hips, clearly puzzled.

"Some other time," Luke said.

Sarah breathed a sigh of relief. Once Luke got going, it was hard stopping him.

"I'll make some supper." Mrs. Navis headed for the kitchen. "Since that oppressive heat is gone, maybe our appetites will return."

"Hold off a few minutes, Bea." Mr. Navis wheeled himself across the living room and lifted his Bible from off the end table. "Speaking of captive audiences, allow me to read from Isaiah chapter twenty-five. It's one of my favorite passages." He leafed through the pages until he found it. "'For thou hast been a strength to the poor, a strength to the needy in his distress, a refuge from the storm, a shadow from the heat, when the blast of the terrible ones is as a storm against the wall.'"

"Amen!" Both Luke and Jake exclaimed.

"Let's bow our heads and give God thanks for protecting us today. Reverend Jake, why don't you do the praying?"

"Be honored to."

Sarah lowered her chin as a hush fell over the group. Just then Libby tugged on her skirt.

"Miss Sarah," Libby whispered, loud enough for all to hear, "Jesus really did keep us safe, didn't He?"

"Yes, He did." Gratefulness spread through Sarah. "Yes, He most certainly did."

Arm in arm with her brothers, Sarah strode to the large fountain in the Navises' front yard. The air was so cool now that she wore a shawl around her shoulders.

"So do you understand now why I can't go home?" After relaying the entire story to her brothers, she glanced from one to the other. She lowered herself onto the ledge of the brick fountain. "What do you say? Can I stay in Milwaukee?"

They answered in unison. "No."

"For the children's sakes?"

"Sarah," Jake began, "for all you know the captain has a governess hired to begin tomorrow morning."

"He doesn't. Richard confirmed it."

"I don't want you living in the same dwelling as Captain Sinclair," Luke said. "I know Pa wouldn't allow you to return to that man's home."

Sarah wetted her lips. She had one last shot in her arsenal. "Richard can attest to the fact I'll be safe from now on. I learned yesterday that he and the captain made a deal. I'm not at liberty to share the particulars, but what's important is that Captain Sinclair agreed to be a complete gentleman around me from here on in."

"Is that a fact?" Jake folded his arms. He didn't seem impressed.

"We like Richard," Luke began, "but he works for Sinclair. He gets bamboozled too. Just look how the captain managed to fill up his weekend with work. He knew Richard wanted to spend time with you."

Sarah sighed. Perhaps they were right. Richard might not be able to protect her—or even be willing to anymore. Yesterday evening he'd said such cruel words. Could he really believe those things of her? Or had he simply been overly exhausted and couldn't think straight? Why, then, wouldn't he speak to her today?

Jake set his arm around Sarah's shoulders. "Baby sister, we've got our orders from Pa. You're coming home with us."

# THIRTY-ONE

SARAH AWAKENED TO THE ROOSTER'S CROW. CLIMBING FROM beneath the warm covers, she shivered as she dressed. The cool weather that moved in yesterday lingered, bringing with it a feeling of fall.

Sarah read from her Bible. She read from the book of Esther and felt amazed at the young queen's courage. Her belief saved her people.

Closing her Bible, Sarah prayed, *Lord, I'm no queen, but those children need me. My brothers are refusing to let me stay. Please turn their hearts, just as You did King Ahasuerus. I'm petitioning here for four young lives. I know without a doubt that it's Your will, Lord. Now I only have to rest and believe it.*

But at breakfast Sarah's faith was shaken. Jake and Luke were still adamant about taking her home this morning. Once finished with her meal, she packed up the children, instructing them to pray but reminding them that God answered in His time, not theirs. She knew that once home in Jericho Junction, she could talk to Pa and he'd understand the children's need and her desire to care for them. He would allow her to return to Milwaukee.

Richard hitched up the horses, and the wagon was packed. Suddenly it was time to go. Sarah hugged Mrs. Navis good-bye and shook Mr. Navis's hand. "You both have been so good to me…me and my brothers. Thank you."

"You are welcome here anytime." The older man's gaze bore through her. "My home is your home."

Sarah realized she'd come to love it here on the farm. "Thank you." She would sorely miss this place—and the Navises too.

"Have a safe trip, honey." Tears rimmed Mrs. Navis's eyes as she hugged Sarah before bestowing the same show of affection to each Sinclair child.

Luke assisted her into the wagon, and Sarah felt a weighty emotion settle over her. The boys sat in the flatbed with the luggage while the girls wiggled in between Sarah and Luke in the backseat. Richard and Jake were perched on the front bench.

"Did God answer our prayers yet?" Libby asked.

"Not yet." Sarah stroked the girl's dark, silky hair.

"Does that mean you're leaving us?"

"It appears so."

"When will you come back?"

"Soon, I hope." Sarah pulled the child close and forced her attention to the landscape. Everywhere she looked, she saw evidence of yesterday's storm. Sticks and twigs littered the road, but none of the felled trees blocked their route. An overturned plow lay in a damaged cornfield. Sarah's heart seemed heavier as she realized a farmer had lost much of his crop to the tornado.

"That was some storm," Jake said.

"Sure was."

Sarah listened as the two men conversed. Luke distracted Libby and Rachel by asking them their favorite colors and ice cream.

Only too soon did the wagon pull alongside of the captain's large home. Sarah was glad Richard had decided not to take the children to Union Depot. Good-byes here would be painful enough.

Eyeing the mansion, Sarah wondered if the captain was still home. She no longer despised him. If she couldn't love others, then the love of God wasn't in her. She felt total peace now where the captain was concerned. But perhaps saying good-bye would help to close this chapter of her life.

The boys jumped out of the back. Luke lifted down the girls, and Jake reached for Sarah's hand, helping her from the wagon. Before Sarah's feet even hit the ground, Mrs. Schlyterhaus ran from the house. She frantically shooed the children into the house as Gabe called to Sarah.

"I won't leave without saying good-bye," she promised.

He reluctantly followed his siblings into the home.

*Lord, if I leave, what will happen to that boy?*

Richard hopped from the wagon, and the housekeeper reached him in seconds.

"Mr. Navis." She wrung her hands. "Zer is something you should know."

"What is it?" He stood next to Sarah.

"Is the captain. He vas sailing on the lake yesterday. He did not make it to safety before the storm hit. Pieces of *The Adventuress* vashed up onto shore. All who vere aboard are"—her voice cracked with emotion—"presumed drowned."

Sarah inhaled sharply. "No! It can't be true!" She looked at her brothers. "He was just here...so very much...alive."

Jake slung a protective arm around her shoulders.

Sarah knew God promised the future to no one, but it seemed so unreal. "The captain can't be—" dare she say it?—"dead!"

Through tears of shock and grief she caught Richard's gaze. She read blazing anger in his eyes—or was it something else?

Mrs. Schlyterhaus brought the skirt of her apron up over her mouth, covering a sob. She turned and ran for the house.

Silently Richard followed.

# THIRTY-TWO

RICHARD PACED THE CAPTAIN'S DARK, RICHLY PANELED study. A permeating smell of stale tobacco tickled his nostrils. He'd moved the conversation indoors so the children wouldn't overhear, and Sarah remained outside with her brothers. She seemed devastated by the news. Why? Had he been correct in assuming she harbored deep feelings for the captain?

Shaking off his perturbing thoughts, he focused on the matter at hand. "Sit down, Mrs. Schlyterhaus. Please tell me everything."

"Well, earlier this morning the authorities came by. They said there is no telling vhen the bodies vill be recovered. *If* they are recovered." Mrs. Schlyterhaus sniffed and dabbed at the corners of her eyes. "Lake Michigan doesn't often give up her dead."

She began to cry.

"This is terrible news. How can it be?" Richard's mind couldn't seem to grasp it. "Perhaps the captain and all on board made it safely to shore, and we just don't know it yet."

"Ve can only hope." Mrs. Schlyterhaus blew loudly into her hankie. "Meanvile, I had to give the authorities the names of those aboard *The Adventuress*, and I vasn't sure..."

Combing his fingers through his hair, Richard thought back on what the captain had told him on Saturday before he left the store. "Aurora and Mrs. Kingsley?"

"Yes, yes. Captain Sinclair mentioned both the ladies yesterday morning before I left for church with the Schmidts. And Mr.—oh, vhat vas his name again? He vas going too."

"St. Martin? He's Aurora's friend."

"That's the man."

"Any others?"

"I believe there vere only the four of them going out on the vater yesterday afternoon." Mrs. Schlyterhaus fell silent. Finally she said, "It's all over. The captain is dead, and my life's vork has drowned in the lake vis him." Her German accent sounded thicker from her emotion. She stood, her bottom lip quivering. "Life is so unkind!"

She ran from the study.

Richard sank into the captain's desk chair, contemplating his next move.

No. He'd do nothing right now. He had to wait. Wait and hope…and pray. Perhaps the captain and all on board would turn up safe.

"I knew yesterday afternoon that I couldn't leave, and I'm more than certain of it now." After Richard and Mrs. Schlyterhaus went into the house to talk, Sarah stayed behind to discuss the situation with her brothers. Still standing near the wagon, she refused to back down on what she felt was the right thing to do. "Jake? Luke? I'm staying. The children will need me more than ever."

"Look here, baby sister, Luke and I have work to get back to in Jericho Junction." Jake leaned on his cane. "We can't put it off any longer."

"I'm not asking you to." She squared her shoulders. "You'll just have to go on home without me." She glanced from one to the other. "I won't have it any other way. I'm staying here for the children, and that's that."

"I imagine Richard will need you too." Luke regarded her askance.

"Richard and I aren't…well, we've had a misunderstanding, and he's not speaking to me."

Her brothers stood quietly by for a long minute, and Sarah thought she'd rather hear their reprimands than their silence.

"Do you love him, Sarah?" Luke finally asked.

"Maybe." Memories in bits and pieces of Richard's gallantry scampered through her mind. Like the way he'd purchased a glass of lemonade for her on that insufferably hot Fourth of July day because he sensed she was thirsty. Like the way he always anticipated her needs before she herself was even aware of them. "Actually, yes, I believe I do love him. But I think it's too late." Did she tell her brothers that Richard believed the worst of her now?

Luke bobbed out a few short nods. "God might use this crisis to bring you together."

Sarah hadn't thought of that. She hadn't been able to even digest the news. *The captain is presumed dead?* It seemed incomprehensible.

Luke turned to their older brother. "I imagine we could stay on one more day. We'll wire Pa and figure things out once we get his reply."

"I reckon that's the best way to handle this situation." Jake didn't sound too enthused.

"I'll let Mrs. Schlyterhaus know." Lifting her hems, Sarah ran to the door and let herself into the house.

She'd made it to the foyer when she saw the housekeeper scurry from the captain's office with her hand over her mouth. Sarah bit back the urge to call out to her, realizing Mrs. Schlyterhaus wouldn't likely accept comfort from her.

But what about Richard?

Carefully, she made her way into the study. She found Richard sitting behind the captain's desk.

"Can it really be true?"

His gaze slid to her. "I don't know." He seemed to be searching her face, examining her…for what?

She steeled herself. "I've convinced my brothers to let me stay, Richard. I can take care of the children—and I'll help you in any way I can."

He stood and pushed back the chair. "In that case I'd better get that wagon unloaded." His voice sounded wooden, indifferent.

Sarah caught his arm as he moved toward the door. "Are you all right, Richard?"

He pulled free of her grasp. "What do you think, Sarah? This is a crisis. People will be counting solely on me."

"I know." She concealed her hurt feelings. "Let me know how I can help."

He strode from the room, then backtracked. "Are you sad, Sarah?" His voice was but a whisper.

She did feel sad, but she sensed that wasn't what Richard meant.

"Will you be devastated if the captain's dead?"

"Will you?" She stared hard into his blue eyes, refusing to acknowledge his despicable insinuation. Then she pushed past him.

Richard was right. This was a crisis, and it would take everything in them both to deal with it.

Those children . . . alone. Orphans.

If both the captain and his mother were really gone, who would care for them? Who would raise them?

Her heart seemed to stop at the grim thoughts.

Richard was gone all day, but he left the wagon hitched. Once Jake and Luke were settled in their bedrooms and the children's luggage was unpacked, they all climbed back into the buckboard. Jake drove and Sarah showed him how to get into town so he could send a telegraph to their pa.

After that they rode slowly back home. No one except the children said much. Sarah hadn't told them the news, hoping they'd learn more details as the day wore on. Instead she'd said only that their father had been called away on business and that she was staying 'til he returned.

By suppertime Richard returned, and Sarah noticed the slight droop of his broad shoulders.

"Two bodies have been recovered," he told Sarah, her brothers, and Mrs. Schlyterhaus. They had gathered in the captain's study while the children ate their dinner. "I've been asked, as the captain's steward, to go and identify them right now." He raked a troubled hand through his blond hair. "This is not something I relish doing."

"I'll go with you, brother," Jake said.

"If it'll help, I'll go too." Luke sent him a reassuring smile.

Richard looked appreciative.

The men left, and Sarah tried to stick to the children's routine. By nine o'clock that night she'd tucked them into bed. Downstairs, Sarah lit a fire in the reception parlor's hearth to stave off the damp chill in the house. Richard and her brothers returned a short time later.

"It's bad news." Jake shook his head.

Sarah looked at Richard.

"We identified Aurora and Mrs. Kingsley."

Immediate tears stung Sarah's eyes as she sat down heavily on a chair. *Aurora. Dead. The children's grandmother. Gone.*

Standing off to the side, Mrs. Schlyterhaus sobbed softly.

"The logical next step seems to be to tell the children." Richard lowered himself onto the settee. "Then we'll have some sort of memorial service for Aurora. I've already contacted Mrs. Kingsley's relatives. It's a good thing I had the invitation list for the wedding."

Sarah couldn't find it in her to feel sorry that there wouldn't be a union between Mrs. Kingsley and the captain. She felt God had wrapped the Sinclair children in a fold of protection by not allowing the marriage to take place. On the other hand, she hoped the woman—and everyone on board *The Adventuress*—had made peace with their Creator.

Jake sat down next to Richard. "Luke and I want to offer our assistance with the memorial service. Our pa always said you find ministry where you least expect it."

Sarah knew the saying well. She'd heard it often enough.

"Thank you," Richard said. "Both of you. I'm glad you're here."

"I am too." Pushing to her feet, she grabbed Luke's hand and squeezed.

He squeezed back.

Jake sent her a sideways glance. "Bet you never thought you'd say that, huh, Sarah?"

In spite of the bleak circumstances, she smiled. "Not in my wildest dreams."

# Thirty-Three

Lake Michigan looked as sleek as glass. Richard found it amazing that this beautiful body of water could also be a deadly, destructive force.

"So what's gonna happen to us?" Gabe asked.

Swiveling on the bench, Richard glanced at Gabriel, who sat on his right-hand side. Michael sat to Richard's left. Richard had just finished telling the boys the news. Back at the captain's house, Sarah and her brothers were informing the little girls.

"As soon as the lawful amount of time passes," Richard said in answer to Gabe's question, "your father's attorney will read the will and name your appointed guardians. In the meantime, Sarah will stay with you, and, of course, I'll always be nearby."

"Can't you and Miss Sarah be our parents now?" Michael's voice held a vulnerable ring.

"Yeah, you could be like a dad to us." Gabe stared at his feet. "It's not like we had a *real* dad."

"Of course you did. Your father loved you very much. He talked about you often and mentioned how proud he felt of his children."

"How come he never told us that?"

Richard set a hand on Gabe's shoulder. "I don't know. Maybe he thought he said those things, but they never really came out."

"He probably just forgot," Michael put in. "He had a forgetting problem."

"Quite true." Richard shifted his weight on the hard bench. He carried an enormous load on his shoulders. Even though Sarah was staying in Milwaukee, he couldn't find happiness in it. His jealousy had kept him angry all weekend, and now his worry over what Sarah might feel about the loss pulled him deeper inside himself with each passing minute. He could hardly gauge the boys' feelings over the news of their grandmother's death and their father's disappearance.

"The funeral for Aurora is tomorrow," Richard said.

"What about our dad?" Michael peered up at him.

"He's missing and presumed dead."

"He's not dead." Gabe leaned back and folded his arms. "I just know he isn't."

"Yeah, Dad's not dead." Michael agreed with Gabe. "He made it through the war."

"Boys, I'm afraid I fear the worst." Richard closed his eyes, willing the demons off his back. However, he just couldn't shake them.

Why couldn't he have acted like more of a Christian where the captain was concerned? Sure, he'd invited the captain to church numerous times over the last seven years. He'd done his best to be a good steward, advisor, often errand boy, and driver. He'd done his all to be a good testimony to the captain.

But in the past month he'd come to almost despise the man. He abhorred the way Captain Sinclair wooed Sarah for his own amusement. He loathed the way Sarah had so easily fallen for the captain's charm while considering Richard just a friend. But more, he detested the manner in which the captain had manipulated him, forcing him to choose between his life's ambition or Sarah's honor and reputation.

Captain Brian Sinclair had been an irresponsible rogue for the most part. But until Sarah's arrival, he'd always been good to Richard. Like the older brother Richard never had.

And now he was gone.

"Mr. Navis?"

Michael's voice dragged Richard back to the present. "Yes?" He looked at the boy.

"Can we go home now?"

The week passed. Aurora's memorial service came and went. Sarah thought her brothers did a fine job with the eulogy. It was hard to kiss them good-bye and see them board the train this morning. But they had to leave. Pa and Ma would arrive in a few days, and hopefully soon they'd learn the names of the children's guardians.

Sarah swayed slightly as Richard drove the buggy back to the captain's house. The children had gone to school this morning, all except Rachel, who sat in between them on the leather seat. As usual Richard kept his silence. Sarah felt like he barely acknowledged she existed unless the topic she broached involved the children.

To be near the children, this past week Richard had carried out business from the captain's study. He often stayed overnight in one of the guest rooms. Sarah wondered if he wasn't subtly looking out for her as well—or perhaps it was only wishful thinking on her part.

She sent a glance his way now, noticing his even expression and the slight downward tug of the corners of his mouth. She missed the man he used to be. The man beside her was a true puzzle.

Occasionally Sarah glimpsed Richard when meetings spilled into the foyer. She admired his diplomacy and found herself attracted more and more to his easy manner when dealing with the city's rich and powerful businessmen. He was professional and dignified.

But once business was through, Richard seemed so hopelessly lost in himself.

The buggy wheel hit a rut, jostling Sarah. She heard Richard's murmured apology but didn't think it deserved a reply. Glancing off into the distance, she hoped Gabe, Michael, and Libby would be able to concentrate on their studies. She and Richard had decided to keep the children's lives as normal as possible, and that meant going ahead with enrolling them at school. To forestall any problems, they had talked with their teachers about how to handle them as well. What a blessing that Lina Johnson was Gabe's teacher this year.

Sarah folded her gloved hands in her lap and tried not to give in to worry. But it seemed if she wasn't fretting about Richard and the cool distance between them, she worried over the children. They were almost in a state of denial. The boys kept saying their father was still alive. Jake said as long as there wasn't a body to prove otherwise, the kids were entitled to hope.

Richard pulled up in front of the house and let Sarah and Rachel off.

"Thank you for the ride." She gave him her best smile.

He inclined his head, averting his gaze.

"Bye, Mr. Navis." Rachel waved.

He afforded the little one a grin. "Bye, honey."

Once more Sarah felt cut to the quick by Richard's neglect. Her only consolation was that Jake said men have different ways of mourning—

Except Sarah knew the trouble between them began before the captain disappeared.

The day progressed, and Sarah went about her usual routine. Gabe, Michael, and Libby walked home from school late in the afternoon. They prattled on about their day, and Sarah listened with interest. They didn't act like the sorrowful orphans that they doubtless were, although Sarah wouldn't dare dash their hopes.

Once the children were settled for the night, she ambled downstairs to the music room. Sitting at the piano, she diddled around with different keys and chords before playing a melody she'd written. The words she sang were taken from the last chapter of the book of Zephaniah.

I won't be afraid. Why should I be sad?
The Lord, my God, is in my midst.
He is mighty.
He will save and I will rest in His love.
I will be glad.
And He'll rejoice over me with singing.

Sarah played through another stanza but suddenly felt a presence behind her. She turned and saw Richard in the doorway. He hadn't shed his black jacket, but he loosened his tie.

"I don't think I've ever heard you play."

She was amazed he even deigned to speak to her. But she hid her reaction. "No?"

He shook his head and stepped farther into the room. "Did you ever play for the captain?"

"As a matter of fact, yes, I did." She smiled, remembering. "I gave him and the children a mini recital shortly after I arrived in Milwaukee. I wanted to show off my skills and prove myself a gifted music teacher."

"Ah..."

Sarah knew he wasn't much of the conversationalist anymore. However, the sadness exuding from Richard broke her heart.

"Come over here." Sarah gestured to the place beside her on the piano bench. "Sit down." She touched three keys. "Now you play these, one after another, while I play the melody."

He turned away. "Sarah, I'm twenty-three years old." His tone was reprimanding. "If I wanted to play the piano, I would have learned by now. All right?"

"I just thought music would make you feel better."

"It won't."

"Fine." *Lord, I'm at my wit's end with this man!*

Sarah stood and crossed the room, intending to leave and not look back.

Richard caught her arm. His grasp was firm, almost biting. He pulled her toward him. "Do you miss the captain, Sarah?" The note of sarcasm in his voice was clear. "Do you cry into your pillow every night?"

How dare he goad her! She whirled on him. "Yes, I'm sorry the captain is missing. I pray for his soul. I'm sad for his children, who may not be dealing well with this situation. And, yes, I cry into my pillow. But not for the captain. For my best friend." She ground out those last four words. "You see, he's gone, and I miss him." Sarah shrugged off Richard's hold and clutched his lapels. "What did you do with him? I want him back." Tears threatened. "He's the man I've been falling in love with all these months. He was filled with joy and made

Uncertain Heart

me laugh. I loved his ever-present smile and sense of humor. I never worried when he was around. I knew he loved me and he loved God." She gave him a push. "But I don't know who you are, and...I don't like you very much."

A sob lodged in her throat as Sarah ran from the music room. Suddenly she couldn't wait for her parents' arrival. She felt torn in two. She loved the children, but she was ready to go home.

# THIRTY-FOUR

THE NEXT MORNING SARAH FELT EMBARRASSED FOR HER outburst. She dressed, helped the girls, then walked with them downstairs for breakfast in the dining room. She was shocked to find Richard at the table eating with the boys.

"Good morning," he said, furthering her surprise.

"Morning." She sat down, feeling wary.

"Isabelle has our lunches packed," Gabe informed her, "and Mr. Navis put candy sticks in our sacks. We can share with our friends at school."

"How nice." She eyed Richard. "And how very thoughtful of Mr. Navis."

A slight tip of his head and arch of one brow said the matter might be debatable. Sarah glimpsed sight of her best friend at last and smiled.

Once they'd eaten, Sarah finished readying the kids for school. Then she and Rachel walked Gabe, Michael, and Libby up the block. The large, brown-brick public school was less than a mile hike, and today the weather was fine.

Back at home a visitor arrived. Sarah recognized him from his attendance at Aurora's funeral.

The tall, balding man removed his hat. "Miss McCabe, I presume." He grinned at her nod. "I'm Horacio Craine. Captain Sinclair's attorney."

"Please come in. I'll find Richard."

"He's expecting me, and I'll need to speak with you as well."

Those last words sounded ominous, but after leaving Rachel in the care of Mrs. Schlyterhaus for the time being, Sarah bravely made her way to the captain's study.

Richard was already there, and he and Mr. Craine stood as she entered.

"I'm sorry this is abrupt. I had meant to warn you."

"Warn me? About what?"

"Let's get right down to business, shall we?" Mr. Craine said.

Sarah took a seat as Mr. Craine pulled documents from his leather valise.

"As you're both aware, three of the four persons believed to be aboard *The Adventuress* that fateful day, aside from her crewmen, have been found dead and identified. The last body being that of Mr. St. Martin."

"Oh, dear..." Sarah hadn't heard that bit of news yet. Would the captain's remains be discovered next?

"Therefore I filed a petition to declare Brian Sinclair's disappearance a death of absentia. No human being could survive in Lake Michigan for this length of time. It's been nearly two weeks. His mother and friends are dead..."

Sarah's hand flew to her throat.

Richard's voice broke in. "I hate to agree, but I must."

She glanced at Richard. "Really?"

He nodded sadly. "We can't move forward otherwise."

Sarah understood.

Mr. Craine eased back and stroked his jaw. "The Sinclair children seem to be faring well. I saw them at Mrs. Reil's funeral."

"Amazingly, the kids are handling this tragedy better than I'd expected," Richard said.

"It was a lovely service, by the way."

"Thank you." Richard glanced at Sarah. "I hope the captain would have thought so."

"I think he would have." Sarah felt confident in the reply.

Mr. Craine cleared his throat. "But now we come to the grave task of reading Captain Sinclair's will." He opened a sealed parchment. "Ironically, the captain had updated this just last month."

Sarah didn't know what to make of that, but she prayed the captain remembered to make provisions for his children.

Mr. Craine began reading aloud. "I, Brian Sinclair, being of sound mind and body..."

Sarah took it all in. Richard was named to oversee all financial matters, including the sale of the captain's business "if applicable." Trust accounts were to be set up for the children and left untouched until each child's twentieth birthday, barring any mishaps or misfortunes, in which case the funds could be withdrawn sooner. The captain's attorneys would be the judges of what constituted a "mishap or misfortune."

"As for guardianship, of course Brian named his mother first. But since Mrs. Reil is now deceased, God rest her soul, you, Mr. Navis, have been listed as guardian along with you, Miss McCabe."

"What?" Sarah sat upright. "Me? And Richard?"

"That's right."

"But it's not possible. How could such an arrangement work?" She shot a glance at Richard, noting he didn't look astounded in the least.

"I think perhaps," Mr. Craine said, "I'll find a cup of coffee while you two discuss this matter." He headed to the door. "I'll return shortly."

Sarah stood and began to pace. "We've both been awarded guardianship over the captain's children. Why would he choose such an arrangement?" She paused in front of Richard. "Unless he thought we'd get married one day."

Slowly Richard got to his feet, his gaze on hers. "Funny that he'd arrived at such a conclusion."

She saw the remorse in his blue eyes. Remorse and something else. Something she'd hoped to see again in these last awful weeks. Love. He still loved her.

"Well, yes, I made my decision, and yes, I can." She gave a nod and smiled.

"You can?" Confusion wafted across his face. "Accept the guardianship?"

"No, the offer you made me this summer. Remember? You asked if I could ever be a farmer's wife, and now I know I can. So I accept your marriage proposal."

Richard drew his chin back. "I don't recall proposing, and—and I'm not a farmer."

"You could be if you wanted to. If you sell the captain's business and set up trusts for the children with the money, you'll be free to return to doing the work you most love—and what you're called to do. Farm."

"Sarah, it's not that easy."

"You don't love me anymore?" She swallowed hard, knowing that if she was brave enough to ask, she'd have to muster the courage to hear the reply.

Richard inhaled deeply. "Sarah, I love you so much it hurts."

"It shouldn't hurt." She stepped closer and took his hand.

"My jealousy robbed me of all happiness and clouded my judgment. I know you are a woman not only of strong passions but also of strong character, and it was wrong of me to think the worst of you. I'm sorry, Sarah." His eyes glimmered with sorrow. "And not only that, but I have to confess that I miss the captain. He hired me when I was sixteen. We went through a lot together. I was the one who wired him to tell him Rachel was born. I was with him when his wife, Louisa, passed. I was always a friend to him, and he treated me fairly—until I let jealousy rule my life."

"I'm sorry I caused it. I was figuring out my own heart."

"You have it figured out now?" A hint of a grin lifted the corners of Richard's mouth.

"Not all of it. My brothers helped some, and I know my parents and I have a lot of talking to do. But the one thing I have learned is…I love you."

Richard stared off in the distance. "I can't believe I'm hearing you say that. Am I dreaming?"

Sarah stepped even closer, enjoying the feeling of finally being near him again. "You've seemed so far away, and I've missed you." She lifted her face, and her cheek brushed against his chin.

Richard lowered his head and their gazes met. The impact set off a spark inside Sarah, and she suddenly recalled something similar occurring the very first day she met Richard. "So will you marry me?"

His blue eyes twinkled. "I think we're supposed to go through a proper courtship first, if memory serves correctly."

"All right, I accept." She smiled up at him.

"Your parents haven't even met me yet. Will they approve?"

"They'll love you because I do. You'll see. So will you marry me?"

For a heartbeat, Richard was speechless. His lips moved, but no words came out. Finally he said, "You're incorrigible."

"I think I'm supposed to say that." A little laugh escaped her. It felt so good to banter with him again.

At last Richard chuckled, a sound Sarah had been pining to hear again.

She slipped her hand around his neck. "I do love you, Richard."

"I love you. But if you think I'm going to kiss you, Sarah McCabe, you're wro—"

She pressed her lips to his, and a flood of happiness surged through her.

And then Mr. Craine opened the door and reentered the study. "Well, well…"

Thoroughly embarrassed, Sarah quickly moved away from Richard.

"I see you two have come to an agreement." He grinned.

A wide smile split Richard's handsome face. "Yes, sir." He winked at Sarah. "We certainly have."

*Coming in January 2011—*

UNEXPECTED LOVE

*Book 3 in the Seasons of Redemption Series*

# ONE

*Chicago, Illinois, September 1866*

"DO YOU THINK HE'LL LIVE, DR. HAMILTON?"

The gray-haired man with bushy whiskers pondered the question for several moments, chewing on his thick lips as he weighed his reply. "Yes, I think he will," he finally said. "Of course, he's not out of the woods yet, but it seems he's coming around."

Lorrenna Fields breathed a sigh of relief. It had been almost a week with nary a sign of life from this half-drowned man, but finally—*finally* he showed signs of improvement.

"You've done a good job with this patient, Nurse Fields." The physician drew himself up to his full height, which barely met Renna's five feet six inches. "I don't think he'd be alive today if you hadn't given him such extraordinary care."

"Thank you, Dr. Hamilton, but it was the Lord who spared this man and the Lord who gave me the strength and skill to nurse him."

The old physician snorted in disgust. "Yes, well, it might have had something to do with the fact that you've got a brain in your head, Nurse Fields, and the fact that you used it too, I might add!"

Renna smiled inwardly. Dr. Hamilton always disliked it when she gave God the credit for any medical advancement. Especially the miracles. Yet Renna's intelligence and experience weren't typical for a woman her age, and she determined to use them to God's glory.

The patient moaned, his head moving from side to side.

"Easy now, Mr. Blackeyes." Renna placed a hand on the man's

muscular shoulder. "It's all right." She picked up the fever rag from out of the cold water, wrung it once, and set it on the patient's burning brow.

Dr. Hamilton snorted again, only this time in amusement. "*Mr. Blackeyes?* How in the world did you come by that name, Nurse Fields?"

She blushed but replied in all honesty. "It's his eyes, Doctor. They're as black as pitch and as shiny as polished stones. And since we don't know his true identity, I've named him Mr. Blackeyes."

"I see." Dr. Hamilton could barely contain his laughter.

"Well, I had to call him *something*, now didn't I?" She wrung the fever cloth more tightly.

"Ah, yes, I suppose you did." Dr. Hamilton gathered his instruments and put them into his black leather medical bag. "Well, carry on, Nurse Fields." He sounded tired. "If your patient's fever doesn't break by morning, send for me at once. However, I think it will, especially since we got some medicine and chicken broth into him tonight."

Renna nodded while the old man waved over his shoulder as he left the hospital room.

Returning her attention to her patient, Renna saw that he slept for the moment. His blue-black hair, which had just a slight wave to it, shone beneath the dampness of the fever. The stifling late summer heat of the room threatened to bring his temperature even higher.

Wiping a sleeve across her own beaded brow, Renna continued to sponge down her patient as she sat at his bedside. Tomorrow would be exactly one week since Mr. Blackeyes was found floating in Lake Michigan after a terrible storm. The crew of the passing ship that found him had thought he was dead at first. But they pulled him aboard anyway. The ship's doctor immediately examined him and detected a heartbeat, so he cared for him until the ship docked in Chicago's harbor a day later. Then Mr. Blackeyes was deposited at Lakeview Hospital. From there he was admitted to the second floor and into Renna's care, and now, finally, he showed some improvement.

Pulling the fever rag from the round porcelain bowl filled with cool water, Renna replaced it carefully across Mr. Blackeyes's forehead. She could tell this man was different from the usual "unknowns" that the hospital acquired. His dark features somehow implied sophistication, even through a week's worth of beard. And his powerful, broad shoulders and muscular arms indicated the strength of a man accustomed to lifting or hoisting. And he was handsome, all right. A lady's man, no doubt.

"But who are you, Mr. Blackeyes?" Renna murmured, gazing down at him.

As if in reply, the man groaned.

Renna settled him once more and then slowly stood from his bedside. She forced her mind to dwell on her other patients as she made her rounds through the sick ward, a large room with whitewashed walls and a polished marble floor. Eight beds, four on each side, were neatly lined in rows, leaving a wide area in the center of the ward.

Moving from bed to bed, Renna began checked each patient, thankful that this ward wasn't full. Mr. Anderson, suffering from a farming accident in which he lost his left arm; Mr. Taylor, who had won his battle with pneumonia and would soon be discharged to go home; and, finally, young John Webster, who had been accidentally shot in the chest by his brother. It appeared the wounded young man wouldn't live through the night, and his family had gathered around him, his mother weeping.

Taking pity on the Webster family, Renna set up several wooden screens to allow them some privacy. Then she checked on John. She could see death settling in, and even being somewhat accustomed to the sight, as she'd trained in an army hospital during the Civil War, it never got easier. Renna was heartened, however, that the Websters were people with a strong faith. Young John would soon go home to be with his Savior.

"Can I get anything for you, Mrs. Webster?" Renna asked the boy's mother now.

A tall, very capable-looking woman, she shook her head. Several brunette curls tumbled from their bun.

Renna asked the same thing of the boy's brother and father, but both declined.

"I didn't mean ter shoot 'im, Ma!" the brother declared. He suddenly began to sob.

"Aw, I know ya didn't mean it, son," Mrs. Webster replied through her own tears. "It was an accident; anyone can see that!"

"Tell it to Jesus, boy." His father's eyes were red, his jaw grizzled. "Then give the matter to Christ, just like we done gave John over to Him."

Renna's heart was with the family, but she suddenly felt like an intruder. The Websters needed their privacy. Stepping back, she gave them each a sympathetic smile before moving away.

Walking to the other side of the room now, Renna sat down on the edge of Mr. Blackeyes's bed and sponged him down again. Afterward she checked his head wound. Nearly a three-inch gash above his left ear. It had needed to be sutured, and Dr. Hamilton had seen to that when Mr. Blackeyes was first admitted. "Unknown Male" was the name on his chart. Most "unknowns" didn't survive, so Renna was heartened that Mr. Blackeyes's prognosis seemed promising.

Now if only his fever would break. If only he'd regain consciousness and pneumonia didn't set in.

Momentarily closing her eyes, Renna prayed for God's healing of this man. She had been praying earnestly for the last week. Why she felt so burdened for him, she couldn't say, but she was.

Suddenly an abrupt command broke her thoughts. "Nurse Fields? Nurse Fields, you may go. I'm on duty now."

Renna glanced at the doorway where the night nurse, as well as her supervisor, Nurse Ruthledge, stood. She was a large woman with small eyes and a stern disposition that kept her lips in a perpetual frown.

"As usual, your charts are in order."

Was that a hint of a smile?

"You're excused."

Renna guessed not. She replied with a nod. She didn't dislike the night supervisor, although she wasn't fond of the woman's overbearing manner. Still, Nurse Ruthledge was in charge. "Thank you, ma'am. I'll just finish up here and then I'll be on my way."

The older woman came up alongside her. "The first rule in nursing is do not get emotionally attached to your patients. You know that."

Renna rinsed the fever rag once more and draped it across Mr. Blackeyes's forehead. "I'm not getting emotionally attached." Renna felt her conscience prick. "I'm just...well, I'm burdened for this man. In the spiritual sense."

"Humph! Call it what you will, Nurse Fields, but I happen to think you're much too emotional and far too sensitive. It's a wonder you've lasted in nursing this long. Why, I heard from the other nurses on duty today that you were crying with the Webster family over their boy." She sniffed in what seemed like disgust. "A nurse must never let her emotions get in the way of her duty, Nurse Fields."

"Yes, ma'am." Renna endured the rebuke. She'd heard it many times before.

Nurse Ruthledge squared her wide shoulders. "Now, may I suggest that you leave your burden right here in this hospital bed and go home and get some rest? You're due back here at 6:00 a.m., and I'll expect you promptly!"

Renna nodded. Then, with a backward glance at Mr. Blackeyes, she left the sick ward. She gathered her things and made her way to the hospital's main entrance. Outside, she paused and breathed deeply. The air was thick and humid, but it was free from the chloroform and antiseptics that she'd smelled all day.

She spied a hired hackney, and within minutes, Renna rode the mile to the home she shared with her parents. She was the oldest child in the family, but at the age of thirty, Renna was what society termed a spinster. Her two younger sisters were married and producing children galore, and her one younger brother and his wife were just now expecting their first baby.

Renna loved all her nieces and nephews. They filled her empty arms when she wasn't at work nursing, and Jesus filled her heart.

Time and time again, however, Renna was asked by a young niece or nephew, "Why didn't you ever get married, Auntie Renna?" And her reply was always, "I never fell in love."

But the truth of the matter was no man would have her—even if she had fallen in love. The large purplish birthmark on the right side of her face deterred every eligible bachelor. The unsightly thing came down her otherwise flawless cheek to the side of her nose and then around and down to her jaw, like an ugly, purple horseshoe, branded into her face. One would think she'd be accustomed to the gawks, stares, and piteous glances sent her way at social functions, but they unnerved her. All dressed up and looking her prettiest, Renna still felt marred and uncomely under the scrutiny of her peers—but especially when she was in the company of eligible men to whom she was supposed to be attractive and charming. Renna never felt she was either of those.

Nursing, however, was different. In the hospital Renna felt confident of her abilities. Moreover, her patients were usually too sick or in too much pain to be concerned with her ugly birthmark. Rather they just wanted her care and sensitivity, and that's what Renna thought she did best...in spite of what Nurse Ruthledge said about her being too emotional and too sensitive. God in all His grace had given Renna a wondrous work in nursing, and it pleased her to be used in that way. What more could she want? And yet lately—lately Renna desired something more. Was it a sin to feel discontented after so many happy years of nursing?

The carriage stopped in front of Renna's house. She climbed out, paid the driver, and then turned to open the little white gate of the matching picket fence around the front yard. A slight breeze blew, and Renna thought it felt marvelous after her sweltering day on the second floor of the hospital.

"Well, there you are, dear." Her mother, Johanna Fields, stood with a pair of shears in her hand. She had obviously been pruning the flowers that graced the edge of the wide front porch. "You're late tonight, Renna." She studied her daughter. "Mr. Blackeyes? Is he...?"

"He's still alive." She stepped toward her mother. "Dr. Hamilton thinks he may even live, except he has an awful fever now. We're hoping it breaks by morning and that pneumonia doesn't set in."

"Oh, dear…" Mum shook her head sadly. "Well, we'll keep praying, won't we?"

Renna gave a nod before Mum hooked arms and led her into the house.

"I've made a light fare tonight, Renna. Help yourself."

"I appreciate it, but I'm too tired to eat."

"But you need some nourishment." Mum fixed a plate of cold beef, sliced tomatoes, and a crusty roll. "Here, sit down at the table."

Renna allowed her mother to help her into the chair. After one bite she realized how ravenous she was and cleaned the plate.

Minutes later, her sister Elizabeth walked in with her twin daughters, Mary and Helena. Delight spread through Renna as the girls toddled into the kitchen.

"Hello, darlings." She gave each a hug before smiling up at her younger sister.

"Renna, you look exhausted." Elizabeth shook her head vehemently, causing strands of her light brown hair to escape their pinning. "You'll be old before your time."

"And what would you have me do? Sit around the house all day, twiddling my thumbs?" Seeing her sister's injured expression, she softened her voice. "I'm sorry. I guess I'm more tired than I thought."

Elizabeth smiled. "All's forgiven."

Renna struggled to her feet. Her entire body ached from her long shift. "I'll have to visit another time. I'm going up to bed."

After bidding everyone a good night, Renna climbed the steps, one by one, leading to the second floor. Entering her small bedroom, she poured water from the large pitcher on her bureau into the chamber basin and then washed away the day's heat. She pulled her cool, cotton nightgown over her head, then took her Bible off the nightstand and continued her reading in John chapter nine. Renna realized as she read that physical ailments allowed God to show His glory, and she marveled as she read about the blind man who by simple faith and obedience regained his sight.

She bowed her head. *Oh, Lord, that You might heal Mr. Blackeyes. That You might show Your power to those who don't believe by healing him.* Renna paused to remember her other patients then. *And please rain down Your peace that passeth all understanding on the Websters tonight.*

Despite the fact her eyelids threatened to close, Renna finished her Bible reading. She turned down the lamp as a breeze ruffled the curtains. Somehow Renna knew that John Webster would not be in her sick ward tomorrow morning. Nor would his family be there. Somehow Renna knew that John was with the Savior already.

But Mr. Blackeyes...why, he might not be a believer. It pained Renna to think of him spending an eternity apart from God.

*Please heal him, Lord*, she prayed as she crawled into bed. She allowed her eyes to finally shut, and the darkly handsome stranger who lay fighting for his life was the last person on Renna's thoughts as she drifted off to sleep.

## Go back to the inspiring beginning of the McCabe family story in book one of the *Seasons of Redemption series*

Amid the dangers of the Civil War, Valerie Fontaine longs to know she is loved. Her father, against her wishes, is prepared to sell her into a loveless marriage. Can she find the strength to fight for who she is and find her true love?